'Suspense, followed by even greater suspense, is the hallmark of this fast-moving, tightly plotted and timely story of American big business terrorism in the Far East. It starts with the frame-up of William Corbett, vice-president of ESK/International, who is accused of illegally selling millions of dollars worth of weapons abandoned in Vietnam . . . Another winner from the author of *Dragons at the Gate**'

Publishers Weekly

* Also available in Sphere Books.

Temple Dogs

ROBERT L. DUNCAN

SPHERE BOOKS LIMITED
30/32 Gray's Inn Road, London WC1X 8JL

First published in Great Britain by Michael Joseph Ltd 1978
Copyright © 1977 by Robert L. Duncan
Published by Sphere Books Ltd 1978
Reprinted 1979

Set in Intertype Times

Printed in Great Britain by
Hunt Barnard Printing Ltd.,
Aylesbury, Bucks.

To
JAMES HENRY HOLMES,
of New York and Holdenville,
dear friend,
a man with a keen eye,
an articulate rage,
and an abundant heart

Temple Dogs

PART I

Chapter 1

Ah, he was tired and that was the truth of it. He sat in the back of the limousine, feeling the faulty flow of air conditioning wash over him, looking out at the streets of Seoul, a stinking dirty city. He was aware that Abernathy, sitting on the left side of the car, was highly nervous, his lean fingers in constant motion, now opening and closing a gold cigarette case that made a distinct click. 'Do you realise that they are following us?' Abernathy asked in a bewildered voice.

'Yes,' Corbett said.

'My God, they follow me every place I go.' Abernathy removed a cigarette from the case and tapped it against the polished surface. 'Every time I leave the plant, there they are, the same goddamned jeep, the same goddamned soldiers.'

Corbett turned his head slightly until he could see the jeep through the rear window. An American jeep with a driver and a couple of Republic of Korea soldiers in the back, carrying automatic weapons, wearing sunglasses against the glare of the summer sun. Young, yes, not more than twenty, twenty-one years old, and even from here he could detect that implacable smugness of the oriental soldier.

'It's not uncommon,' Corbett said. 'They're trying to throw you off balance.'

'They're succeeding.' The smoke drifted out of patrician nostrils. Abernathy was the wrong man for the job, Corbett thought, a poor choice. He had the breeding

11

for the San Francisco slot, the air of elegance and urbanity needed for that city, with a slightly nasal accent, an orderly mind. But now he sat in alien territory, face grimacing as he exhaled smoke from a cigarette, a smudge of brown dust on the arm of his linen jacket, which he did not even notice. 'I must say, our Embassy has not given me one goddamned bit of help.' There was a note of petulance in his voice.

'What did you tell them?' Corbett said.

'I explained the situation. I asked them to do something to keep the Colonel out of the internal affairs of our plant.' He smiled slightly, humourlessly. 'They gave me a GPO pamphlet on how to understand the Korean mind.' He sighed, snuffing out the cigarette, immediately lighting another. 'My wife is planning a dinner party for you this evening. Nothing elaborate, a few key personnel.'

'I won't be able to stay,' Corbett said.

'You expect to take care of this in an afternoon?'

'I have to be in Tokyo tonight. Now, before we meet the Colonel, I need to know exactly what's happened.'

'It's all in the report.'

'I want to hear it from you.'

Abernathy shrugged slightly, removed a handkerchief from his pocket and caught a sneeze. 'My damn sinuses can't stand this dust,' he said. He folded the handkerchief, replaced it in his pocket. 'There's not a great deal to tell,' he said. 'One day the Colonel demanded to see me. He intimidated the hell out of my secretary, reduced her to tears, and then came into my office with an interpreter and two armed soldiers. I lost my temper and demanded to know what in the hell he thought he was doing. He informed me that investigation revealed that ESK/KOREA was guilty of subversive activities and that there would be a complete investigation.'

'Did he speak to you in English?'

'No. He used his interpreter.'

'Go on.'

'I was nervous, to say the least. Armed men in my office, charges against the company I couldn't understand. I offered them coffee, asked for particulars. I couldn't make any sense out of it, I'll tell you that. The Colonel refused to give me any specifics. He just insisted that unless conditions were corrected, he would close down the plant. Then he left.'

'I see. And you contacted the Embassy.'

'Yes.' Following the rejection of help from the Embassy, Abernathy continued, it seemed that nothing more was going to happen. A week passed and there was no more communication from the Colonel and things went on as usual. Then, for the first time, Abernathy noticed that whenever the limousine came to his house to pick him up and take him to the plant, the jeep full of soldiers followed him, always at a respectful distance, but omnipresent. Then one day two of his employees, Korean middle managers, were picked up by the police. Both were questioned extensively, accused of subversive activities, again with no particulars. One was released and the other was beaten regularly for two days and then freed. At that point Abernathy had called the Colonel's office, demanding an explanation. 'He refused to discuss it with me,' Abernathy said. 'He said that since I was suspected of subversion myself that it would not be proper to discuss any aspects of the case with me. He demanded that I bring in an official from the parent company. Do you know what in the hell is going on here?'

'We'll see shortly,' Corbett said. The limousine was climbing a hill, following a winding street, the horn blaring to clear the way. He leaned his head back against the seat, wanting to close his eyes, rest, but knowing that he would have to be up for the Colonel, he did not. He had been fully briefed on Colonel Pak, an official in the Public Information Ministry, and the Colonel would certainly be fresh, alert, looking for any signs of weak-

13

ness, any evidence of weariness on which he could capitalise.

It was a game and Corbett had played it a hundred times before, in Singapore, in Malaysia, in the Philippines, wherever there were local men with power and the presence of a large foreign company with all the visible signs of affluence, a company vulnerable to harassment. This was Corbett's specialty, this bargaining under pressure, this negative negotiation, and in a matter of hours he would be back on the jet again, lifting off, this business behind him.

The limousine slowed now, turning from a narrow lane on to a wide boulevard across from the crumbled walls of an old temple. War? A National Historic Site? It made no difference. Ruins were ruins. The limousine pulled into the driveway of a small business building, an ugly cube of modular concrete, one of the hundreds of new buildings springing up over the Korean landscape. A small sign near the door proclaimed it to be a REPUBLIC OF KOREA PUBLIC INFORMATION OFFICE. The Korean chauffeur sprang to open Corbett's door first and Abernathy was left to slide across the rear seat before climbing out. He stopped a moment in the bright sunlight to smooth his linen suit and grimaced towards the jeep parked down the street.

Corbett put on his sunglasses. 'In this negotiation you will follow my lead,' he said. 'He'll work on the principle of surprise and come at you out of left field. But you will admit nothing and you won't appear to be startled.'

'Very well,' Abernathy said.

Perhaps Abernathy was going to be able to pull this off after all, Corbett realised, for he was now undergoing a metamorphosis, his back straightening. He clasped the leather envelope briefcase beneath his left arm and preceded Corbett, opening the door into an anteroom dominated by colourful political posters on the wall and a metal desk (American army surplus, Corbett

14

reasoned). A lieutenant stood up behind the desk, bowing slightly, formally, as Corbett approached.

'I am Lieutenant Tae,' the young man said, 'adjutant to Colonel Pak. You are Mr Corbett?'

'Yes,' Corbett said. 'Please let the Colonel know we are here.'

The Lieutenant picked up the telephone, spoke into it, and then replaced it on its cradle. 'I am sorry, sir,' he said. 'But at the moment the Colonel is otherwise engaged. If you will be kind enough to have seats, the Colonel will be with you as soon as possible.'

Corbett made no move toward the two seats against the wall. He removed a card from a leather case. 'I don't intend to wait,' he said. 'You'll notice that my Tokyo number is on the card. Have the Colonel get in touch with me when he's ready to talk.'

The first gambit had been made and the Lieutenant blinked, a blank expression on his face. 'You cannot wait?'

'No.'

The Lieutenant picked up the telephone again, his voice more urgent now. 'The Colonel will take the time to see you now.'

Corbett said nothing. He waited until the Lieutenant had opened the door into an inner office and then followed him into a spacious room with bookcases along one wall and the Colonel's desk sitting beneath a large window so that anyone sitting opposite the desk would have to face into the light. The Colonel himself was a small, stocky man, the back of his neck thick, shaven to a tapering of short black hair on his scalp.

'Do you speak English?' Corbett said to the Colonel, abruptly.

'The Colonel prefers that this conversation should be conducted in Korean,' the Lieutenant said. 'I serve as his official interpreter since I have satisfactory command of your language.'

Corbett was aware that the Colonel was studying

15

him, the stolid face expressionless. He said something in Korean, made a slight formal bow to Corbett and then to Abernathy before he sat down, his hands clasped before him on the bare desk.

'He wishes you to be seated,' the Lieutenant said. 'He welcomes you to Korea and hopes that your stay here will not be an unpleasant one.'

Corbett pulled the chair to the side of the desk where he would not be facing the light and then removed his sunglasses, carefully folding them, placing them in the top pocket of his jacket. He sat down, aware that Abernathy was following his lead and going him one further, moving his chair and placing his briefcase on the Colonel's desk, an intrusion upon the Colonel's sense of space. If the Colonel was disturbed, he did not show it. The Lieutenant stood beside him at a proper distance. Tae would be the barometer, Corbett thought, and at the moment he was clearly uncomfortable. 'Now,' Corbett said. 'Tell the Colonel that this is to be an informal meeting as far as the Erikson Company is concerned. If he is making a recording of our conversation, we have no objections. But our notes will clearly show that we consider this informal.'

The Lieutenant relayed the information to the Colonel, whose hands shifted slightly, almost imperceptibly. As he spoke, the Lieutenant began a simultaneous translation, smooth, coherent. 'The Colonel wishes to state that there are grave charges against your company which are not as yet official. He is willing to concede that such offences may have occurred through ignorance of the customs and traditions of this country. Therefore, he has requested this meeting. But you are to be advised, sir, that the charges are serious ones and, unless resolved here, may be taken to a formal hearing at an appropriate time and place.'

'I see,' Corbett said. He took out a cigarette, pulling the Korean Lieutenant into the subservient position of lighting it for him and providing him with an ashtray.

16

He leaned back in the chair, inhaling the cigarette smoke, saying nothing, his eyes not moving from the Colonel. Pak murmured something to the Lieutenant.

'He wishes to know your position in the company,' the Lieutenant said.

'In which company?'

'ESK, International,' the Lieutenant said.

'I am a vice-president,' Corbett said.

'ESK is the international name for the Erikson Company.'

'That is correct.'

'The Colonel says he is aware of the gross and net amounts generated by ESK/KOREA and that these amounts contribute a large share of the net profits of ESK, International.'

Corbett nodded, tapping the ashes from the cigarette into a shallow bowl. 'The Colonel should also be aware of the number of people we employ in our Korean operations.' He spoke directly to the Colonel. 'I am sure he knows the enormous taxes, fees, and licences we pay directly to the Korean government. He should also be aware of our flexibility as a corporation. Six months ago, for instance, we liquidated a large plant in Singapore and moved it to Australia, where the business climate was more favourable. We appreciate the opportunity of contributing in legitimate ways to the growth of countries who do not abuse our goodwill.'

The Colonel had received the message, fully understood, for he said something to the Lieutenant, who immediately removed glasses and a bottle of wine from a cabinet and proceeded to serve Corbett and Abernathy. The Colonel was more relaxed now, placing his hands palms down on the table. They were large hands with prominent knuckles, the hands of a labouring man who had risen through the ranks of the military, a street-smart man who knew the parameters of the game. Corbett tasted the wine, noticing with satisfaction that Abernathy was settling in now, following his lead.

It was time for the Colonel to make his move, Corbett realised. The Colonel opened a drawer and placed two books on the desk. Corbett picked up one of them, thumbed through it. It was printed in Korean, unintelligible. The Colonel's voice was stronger now, full of inflections. Lieutenant Tae rubbed his chin. 'The Colonel wishes you to deny that these two books were carried in the library of ESK/KOREA, and that they were there circulated and read by many Korean employees of the company who proceeded to discuss their contents in the library of the aforesaid company.'

'Are you a lawyer, Lieutenant?' Corbett said with a disarming smile.

'I am studying law,' the Lieutenant said uneasily.

'You use the language very well.' Corbett handed the book to Abernathy. 'Do you have a library at your plant?'

'We have a technical library,' Abernathy said. 'We also have an informal library in the employees' lounge.' He looked to the Colonel. 'What book is this?'

The Colonel stood up, affecting a military posture, hands clasped behind his back as he turned to look out of a small window. The words tumbled out of him with the smoothness of a speech repeated many times. 'The Colonel says that these are perilous times,' the Lieutenant began. Corbett watched the grey smoke curl up from his cigarette, only half listening. The Colonel was wise in the ways of business politics, refusing to confront head-on but choosing instead to attack from the periphery, manufacturing a grievance to which there could be no solution. The book, it seemed, was a volume of poetry by a young man named Kim Cha Ha, who at one time had been sentenced to death for writing seditious literature. By maintaining his books in the company library, the company had exposed itself to the charge of fomenting unrest and rebellion among the Korean people.

'Nonsense,' Abernathy said, interrupting the Lieuten-

18

ant. 'The whole thing is a bunch of goddamned nonsense.'

'I'm afraid not,' the Lieutenant said, almost apologetically. 'We have the names of many employees who admit to reading these books and discussing the contents on company premises. This is in direct defiance of Executive Directive Number Nineteen. It would be to your extreme disadvantage to require proof of this in open testimony.'

'Our company has never encouraged any sedition,' Abernathy said. 'I resent the hell out of the accusation.'

'What does the Colonel suggest?' Corbett said calmly.

'He suggests that there must be new procedures to guarantee mutual support.'

'I see,' Corbett said reflectively. 'Tell the Colonel I will guarantee a company payment of five thousand American dollars a month to the Colonel to avoid further harassment. To allow him to cover his ass, I will authorise a one-time payment of forty thousand dollars to any national welfare fund he chooses and let it be known that the money was paid as an apology for any affront the company inadvertently made to the Korean government.'

The Colonel's body position was unchanged; his expression was fixed. And quite suddenly, Corbett realised that there was much more involved here than a simple graft. He did not know how he knew, something in the Colonel's attitude, perhaps, as if the Colonel had expected this response. The Colonel rubbed his chin thoughtfully, spoke through the interpreter.

'The Colonel is not insulted because he realises that such business has been conducted in the past. But these are new times.'

'What does he have in mind?'

'The Colonel states that he is pleased with your willingness to discuss. The offence of your company has forced the government to reassess the relationship of the republic with your firm. The current tax structure does

19

not represent a fair return to the people of Korea and therefore your company will be expected to agree to make payments based on the value of your investment here.'

Ah, here it was, he thought, and he had been caught off guard. The company had been expecting something like this from the new alliance of Asian nations but he had not expected the first demand to come from this quarter, under these circumstances, with a major shift in foreign policy being presented by a colonel in a rumpled green uniform. The Korean Foreign Ministry had moved this one very cleverly. He stubbed out his cigarette, suppressing any sense of surprise. 'I think we had better clarify,' he said. 'The Colonel is speaking for the Korean government in this matter?'

'That is correct,' Lieutenant Tae said.

'Does this new policy apply to all companies or just ours?'

'It will eventually apply to all. The Colonel suggests that the Korean people will take matters into their own hands if an agreeable solution is not found. The labour organisations will call for a general strike against any plant that has made itself known as subversive to the general welfare.'

'No,' Abernathy said, quietly but firmly. 'I won't have any part of this.'

The Lieutenant looked to Corbett. 'Does he speak for the company?'

Corbett removed a business card from his pocket and handed it to the Lieutenant. 'This is my address in Tokyo,' he said.

'I don't understand,' the Lieutenant said.

Corbett stood up. 'You can explain to the Colonel that I consider this meeting a personal affront. If harassment continues, we will either make a formal complaint through our government or we will move our business interests elsewhere. If the Korean government wishes to negotiate new tariffs, it will have to do it through the

Foreign Ministry.' He nodded to Abernathy and then looked directly at the Colonel. 'Good day, Colonel.'

Once they were outside, Corbett put on his sunglasses against the hazy glare of the sky. Abernathy bore up very well until he was in the limousine and then he slumped against the seat. 'Fucking orientals,' he said. 'How in the hell am I supposed to keep a plant running in an atmosphere like this? Extortion. My God.'

'How long have you had an overseas post?'

'This is my first.'

'They all expect baksheesh in one form or another,' Corbett said. There was a fleck of dust on the right lens of his glasses. He removed them to polish the glass with a linen handkerchief. He would not discuss the full implications of the Colonel's demands with Abernathy. 'They're more brazen now than they used to be, all around the world, but it's always been the same.' He held the lens up to the window, a clean and tinted view of a slight man on a bicycle loaded with trays. He put the sunglasses on. 'You can expect trouble from this point on for a while. You'll have labour problems, work stoppages.'

'My God,' Abernathy said quietly, almost as a litany. 'Our house in San Francisco is rented. It was on the market for a while but I'm glad it didn't sell.' He shrugged. 'We might as well make it definite,' he said. 'I want to go back to the States. I'll send in an official request tomorrow morning.'

'No,' Corbett said. 'This is going to be one hell of a fight, you can count on that, and if you left now, it would be interpreted as a sign of weakness.'

'I'm a businessman, not a politician. I'm giving you my notice. I'll stay here thirty days and then I'm going home.'

'I don't think so.' He felt the slight bristling, the almost imperceptible intake of breath. There was a long pause while Abernathy apparently got himself under control.

'Are you telling me you would turn down an immediate transfer?' he said.

'Yes.'

Abernathy leaned back against the seat, staring out of the window at the gun emplacements fringing the airport, the clots of soldiers in mufti, the sun glinting on rifle barrels. He probed gingerly at his teeth with the tip of an index finger. 'I'm having some dental work done. Damn clever dentists, these Koreans.' He shifted in the seat. 'Perhaps you had better clarify,' he said. 'I've handled work stoppages before, strikes. You know my record in dealing with the unions in California. But I have a wife to consider. Now, if there are any terrorist activities in the plant, any bombings, any rough stuff at all, then you'll have my resignation before the smoke clears.'

'I don't think you fully understand what's going on here,' Corbett said. 'If that bastard in there is really speaking for the government, then there's a major shift in the offing. I'm going to need time to put something together. And that means that you're going to stay tight for the time being.'

Abernathy shook his head. 'I realise that company interests have to come first with you. They don't with me. Now, you can disapprove a transfer for me and probably queer it, but that's as far as you can go.'

'I can go further,' Corbett said without rancour.

'I don't think so.'

'You're in no position to quit,' Corbett said with a sigh. 'You owe seventy-six thousand dollars on your San Francisco house and another sixty-odd in various debts. You're forty-nine years old, without contacts for another top level position and you're eleven years from any kind of retirement. So you'll sit tight.'

'You are a son of a bitch,' Abernathy said.

'I do what I have to.'

'For the company.'

'It's my job,' Corbett said. They were passing through

22

a checkpoint now, an ROK soldier examining papers presented by the chauffeur, peering into the back seat before he waved them through. The soldier's face was almost moon-shaped, almond-coloured, wearing over-sized sunglasses. Was this the mark of the new oriental soldier, Corbett wondered, the mirrored sunglasses?

The company jet was waiting on the runway, and the hatch steps lowered as the car approached. In a few minutes he would have a drink in his hand and be looking down on the Strait but there was peace to be made here first. He must allow Abernathy to salvage some of his self-respect. 'Look,' Corbett said. 'I'm in a bind here because you're a key man and I can't replace you that quickly. I can't guarantee that things are going to get any calmer here, because they're not. So if the heat gets too much for you, call me in Tokyo, personally, and I'll pull you out of here immediately. In the meantime I'll be looking for a replacement just in case.'

Abernathy nodded quietly. 'I'll give it a try,' he said. 'And I apologise for the language.'

'It's not needed,' Corbett said with a smile. 'I am a son of a bitch.' He shook Abernathy's hand. The skin was cold. 'I'll call from Tokyo to keep you updated on our progress. And you have my number.'

'Right.'

Corbett left the car and climbed the steps into the plane, a plush blue and russet office designed for his every comfort. Wilson's timing was impeccable; the moment Corbett was aboard the jet engines began to whine up to full power and the hatch closed. Corbett liked Wilson. He was a bright, taciturn man with a glossy athletic look about him. After another year as Corbett's assistant he would be ready for a territory of his own and Corbett would see that he got it.

Corbett removed his jacket and his tie before he sat down and Ellen came in from the galley area, cheerful as usual, bringing him his bourbon and water. 'Has

Stevens sent his reports yet?' he said, taking the drink from her.

'They're coming through on the Telex now.'

He nodded. 'I want them the minute they're ready. I'll have some memos to go out later.'

'Fine.'

He watched her as she went back into the communications compartment. 'Give the pilot a green,' he said to Wilson. He sipped the drink, the bourbon strong. He would take care of business and then try to sleep a couple of hours before the jet reached Tokyo. The jet began to move. Wilson sat down opposite him.

'How did it go?' Wilson said.

'Poorly,' Corbett said. 'They threw me a curve.' The jet was airborne now and he could see the gun emplacements ringing the airfield like hollowed pockets. Always one step short of war, a natural way of life in the Far East nowadays, military politics. 'I think the Asian countries are going to use ESK/KOREA for their first test case. Hell, I should have seen it coming. The Colonel wasn't looking for personal baksheesh. I won't be surprised if the Korean government issues a statement that official talks have opened.'

Wilson whistled softly. 'Are you sure he speaks for the government?'

'No doubt at all.'

'How's Abernathy doing?'

'He'll settle down. He's a good man but out of place.' The whisky was beginning to relax him now, loosening him. 'What do you have?'

Wilson placed a stack of papers on the small table. 'The most important of the lot are the position papers for the Chinese banquet tomorrow. While you're going through them, I'll check the Telex. Stevens is currently sending.'

He left Corbett alone. Corbett went through the teletypes first.

For twenty years Erikson had been sending a daily message to all of his key employees – epigrams, essays, exhortations, definitions of company policy. Lately the old man's messages had been diatribes against the scandals in Washington, comments on the illegality of Senate examination of multinational corporations and a kind of gearing up of the corporate spirit against the new nationalism rising in the small Asian countries and their new coalition. Today's message exhorted the members of the ESK family to meet their quotas and ignore any rumours that might be disruptive to morale.

At times, during informal meetings in bars, in places of relative safety, the daily communiqués were interpreted as an indication of approaching senility, especially since Erikson had recently passed his seventy-second birthday, but Corbett had never agreed with such opinions. The old man had immense power and he was particularly astute at outguessing international trends long before they became apparent to anybody else. The computer managers did not agree with him but he was right far more often than they were. And if he chose to demonstrate his ability to communicate instantly with his people, he could not be faulted for that.

The jet reached altitude, levelled, and Ellen came into the compartment. 'If you're hungry, I have cold cuts in the galley,' she said. 'If you don't like cold cuts, I have soup. But you should eat something.'

He had not noticed the colour of her eyes before, a blue that almost matched her suit, which just missed being a uniform. 'I'll have something to eat later,' he said. 'Sit down. Keep me company.'

'Sure,' she said. She sat down in the chair across from him, and he could tell that she was checking his glass, making certain that his drink did not need refueling. She had been with the company eight months now and despite the fact that he had hired her himself he realised he knew little about her other than that her efficiency had turned into a kind of professional devotion. 'Tell me something,' he said abruptly, not even knowing he was about to ask the question. 'How do you see all this? What sense does all this make to you?'

There was a quizzical expression in her eyes. 'In what way? I don't understand.'

'You must have some feelings about this business you're in,' he said. 'How would you describe what you do for a living if somebody asked you?'

'I would tell them that it's exciting,' she said instantly. 'Exciting and bewildering.'

'How?'

'Exciting because we're always on the move,' she said. 'Bewildering because I sometimes wonder why you do it.' She looked at him directly, openly. 'This isn't supposed to be a conversation where I tell you something you want to hear, is it? I'm no good at that.'

'No,' he said. 'I'm interested.'

'I get concerned about you sometimes,' she said. 'But I'm also very curious. You seem to go twenty-four hours a day. You don't eat regular meals and you don't appear to get much enjoyment out of life. Excitement, maybe, but not enjoyment. I think sometimes you're completely involved with the company so you won't have to be involved in anything else.'

She refilled his glass and he felt challenged, as if in this instant she had cut through to the central issue in his life. It made him uncomfortable. 'You work for the company too,' he said.

'Not in the same way. I enjoy what I'm doing but I'm not consumed by it.' Now Wilson came in from communications, bringing the Stevens material, and she appeared to be grateful for the interruption. 'When you get hungry let me know,' she said.

'I'd like to continue this conversation later,' he said.

'Anytime.'

Corbett took the Stevens material from Wilson and then settled back to go through the pages. They were summaries of news dispatches concerning the Vietnamese arms business. Obviously, Stevens had done his work well. The findings were concise, objective.

First, the Senate Committee on Multinational Corporations had concluded that ESK/INT was involved in the purchase, for an indeterminate amount of money, of all the tanks, weapons, miscellaneous missiles from the Vietnamese government, all of the heavy equipment abandoned by American forces that could not find a ready market in Southeast Asia. The Senate committee was following a popular tack Corbett realised, for they had scored heavily against the multinationals by humiliating corporate officials for overseas payoffs, but he felt they were overreaching on this one.

They were following a tenuous trail but it was not outside the realm of possibility that such a transaction had been made. One American tank had been discovered in Biafra with a serial number designating it as one of the tanks abandoned in South Vietnam, and the prevailing theory had it that the arms had been transported from Vietnam to Africa by two ships under Liberian registry, *The Quarter Moon* and *The Liberty Sentinel*.

Repair parts were presumably finding their way to Africa via sub rosa sales authorised by the Department of Defense. The only witness for the Senate committee was a staff member at DOD, an under-secretary of sorts named Kukler who, from newspaper pictures and television interviews, appeared to be a wild-haired young conservative determined to make a name for himself as a watchdog of global corruption.

Corbett's interest in the investigation was only peripheral. The old man had asked him to have an informal look at the cash flow of ESK/JAPAN to prepare a defence against Senate charges, should it come to that point. And the most that Corbett could offer Erikson was a qualified opinion that no money in large numbers could have been diverted from Japanese operations to the Vietnamese government because he could find nothing amiss.

27

He leafed through the teletypes until he found an answer from Swanson in Liberia concerning the ownership of the Liberian ships. He was not surprised that Swanson had come up with very little. After all, Liberian registry and a flag of convenience were designed to protect the anonymity of the owner. In this case the vessels were listed as being owned by Ludlow, Limited, a holding company that was not listed elsewhere as a corporation and whose home address was no more specific than Hong Kong.

Corbett abandoned the report from Swanson and with a sense of distaste picked up a long communiqué from Klein. Corbett had met Klein infrequently in the six months Klein had been with the company as a policy adviser to the old man and he disliked him immensely. He saw Klein as a rigid, inflexible man, full of disguised paranoia, operating according to the omnipresent-enemy concept. He had been in the military too long.

TO: CORBETT
FROM: KLEIN
SUBJECT: ARMS
WE HAVE RECEIVED STRONG ADVICE FROM WASHING-
TON CONTACTS THAT ERICKSON WILL BE SUBPOENAED
BY SENATE COMMITTEE – MULTINATIONALS WITHIN
TWO WEEKS. NEED ALL INFORMATION YOU HAVE
COLLECTED SOONEST, PLUS GUARANTEE OF YOUR
PERSONAL CAPABILITIES TO CLEAR ANY POTENTIAL
CHARGES. OUR POSITION HIGHLY VULNERABLE. COM-
MUNICATE SOONEST AND REPORT ON ARRIVAL IN TOKYO.

He put the teletype on the table and scratched his left eyelid, aware that Wilson was watching him, observing his reaction to the high-handed language of the message. At one time he had been very careful to preserve a façade of cool neutrality in the presence of subordinates – it paid to have a reputation for nervelessness – but he realised that such pretences were no longer necessary.

'Shit,' he said. 'The Asians are getting ready to eat us up alive and this military son of a bitch wants to concentrate everything on how we're going to look in the Senate committee.' He sipped his drink, looked out the window. He was level with the towering tops of cumulus nimbus clouds over the obscured Strait of Korea. It would be raining far down below. 'Klein would like to make this a full-scale battle, provoke the Senate, and then launch a counteroffensive and tromp the hell out of them. He would also like to cut the ground out from under me.'

'Why?'

'Because I don't want to play war.'

'Then you don't think the charges are serious?'

'No,' Corbett said. 'Somebody cashed in on an American mistake, I don't doubt that. Somebody bought the leftovers from the Vietnam War and peddled them in Africa. But I don't think it's connected with ESK in any way.' He finished the drink, then took out his pen, blocked out a message below Klein's.

TO: KLEIN

FROM: CORBETT

SUBJECT: ARMS

I HAVE SURVEYED THE TRENCHES. IF THERE IS AN ENEMY, HE DOES NOT BELONG TO US. MY PERSONAL CAPABILITIES NEED NO GUARANTEE. I AM WILLING TO TALK, TO DISCUSS, NOT TO REPORT.

He examined what he had written and struck out everything beyond the word *guarantee* and then handed the paper to Wilson. 'Send this,' he said.

'There's something I think you ought to know,' Wilson said tentatively. 'There's a rumour going around the middle-management area. I think you should be aware of it.'

'All right, make me aware,' Corbett said.

'Middle management sees Klein as the new Far East

wheeler-dealer. They think he's out to reorganise our operations in this part of the world.'

'Do you know what's really going to happen?'

'No.'

'I can give you an educated guess, no more than that, but I think I can come pretty close to it.' How to distill what he felt, what he saw, what he sensed was happening here in a world gone crazy, the old values turned upside-down, that was the problem. 'On our present course I'd say we have another ten years in the Far East, not just us but any corporation with an American base. American stock is falling, that's the long and short of it.'

'I don't see any weakening in the Japanese area,' Wilson said.

'Japan may be the last stronghold,' Corbett said, 'but I'm not even sure of that. Hell, the Koreans aren't just testing the company, they're testing the United States and the government's not going to back us anymore. Now, I may be able to negotiate with the Koreans and bring them down in their demands, but the camel has his nose in the tent and the minute we pay there, we pay everywhere. And it won't be too long before they're able to operate without us.' He lighted a cigarette, leaned back in the seat, feeling the vibration of the jet, the sense of movement. 'There are hundreds of very bright young Koreans in business schools all over the world. They're grooming managers and when they're ready they can operate as efficiently as we can. But Klein underestimates them, that's his trouble. They walk around in mirrored sunglasses and their soldiers swagger and look undernourished and he figures none of them are quite bright. But there's no way that Klein's going to improve our position with his military thinking.'

'Then you think Klein is fighting a losing battle,' Wilson said.

'I know damn well he is.'

Now Corbett could see that Wilson did not agree with

30

him. There was that slight flicker of doubt within himself that he could not conceal. He would have to watch that. He could not afford to have his feelings displayed so transparently.

Wilson stirred. 'I'd better get this on the Telex.'

'Yes. Do that.'

And then Corbett found himself alone. He could not sleep. He would have to get together with Erikson for a strategy session and the old man preferred to meet late at night or in the early hours of morning, as if he needed no sleep at all. And when Corbett arrived in Tokyo, the suite would be ready at the hotel, the rooms set aside for his use whenever he was in the Far East. His wardrobe would be freshly cleaned, replenished by staff members retained only for their ability to make arrangements, to take care of any details that might otherwise distract a high-level official from the necessary single-minded company dedication. It had been many years since he had had to take care of anything for himself and he wondered now if he could adjust to it again, removing his mind from the hard bright world of financial reports and company policy to the area of his own needs.

Cristina came into his mind. She would be in Tokyo tonight. He would have to talk to her, come to some decisions, because their present relationship was an untenable one and it was only a matter of time before it became an issue in the company. There were few secrets at ESK, not in an organisation with a quarter million employees scattered around the world and ambitious men busily collecting data that could aid their climb in the company.

Abernathy. He could see Abernathy's pallor as he stood outside the ROK headquarters, the slight tremor in his fingers, and he could remember the precise tenor of his voice as he exploded at the Colonel. No great strength there, no, a pitch of desperation rather than strength. It had been a mistake to move him from San Francisco to Korea, to throw him into rough and tumble

31

when he was accustomed to smooth, and yet if Corbett made an accurate report of what had happened, Erikson would have no qualms about removing him immediately, without recommendation, so that Abernathy would be left stranded on the sandspit of middle age, with few alternatives. Ah, hell, what was the difference? Corbett would say nothing. He would retain Abernathy here for a while and then carefully ease him back to San Francisco, where he could run the plant there and live in his fine house overlooking the bay and come home at night to a fire in the hearth and a wife content to be where she was.

He submerged himself in the preparation of the report on the meeting with the Colonel and its implications, then dictated it to Ellen and asked her to have a copy put on the Telex immediately so Erikson would be briefed by the time of their meeting. Once the report was cleared away, he looked out the window to orient himself, found the clouds had disappeared, the jagged peaks of the Japanese alps below him and in the far distance the cone of Fujiyama rising out of the yellow layer of smog that clouded the horizon.

Wilson came in from the communications compartment. 'We have a delegation of newsmen waiting at Haneda,' he said.

'Oh? What's the occasion?'

'I just had a call from Stevens,' Wilson said, sitting down, pouring himself a cup of coffee. 'You hit it right on the nose. While you were meeting with the Colonel, his boys were releasing a statement to the press, stating that first talks had opened between the Republic of Korea and ESK/INT towards a formula for payment of what he terms "obligations".'

'Do you have a text?' Corbett said.

'Yes, sir.' Wilson handed him the sheets. Corbett smiled as he read them. The Koreans were handling this with considerable sophistication. If Corbett had been summoned to the office of the Foreign Minister, he would have been accompanied by a staff of Korean lawyers and experts from the American Embassy and there would have been no discussion whatsoever, merely a presentation of Korean demands that would have been carried away for a time-consuming study and a subsequent protest from the American State Department. 'It's goddamned clever,' Corbett said. 'It has the same effect as if we had agreed to a full-scale meeting.'

'What are you going to say to the press?'

'Nothing. I want you to handle it for me. Tell them there was an informal meeting concerning the diode plant and some internal troubles but that there was no discussion of either payments or formulas. Tell them the company has the greatest respect for the Republic of Korea and its people and that there has been a misunderstanding here.'

'If you'll excuse my saying so, I don't think that's going to get it,' Wilson said.

'Obfuscation is our greatest strength,' Corbett said. 'Has Abernathy made any statement?'

'No. So far he's been inaccessible to reporters.'

'Send a message and tell him to stay inaccessible,' Corbett said. 'He's to make no comment to anybody. Also tell him to remove the library from the employees' lounge and to maintain a very low profile. I do want to hear from him the second the Korean government makes any move against the plant, either directly or indirectly.' He accepted coffee from Wilson, sipped it, allowing himself time to think. 'See if you can get us permission to land at a freight terminal. And have a car meet us there.'

'Will do,' Wilson said.

Wilson disappeared towards the cockpit. The pressures were beginning to build again. He had allowed the Koreans the advantage once; he must make certain that did not happen again. He opened his attaché case and went back to work.

3

The traffic in the city was frantic as usual, the expressway crowded, the air dirty. He used the telephone in the limousine to call the hotel, asking for Stevens, who came on the line with an air of urgency.

'Where are you, Willie?' Stevens said.

'I'm in Tokyo, on the way to the hotel. Is Erikson there?'

'I don't know where the hell he is,' Stevens said, a frenetic tone to his voice. Stevens was the worrier, the purveyor of small informations, the computer technician elevated beyond his capacities. 'He's been with the Chinese all afternoon. Klein wants to see you immediately.'

'I'm sure he does,' Corbett said. 'When will Erikson be back?'

'I'm not sure,' Stevens said. 'I try to keep an accurate schedule but I'll be damned if I can. What time will you get here?'

'I don't know. As soon as possible.'

'Please check in with me. I've got some other stuff but it will wait.'

Corbett severed the connection, leaned back against the seat of the limousine, setting his watch back to Tokyo time. In the next day or two he would have to find time to get back to his regular regimé of exercise and sleep. At one time he had been able to operate a full twenty-four-hour day with no more than a few catnaps to sustain him, but that time had passed.

The twin towers of the Sakura-Erikson loomed ahead of him, over the bank of lesser buildings in the Marunouchi district, a monolithic complex of buildings with marble and glass façades. Erikson had boasted once that there was so much glass in these buildings that they would require a crew working continuously around what he considered to be the capstone to his empire. Even now there were window washers on scaffoldings near the top floor, gradually working their way down, a perpetual task. The smog would guarantee that; there was rarely a time when the glass was not covered with a fine layer of soot.

The limousine pulled into the parking basement and he took the elevator to his suite on the eighth floor. Standardisation, he thought, closing the door behind him. Standardisation was the secret of Erikson's success, for the hotels the old man had built around the world contained identical rooms, the local culture of the host countries reflected only in the lobbies. But the suite was the same as Corbett's suite in Rome, dimensions identical, an ornate bathroom to the left, a sizeable sitting-room opening to a rarely used terrace, and to the right a door that led to the bedroom and a dressing-room.

There were flowers on the coffee table and a note in a small envelope, no writing on the outside, and he smiled slightly as he read the impersonal block letters on the card, CALL WHEN READY, nothing else. Cristina was in another of her paranoiac moods and there was no telling how elaborately she had planned to get the card into his room without the possibility of having it traced back to her.

He found a bottle of bourbon in the liquor cabinet, the seal unbroken, and he was tempted, but he let it be for the time being. Instead he called room service and ordered a rare steak. Then he checked in with Stevens, who said he would drop by shortly. Corbett was washing his face when Stevens arrived. He was a small, balding man in middle age who wore round glasses with steel rims that gave him the appearance of an anxious owl.

'What's your schedule?' Stevens said from the sitting-room. 'It's six now and Erikson won't be back until seven but he's eager to get together with you.'

'I'm available,' Corbett said, drying his face, moving back to the sitting-room. 'What do you have for me?'

'Let me see,' Stevens said, consulting his notebook. 'In

the first place, legal wants to talk with you as soon as possible. Klein's been waiting all day. He's in twelve forty-seven. Transportation would like a schedule. Also Stedman wants you to call him in Munich.'

'There's nothing there that can't wait. I'll see Klein after a while and legal in the morning.'

The messages had been delivered and still Stevens stayed where he was, obviously uncomfortable. 'I just want you to know that I'm behind you a hundred per cent,' he said. 'This is off the record, but I think you have grounds for a suit.'

'What's happening to me that calls for a suit?' Corbett said. There was a tap on the door and a Japanese waiter wheeled a cart in with his dinner. 'Just put it on the table,' Corbett said. He sat down, unrolled his napkin, waiting until the waiter was gone, feigning an ease now that he did not feel. 'Now, what seems to be the trouble?'

Stevens placed a newspaper on the table beside his plate. 'I thought you would have seen it by now. It's a story in *Asahi*. Page three.'

'Thank you for your concern,' Corbett said.

'If there's anything I can do . . . '

'I'll get back to you after I've read it.'

'Let me know about the calls.'

Ah, the tidings of bad news, and Stevens was a natural carrier. He abandoned the steak for a moment in favour of the coffee and the newspaper, which had been folded to page three and a story credited to *The New York Times*. Hell, it was bound to come, he knew that, because a company was difficult to attack and investigating committees always seized on a name, a person, but the sense of shock was there nonetheless. This time he was it, singled out in a fiction with the absolute ring of truth to it. He knew it was false because it had not happened, but he realised that if he had been reading the name of an unknown person in place of his own, he would tend to believe it.

The story was simple and at the same time complex. It described him as a close personal friend of Erikson's who had done so well in European middle management that he had been promoted to an international trouble-shooter for ESK/INT and a possible successor to Erikson once the old man decided to retire. It mentioned the attacks being made on multinational corporations, which were assuming the power of separate political entities attached to no country, and rehashed the alleged misconduct of Erikson in Argentina and collaborative efforts between ESK/INT and other multinationals to circumvent any government regulation.

But Corbett found himself described as the man responsible for the purchase of American arms from Vietnam. According to the account, the Vietnamese government had long been looking for a market for American equipment that was useless to them, a stockpile that included several Phantom jets in various stages of disrepair along with dozens of tanks and literally hundreds of thousands of small arms. They had managed to sell five million dollars' worth of the small arms to neighbouring countries in Southeast Asia but they had been unable to sell the larger equipment to any single government, not only because repair parts were inaccessible, but because the United States were exerting considerable international pressure to block sales.

Allegedly, Corbett had formed his own holding company, Ludlow, Limited, in Hong Kong, and borrowed funds from ESK/INT, which he paid to a Vietnamese representative in Paris. The armaments were removed from the port of Da Nang on August 12, 13, and 14 and taken to a port in Africa. Corbett had then bribed an official in the Department of Defense to authorise sale of repair parts ostensibly bound for Israel under a standing military agreement. Instead, the parts were shipped to Africa, where they were used to restore what was a formidable arsenal. It was alleged that Corbett was sell-

37

ing these armaments to the highest bidder, piecemeal, to buyers all over the world.

Somebody had gone to a great deal of trouble for nothing because in his career with the company he had been a highly visible man and across the world could be found a trail of landing and departure times at airports, stamped visas, expense accounts, a daily journal, tons of trivia with which he could prove beyond the shadow of a doubt that he had not been involved. He decided to have a drink after all. He mixed bourbon with bottled water and then he picked up the telephone and called Fenster in legal.

'Willie,' Fenster said, with great relief. 'I've been waiting for you to call. Do you know what's happening? Are you in the hotel?'

'I'm here. I just read the account in *Asahi.*'

'Come on up.'

Corbett felt comfortable with Fenster because Fenster had a quick mind, an alertness to countless alternatives, which tended to minimise any crisis, regardless of how grave it seemed at the moment. As Corbett entered his suite he was leaning over the coffee table, scribbling something on a yellow legal pad, looking up over the rims of his half-glasses with a frown, tapping the pencil against his chin, scribbling a final word before he sprang up from the divan, displaying a smile that was almost a grimace. He shook Corbett's hand. 'I was going to offer you a drink but I see you're carrying. I think I'll have one for myself.'

He mixed himself a drink at the bar, delivering a monologue that encompassed the dissolution of the world, the collapse of cities, and the disintegration of international law. He moved among the papers strewn across the chairs, clearing space for Corbett to sit. 'Ridiculous, of course,' he said. 'Absolute shit. So goddamned time-consuming, simply because somebody wants to score some political points.'

'All right, Al,' Corbett said. 'What am I up against?'

'A massive fucking misunderstanding along with a good dose of malice. They could be out to get the company or they could be out to sink you. Okay, who has it in for you?'

'Dozens of people. Inside and outside the company.'

'They'll get flushed out along the line. But right now, we have to cover your ass.'

'From what?'

'The Senate committee. But if we beat them to full disclosure, we can head that off.' He threw up his hands at the jumble of papers on the coffee table, then leaned back and rattled the ice in his glass. 'All right, we begin with all the cards on the table. Is there anything to the charges?'

'Hell, no.'

'If there's the slightest connection, there's no need to conceal it from me. If the company's involved, then we take a different tack, that's all.'

'The company is not involved.'

'You're in a position to know that for sure?'

'The old man asked me to see if I could find any connections. I can't.'

'Klein thinks there's a connection.'

'He's wrong.'

'And you have had absolutely nothing whatsoever to do with the fucking Vietnamese?'

'Absolutely not.'

No judgements, yes, and Corbett had the feeling that if he admitted murder at this point, a heinous and bloody crime, Fenster would continue to sip his drink and frown over his glasses, displaying no regard at all for the act itself but only for the best line of defence.

'All right,' Fenster said. 'Any skeletons?'

Corbett took a drink from his glass, thinking of Cristina. 'What kind?'

'Any kind. You're going to be run through the journalistic mill. My God, the world's an angry place. Everybody's frustrated, looking for scapegoats, and you have all the qualifications for a dandy one. If they find anything to seize on, believe me, they'll do it. If they find anything dirty, kinky, massively illegal, you have the makings of a number one national villain.'

'Nothing,' Corbett said. 'Nothing like that.'

'All right,' Fenster said, sitting on the edge of the divan, picking up a folder of loose papers. 'How many times have you been in Paris this year? I need dates.'

'Very often,' Corbett said. 'At least once a month.'

'Dates.'

'Wilson can supply them. Or the Paris hotel.'

'Africa?'

'No.'

'You're sure of that?'

'Yes.'

'Could the money for this deal have come from any place in ESK/INT?'

'Shit,' Corbett said, leaning back in the chair. 'Sometimes I fool myself. You know what the company's like, Al. I can guarantee that the money didn't come from the Japanese end. But there are enough ESK deals floating around Europe and the United States that I'd have to say it's possible. Jesus, we have auditors in every country in the world, all of them using different auditing methods.'

'Then company money could be involved.'

'I'd have to say yes.'

'Trackable?'

'Given time. Why not give the problem to Klein? It would occupy him for six months at least, get him out of the mainstream.'

'Klein is a horse's ass,' Fenster said, without emotion. 'Tell me something, Willie. Could you have done it?'

'Certainly.'

'Then the scenario in the paper is a valid one.'

'It's not that good,' Corbett said. 'In the first place, I wouldn't have had to use any company funds at all. There's lots of money available in the Arab countries and I could have bankrolled the whole operation from a single source and washed the money through dummy companies in the Bahamas and made the trail so damned complicated nobody could ever trace the funds. And secondly, I would never ship materials to Africa in the hopes of holding a stockpile and selling piecemeal. There's no place in Africa where it would be safe.'

'Right,' Fenster said, more reflective now. 'But simply because something is stupid doesn't mean that it can't be or hasn't been done. If you could have done it, then other people in the company could have done it as well.'

'A few, maybe,' Corbett said. 'But any global manager would know he couldn't keep the lid on a transaction like that for very long, not if he tapped company funds. It would blow wide open the second one of the jets showed up. The American government wouldn't stand still for it.' He realised that was not completely true, even as he said it, because scandals continued to crest and break, with revelations of domestic assassinations, sexual misadventures in high places, the shattering of the old values, and when it came right down to it, who gave a shit anymore about Vietnam or what had happened there or where the abandoned arms had gone. It was past history, as remote as Antietam in many ways.

Suddenly he was aware how silent Fenster had become, sitting on the divan, studying him quietly, almost motionless, and Corbett knew why he was here. He was more amazed than troubled by the realisation. 'How long have we known each other, Al?'

'Seven, eight years, maybe.'

'And still it took me a while to catch on.'

'I don't get what you mean.'

'This isn't a simple exploratory conversation, is it? I mean, you have had orders to pinpoint my complicity in this deal and then protect the company, right? Because in somebody's mind, at least, there's no doubt that I'm guilty.'

'Not in my mind,' Fenster said.

41

'Then Klein. He's the one.'

'Yes. But I wouldn't worry about him. He doesn't have the clout.'

'He had the clout to get you assigned to this.'

'Oh, come on,' Fenster said, attempting to dismiss it. 'It's my job to look into anything that has a bearing on the company and the courts. You know the way Klein operates. Bogie at twelve o'clock high, enemies in the woodwork. Shit, you can't take these things personally.'

'I do take them personally,' Corbett said. 'But that's neither here nor there. I have nothing to hide. I can provide you with shortcuts if you like.'

Fenster shook his head, slowly. 'Perhaps a few questions as we go along.' He became more animated now, as if his inactivity had been temporary. 'I'll go through the motions, that's all. But I would advise you to do two things. First, don't go back to the States until we see what's going to develop. And secondly, keep a low profile, a vacation perhaps, at least officially, so that everybody around here can go blank when they're asked where you are.' The telephone rang. He picked it up and then handed it to Corbett.

It was Mrs Seagraves. 'I just had a message from Mr Erikson,' she said, her voice laden with forbearance. 'He won't be back until quite late and wonders if you could meet him in his suite at eleven o'clock tonight.'

'Certainly,' Corbett said. 'Eleven o'clock.'

3

When he called Cristina she answered on the first ring, her voice restrained.

'I'm here,' he said.

'All right,' she said. 'Leave the hotel by the front entrance and walk to your right. I'll pick you up. But you'd better give me about a twenty-minute head start.'

He was about to ask her if all these precautions were absolutely necessary but the line had gone dead. He waited twenty minutes and then left the hotel, walking along the crowded sidewalk. He had walked about a half mile when a small Datsun swooped from the traffic to the curb and he climbed in just as it moved away again, Cristina at the wheel, her black hair hidden beneath a large hat with a floppy brim, her face engulfed by an oversized pair of dark sunglasses.

'Were you followed?' she said, manoeuvring the car away from a truck, into a faster lane.

'Hell, no, I wasn't followed,' he said tolerantly.

'Make sure.'

He was humouring her now and he knew it, peering back at the maelstrom of automobiles and trucks on the boulevard. She made a sudden turn, careening across the path of the truck and into a side street, the truck braking suddenly, horns blaring. Her speed did not slacken.

'You have my guarantee,' he said. 'No one could follow you.'

'I don't think you're taking me seriously, darling,' she said. 'How are you, anyway?'

'Ragged ass tired,' he said. 'What's going on with you?'

'Do you remember Paris, a couple of months ago?'

'Sure.'

'Well, there's an investigator there who's trying to prove we were together.'

'How do you know that?'

'Elsie,' she said. She stopped suddenly at a light, peering ahead before she urged the car into a sudden turn, continuing to talk while he tried to remember who Elsie was. 'You remember Elsie. She's that stunningly beautiful German girl you liked so well, the one with the long legs. I had a letter from her waiting for me here. She said that a private investigator approached her last week and asked about me and the time I had spent in Paris. He was pretending that it was connected with an automobile claim. Elsie told him nothing, absolutely nothing, but she thought I should know what was happening. I'm convinced it's Erik. I know it is.'

'You're making broad leaps,' he said.

'I don't think so,' she said, driving past the Diet Building. 'I can't prove it, of course. I simply can't confront Erik with it, but I think we have to be more careful.'

'All right,' he said. Games, yes, one of Cristina's elaborate games, needing to believe that in some way she was deceiving Erikson when Corbett knew with almost absolute certainty that she was not. He felt sure that Erikson knew of the relationship and had given his silent approval simply by not interfering. For the old man had undergone surgery four years ago under such security that few people in the company knew anything about it. Even Corbett did not know the exact nature of the surgery but he did know that since that time Erikson had demonstrated no interest whatsoever in sexual matters. Cristina was simply window dressing.

But at the same time if Cristina's movements had been charted in Paris, it was highly significant. He could not help but believe that he himself was the main subject under investigation and that she was simply a means to track him.

She fell silent, following an indirect route towards the house that Erikson maintained in Tokyo, a European-style villa set in the heart of the Shinanomachi district. There were at least half a dozen houses scattered around the world that Erikson had personally selected, one in Rome, another in London, one in Geneva, another at Cuernavaca, one twenty miles outside of Paris, all of them ostensible sites for elaborate entertainments should the occasion arise, but as far as Corbett knew, they had never been used for any other purpose than to accommodate Cristina on her travels.

The traffic thinned near the athletic stadiums that had been built for the Olympics and the car moved down a

44

tree-lined boulevard on which there was little traffic at all, finally turning to dip beneath a railroad underpass into a narrow lane flanked by the grounds of a detached palace on one side and houses on the other.

Cristina parked the car by the gate and Corbett led the way into the garden courtyard in front of the house. The garden had changed little since he had seen it last except that now there were two large ceramic dogs mounted on pedestals along the tree-lined path, oriental, ferocious in a passive, stylised way. Cristina unlocked the door and pushed her way into the house, dramatically, as if preparing for a scene with her enemies, but the house was quiet. She took off her hat, shaking her hair, removing her sunglasses. 'Why don't you fix the drinks, darling?' she said. 'I need to freshen up.'

'Sure,' he said.

He occupied himself at the wetbar with the crystal glasses and the ice, and the moment Cristina left the room he found himself thinking about his schedule. He tried to clear his mind of all the business he would have to report to Erikson tonight, sorting it out, compartmentalising, trying to let go of the concern for his own welfare. It was Fenster's role to be thorough and in that thoroughness lay protection.

She returned to the room just as the telephone rang, the change complete, the suit replaced by a gown, her hair brushed, the franticness of the drive giving way to the insulated peacefulness of Cristina at home. She answered the telephone, which lay on an ornate refectory table, sitting on the edge of it, her long and perfect legs extended to the floor, her fingers brushing one strand of fine black hair away from her face.

In this room, he thought, in the almost European elegance with its pale white walls and the ceilings with the massive beams, she took on a fragile air, looking very small and very lovely and he felt a brief pang that this was not his house and that she was not his wife, that whatever claim he had upon her was very tenuous in-

45

deed, the relationship to be sustained only as long as she wished to preserve it.

He handed her a gin and tonic, sticking with bourbon himself, listening to her half of the conversation. She was speaking French, he realised, cajoling somebody to provide something for tomorrow night, and whoever it was would be unable to resist her. He took off his suit jacket before he sat down on a long, low divan. It seemed very natural for him to be here with her, watching her smooth the fabric of her gown across her thigh. She said a few more words into the telephone, then came to sit beside him, kissing him, settling in.

'Did you know that the chef at the hotel is French?' she said. 'He's being very difficult about the dinner tomorrow night. But then, if Erik was really upset with me, the chef wouldn't be calling me at all, would he?'

'No,' he said. 'I don't want to talk about Erik. When did you get in from the States?'

'This morning,' she said, tasting the drink. 'Just in time to hear about you. Did you do it?'

'No.'

'Are you in serious trouble?'

'I don't think so,' he said.

'I think something's about to happen in the company. Everybody is so on edge, restless.' Her hand rested on his leg. He could feel the warmth of her palm.

'To hell with the company,' he said. 'Are the servants here?'

'No,' she said.

He smiled slightly, put his drink on the low coffee table, then he kissed her. 'It's been too long,' he said.

'Yes, much too long.'

They went upstairs, into a large room with dormer windows, and he lay down with her on the bed, caught up in the scent of her, the taste of her mouth, the feel of her body beneath the gown. But he found in the midst of the undressing, the mutual exploration of flesh, that despite the apparent eagerness with which she opened to him, joining him, that there was a resistance in her that he could not overcome. He would wait; he knew her well. She lay beside him on the bed, naked, her arm across his chest.

'Where are you?' he said.

She was quiet for a moment, thoughtful. 'Would you give up the company for me?'

'Yes,' he said. 'I think so.'

'But you're not sure.'

Ah, the pattern and drift of words that had been said before and sometimes he felt as if he were playing out a kind of drama for which the script had already been written. He lighted a cigarette. 'No, I'm not sure. I stay with the company because it's the most exciting game in the world.'

'And where do I fit?' she said.

'I'm not exactly sure,' he said. 'Maybe you don't. I love you. I like being with you. You're an intelligent, exciting woman. Just for the hell of it, reverse it. Would you give up the company for me?'

'No,' she said, amused. 'How much are you worth, William?'

'I don't know. I haven't counted lately.'

'Be serious.'

'I honestly don't know. Maybe a half million. Plus some stock options that may or may not be worth another quarter, depending on the day.'

She stood up now, totally naked, restless. In the soft light of the room her flesh was aglow, her breasts full, hips tight, hair only slightly dishevelled, falling down across the smooth slope of her shoulders. She stopped in front of a full-length mirror, examining herself dispassionately, with a critical eye. She put the flat of her hand against her stomach. 'I'm thirty-six, William.'

'So?'

'Have you ever noticed the patina of the very rich? I mean, you can see it even in the children. Glossy skin, hair that's alive, a special quickness to the eyes. They

47

have a head start and their women are always beautiful. How could they keep from being beautiful?' She concentrated on her breasts. 'Do you know how much it costs to fly Alice around, just to massage me? About twenty-five thousand a year. And that gown on the floor? About a thousand dollars. I spend about fifty thousand dollars a year on my body. Could you afford that?'

'Why in hell are we sitting around balancing books?' he said.

'Because we have to consider the future,' she said. 'And the future means money.'

'Why is it so important to you?'

'Last month, in Paris, I was mistaken for one of the very rich. I was approached for an interview by an editor of *Réalités*. I turned it down.' She reached out and put the palm of her hand on his chest. 'I can feel your heart beating.' She withdrew into herself, taking the cigarette away from him. 'It costs about two hundred thousand a year to support me. I would like to be very, very rich and never grow old, older, oldest.'

The race against time, he thought, but there was no way she could know it until she experienced it for herself. This was one battle she would eventually lose. In many ways she was a personification of the propaganda engendered by the three hundred-odd companies that formed the corporation, so many of them selling protection against age as if age were a blight that could be controlled, a progressive disease that could be arrested.

'You're a beautiful woman,' he said. 'Sometimes I think you work too hard at it, but that can't be helped. Now, what do you want out of me?'

'Could you take over the company?'

'When?'

'Now.'

'No. I'm not sure I would want to if I could.'

'Why not?'

'That takes absolute commitment.'

48

'Are you sure the rumours about you aren't true?'

'You sound as if you would like them to be.'

'Yes,' she said. 'If you had done that, we could live in Monaco and go to the casino every night and make love on our own private beach.' She shrugged slightly. 'I could always marry him briefly, couldn't I?'

'He has a wife.'

'In Key Biscayne. A very old wife.'

'You're forgetting. He's a practical man.'

'She's of no use to him.'

'Hell,' he said. 'You're being naïve. She gives him respectability when he needs it. When he's with a conservative President or dealing with a Member of Parliament, she gives him a credibility and legitimacy he couldn't have any other way.'

'And what do I give him?'

He was in a touchy area now and he knew it. 'I don't know what kind of personal feelings he has for you and I don't want to know. But tomorrow night, with you around, he'll be the envy of all his Asian managers, men harassed out of their gourds by the pressures of business, most of them trapped in terrible marriages because he demands everything from them and keeps them so off balance most of the time that they're ulcerated and impotent.'

'Which you're not,' she said with a half smile.

'You're his goddamned status symbol,' he said. 'The men in the company see you as the symbol of what a real success means.'

'I'm afraid of him,' she said. 'What do you think he would do to me if I told him I was leaving?'

'If you confronted him?'

'Yes.'

He had reached a line that he refused to cross. He felt that if Cristina went too far with Erikson, he would simply shed her as he would a raincoat, with about as much emotion. But to express what he felt would demean her and he had no desire to do that. 'I don't know,' he said.

She lay beside him again and he could tell that the time was right for her now, that she wished for him to make love to her again. 'How long will you be in Tokyo?' she said.

'I don't know. How about you?'

'Erik said a few days. Then I've been thinking about Hong Kong. Wouldn't it be heavenly to have a week together, just the two of us?'

She lay separate from him, not touching, but he felt his desire returning. 'Not in Hong Kong,' he said. 'Hong Kong is a glass house.'

'Then somewhere else.'

'I'd like that,' he said. 'They're suggesting that I take a vacation. They'd like to get me out of here for a while.'

'Where can we go?'

He reached out his arms and gathered her in.

Chapter 2

The Esk hotel system had never ceased to amaze Corbett, the whole concept of corporate enclaves in every
major foreign capital. The idea had not been original
with Erikson, of course, for Geneen of ITT had begun
the trend and Erikson, with his usual perspicacity, had
only picked up the idea and refined it, capitalising on
the opportunities it offered. The Sakura-Erikson was a
perfect example; an immensely profitable operation
with all of one tower and part of the other open to
the public and corporate headquarters occupying the
major part of one building. Four excellent restaurants
were scattered over the lower floors, and multiple bars
and clubs, all cloaked under an absolute security in a
city renowned for the lack of it. It was not publicly advertised, of course, but it was known in business circles
that the hotel was clean of electronic devices, swept daily
by monitors in the hallways, and that all hotel personnel were carefully screened to insure an absolute
privacy. Whatever was said within the hotel, whatever
happened here would be contained within the building.

It was now ten thirty. Sitting in the bar he could
spot at least a half dozen of the Asian managers in
the candlelighted recesses of the booths, two of
them hunched conspiratorially, jotting down figures,
obviously working against time to come up with a presentation of unshakable facts, as Erikson called them,
hard financial situations. The Japanese manager of an
electronics branch was in the shadows with a woman

51

who was obviously not his wife. It was a peculiarity of the Japanese managers that they allowed themselves to get drunk so easily. He was singing along with the piano player, his voice shrill, obtrusive.

Very shortly Corbett would go up to the executive suite for a meeting with a man who never appeared to sleep, who needed no rest. Corbett summoned the bartender and ordered another cup of coffee. He was not nervous about the meeting. Fenster would already have made his report and Corbett would be absolved by reason of impossibility, for he had been in the wrong places at the wrong times to have been able to bring it off. And the final proof would be in a close examination of his own money flow, something the accounting staff would have researched by now.

He took the nonpublic elevator to the quietness of the eighth floor, putting on a fresh shirt, adjusting his tie, examining his weary face in the mirror. Somewhere in the hotel Klein would be fuming because Corbett had not yet seen fit to make an appearance. So be it. He went into the sitting room and turned his attention to the attaché case, laying out the folders in proper order. The Colonel Pak folder was top priority and the old man would have to make a quick decision on it. Of lesser importance were the objections of the Japanese managers to the new concept of the zero-base budget (they operated well under a paternalistic system but did not like the idea of having to justify a total budget every year). It was not likely the old man would choose to discuss that tonight but Corbett knew better than to enter a meeting with him unprepared.

On impulse he picked up the telephone and called Wilson's room on the chance he might be in. Wilson answered the call almost immediately.

'What happened with the Japanese reporters?' Corbett said.

'I played the whole thing down,' Wilson said. 'I told them it must have been a political move, that there was

52

nothing to it, that we had far more important things on our corporate minds. I also told them we would have a full statement to make on the matter in the next few days. As a matter of fact, I'm working on it now.'

'When will you have it?'

'Tomorrow, sometime.'

'Good enough.'

He severed the connection and went back to the folders. He decided against beginning to amass any materials in his own defence. If Erikson made the request, he would act upon it, but not before.

A few minutes before eleven he took the elevator to Erikson's suite, where he was met in the anteroom by Mrs Seagraves, a self-effacing grey-haired secretary who had been with Erikson as long as Corbett could remember. She insisted on offering him a cup of coffee poured from a silver pot, informed him that Mr Erikson would be a few minutes late and then left to answer a muted telephone in another room. Corbett lighted a cigarette and sat down on the narrow sofa, studying the paintings on the wall, all early French, from an age of stylised religiosity. He wondered if this room had been designed to effect an uneasiness in men waiting to be summoned, for there was nothing in this room that did not suggest fragility and coldness, all of the furniture balanced on insubstantial legs.

At precisely eleven o'clock Mrs Seagraves reappeared to conduct him into a spacious and much more comfortable room, where Erikson stood examining a large ceramic oriental dog on a massive table, his face thrust within inches of the ceramic surface, his weight resting on his arms. He was a short man, wiry, but even at this hour he reflected a placid easiness, his Italian suit unrumpled, an unlighted cigar clenched in his even teeth, his grey hair perfectly in place.

'Come in, Willie,' he said with a smile. 'We'll talk about the Colonel pretty soon, but first I want you to see something.'

Corbett approached the table. Erikson picked up a magnifying glass, examining the grimace on the face of the dog, the ferocious eyes. 'What is it?' Corbett said.

'It's a temple dog, quite old, one of the original Korean pieces from which the Japanese adapted their model. Now, I'm being asked a great deal of money for this piece and I like it. But the question is whether this is an original or a copy that was made a couple hundred years ago. How would you go about verifying it?'

Another of Erikson's famous ideological mazes, Corbett realised. He was noted for them in the company, elaborate mental exercises that spiralled around some concealed and central point Erikson would eventually reach. And quite suddenly, Corbett had no desire to indulge the old man. 'Are you really interested in my opinion about this?'

'Assume that I am.'

'Then find an expert and take his advice.'

'It is an expert who is trying to sell me this piece.'

'Then get another opinion.'

'With no assurance that there won't be collusion among the experts.'

'Then you either find an expert you can trust or you take the chance because you like it and can afford it,' Corbett said. He sat down on the sofa. 'I'm not fond of oriental art.'

Erikson nodded slightly. 'Will you join me in a brandy?'

'No, thanks,' Corbett said. 'I don't like brandy either.'

Only now did Erikson smile, a dry leathery smile, a genuine expression of being pleased. He moved to a sideboard of crystal decanters. 'That's one of the things I like about you, Willie, your sense of independence. You have no idea how many men accept the brandy when they don't even like the damn stuff. I want us to have a chat.'

'This Korean business can't wait,' Corbett said.

'This is their straw in the wind,' Erikson said, sitting

down opposite him, his face half in shadow, the brandy glass held in both hands. It was not just an ESK problem, he went on, because all of the multinationals were in trouble in the Far East. He had been in informal communication with a number of them in the past week, setting up committees to assess the situation and come up with possible solutions. Many countries were in economic trouble, that was the long and short of it, and the multinationals were expected to take up the slack. The five-member Association of Southeast Asian Nations had signalled the first danger to the companies, but the internal conflict between Singapore and Indonesia over a free trade zone had prevented any unified movement against the globals. But now that the All Asian Coalition was being formed, the threat was a tangible reality. Next week the AAC would be meeting in Japan. Erikson had no clear idea of their agenda but he was reasonably certain the primary item under discussion would be the establishment of either an annual levy tied to the gross income of any company doing business within their borders or an added value tax. 'A confiscatory levy,' Erikson said, sipping his brandy. 'That's what it amounts to. No country can move unilaterally against us because we would simply shift operations. The question is, what do we do if they come together with a plan? What do you think?'

'I think we have to deal with the Koreans first, immediately,' Corbett said. 'The Koreans have to be pretty goddamn certain of the rest of the countries in AAC or they wouldn't dare to try this.'

'Very likely.'

'What kind of response do you want me to give the Colonel?'

'What would you recommend?'

Back to the Socratic questions and back to the answers that would be useless since Erikson would make the final decisions. 'I suggest we give the Colonel an opening and find out what ROK wants. Not on his turf, but on ours. I can invite him here to talk and find out what he has in mind.'

'Fine,' Erikson said. 'I agree. Do it right away. Now, I have some fine bourbon if you would really like a drink.'

'No,' Corbett said. 'I don't think so. We need to discuss the charges against me.'

'Yes. Have you talked with Klein?'

'Not yet.'

'Why not?'

'I don't like him. I don't see him as the kind of man who can tolerate dissent.'

The old man was quiet for a moment. 'I have confidence in him,' he said flatly. Ah, so be it. 'The charges against you are nonsense, of course. Nobody in this corporation believes you did anything dishonest and neither do the responsible people in Washington. Klein has launched an extensive investigation into the matter and he tells me we should have hard evidence within the next couple of weeks to feed the American government. And that should clear you.'

'I want to release a statement.'

'I'd prefer that you wouldn't,' Erikson said. 'I don't think you would gain anything by taking the accusation seriously. I want you to go full time with the Korean business. I want to know what they're after.'

'All right,' Corbett said. 'I'll get in touch with him in the morning.'

The telephone rang. Prearranged, yes, the transition from one meeting to the next. Erikson moved to answer it. 'Ask him to wait, please,' he said, into the telephone. 'I'll see him shortly.' He put the telephone back on the cradle. 'How soon do you think you can give me a response?'

'I'll let you know as soon as I talk to him.'

'Thank you for coming,' Erikson said, extending his hand. 'I'll look forward to your call.'

There was an art and a science to dealing with the foreign military and Corbett could not contact the Colonel directly, not without putting himself at a disadvantage. Instead, he instructed Wilson to put in a call to Lieutenant Tae at eleven the next morning, explaining that Corbett would be willing to talk but placing a time limit on his availability. Unless the Colonel could come to Tokyo, Corbett might change his mind for Corbett had developed a personal dislike for the Colonel and was at the moment looking for strength within the company to resist Korean demands altogether.

Corbett was not sure whether it would work and while he had breakfast in the hotel dining room he was outlining an alternative strategy in which he would meet the Colonel at one of the towns along the west coast of Honshu, should the Colonel demand a compromise site. But from the expression he saw on Wilson's face as he crossed the dining room Corbett gathered that he had not been unsuccessful.

'Have you had breakfast?' Corbett said.

'No, and as a matter of fact, I'm hungry,' Wilson said, sitting down and summoning a waitress. He ordered ham and eggs and then picked up the coffee cup. 'The Colonel will be in Tokyo this afternoon,' he said. 'But I had to make a minor compromise.'

'What kind?'

'There's a Korean section in the Aoyama Cemetery,' Wilson said. 'The Colonel's sister lives in Tokyo, or she did up until two months ago when she died. She was cremated and the ashes have remained here until the Colonel could come to inter them. It turns out that he will be coming to discharge this family obligation today. If you could happen to be in Aoyama at two this afternoon, the Lieutenant thinks the Colonel would talk to you.'

'That's good enough,' Corbett said, finishing a piece of toast. The night's rest had refreshed him and he felt more buoyantly cheerful than he had in weeks. 'Is there anything in the morning papers about the Vietnamese arms?'

'I talked with New York just after I called the Lieutenant,' Wilson said. 'There doesn't appear to be any follow-up story today. The opinion seems to be that the Senate committee is waiting for some sort of response from the company.' He was interrupted by the arrival of his breakfast and he said nothing until the waitress had served him and gone. 'Do you think they're really serious about pinning you with this business?'

'The old man says not,' Corbett said. He stood up. 'Two o'clock. Can you drive me out there?'

'Certainly,' Wilson said.

'Enjoy your breakfast.'

He thought about walking over to the convention rooms to see if everything was in order for the Chinese banquet but on impulse decided to see Klein instead. The old man's message concerning Klein had been quite clear, so Corbett would make his peace and do his best to get along with him.

Klein had established his headquarters in the area business offices on the twenty-second floor and Corbett never entered his reception room without the feeling that he was moving backward in time, for the offices were almost Spartan, with the feel of a government bureau about them, or the cadre room in a barracks. Klein's secretary was named Miller, a man in his fifties with an air of perpetual good health about him. It had been said that Miller had been Klein's aide-de-camp in the army and had resigned his commission at the same time Klein had made his exit so he could continue service with a man he believed in. Miller rose from his desk as Corbett came in.

'I've been trying to reach you, Mr Corbett,' he said.

'I'm sure you have. Is Klein in his office?'

Miller picked up the telephone, pressed a button with a spatulate finger. 'Mr Corbett is here.' He nodded, replaced the telephone. 'Mr Klein will see you now.'

As Corbett entered Klein's office he was startled to find Klein in what appeared to be a good mood. Klein had already risen from his desk and was approaching the door to meet him. In many ways Klein was as anachronistic as his offices. In his late fifties, having served in the military for over twenty years, he was unable to escape the old image. Despite the tailored suit he wore, he still projected the confidence of a commanding officer.

He shook Corbett's hand. 'I'm glad you could take the time to drop by,' he said. 'Would you care for coffee?'

'No, I just finished breakfast.'

'If you don't mind, I'm in the middle of making a pot.' Klein moved to a sideboard where a pot of water was boiling on a recessed electric burner. 'I find that if I want coffee as I like it, I have to make it myself. Even Miller could never get the hang of it.' He measured ground coffee into a filter, occupied himself with an elaborate procedure. 'I think I owe you an apology,' he said.

'For what?' Corbett looked at the photograph on the wall above a leather divan, all faces of Presidents with scrawled inscriptions in the corners, dedications to Klein, reflecting the collective power of the past.

'I spent too long in the military to maintain any sense of good manners,' Klein said. 'I realised when I came with the company I was going to have to change my administrative approach, but Miller tells me I'm still coming across pretty strong and that an approach like that can be offensive. I apologise for the teletype I sent you yesterday, for the language. But this arms business upsets me. Are you sure you wouldn't like to try this coffee?'

'No, thank you.'

Klein removed a sheaf of papers from his desk, sat

59

down across from the divan, placing his coffee cup on the conference table in front of him. 'I think it might be a good idea if I let you know exactly why Mr Erikson asked me to join the company.'

'That's not necessary,' Corbett said. It was beginning to occur to him now why there had been this change of face since yesterday. The old man had talked to Klein, he could almost be certain of that, the old man had talked to him and asked him to soften his position and now Klein was obediently carrying out the orders from a superior.

'I think it is,' Klein said. 'Did you hear what happened in Argentina last week? Do you know a man named . . . ' He paused, sifted through the papers in search of a name, found it. ' . . . Frederickson, chairman of Telecon.'

'South America isn't my area.'

'If you haven't heard of it, then it proves I'm doing my job,' Klein said. Frederickson had been kidnapped from the Telecon office just as he was arriving for work. It followed the classical pattern for Argentina kidnappings, with a band of terrorists swamping the car and shooting the chauffeur and pulling Frederickson into a closed van. 'But we managed to get him back within twenty-four hours,' Klein said. 'They demanded two million five for his release, but we didn't pay a penny. We've installed a new security system in Argentina, the total operation of which runs considerably less than two million a year.'

'How did you get him back?'

'We had sufficient contacts to know where he was and sufficient force to remove him from a dangerous situation. Hell, ten years ago it wouldn't have been necessary. Under Eisenhower, Kennedy, we were well protected abroad and the whole business community was considered to be an extension of the United States. It went downhill with Johnson, was mishandled under Nixon, and totally degenerated under Ford.' He drank

60

from the cup briefly and set it aside, standing up again as if he were too restless to sit still. 'Mr Erikson brought me in to establish a security system,' he said. 'An extensive one, worldwide. And that's all I'm doing. I don't have any political ambitions within the company nor any desire to reshuffle the current lineup.'

'Why are you telling me all this?' Corbett said.

'Because I need your cooperation, the cooperation of all the top-level people. There's no intelligence community worth a damn anymore. The CIA is limited to a couple dozen men in the Embassy and their names are common knowledge. That reduces their effectiveness to zero. It also places us in the position of having to protect ourselves. Do you agree?'

'In principle,' Corbett said.

'Good. That's all I ask. Now, to the business of the Vietnamese arms. I'm going to need your cooperation on that one.'

'We'd better get one thing in the open,' Corbett said. 'If you have a direct accusation, make it now.'

'I'm not accusing you,' Klein said. 'Washington made that accusation, not me.' He crossed the room to a small computer terminal and a microfilm reader and Corbett noticed that he had a slight limp in his left leg and wondered if the wound had been battle-inflicted. He rather imagined that it was. 'A company is really too large to scapegoat. Two hundred fifty thousand people scattered across dozens of countries, headquarters diffused. They can't sustain an attack on Erikson himself. So they picked you.' He opened a locked file drawer and removed a box of microfiches. 'Have you come up with any leads?'

'I had a report from Swanson, in Liberia.'

'About *The Quarter Moon, The Sentinel*.'

'Yes,' Corbett said, with some surprise. 'Did he also report to you?'

'No. We had that information three days ago.' Klein inserted the microfiche card into a reader, projected the image on a screen mounted in the wall. 'I think you should be fully briefed on what we have.' He turned his attention to the image on the screen, a photograph of the Phantom jet that had been in operation in Vietnam and on the lower edge of the screen an estimate of the number of jets assumed to be in a reparable state. 'As far as we know,' Klein said, 'the majority must be considered reparable. Sold as a group, including necessary repair parts, they should find a ready market.'

Corbett endured the presentation through helicopters and tanks. 'I'd like a printed list of the inventory.'

'Certainly,' Klein said. He pressed a button on the intercom, summoned Miller with a list that filled seventeen pages. 'If you'll notice,' Klein said, as if reading his mind, 'each category is followed by a list of serial numbers that is distinctive. For instance, on the Phantom jets, the last four digits are in the five thousand–eight thousand range. These were jets supplied to the South Vietnamese. The jets supplied to the Israelis carry a two-letter designation such as BZ affixed to a four-numeral range from two thousand to three thousand. In that way we can have a partial fix on the origin of this equipment as it surfaces any place in the world.'

'All right,' Corbett said, impressed. 'But how do you know the Vietnamese peddled the stuff in the first place?'

'That's their catalogue of the material,' Klein said. 'They offered it on the open market. We do have a record of small purchases, a hundred thousand M-16 rifles to one country, smaller numbers to others, but none of the small countries had either the financing or the expertise to be able to buy the more sophisticated equipment.' He pressed a button. The screen was filled with a high-altitude photograph of what appeared to be rows of equipment on a field. 'This was taken at twelve hundred hours on August ten near Phan Thiet. Another picture was taken on August eleven, at about twelve hundred hours.' He pressed a button again and the same field appeared again, the rows more closely crowded, piles of equipment on the periphery of the photograph. 'Unfortunately, there was heavy cloud cover on August twelve and thirteen, and we have no pictures. On August fourteen, at twelve hundred hours, we got this.' The screen went temporarily blank and then a picture of a bare field appeared, not a scrap of litter, not a sign of machinery.

'So they moved everything in forty-eight hours.'

'Correct. They must have been aware that they were under surveillance so after they made their deal they simply waited for a suitable cloud cover. Now, we have records of ships that were in the port that day and all of them can be accounted for except *The Quarter Moon* and *The Sentinel*. We had a good idea those were the ships but we weren't sure until the tank showed up in Africa.'

'Do you have the ports of call for those freighters?'

Klein nodded. 'Tel Aviv, Cairo, and Johannesburg. But that makes no sense, not from any political standpoint. The Israelis have the Kfir, a fighter plane they've developed themselves. The Arabs are well supplied with the new MIG-23's, a hell of a fine aircraft, and South Africa isn't stockpiling American arms. So we have to conclude that the freighters pulled into a port in West Africa and unloaded.'

'This is all very interesting,' Corbett said. 'But I have no connection with any of it. If you have any specifics putting me in the picture, I want the chance to respond. If not, then I want a statement by the company detailing a denial.'

Klein pinched the bridge of his nose as if he had a headache. He said nothing until he had retrieved the coffee cup from the table. 'I suggest you come up with a list of enemies you might have either inside the company or in the private sector.'

'Then you do have evidence.'

'There is an indication that evidence exists.' Klein moved to a small bar sink, poured out the cold coffee, and refilled the cup. 'The Senate committee has a witness who claims that it does.'

'Kukler.'

'Yes. Do you know him?'

'Not to my knowledge. No.'

'Then it's quite obvious that someone is backing him.'

'Kukler is the high-level source who fed the story to *The Times*. Is that what you're saying?'

'I'm not saying he's the direct leak,' Klein said. 'But he testified before the Senate committee in a closed session. Either one of the Senators leaked it, or a stenographer, or a dozen other people. I have a transcript of his testimony, or at least a part of it. I'd like you to see it.'

'Yes,' Corbett said. He watched Klein as he approached his desk, favouring his leg. He opened a drawer and removed papers in a binder marked CONFIDENTIAL. Corbett lighted a cigarette before he opened it.

The first questions in the transcript did little more than establish Kukler's background. He had come from a small town in Pennsylvania, graduated with a law degree from George Washington University, served briefly with a law firm, joined the Department of Defense as a contract lawyer, and at the moment was deputy to the Undersecretary of Defense for Procurement.

The questions and answers seemed to be vaguely wandering but as Corbett scanned them the point to the testimony was quite clear. Kukler had been in Paris in July on another matter when he was approached by a Nigerian government official who wanted Kukler to expedite delivery on military repair parts that had been authorised by the Department of Defense. Kukler was flabbergasted because he was not aware that there was any American military equipment in Nigeria but he was told that the Nigerian government was acting as broker for certain other African governments who did have surplus American material.

64

Kukler took the contract number and the name of the DOD liaison who had authorised it, a man named Harry Saperstein who, when Kukler called him in Washington, verified that he had authorised the contract and that the shipment was already on its way to Nigeria. Saperstein, in turn, revealed that he had executed the contract on the request of William Corbett of ESK/INT, a company that was listed as a prime contractor for DOD in a project to revitalise certain surplus military equipment to be turned back to DOD for resale. Kukler had been alarmed, suspecting an illegal deal of massive proportions.

Q: Did you report this meeting and your suspicions to your superiors?

A: I did. Yes.

Q: And what action was taken?

A: I was told that the matter would be investigated but that such things took time. I asked if the shipments to Nigeria were to be stopped pending an investigation, but I was told that nothing could be done until the matter had been looked into and it was proven that the allegation was true.

The transcript ended abruptly. Corbett looked to Klein, quizzically. 'Where's the rest of it?'

'That's all our source in Washington was able to get. I assume from *The Times* account that either Kukler was able to supply additional information or they had another witness. Have you ever met Saperstein?'

'Yes, I know Saperstein,' Corbett said. 'I know a lot of men at DOD.'

'Did you see him in Washington any time last summer?'

'I may have,' Corbett said. 'I honestly can't say whether I did or not. If I did, it was on a social basis, at a reception, a dinner party. I didn't do any business with him.' He flicked the ashes of his cigarette into a silver

5   65

tray. 'Saperstein must have made some comment. He must have denied the whole thing.'

'He's currently on sick leave,' Klein said. 'Somewhere in South America, although nobody seems to know exactly where. Now, were you in Paris on the first of July?'

Paris, late in June, yes, he had been there on a week's stop-over between Beirut and New York, with Cristina, who had left Erikson in London and come to be with him for a few days. 'Yes,' he said finally. 'I arrived in Paris the last week in June and left, I believe, about the third or fourth of July.'

'Do you have a schedule of your meetings during that time?'

'Hell, I was on vacation. I may have met with some of the people from French companies and I will have a record of those, but for the most part, I was visiting museums, going to restaurants, nothing unusual.' Was his tone defensive now? Was that the way he was coming across? Hell, it made no difference. He had never met with any representative of the Vietnamese government, never discussed any arms deals. 'I don't like this,' he said. 'Now, I don't know why Kukler has chosen to involve me in this but I would like to have a meeting arranged, either with Kukler or members of the Senate committee.'

Klein rubbed his chin, thoughtfully. 'This is a very tricky business,' he said. 'I wish it were as simple as you seem to think it is.'

'What does that mean?' Corbett said. 'Of course it's simple. The man is obviously lying. Now, I don't particularly give a shit why he's lying, but the implications for me are enormous. In the first place, with this kind of accusation hanging over my head, my efficiency is going to go down the drain.'

'I know how you feel,' Klein said. 'Nevertheless, there is one coincidence that we have to overcome. Now, I don't think the Senate committee has this information but they're bound to uncover it and we have to be ready for them.'

'What information?'

'You attended a reception given by the Concorde people in Paris on June thirtieth, at a restaurant on the Place Vendôme. Do you remember it?'

'Vaguely,' Corbett said. 'Where did you get the information?'

'You wrote a memo concerning the dinner. You stated that you didn't get a chance to talk with the chairman of the Federal Aviation Administration, who was also present at that meeting.'

Now it returned, the scene with Cristina as she sat on the edge of the bed in the hotel, wearing a new black gown that had just been finished for her that afternoon. She was pale, silent, caught up in a kind of petulant dilemma between going out with him and running the risk of recognition or staying in the hotel by herself. In the end she had stayed in the hotel and drunk too much and there had been an argument when he returned, followed by a night of lovemaking. 'Yes, I was there,' Corbett said. 'I don't remember any of the details. I must attend a hundred receptions a year.'

'There was a Vietnamese official at the meeting. Than Duc Hu.'

'If he was, I didn't meet him.'

'I'm afraid you did,' Klein said rather unhappily. 'I had a man in Paris check out the guest list, not openly, of course, not connected with you in any way, but a number of people remember your having a rather earnest conversation with the man from Vietnam.'

Corbett could vaguely remember a conversation with an Asian, a diminutive little man, nattily dressed and covertly hostile. 'It's possible,' he said.

'So there you are,' Klein said. 'It makes it more difficult, doesn't it? We're not dealing with truth here, but with appearances. There is enough evidence of appearances to make any story Kukler comes up with

67

quite credible. So, for the time being, I think it's wise that we continue to investigate and make no public statements of any kind.'

'Do you have anything else?'

'Nothing,' Klein said. 'The moment we get anything I'll let you know. I'd like to consult with you on another matter, if you have a moment.'

'Yes,' Corbett said. He only half listened as Klein entered a discussion of terrorist activities over the globe, the increasing trend towards kidnappings in South America. Klein was certain the abduction of company officials was bound to spread into other parts of the world. He was convinced the company had to put countermeasures into effect. 'It's only a matter of time until we have an incident in Japan,' he concluded. 'The Japanese terrorists have been quite effective in other parts of the world, very active.'

'I don't believe it will happen in Japan,' Corbett said.

'But you would have no objection if we take precautions against it?'

'What kind of precautions?'

'I intend to assign a liaison to every top official here.'

'Are you talking about a bodyguard?'

'In a manner of speaking, yes.'

'I don't want a bodyguard,' Corbett said. 'I've operated all over the world for a long time and I'm not afraid of any violence against me.'

'All that I'm asking at this point is that you consider it,' Klein said. He stood up, an obvious signal that he had no further business at this point. Corbett stayed where he was for a long moment and found as he stood up that there was a certain stiffness in his joints, a reluctance somewhere within him to move at all.

Once he left Klein's office, he considered the work that needed to be done and decided to pass it in favour of a walk. He felt oppressed by the closeness of the building, experiencing the peculiar visceral sensations of a kind of dumb panic. He had been in the business world long enough to have seen a hundred different machinations by which one man or one company gained ascendancy over another, but there was always a deal involved, a potential profit, a point to the moves and countermoves. He could see no such point here. It was as if a plot that had been carefully hidden over a long period of time had surfaced overnight, his personal history rewritten to fit its demands. And if the one incident in Paris could be interpreted in a totally erroneous context, there could be others as well.

After making certain there were no Japanese newsmen in the lobby he left the hotel and walked into the Ginza district, aware of the people around him, the great hordes of Japanese in every conceivable form of dress, the workingmen in their jackets emblazoned with the symbol of the company that owned them, the personification of a national business ethic. Quite suddenly, it occurred to him how thoroughly he was bound to the company, how much of his thinking was occupied with company business, how his life as a whole was encapsulated within the company.

And now the threat to him was far more personal, far more real than any of Klein's terrorists in the business of abduction. For unless the evidence were reversed, unless he was able to contradict what was happening, his removal from the company was inevitable, all of the old man's reassurances to the contrary notwithstanding. ESK would have to protect itself either by demoting him to a less critical area where he would not be a liability or by settling his contract and allowing him to cash in his stock options before he was dismissed.

'Mr Corbett.'

He heard his name called and he turned to see a woman in a yellow dress coming towards him. It took him a moment to realise that it was Ellen. She was slightly breathless when she caught up with him. 'Well, isn't this a coincidence?' she said.

'A pleasant one,' he said. 'Come along. I'll buy you a drink.'

'I don't know,' she said. 'I was just doing some shopping.'

'I'd like to,' he said. 'I'll probably be lousy company but I need protection from the hostesses.'

'In that case, I can't turn you down,' she said.

He spotted a bar with a small sign in English above a row of Japanese characters and moved gratefully into the darkness. He seated her at a small table lighted with a single candle. 'I'm going to have a bourbon,' he said. 'If it's too early for you, you can have coffee.'

'Bourbon's fine,' she said. He gave the order to the waitress and then turned his attention to the woman across from him. He had always been drawn to Ellen without ever taking the time to discover why, but now, sitting here in the bar, she reminded him of his ex-wife, that proudly defiant young woman so far in his past he could not specify her face in his mind. There was something of her in Ellen perhaps, a quality of honesty, directness, tempered here by a lack of possessiveness, for Elizabeth had demanded that he choose between the company and her and he had made his choice.

'Have you ever been married?' he said.

'Once,' she said with a smile. 'A long time ago.'

'What happened to it?'

'Do you really want to know?'

'Yes.'

'He was a struggling young accountant and he needed an accountant's wife. I was far too restless for that. What happened to your ex?'

'How did you know I had one?'

'I asked. As a matter of fact, I think I know you pretty well. That is, I know the basics. I know what you think, what you say in your cables, what you like to eat, what you drink, some of what you're doing. So I know you were married.'

'I was a company man, constantly being shifted

70

around, and I needed a company wife. She wanted a nest.'

The waitress came with the drinks. He had broken a pattern he did not even recognise by coming here, to this strange little bar, for there were established watering holes where American businessmen congregated, and there was no drink without at least the dim prospect of doing business. He suddenly realised how ingrown he was, for this woman certainly had a life outside the company and he did not. He raised his glass. 'To the future,' he said.

'I'll settle for the present.'

'Then you must be satisfied with it.'

'Not altogether,' she said. 'I like travelling – I used to be a stewardess – but I'm never in one place long enough to form any relationships. I get propositioned at least once a week by company men and I see a lot of places I haven't seen before.' She brushed a wisp of blonde hair back from her face. 'Do you have any involvements outside the company?'

'No,' he said.

She finished her drink, grinned. 'Strong,' she said.

'Do you want another?'

'Yes, please.'

He signalled the waitress and ordered another one for her, then studied her face in the candlelight. How old was she, twenty-eight, maybe thirty, a beautiful woman in her own way, not like Cristina but beautiful nonetheless and somehow terribly vulnerable. And yet here she was, sitting in a bar in Tokyo, between flights, and the situation struck him as grotesque.

'I've never understood the company,' she said. 'I look at it from the outside, of course, just from the teletypes I send and the people we carry on board. And I wonder what makes you tick. I don't think it's the money because I imagine you already have all the money you can ever use. And yet I see you running all the time as if everything is at stake.'

71

'Maybe it is,' he said. 'What would you do in my place?'

She smiled. 'I've thought about that. Actually, I would be quite good as an executive. I'm a very good organiser.' She studied the flame of the candle. 'And the problem is a pretty simple one, right? These countries want more money from the companies and the companies want to pay as little as possible.'

'Basically, yes.'

'But the companies could afford to pay more than they're paying now. And the countries could afford to take less than they're going to demand. So it becomes a negotiating game, doesn't it?'

'A very complex game.'

'I think I would enjoy it once, no more than that.'

He ordered himself another drink, realising that the alcohol was having no effect on him at all. He was too strung out for that, in one of those states in which he could relax in any way until after the meeting with the Colonel. 'You must have some long-range plans,' he said. 'Something you want. I don't believe anybody can exist without a direction.'

'I know my direction, the north shore of Oahu.'

'When?'

'Someday. I want to live there, when I can afford it. Until then I want to try different things, see different places, be good at what I do as long as I'm doing it. Can you understand that?'

'I think so. Sure.'

'I shouldn't drink in the middle of the day,' she said. 'I'm not used to it and I say things that embarrass me later.' She reached over and put her hand on his, almost a gesture of reassurance. 'I suppose what I want to say is that I like you, Willie, and I don't want anything out of you, absolutely nothing. And now that I've said it, I think I had better go on with my shopping. I have an aunt who's having a birthday and I promised her a string of pearls the next time I came to Japan.'

He watched her make her way across the bar and he felt the vague sense of uneasiness that had become a way of life with him. She had wanted nothing from him, a chance meeting, a drink, and yet he found himself disturbed. Cristina was not that much older than this girl, he realised, yet he felt much more comfortable with Cristina because there were few subtleties in their relationship. He might lose her in the end, no, probably would lose her, because she was as much a part of the company as he was and if he managed to extricate himself from his current predicament he would continue to make the rounds, moving from one part of the world to the next and he could expect to see her every few weeks.

He was suddenly dissatisfied with that glimpse of a possible future. He paid the bill and called Wilson to pick him up, then went out on the street to wait. The limousine arrived within minutes. Wilson opened the door for him, a satisfied expression on his face. 'I think I've run across something,' he said, as the car pulled into the stream of traffic. 'I think I know why Kukler is doing this, at least partially. He was up for a job with ESK once. We passed him over.'

'Possible,' Corbett said. 'Did you bring the Korean figures?'

'Yes,' Wilson said, opening his attaché case, removing a looseleaf notebook full of neatly printed sheets. 'The first is the report we submitted to the Korean government for tax purposes. Then I've included the balances, which cover our real net, including amortisation. And finally, the report we made to the SEC.'

Corbett glaced over the figures. There were three companies in the Korean complex, Abernathy's, which had shown a net of $17 million for the year, a smaller phosphate company in its second year of operation with a gross of $8.5 million and a loss of 10, and finally a smaller diode plant with a net of $10 million. There was an aggregate margin of approximately $7 million between the actual figures and those reported to the Korean government.

The cemetery lay beyond the new stadiums, and the traffic became more congested as they took the bypass street to the west. The cemetery was tucked away in the midst of buildings, a series of humps and ridges covered with rising tiers of vertical stones, obelisks, some with scalloped surfaces into which were set stone figures of passive buddhas. Wilson instructed the driver to park at the foot of a rise of cobblestone steps leading into a forest of markers. There was no sign of the Colonel, only an ancient Japanese couple slowly descending the steps.

'Do you want me to go with you?' Wilson said.

'No,' Corbett said. He left the limousine, finding the air muggy and oppressive, heavy with incense and the moulding smell of ancient stones. He climbed to the top of the steps and paused to get his breath, looking around in the hope of spotting the Korean party, but the cemetery was deserted and his view was limited by a row of staggered obelisks, black with age, cut deep with Japanese inscriptions. He followed a winding path, working his way towards the top of the next ridge, and then he saw the Colonel and Lieutenant Tae, both dressed in ill-fitting Western suits, standing somewhat below him, near a granite slab with a monument above it.

'Good afternoon,' Tae said when he saw him. 'The Colonel wishes to express his appreciation for your promptness.'

'I take it you have completed your ceremony,' Corbett said. 'The interment of the ashes.'

'Yes,' the Lieutenant said. The Colonel said nothing, made no sign that he recognised Corbett's presence here. He looked oddly stocky in his Western clothes and his expression was as passive as ever, the eyes hidden behind sunglasses, his mouth a rigid seam across a powerful face. Corbett looked at him directly.

'I am prepared to talk with you, Colonel,' he said.

74

'Now if you speak English I would prefer to have our discussion without an interpreter.'

The Colonel hesitated a moment and then nodded to the Lieutenant, who walked on down the pathway towards the steps. 'Would you care for a cigarette?' the Colonel said in very good English with just a trace of a British accent.

'Thank you.' Corbett accepted one, lighted it. It was one of the Japanese brands, harsh.

'The question is whether you are now recording this conversation,' the Colonel said, flatly, as if it were not really a question at all. He began to stroll down the path, waiting until Corbett moved to join him.

'No,' Corbett said. 'We've reached the point where we both must act on good faith.'

'Good faith,' the Colonel said with a wry smile. He looked up as a flock of birds flew overhead. Corbett could see them reflected in the lenses of his sunglasses. 'The question is whether the Americans are really acting in good faith for our protection.'

'I can't speak for my country,' Corbett said. 'I represent ESK, not the United States.'

'And your interests are not always the same,' the Colonel said. He sat down on a stone bench. 'We don't think the United States is reliable anymore. They put on a good display of force when necessary but it is our opinion they will find very good reasons not to fight if the North invades us. Personally, I don't blame your country for this. Because your public sentiment is very much against another war.' He exhaled the cigarette smoke. It hung like a pall in the motionless, hot air.

'I have no idea what the American military would or would not do,' Corbett said. He was not being entirely truthful, of course, because the company had run such a possibility through analysis and determined that American policy would not go beyond a display of force into an actual large-scale military involvement. 'I don't think you came all the way to Tokyo to discuss a possible military situation.'

'I came today to inter the ashes of my sister,' the Colonel said. 'But the point I wish to make to you is that my country is prepared to defend itself at any cost. And so we must insist that any foreign company that does business on our soil is a part of our country and therefore must share the cost of preparedness. It would be foolish if, under the present danger, we allowed excess foreign profits to be made in business that would simply be removed in a time of crisis. And I will tell you frankly, although I think you are already aware, Mr Corbett, that there is a strong sentiment in my country and many countries in Asia towards the nationalisation of foreign industries.'

The Colonel was most effective, Corbett thought. 'We're aware of those sentiments, Colonel. I suggest we get to it. What figures does your government have in mind?'

'Four million,' the Colonel said quietly, his thick fingers with the cigarette at his mouth so that Corbett could not be sure he heard correctly.

'Beg your pardon?'

'As of the first of October, your international corporation will pay the Republic of Korea a surcharge of four million dollars a year to allow your various enterprises permission to continue to do business in Korea.'

Corbett looked up. A couple of Japanese university students were moving down the path, dressed in rumpled uniforms, shaggy-headed, taking pictures of tombstones, chattering in Japanese. They bowed slightly as they passed Corbett and the Colonel and then moved on.

'Without cameras, I think the Japanese would fall apart,' Corbett said.

'Four million dollars,' the Colonel repeated.

'Out of the question,' Corbett said evenly. 'Our company would never go for that figure.'

'It will be paid at the rate of approximately three hun-

76

dred and thirty-three thousand dollars a month directly to our Ministry of Finance, beginning October first.'

'Are you proposing this instead of the taxes our companies already pay?'

'In addition to. As I say, it is a surcharge.'

'I'm curious to know what the American State Department will say about this new plan of yours.'

'It makes little difference to us,' the Colonel said. 'I say that frankly. I do not look forward to any ill will, but we don't need permission from any foreign government to levy additional charges.'

Corbett looked at him, steadily. 'And suppose we refuse to pay?'

'The Republic of Korea is prepared to nationalise any industries considered essential to our national survival,' the Colonel said. He had finished his cigarette and with an innate sense of tidiness was field-stripping it, pinching the coal loose with his thumbnail, tearing the paper and scattering the tobacco on to the cobblestones. 'The South American countries have been successful. The Arab countries have also been successful. I have no reason to believe we will not be.'

'And if we decide to shift our companies elsewhere?'

'You can't shift men,' the Colonel said in a heavy laboured voice. 'We won't allow you to remove any of your machinery. The natural resources are beyond your power to export. The question is, where would you move? Very shortly there will be full accord among Asian nations.'

Nothing new, no, he had expected this and been prepared for it and yet the actual demand left him short of breath. For if the Koreans began at four million, it was doubtful they would come down past the three level, and he was not certain, considering the Colonel's sureness, that they would move a dollar off the mark they had set. He watched the Japanese students at a distance now, measuring the distance between lens and stone in centimetres, cameras on tripods.

Corbett shrugged. 'Your deadline is impossible. I'll talk with my superiors, but frankly I think they will consider your demands outrageous. I can meet you in Seoul next week and provide you with a full audit of our operating expenses at the plants in question and show you why what you suggest is impossible.'

'No.'

'No to what? The meeting?'

'There will be no adjustment of the figure,' the Colonel said. 'And I would offer you one further piece of advice. We are aware of the propaganda capabilities of very large corporations such as yours. We would regard any such effort on your part as a categorical rejection of our new regulation. And we will begin to press against your companies immediately. You understand what I'm saying?'

'In my personal opinion, your country is making a grave mistake,' Corbett said. 'I'll get back to you with a company response, one way or another.'

By the time he reached the car the fatigue had begun to set in. As he told Wilson what had happened, putting the whole thing into words, he could see quite clearly that the Colonel was not bargaining. He had his government behind him.

'So what will Eriksen do?' Wilson said when Corbett had finished.

'That depends on what I can come up with,' Corbett said. 'Have the driver take us back to the hotel. I have a hell of a lot of research to do.'

3

The papers covered his desk and he leaned back in his chair, considering the next move. He had before him a complete file on the Colonel, records back to the date of his birth, his slow rise through the military ranks, his two wives, his mistresses, his political indiscretions, but he had already mentally discarded this material. For to discredit the Colonel would be to see him replaced by another man. No, the leverage had to be economic, massive, sufficiently so that they could not afford to press the matter now.

He called Erikson's suite again and was informed by Mrs Seagraves that she expected him any time and that she would call him the moment Mr Erikson arrived. She was full of patient forbearance and as he put the telephone down he was aware that he was on edge. It was imperative that he get to Erikson before the Chinese banquet because he was convinced that this was one ultimatum they could not stall.

Wilson came in, carrying the computer printout he had requested, and Corbett paced the room, leafing through the figures. There was a possibility here, yes, a rather simple but drastic action. He stared out the window at the city sprawled below him. From here he could see the moat around the Emperor's palace, which even on this bright and hazy day shone like dull pewter. 'I think we have a chance for an end run,' he said to Wilson. 'They will expect us to take some action on the threat to Abernathy's plant. But suppose we close down the phosphate production. Now, that whole operation is computerised and it's a very simple matter to foul it up so that they will have to start over. Too, they don't have a merchant fleet and I think we still have enough clout to make it hard for them to get carriers.'

'Then you intend to call their hand?' Wilson said.

'Only if it comes to that. But we can't go into this thing defenceless.' The telephone rang. He picked it up. 'You have a call from a Mr Rodriguez in Mexico City,' his secretary said. 'Do you want to take it?'

'Yes,' Corbett said. He sat down behind the modernistic desk, propped his feet up. 'Hello, Rodriguez,' he said, 'how goes it?'

'Not so good,' Rodriguez said. 'Have you had a look at the Mexican stock market today?'

'No,' Corbett said. And he knew what was coming even before the words because there was a shorthand with Rodriguez, a tone of voice that communicated bad news even before he articulated it. The Mexican government had just announced that it was considering the suspension of Petrosur from the stock exchange, pending a resolution of offshore drilling rights with the Guatemalan government. Consequently, the price had plummeted from 1,396 pesos per share of common stock down to 453. 'Are you there?' Rodriguez said. 'Do we still have a connection?'

'I'm still here,' Corbett said. 'How firm is the Mexican government in their intent to take over?'

'God only knows,' Rodriguez said with a sigh. 'Gulf and Shell haven't dumped any of their holdings. But in my opinion, amigo, it's a hell of a gamble to stay in the game.'

'How long are you going to be in your office?'

'I can wait here as long as you please.'

'I'll call you back in a few minutes.'

He severed the connection, looked to Wilson. 'I want you to get hold of Anderson in Mexico City,' he said. 'I want to know how close Mexico and Guatemala are to settling the offshore drilling rights claimed by Petrosur. I want his estimate of a probable resolution.'

'That may take a little time.'

'I want it to take very little. I need the information now.'

'Will do.'

Once Wilson was gone, he stood at the window again. No ground was ever gained except by taking a risk, but there had to be an alternative in case the risk went sour. If he was forced out of the company, he would need money and the Petrosur deal might provide it.

In a few minutes there was a brief rap on the door and Wilson came in, carrying a sheet torn from the teletype. 'We're in luck,' he said. 'Anderson's looking into a possible ESK deal with Petrosur so he's on top of the situation.'

Corbett glanced at the teletype.

SLX 464/GA-7499
SETTLEMENT IS CLOSE BETWEEN THE GUATEMALAN AND MEXICAN GOVERNMENTS, EVENTUAL RESOLUTION TO CONSIST OF COPRODUCTION VENTURE BETWEEN PEMEX AND PETROSUR, WITH OWNERSHIP FORMULA OF 53-47 PEMEX. ACCORDING TO HIGH-LEVEL PRI CONFIDENTIAL INFORMANT, THE GOVERNMENT ANNOUNCEMENT WAS DESIGNED TO DEPRESS THE MARKET AND ALLOW HEAVIER PARTICIPATION PROFIT BY MEXICAN AND GUATEMALAN OFFICIALS. EXPECT HEAVY LARGE-SCALE BUYING FORTY-EIGHT HOURS IN LARGE NUMBERS. EXPECT LEVEL TO REACH 1500 (FIFTEEN HUNDRED) PESOS BY END OF TRADING FRIDAY. PLEASE HOLD INFORMATION TOP PRIORITY CONFIDENTIAL, COMPANY EYES ONLY.

ANDERSON

There it was, appearing before him at a time when he needed it most and if he had been superstitious, he could almost interpret it as a sign. He tore up the teletype, dropped it in a bag that would be run through the shredder.

Wilson was obviously curious but he did not press it. 'What else can I do for you?' he said.

'Nothing,' Corbett said.

'Then I'll see you at the dinner.'

'Right.'

He waited until Wilson had left the office and then reached for the one telephone he knew was kept clean of interceptive devices. He buzzed the overseas operator and placed the call to Rodriguez.

'Yes,' Rodriguez said, answering the call immediately.

'This is Corbett. I want you to buy ten thousand shares of Petrosur for me, at the opening of the exchange tomorrow.'

'Ten thousand?'

'Yes. I'll have the money transferred to you by tomorrow noon.'

'May I ask if you are acting on strong information?' Rodriguez said.

'No information. I just believe the spirit of reason is going to prevail.'

'I don't,' Rodriguez said, a tone of desperation in his voice. 'I would give this matter second thoughts, amigo. I think the bottom is going to drop out, so if I were you I'd sell what I have and take the bruises. My feeling is that Petrosur common will drop to a hundred fifty tomorrow.'

'I appreciate your advice,' Corbett said. 'But I'm willing to take the gamble.'

'That's up to you,' Rodriguez said. 'How's the weather in Tokyo?'

'Hot,' Corbett said. 'Muggy, smoggy.'

'Sometimes I think we should give up the cities,' Rodriguez said. 'We've had a smog alert here all week. Travellers are being dissuaded from driving into the city.' He paused slightly. 'If you're sure that's what you want to do.'

'I'm sure.'

The moment he severed the connection Mrs Seagraves called to inform him that Mr Erikson did have a few free minutes and would be glad to see him. He put the print-out into his attaché case and caught the express elevator to the twenty-fifth floor, where he was again temporarily detained in the anteroom while the old man completed a telephone call. As he waited he saw that the temple dogs had been installed on pedestals near the door to Erikson's private office and for the first time he realised that the old man was indeed superstitious, that these grimacing ceramic animals that were supposed to ward off evil had been installed to protect Erikson.

When Mrs Seagraves ushered him into the office Erikson was sitting at his desk, punching out figures on a calculator, a frown on his face, and Corbett could almost see him as he must have been at the beginning of his career, an accountant in a small hotel in New York City, spending his hours punching figures into an old-fashioned adding machine. His world was made of numbers, balances, margins. He glanced up at Corbett, continued to work the machine until he had reached a total, tearing off the tape, laying it flat on the surface of his desk to study it. 'There are times when the fish is worth catching,' he said enigmatically, 'and there are times when it's better to cut the line. I had two heroes when I was a young man. Can you guess who they were, Willie?'

'No,' Corbett said.

'An unlikely pairing,' Erikson said. 'Frederick the Great and J. C. Penney. They both conquered the world, each in his own way.' He picked up the tape. 'The Chinese business is especially important to me. That's the reason why I have handled the whole thing personally. Relations between China and the United States may blow hot and cold for a long time, so we have to make our own alliances. Lacking the backup of our government, we have to become more resourceful, take care of ourselves. How much do the Koreans want?'

'Four million a year,' Corbett said.

'We won't pay, of course,' he said quietly. He picked up a sheaf of papers from his desk. 'I have here the names of all the delegates to the All Asian Coalition meeting that will be held next week. The Japanese will participate but they won't dominate. We have to keep that in mind.' He removed a cigar from the humidor on his desk, placed it between his teeth but did not light it. 'The meeting is to be held at Atami and most of the delegates will be arriving at least twenty-four hours before the meeting. I want each of them assigned to an Asian manager. You'll need to get somebody to coordinate because I want every one of those delegates to be contacted personally before the meeting. Our approach will be that we intend to contribute greatly to the welfare of each country in which we have plants, but that we won't be coerced.'

He handed the list to Corbett, who did not look at it but instead sat down on the leather sofa. 'I have always given you my straight opinion, Erik.'

'Yes.'

'We can romance the delegates,' Corbett said. 'We can provide them booze, women, money, anything they want, and in the end it won't do a damn bit of good.'

'How did you arrive at that opinion?'

'The Koreans wouldn't risk the demand unless they had agreement with the rest of the countries in AAC.'

'Did I ever tell you about my meetings with FDR?' Erikson said obliquely, apparently unperturbed. 'It was at the height of the Depression. I had a controlling interest in a number of banks in the Southwest and a scattering of hotels around the country at a time when few people could afford to stay in hotels. But I knew Franklin from his days as Secretary of the Navy and occasionally I dropped by the White House to chat with him. He was always seeking support for one or another of his socialistic policies. I remember once he asked me to advance a line of credit to somebody or another, I don't remember who or what, and I voiced my doubts. I told him we were at the depths of bad times and I felt the bottom had truly dropped out of everything. And there he was, that crippled, powerful man in the wheelchair, and he told me something I never forgot. "The bold man always wins", he said to me. And that was all.'

'This is a different ball game, Erik. We are dealing with nationalistic countries who don't give a damn for bold men. They are not to be persuaded.'

'Then you think they'll drive us out?'

'If it suits them, yes.'

'And what would you recommend?' There was a cold tone in the old man's voice, an audience from courtesy only, and Corbett realised that any recommendation would scarcely be heard, much less acted upon, but he felt compelled to make it.

'First, we show that we will not be coerced. We reject the Korean demands and if necessary we close down the phosphate operation. We have leverage there. Then we offer our own proposal, something totally different, something to accommodate the pride of the new nationalists. Shit, no more payments, no more baksheesh, no more negotiating sessions with people like the Colonel. We simply announce that as far as ESK is concerned there will be no more operations that smack of colonialism. We announce in advance that all our Asian operations will begin the gradual transition to all indigenous staffs, that within ten years, *they* will determine policies, run everything. They will become a strong stabilising force within their own countries.'

The old man glanced at him. 'Do you expect me to give this serious consideration?' Erikson said.

'Yes,' Corbett said. 'You're a realist and you don't have any other choice. You have alternatives but you can't set policy in the Far East. We don't have any influence in government anymore. This way, we salvage profits. By the time we hand over our plants to nationals we'll realise an excellent return as well.'

Erikson clipped the top of his cigar now with a silver cutter, rolling the end of it in the flame from a gold lighter. 'I consider you obstreperous,' he said. 'I don't intend to give away the phosphate. I don't intend to give away anything. If I didn't know you better, I'd say you have taken leave of your good senses and been persuaded by specious propaganda.'

A stone wall, yes, the old man was not going to move from his position. 'There's no sense in this,' Corbett said. 'You built your corporation and you will decide what you're going to do. But if you're counting on American rescue, you're wasting your time.' He heard the muted sound of the telephone on Erikson's desk. The old man picked up the telephone. 'Thank you for reminding me,' he said. He replaced the telephone and looked to Corbett again and Corbett could not tell what he was thinking. 'I appreciate your candour,' he said. 'We'll have to thrash this out in a larger meeting.'

Something was not right here and Corbett could feel it but he could not locate it. He had confronted Erikson and apparently the old man was simply going to let it pass. 'What do you want me to do?' he said, attempting to clarify.

'Let it rest for the time being,' Erikson said. 'And now, if you'll excuse me, I have to get ready for our Chinese friends.'

By the time Corbett reached his office the uneasiness he felt was even more pronounced. For he knew Erikson well and the old man was not one to back away from a challenge, especially in this case when it came from the man who was expected to implement Erikson's policies in the Far East. Had Corbett been in a similar situation, he would have transferred the dissenter to a different area and put Far Eastern policy in the hands of someone who agreed with it.

He sat down at his desk, poured himself coffee from the carafe, and went over his financial position. At the moment he would need approximately $400,000 to carry the Mexican deal for at this point he did not wish to operate on margin. He called Switzerland, arranged for a closeout of an account worth just about $100,000, the money to be sent to his account with Rodriguez in Mexico City. Then he called a friend in the Chase Manhattan Bank, getting him out of bed, arranging for a conversion of his stock options, which would make up the difference. When he put the telephone down he realised there was a slight tremor in his fingers. In five minutes he had committed himself to the limit of his resources.

At 1,500 pesos a share he would stand to gain close to $900,000 on this transaction. At that price his current holding of 2,700 shares would be worth an additional third of a million, which would give him a total of about a $1,250,000. With that kind of financial cushion he could decide for himself whether he wished to go along with Erikson's policy or leave the company and strike out on his own.

On impulse, he asked his secretary to see if she could locate Ellen Benson and in a few minutes he had her on the line. 'I have something I want to talk to you about,' he said. 'Where are you?'

'I'm in the hotel.'

'Fine. How about the roof garden? Say, ten minutes?'

'I'll be there.'

He put the list of names into his attaché case and asked his secretary for a folder on arrangements for the meeting in Atami and then took the elevator up to the roof-garden restaurant. After glancing around to make certain that Ellen was not yet there, he left word with the hostess where he would be and then went out into the open air and an area designed to look as much like a natural garden as possible, with screens of flowering shrubs that blocked off the unsightly vents and stacks of the building.

He had always enjoyed this vantage point, for from here he could see the other tower of the hotel and the tops of the trees in the central courtyard far below, a symbol of Erikson's genius for putting things together. For there was an illusion of wasted space where indeed there was none, and on the roof of the building to the east, concealed by coloured aluminum walls, was a scientific centre for air pollution where Erikson was cooperating with the Japanese government to measure the noxious substances in the air. And terraced on the upper three floors was a golf driving range, and through the boxed trees he could glimpse the rows of frenetic Japanese golfers driving balls into a suspended net that collected them on a terrace immediately below the drivers.

He saw Ellen coming down the path in the late afternoon sunlight and he stood up as she approached. 'Did you find the pearls for your aunt?'

'Yes,' she said. 'I only had to mortgage six months of my future.'

He held the chair for her. 'How about a drink?'

'I had my quota earlier,' she said with a smile. 'What's up?'

'If I were dealing with one of my Asian managers, I would say that it's opportunity time. I want to offer you a job.'

'What kind of job?'

'You said you were very good at organising things. We have a hell of a deal to be organised.' He sat down, opening his attaché case. 'There's to be a meeting of the All Asian Coalition at the New Atami Hotel next week. ESK will arrange a hospitality suite and swamp the delegates with every conceivable service. In addition, each delegate will be covered by a corresponding ESK manager from his country, one on one.'

'You make it sound like a basketball game.'

'Something like that, only we're playing for very high stakes. I have a list of the delegates who will be coming, some of them bringing wives, others coming by themselves. They're all top-level people, Foreign Ministers for the most part. In a day or two you can expect dossiers on each of them, their weaknesses, sexual preferences, whether they drink and what they drink, everything about them.'

She gave the list a cursory glance. 'What do you have in mind for me in connection with all this?'

'I want you to head the whole operation.'

She looked at him quizzically. 'Why?'

'Because I think you can do a good job of it. And I need somebody I can trust. You'll have all the help you need and want. As far as our Asian managers are concerned, they will all have ideas and they know their business. What do you think?'

'I don't know what to think. At the moment I'm startled, a little stunned.'

'You'll have the position of an executive assistant. Forty thousand dollars a year, headquartered here, in this building. When you get through with this meeting there will be others. You will have a chance to get to know very important people, participate in high-level conferences.'

She fell silent now. She looked at the list more carefully, pursing her lips, frowning slightly, nearsighted, he supposed. 'Some of the delegates are pretty kinky,' she said. 'Where did you get all this information?'

'It was gathered as carefully as any government intelligence operation.'

'Then it's accurate.'

'Dead centre.'

'And we cater to their tastes, whatever they want, with no sense of moral judgement, neither approval nor disapproval.'

'Yes,' he said. 'That's the way it is.'

'So among other things, I would be procuring women for certain of these men.'

'You won't have to do that directly,' he said. 'There's a man here who maintains a file of women. You simply tell him what you want and he will provide them for you. Look, I don't mean to compromise you in any way with this.'

'I was a stewardess for a long time,' she said. 'I knew that things were going on all around me, this captain with that girl, another friend with a man in the front office, but I considered myself untouched by any of it.' She looked off at a flock of pigeons landing on a rooftop. 'Oh, hell,' she said. 'It isn't your fault. People screw people, figuratively and literally.'

'There's a lot more to preparing for a meeting than that. You can delegate those chores.'

'I don't know,' she said. 'I enjoy working the jet. It doesn't make any sense to pass up an opportunity like this, does it? But I'd like to think about it.'

'All right,' he said. 'I'm going to need to know by tomorrow morning.'

She looked at him another moment, as if she had another question, but she did not put it into words. 'First thing,' she said. 'I'll let you know.'

4

The reception for the visiting Chinese delegation was an unusually sombre affair, planned with immaculate protocol in the most elegant of the hotel's ballrooms, which had been closed to the public for a week and redecorated in the red and white of the People's Republic. Had this been a Japanse reception, Corbett realised, it would have broken into a loose and friendly hilarity with everybody drunk and singing after the first two hours, for the Japanese were able to enter into alcoholic foolishness with no sense of shame whatsoever, no loss of face. There was no such loosening at the Chinese dinner.

The head of the Chinese delegation was Li Su Pang, perhaps in his thirties, dressed in a traditional blue Chinese uniform, clearly distinguishable from the other Asian managers. He held himself rather stiffly at the head table, all of his movements slow, precise, and when he turned to address a remark to Cristina on his left or Erikson on his right his whole torso shifted rather than his head. A slight formal smile remained on his face at all times, all carefully maintained, a Chinese show of good manners.

It was all bullshit, of course, Corbett knew, for the Chinese never sent a younger man to conclude a deal, operating as they did from a consensus of ageing and ailing leaders. Li Su Pang was window dressing, a sign of good faith and nothing more. Corbett had asked Wilson to sit at his table because Wilson spoke Chinese and

Corbett had been assigned to host Li Su Pang's assistant, a man in his thirties who seemed remarkably uncomfortable isolated from his superior.

His name was Chang, and from the comments that Wilson dutifully translated, it was apparent that he was an engineer assigned the technical evaluation of the plan Erikson was proposing to the Chinese government. He was also a heavy drinker, consuming immense quantities of the Chinese wine Erikson had imported for the occasion, and the more he drank the more loquacious he became until Wilson was providing a running paraphrase of his Chinese monologue.

'He's a member of the old school,' Wilson said drolly, without expression. 'What he is saying without saying it is that all Westerners should go fuck themselves and the dedicated Chinese will survive very nicely.'

'Great,' Corbett said.

'He also says, obliquely, that he does not like Western food. He does, however, have some regard for American industrial equipment although it is not constructed with the same dedication as Chinese equipment.'

'Give him the very best from the Great American Southwest,' Corbett said. 'Tell him the Mojave Desert is better than the Gobi.' He looked towards Cristina at the head table. She was smiling, the thin stem of a wineglass held in delicate fingers, an absolutely exquisite woman, but for this moment he saw her with a detached objectivity and a kind of numbness, which had been with him since the meeting with Erikson. It was a reaction against complexity, he knew that, because he had experienced it before, many times, when he was either overworked or caught up in a seemingly insolvable negotiation. He had developed the capacity simply to remove himself, to witness without involvement.

'He's never heard of the Mojave,' Wilson was saying, thoroughly enjoying himself.

'Tell him of the tremendous oil reserves in the Mojave,' Corbett said. 'That's the reason he hasn't heard of it, because we have been keeping it a secret. He's the first Chinese to know.'

He watched Erikson sipping from his glass, saying something to the Chinese, turning on that supersalesmanship quality that he had. He would not be drinking now, only pretending to do so, refusing to dull his perceptions. Because he was on the track of something absolutely immense, a whole continent into which ESK/INT hoped to extend, virgin territory. God help you, Li Su Pang, Corbett thought, if you had the power to buy, you would be sold despite yourself.

'He wants to know about your training as an engineer,' Wilson said and Corbett turned his attention to the Chinese, who was staring at him, stolidly. 'He wants to know if you are an expert in generated power, if you had a hand in developing the proposal your company is advancing.'

'Tell him I designed the Hoover Dam,' Corbett said, picking up his glass of wine. 'Tell him I also designed the Grand Coulee Dam and the Golden Gate Bridge.'

The Chinese was straining as if by sheer concentration he could extract the meaning from the words. 'I think we had better cool it,' Wilson said matter-of-factly. 'Let's just make it the Hoover Dam.'

'Let's cancel the dams altogether,' Corbett said. He raised his wineglass to the square Chinese face. 'Tell him I toast the cooperative effort for the benefit of the people.'

'That should do it,' Wilson said. He translated and the Chinese nodded and raised his glass. 'He says he toasts any cooperative efforts between people devoted to social change.'

The wine was sweet, heady. Nonsense, Corbett thought, and he had been taking all this much too seriously. Limits, everything had limits, even the games of buy and sell, and he had been projecting futures when he should be content with this moment, a time of ostentatious overkill, phalanxes of Japanese waiters bearing platters and covered dishes and tureens, and flocks of oriental dancers and musicians, all too much, too much food to eat, too much colour, a drenching of the senses and yet despite all this, it was still a sober occasion.

He was aware of Klein watching him from across the room through a swirl of dancers, and he wished to send him a message. He framed it in his mind. To: Klein (what the first name was he could not remember, only the rank, but the single name seemed to fit him well, a tall, compact man, *Klein*, like the declension of a German adjective). Was he Germanic, Teutonic, an Aryan avenger? From: William Corbett. Subject: The seriousness of ambition, the dangers of single-mindedness, the pitfalls of paranoia. Body of the Memo: Relax, Klein, and play it cool because the world is highly corrupt and any individual battle is deceptive and there is no clever man who cannot be out-manoeuvred. We are all vulnerable.

The Chinese lifted his glass again, erupted into a tirade. 'He wishes to toast the power of the mighty Yangtze River, which is symbolic of the unstoppable power of the Chinese People's Republic. He also wishes to toast the triumphs of the people's socialistic endeavour.'

'Shit,' Corbett said, smiling, raising his glass, drinking. 'Tell me something. You hear more in the company than I do. What's the group opinion about who's trying to put my ass in a sling?'

'Straight?'

'Sure.'

'Well, there's a split. A number of the boys are certain you did it and they are very envious of the action. According to them, it was an impossible deal and you brought it off. They expect you to beat the rap and, after a decent cooling period, to take over ESK or split off with a company of your own.'

'And the rest?'

'They're convinced you didn't do it, that you're in the process of being had.'

'By whom?'

'The heavy money's on Klein. Side bets on the American government, CIA maybe, Department of Defense, somebody in the military. Smaller side bets on one of the other big ones, ITT, Intertel, somebody in competition who wants to reduce ESK to a crawl.'

'And what about you?'

'Hell, I've been with you,' Wilson said. 'I know how you operate. This isn't your deal. I think I'd put my money on somebody in the company.' He glanced towards the dancers. 'I don't see how they can make this stick, whoever's doing the planning. On my own, I've been putting out some feelers in the black countries. Angola seems like a possibility. If any American equipment shows up with the right numbers, they'll let me know.'

'I appreciate that.'

The Chinese glass had been raised again; the engineer's voice was slurred. 'To hell with the translation,' Wilson said. 'Just drink.'

Corbett drank.

At eleven o'clock the banquet was finished and Erikson rose at the head table. 'Now that we've shared hospitality with our Chinese neighbours, I think it's time to share plans for the future.' Ah, God, earphones were coming out from beneath tables; the Chinese opposite Corbett was placing one against his ear, simultaneous translations. 'This has been in the planning stage for a long time now and now it approaches the status of a hopeful reality.'

Erikson nodded towards a man who stood at the side of the room; the lights in the room dimmed and the solid wall behind the head table divided in the centre and telescoped into itself and there, in a separate room, glowed the expensive model of a massive dam with miniature turbines humming and power lines stretching from a perfectly scaled powerhouse into a painted backdrop of what Corbett supposed was the Chinese countryside. He knew Erikson; he had seen many of the old man's presentations, but this time Erikson had outdone himself. The dam itself was at least twelve feet wide and there was real water coming down the spillways.

'Jesus,' Corbett said.

Erikson was conducting Li Pang on a close examination of the model and Corbett drifted through the crowd. He found himself standing by Cristina, who put her hand on his arm, maintaining her professional smile but plainly worried. 'What time will you be through tonight?' she said in a low voice.

'Anytime,' he said. 'An hour maybe.'

'Can you meet me?'

'Sure. At the house?'

'No, an inn.' She slipped a card into his hand. 'Give it to a taxi driver. It has directions in Japanese.'

'Are you worried about something?'

'Calamity, darling,' she said, and then she was gone. He worked through the crowd to the model of the dam, watching the water dashing down the spillways, shutting off, to work again as Erikson pressed a button. Erikson spotted him, beckoned to him. 'I want you to meet our distinguished guest. Mr Li, this is William Corbett, one of our executives.'

'Very pleased,' Li said.

Erikson turned, introducing one of the Asian managers, and Corbett moved away. He decided to go to the bar and have a drink before he went to join Cristina in whatever inventive disaster she had planned for tonight.

But as he crossed the ballroom he was intercepted by Klein, who had obviously been waiting for him. Klein was dressed in a black tuxedo with velvet lapels but it did nothing to temper the atmosphere of officiousness he generated. 'I need to talk to you briefly,' he said. 'Do you have the time?'

'Certainly,' Corbett said. 'How about the bar?'

'We have a better chance of being uninterrupted in the lobby.'

'Fine.'

The lobby was enormous, with an expanse of glass on one side overlooking the gardens and the swimming pool, and gigantic banners draping another wall of native stone. Klein picked a grouping of overstuffed chairs near the wall, sat down, laced his fingers as if bracing himself against the weight of his own seriousness. Corbett signalled one of the lobby waiters, ordered himself a bourbon and water.

'Mr Erikson told me about the conversation you had with the Colonel,' he said. 'I thought maybe we should chat about that.'

'I can't see that there's anything to chat about,' Corbett said. 'I feel strongly but I don't make policy.'

'That wasn't exactly what I had in mind,' Klein said. 'I'm interested in the conversation itself. I checked with your office to see if you had prepared a briefing memo but apparently you have not.'

'No,' Corbett said, with some incredulity. 'My God, the world's full enough of incriminating bits of paper and I do not intend to add to that overwhelming number.'

'Nevertheless, it's imperative that I know exactly what was said and what the Colonel's state of mind was when you left him.'

'Why?'

'Proper security depends on it.'

'Hell,' Corbett said with a smile. 'All right, I'll give you his state of mind. He was obdurate, intransigent, determined, and unmovable. They have established four million as their floor and I don't think they're going to budge an inch.'

'But you gave him no indication that the company was willing to pay?'

'I told him I would get back to him. But I left no

96

hope that the company would even consider. That's my standard negotiating posture.'

Klein shrugged slightly. 'That's all I needed to know,' he said. He glanced back towards the ballroom with an attitude of impatience. 'We may need to talk about increased security in our Korean plants, but not tonight. And I would suggest that you consider position memos on your negotiation meetings. They would be very helpful.'

Corbett stayed where he was when Klein left, seduced by the softness of the chair, the almost mesmerising view of the crystalline fountain in the centre of the outdoor pool. He stayed long enough to finish his drink and then he walked outside, temporarily revived by a cool wind blowing in off the bay. At the taxi stand he presented the direction card to a driver and then waited while the automatic rear door of the taxi slid open with a pneumatic hiss.

God, the evening had been absolute insanity and he had recognised it as such even while he participated in it. And the model dam was the greatest insanity of them all, for he had been in planning sessions with Erikson, on the periphery, as the old man was discussing the harnessing of Chinese rivers and the resultant electric power, but never did Corbett have any notion that Erikson had carried this idea to such lengths. The models must have cost at least a quarter of a million dollars and it represented an absolutely irrational flyer against the expressed technology needs of the Chinese.

And suddenly it occurred to him, and he knew why Erikson wanted to move into China. Not for immediate profit, no, not for the sake of a larger gross. Erikson was out to *collect* China, for God's sake, and the hydroelectric dam was the sanest move he would possibly make. He would lose millions if the Chinese accepted his proposal but at the same time he would have the inside track on developing Chinese petroleum, the Chinese automobile industry, the whole fucking thing.

7.

It took the better part of an hour for the taxi to reach the inn and he had absolutely no idea where he was. The inn itself was tucked away in a grove of trees, surrounded by a wall. He rang the bell and was admitted by a small Japanese woman in a kimono who appeared to know who he was. He removed his shoes and followed her down a polished wooden hallway to a sliding door that she tapped with her fingers and then opened to admit him to a pleasant Japanese room. Cristina was standing at a sliding screen that was half opened to reveal a small garden. She was wearing an elegant Japanese gown, a slight smile on her face, and he realised that her whole life had been organised into a series of dramatic tableaus, Cristina Driving, Cristina at Home, Cristina in the Throes of Passion, and as he waited for the Japanese woman to leave the room before he kissed Cristina he was not absolutely sure what this one was to be. She kissed him briefly and then pulled away sufficiently to allow him to look at her.

'It's a new gown,' she said. 'What do you think?'

'I think it's a beautiful gown and that it probably cost as much as a new Mercedes and that you brought me here under false pretences. What's the calamity?'

'I brought you a bottle of bourbon,' she said. 'Why don't you have a drink?'

'Not now. What's going on?'

'There, on the writing table.'

There were some typewritten sheets carefully folded and placed on the low Japanese table at an angle beneath the light of a reading lamp. 'I think I will have a drink after all,' he said. He found the bourbon on a corner shelf and poured some into a glass. He sat down by the table. He did not touch the papers. 'Look,' he said. 'This has been a long day and it hasn't been a particularly pleasant one. So why don't you just fill me in?'

She sat down across the table from him, arranging the folds of the gown around her, and his irritation evaporated. She had an incredible magic about her. 'I had a

98

very strange afternoon,' she said. Erik had given her a call about three to come down and see the model of the dam and after she had expressed a proper awe he took her to the kitchens where he had champagne chilling, wanting her opinion of the vintage since it would be served at the banquet to supplement the Chinese wines. He poured her a glass and then poured aquavit for himself. Then, out of the blue, he asked her how well she knew Corbett and she did not hesitate a moment. Quite well, she said, because very often Corbett had served as her escort when Erik was tied up in one of his business meetings.

It was then that Erik took the folded sheets from his pocket and handed them to her, sitting back in his chair and studying her for any possible negative reaction. Of course, she displayed none.

'What papers?' Corbett said.

She picked up the folded sheets from the table, handed them to him. 'He had a routine check made on us. These are reports of six different occasions when we were together.'

He took the papers, thumbed through them. Nothing damaging, no, nothing to suggest sexual interludes, but a thorough charting of all the public places they had gone together. 'Shit,' Corbett said, frustrated, puzzled. 'Why in the hell should he go to all this trouble now? Was he upset, angry?'

'No,' she said. 'I told you it was all very strange. I thought at first he was just pretending not to be angry and I worried about it. But tonight, after the banquet, he asked me to do a favour for him.'

'What kind of favour?'

'He suggested that I find out your state of mind and keep him informed.'

'My state of mind?' Corbett said. 'What the hell does that mean? If Erik wants to know my state of mind, all he has to do is ask.'

'I don't know, darling, but I'm convinced he isn't trying to make trouble for us. I just thought that you should know what's going on.'

He downed the drink, shook his head. 'That makes no sense at all to me, none. And he didn't say any more than that?'

'No.' She moved away from the table now to some pillows on the reed floor and slowly removed the gown, folding it neatly and placing it to one side, and then she lay down gently, looking towards him expectantly. 'I don't think we have anything to worry about, darling,' she said quietly. 'And we don't want to waste the night, do we?'

He moved over to her and in the stark simplicity of the Japanese room he found her very exciting. He began to kiss her, long slow kisses, her hair falling around his face, and he made love to her, feeling the warmth of her breasts, but a part of his mind remained uninvolved, hanging on the barb of Erikson's peculiar request. And even as his body went through the motions, he tried to sort through the reasons why Erikson would need Cristina's opinions and all he could locate was the Vietnamese business, the one shadow he could not escape.

Once they had finished, he lay beside her, staring at the ceiling. He could feel her hand warm on his stomach, her head nestled against his shoulder. Perhaps something new had happened concerning the Vietnamese arms that he did not know about. He pulled away, sat up. 'Do you have a telephone here?'

'Yes. Who are you going to call?'

'Stevens will know if there's something happening I don't know about.' He found the telephone in a recessed niche in the wall. He dialled the hotel and asked for Stevens. The call was answered immediately. 'This is Corbett,' he said. 'I need some information.'

'That will have to wait,' Stevens said. 'I've been trying to reach you, Willie. Where in the hell are you? You'd better get back here right away.'

'What's the trouble?'

'Abernathy's plant in Seoul has been bombed.'

'Jesus Christ,' Corbett said. 'I'll be right there.'

5

He sat watching the films of the disaster taken from the Korean television coverage (there were always films in this electronic age; every disaster had its immediate chroniclers, the death of a President, volcanic eruptions, bodies buried in an earthquake) and he was aware of Klein and Erikson as they watched the unfolding devastation on the screen, the old man with a set, impassive expression on his face, Klein's attitude openly curious as he leaned forward slightly, his chin resting on his hand.

Stevens was operating the remote-control closed-circuit television, providing a running commentary. The Korean government had an explanation for the existence of this footage because they had sent cameramen to cover a demonstration by a group of students against the exploitative policies of ESK/KOREA and indeed there they were, by the thousands, filmed from a distance in the Korean twilight so they appeared faceless, a welling mass of bodies in black uniforms pressing against the chain-link fence fronting Abernathy's plant, parading signs in front of the gate.

And then it seemed that there was a sudden swelling in the mass of students, the ripple effect of a wave that crested against the fence, and the chain-link sections collapsed, allowing the students to pour in a torrent towards the buildings. Almost at the same moment there was an explosion in the office headquarters building, a low modernistic structure of steel and glass, and a whole corner of the building exploded, shattered, and flew outward in a charged cloud of flying glass and smoke. Another explosion was visible at the far right of the screen, in an assembly area, a sudden fireball, and

101

the students scattered away from the buildings and the screen went black.

'We're making a detailed picture analysis,' Stevens said fatalistically, 'but we have a computerised report that makes more sense than we'll get out of this film.'

'What did you find?' Erikson said.

'The two explosive devices were planted in the early morning hours, one in a currently vacant office in administration, the other in supply for the assembly area. The explosives were Korean army-style, very sophisticated, hardly student tactics. The students were all transported to the plant in government buses. The claim that the demonstration was a spontaneous one is bullshit.'

'Is Abernathy critically hurt?' Corbett said.

'He was cut by flying glass, suffered a minor concussion. First reports say it's nothing serious. He was taken to a hospital to be checked out, but we don't know where yet.'

'How many casualties at the plant?' Klein said.

'Ten dead. We have twenty-three critical and twenty minor, treated and released.'

'Thank you, Stevens,' Erikson said, dismissing him.

'I'll let you have the enlargements as soon as possible,' Stevens said.

Erikson nodded. After Stevens had left the room Erikson looked to Klein. 'What's your opinion?'

'All carefully staged,' Klein said without emotion. 'A beautifully arranged pressure tactic. They know damn well that we understand the significance of the attack and that we can't pin them with it. It's their reaction to our negative answer.'

Erikson began to write figures on a piece of paper. 'Five hundred thousand,' he said absently.

'What?' Corbett said, not understanding.

'That demonstration is going to cost us approximately half a million dollars before we're through. Assembly three is going to be shut down at least seven days.' He continued to enumerate the cost of the damages and Corbett listened to him with a mounting incredulity, not only at the old man's absolute financial memory, his ability to project costs, losses, stopgap solutions, but for his complete lack of feeling as well.

'I want Abernathy out of there within twenty-four hours,' Corbett said abruptly.

'Why?' Erikson said.

'I forced him to stay on as a show of determination on the part of the company. But that's all blown to hell now. I want him on a plane to San Francisco with his wife before the South Koreans decide to use him as a counter. And I want him replaced by his Korean assistant. I don't remember his name, but he's competent.'

'I see no point to that,' Klein said, offhandedly.

'There's a hell of a point to it,' Corbett said. 'Jesus, the handwriting is on the wall and it's bloody. Either we come up with a new way of dealing or we're going to have a whole string of these firecrackers exploding all over Asia.'

'I disagree,' Klein said. 'We can't capitulate.'

'I'm not suggesting capitulation.'

'I think you're out of your area now,' Klein said. Was he playing to the presence of the old man? Corbett could not be sure.

'I'm interested in your view, Willie,' the old man said.

'You already know it.'

'But what are you suggesting here?'

'I'm suggesting that we draft a test policy in Korea, that we reject paying exorbitant blackmail, that we use the phosphate plant as leverage, that we put a Korean national in charge of Abernathy's operation with a view to making this one plant fully Korean-operated within ten years.'

'I'm against that,' Klein said. 'Any way you go, it's still blackmail.'

'Now, you can interpret it any goddamned way you

wish,' Corbett said. 'But I'm saying it's a practical reality.'

The old man was silent a moment. 'All right,' he said finally. 'I'm willing to give you your chance to explore this, but nothing more. Arrange a meeting with the Korean Colonel here in Tokyo. No publicity. Sound him out and if it appears that you might make an arrangement that would be mutually advantageous, draft a rough proposal, a schedule, and submit it to me. But I'm telling you in advance. I don't intend to give anything away.'

'Fine,' Corbett said. 'Now, I want your agreement that Abernathy is to be removed immediately.'

'I suggest we put that off until you meet with the Colonel,' Erikson said. 'That would make the transfer of power to a Korean manager an act of good faith instead of an act of desperation.'

'I'll go with that,' Corbett said. 'I'll meet the Colonel and we'll see what develops.'

Chapter 3

By noon of the third day he was beginning to think that the meeting with the Colonel would not materialise at all. For Wilson's calls yielded a blank as Colonel Pak was not available. The Koreans were obviously playing from a position of strength. The news dispatches that continued to flow in were about what he expected them to be. The ROK government was decrying the student action with one breath and supporting their purported grievances with the next. They were looking for the leaders of this student rebellion and promising that appropriate action would be taken against them. They were also saying that such uprisings of popular sentiment were inevitable until inequities ceased to exist.

He had not heard from Ellen as to his offer but he would need an answer soon as time was running out. A folder arrived, the data on the Asian delegates in a binder marked CONFIDENTIAL, and as he thumbed through the dossiers he realised that he had done Ellen no favour. God, a vast moral shift had taken place somewhere along the line and he could remember the time when women were provided as decorations as much as anything else, and what transpired after the meetings between the visiting officials and the women was not a matter for company concern.

But Klein, through whatever intelligence sources he had, had compiled a cesspool of information, with as much aberrant data on each delegate as he could gather. One of the Philippine delegates was designated as S/M –

sado-masochism, Corbett supposed – and a Thai delegate preferred very young girls and had created minor scandals in certain foreign countries because of his proclivities. Sexual preferences, alcohol, hallucinogenic drugs, and suddenly it occurred to him that Klein's complicity in this had a much deeper significance than catering to the delegates. Whether he was aware of it or not, he was setting a perfect background for blackmail. He wrote a note across the front of the binder. 'THIS GOES BEYOND STANDARD COMPANY PRACTICES. WE WILL FOLLOW USUAL PROCEDURES. WC.' He rang for his secretary, asked her to see that it was delivered back to Klein.

It was late in the afternoon before Wilson came back to his office with the information that Lieutenant Tae was willing to accept a call. 'I need some signals on this one,' he said. 'First, do I lodge a complaint on this level?'

'No,' Corbett said. 'Just let him know that we have a willingness to talk, but that we won't come to the Colonel.'

Wilson nodded, placed the call. God, he was smooth, Corbett realised as he listened to Wilson's side of the conversation, exactly the right tone, full of implications, nothing concrete. No weakness. Mr Corbett was willing to meet with the Colonel. No, Mr Corbett was much too busy to come to Seoul but he would take the time to meet with the Colonel in Tokyo. Wilson listened a while longer, then agreed to something and severed the connection.

'The Colonel will meet you at three o'clock tomorrow morning at the same place you met before. He's playing this very cagey.'

'He'd be a fool if he didn't,' Corbett said. 'This way we will have an off-the-record meeting that officially never took place. He will be prepared to take nothing less than the initial demand, since we're obviously responding to an act of aggression. He thinks he's allowing

106

us to save face.' He took a sheaf of blank paper from a desk drawer. 'We have a lot of work to do. I want to be ready with an informal proposal.'

For the next couple of hours he dealt with the computer projections, which flooded in over his desk, concerning the transition period for Abernathy's section of ESK/KOREA, printouts of equipment and physical plant amortisation, short-range and long-term contracts, labour policies. The more immersed he became in the data the more clearly he could see Erikson's shortcomings, a traditional blindness that valued possessive ownership over cash flow and profits. For in the eventual separation of the Korean plant from ESK/INT the potential for profits was absolutely enormous. In the end, worked properly, the Koreans would be managing a plant and supplying diodes at a reasonable cost to ESK as an exclusive marketing agency.

Finally, at seven o'clock, after Wilson had already retreated to his own office to study position papers on the AAC meetings, Corbett decided that he would put nothing on paper for the Colonel to inspect, for the figures were firmly in mind and it was far better to deal in intent than to provide any specifics to which the Colonel could anchor.

He called Stevens for a daily check on Abernathy and found to his surprise that he was still in the government hospital, feeling quite fit but staying an additional twenty-four hours at the request of the doctors to make certain the concussion was indeed a minor one. Very well, that problem had been solved. He felt quite responsible for Abernathy and once he was assured that Abernathy had been removed to a position of safety, he would breathe easier.

He ordered dinner sent up and worked through the evening clearing his desk. He had lost all track of time when the telephone rang and Wilson informed him that it was time to go. The car was waiting. He found Wilson in the lobby, armed with an umbrella and a thermos.

107

'The forecast calls for showers,' he said. 'And I thought you might need a little reinforcement.'

'Yes,' Corbett said. 'I can use it.'

'The car's right outside.'

Once Wilson had pulled the car out into the very light traffic, Corbett poured himself a cup of coffee. It was black, bitter, sufficiently strong to bring him alert. He was feeling detached now. The car passed a truck. Wilson was an excellent driver and the traffic was extremely thin at this hour.

'Do you want me to go with you on this one?' Wilson said.

'No,' Corbett said. 'At this stage it's better if the Colonel and I have a private conversation. He will be alone and I have to observe the same protocol. Nothing will be resolved. He will simply absorb the new proposal, perhaps make an objection or two, and then he will carry the information back to Seoul. He knows that neither one of us is in a position to finalise anything.'

The car was approaching the cemetery now and Corbett was surprised to see how dark the area was, the hills and monuments almost pitch-black against the reflection of the lights of the city on the low clouds. Wilson pulled up to the steps, killed the motor, and almost immediately a mist began to form on the windshield, the beginning of a light rain. There were no cars in the lane, no people, no signs of activity whatsoever. Wilson opened the glove compartment and removed a flashlight, then handed him the umbrella.

Corbett looked at his watch. 'Hell, I'd better move,' he said. 'This is one of the things you have to guard against in this business, this goddamned sense of melodrama. There's no reason we could not have met in some place private and comfortable at the same time.'

He took the flashlight, checked it to make sure it worked, then climbed out of the car into the light rain, unfolding the umbrella and making his way up the steps. He slipped on the slick stones twice, almost went down before he could regain his footing, and then moved forward again, slightly out of breath.

Shortly he was enveloped in the almost total darkness of the winding paths and he cursed to himself that he had not made a mental chart of the cemetery during the daylight. The beam of the flashlight glinted on stone faces, on obelisks encrusted with mould, and despite the limited protection of the umbrella, he found himself chilled to the bone, his suit damp, clammy. For the first time he was nervous in this city of the dead, aware that he was surrounded by the ashes of perhaps a quarter of a million people, all neatly encapsulated in urns and shelved beneath the ground.

The Korean section lay near the top of a ridge, yes, he remembered that much, and there had been a peculiarly shaped stone near the top, hollowed out, with a broken buddha sitting in the concave opening. It took him a full ten minutes before he saw the glow of a cigarette and realised that the Colonel was here, waiting for him, a dark and shapeless form standing near a stone bench.

'Good evening,' the Colonel said as he drew closer. 'It is a terrible night.'

'Yes,' Corbett said. He clicked off the flashlight, put it in his pocket.

'I am empowered by my government to offer you commiseration for the destruction at your factory in Seoul,' the Colonel said without emotion.

'I'm sure you are,' Corbett said rather sourly. 'Considering the circumstances, I suggest that we cut this as short as possible.' He fumbled with a pack of cigarettes, lighted one awkwardly, having to manage the umbrella at the same time. He could see the Colonel more clearly now, dressed in some kind of Korean rain poncho, quite bareheaded, his face wet and shining in the glow of the lighter. 'Your government moves very quickly, I'll say that for you,' Corbett said.

'It was a student demonstration,' the Colonel said.

109

'Hell, it makes no difference in the long run, does it? I don't think it shows any good faith on the part of your government, but that's beside the point too. I have a proposal I want to make to you with the understanding that this represents no weakness on our part. Because we also have planned a counteraction should your government not agree to what we consider an equitable compromise.'

'We remain quite firm in our demands.'

'All I ask is that you listen to our approach.' And suddenly Corbett realised there was something terribly wrong, for as the Colonel stood there, his body seemed to jerk, almost imperceptibly, and Corbett realised that he had heard a sound, a kind of muted whomp and the Colonel had been shot.

The Colonel staggered against him, a heavy weight in his arms as he dropped the umbrella to support him, speaking incoherently now, in Korean, and there was a second shot, yes, he believed he heard it, believed he felt it strike the Colonel and he was seized by a blind and paralysing panic, for somewhere out there in the rain and the cover of the tombstones was a man with a pistol. He lowered the Colonel to the wet stones and ducked down behind the cover of the stone bench, his breathing heavy within his chest, laboured, expecting at any moment to feel the impact of a bullet, but there was nothing, no sound except for the rain.

Jesus Christ, the Colonel was dead, certainly, and he knew it even before he groped for the wrist, thick, bony, no pulse he could detect, and he felt the artery in the neck, the folds of flesh heavy against his fingers. No life. He stayed where he was, crouched low, as if by remaining perfectly still he would also remain alive. The rain increased. He was aware that the umbrella lay on its side near the bench, that his head was drenched, yet he could not feel it.

Finally, slowly, he stood up, looking around, able to see nothing except the irregular shape of the ridge of tombstones. They had meant to kill the Colonel, not him, that much was clear, for they had an open shot at him now and they were not taking it. He looked down at the inert form of the Colonel lying at his feet and he thought for a moment that he perceived breathing and he knelt down and placed his ear against the broad chest, listening, straining to hear. He heard nothing. The Colonel was dead.

He picked up the umbrella and moved through the winding paths in what he hoped was the direction of the car, not daring to use his light, and in a few minutes he found himself stumbling down the steps and into the door, which Wilson had opened for him. It took a moment to collapse the umbrella. 'Get out of here,' he said almost breathlessly and Wilson shifted into gear reflexively and the car slid away from the steps.

'What's wrong?' Wilson said, alarmed. 'What in hell happened up there?'

Corbett shrugged. He could not speak. Calm now, yes, he needed to be calm, to think it through, to think about what he should do next. He could not leave it here. What had happened called for some action on his part, some response, and he simply could not walk away from it. The pounding of his heart began to subside. 'Jesus,' he said. 'Just like that. I was talking to him one minute and the next minute he was dead. Twenty seconds, thirty seconds, my God, dead, just like that.'

'Dead? How?'

'They shot him while we were standing there. I need a telephone. I have to call the police.'

'Who shot him?' Wilson said. 'Are you sure he's dead?'

He did not answer immediately, bringing himself under control, forcing himself past the shock so that he could think coherently. Impressions: the heavy bulk of the man sagging against him, the feel of the cold, wet flesh of the jowls against his fingertips, the search for

111

pulse. That was death, yes, he had been in the presence of it.

Wilson slowed the car near the great modernistic sweep of an Olympic stadium, a row of red telephone boxes, and Corbett got out of the car and approached one of them, fumbling for change, managing to get an English-speaking operator on the line.

'Connect me with the police, please,' he said, realising how rational his voice was, projecting calmness when he did not feel calm at all. A male voice came on the line; he had been connected with the police. His reason returned. He could not afford to be connected with this killing, not now. 'Do you speak English?' he said.

'Yes,' the voice answered.

'A man has been shot and killed in the Korean section of the Aoyama Cemetery.'

He severed the connection, went back to the car.

'How far are we from Shinjuku?' he said.

'About ten minutes.'

'I need a drink, time to think.'

Improbable, yes, he thought, but the Colonel was lying there in the downpour, the rain washing across his dead face, and Corbett was thinking ahead, covering himself. Wilson said nothing until they reached Shinjuku, the area near the station awash with lights. He parked the car and followed Corbett into a small bar decorated in black leather. Corbett sat down, ordered a bourbon, and then beckoned to a round-faced hostess, who came over to the booth, displaying a pleasant smile. He took out his wallet, removed a ten-thousand-yen note that he folded twice and then tucked into her hand. 'We want to be undisturbed,' he said. 'Do you understand?'

'Yes,' she said. '*Arrigato gosaimasu.*'

He leaned back in the booth and when his drink came he downed it instantly and then ordered another.

'Are you all right?' Wilson said.

'No, I'm not all right. It's really a terrible thing.

112

There's a man lying out there dead and I am sitting in here figuring out how it is going to affect the company.' The whisky had begun to relax him now.

'What happened out there?' Wilson said quietly.

'A crazy goddamned business,' Corbett said. 'Oh, they really screw things around in the Far East. Either one of the Korean factions could have shot him. He could have been killed by the dissenters because he represented the forces of oppression. Or he could have been killed by his own superiors because they did not feel he was efficient enough. Or his own lieutenant could have shot him in order to make room for his own promotion. Jesus, the list is endless, but the Colonel is just as dead in the end.'

Wilson lifted his glass, studied the rim. 'And what do you do now?'

'Business,' Corbett said. He finished his second drink. 'We will go back to the hotel and I will roust the old man out of his sleep and get his instructions.' He looked at the hostesses gathered at the bar, talking, all very pretty young women, animated, yes, and one of them was laughing. One man dead and life was going on. 'There will be a temporary hue and cry,' he said. 'If he was shot by his own people, they will lay it on the opposition and tighten the screws a few turns more. And if he was shot by the dissidents, they will claim it as a victory. And in a couple of days the Colonel will be replaced and the bargaining will continue, right where it left off.'

'A hell of a note,' Wilson said.

'Yes, a hell of a note,' Corbett answered.

2

When he reached the hotel he went directly to his suite and took a shower, trying to dispel the heavy sense of fatigue that had overcome him. He had not slept for

8

twenty-four hours and it was unlikely he would get to bed for another twelve.

As he changed into a fresh suit the wet coat jacket caught his eye and he picked it up and went over it, looking for any traces of blood, but there were none. When he had dressed, he sat down on the sofa and lifted the telephone. It was five in the morning and Erikson would be stirring by now, rising from his bed to spend thirty minutes on his exercise bicycle before he took his shower and checked communications for anything that had happened while he was asleep. He dialled Erikson's suite and was surprised when Mrs Seagraves answered.

'This is Corbett,' he said. 'I need to speak to Mr Erikson.'

'I'm sorry, Mr Corbett,' she said reluctantly, 'but Mr Erikson is not available.'

'I have a great respect for you, Mrs Seagraves, but that answer is not good enough. Now I don't care where he is or what he is doing, my business with him is urgent.'

'I'm sure he would be delighted to talk with you,' she said apologetically. 'I don't know where he is. He and Mr Klein left the hotel about an hour ago for a very important meeting.'

'At this hour?'

'If he checks back with me, I'll certainly give him your message. But he said he would be gone all day.'

He stood up, feeling restless, suspicious, aware that something important was in the wind. He went up to the company offices, where he found Mrs Jordan red-eyed and suffering from strain. She was in charge of reproduction, the one place in the company where everything had to pass through. 'I'm sorry,' she said, the moment Corbett entered her office. 'If you have another rush job for me, Mr Corbett, I just can't possibly do it.'

'I'm looking for Mr Erikson,' he said.

'He came and went,' she said. She had been up all night duplicating copies of position reports on all ESK holdings in the Far East, she went on, and the Japanese office girls had driven her to distraction with their inflexibility. An error on one page, for instance, corrected in pencil by Mr Erikson, had not been reset on the machines but had been painstakingly reproduced, pencilled corrections and all, on twenty-four copies before Mrs Jordan caught it. And Mr Erikson and Mr Klein had both come to pick up the material rather than have it delivered through normal channels.

'I'd like a copy of the material.'

'There isn't a copy, Mr Corbett. You'll have to see Mr Erikson for that.'

He went down the office corridor, the place deserted at this time of the morning, the first secretaries not due until seven thirty. He let himself into his own office and then just sat behind his desk, thinking. An important meeting, yes, important enough to demand an extreme security with not a whisper leaking out in advance, not even a rumour, or he would have heard about it. He had nothing more than a hunch but he followed it, picking up the telephone, asking the operator to connect him with Lawson, the transportation chief in Haneda.

'This is Corbett,' he said when Lawson was on the line. 'I'm trying to locate Erikson. Did he fly out this morning?'

'No, sir,' Lawson said. 'He would have had a hell of a hard time getting his jet prepped. Look, I'm not complaining, but in the future, when our facilities are going to be overbooked, I'd appreciate it if somebody would give me a little advance warning.'

'Overbooked?'

'Hell, we're swamped.' All of the private maintenance facilities were swamped, he went on, and the ESK facility was catching the overflow. There had been a heavy influx of corporation jets from the United States beginning about midnight, at least thirty of them, all of them filled with high-ranking executives from Exxon, Intertel, Citibank, all of the major companies with interests in

115

the Far East. Lawson had tried to find out what was going on and he had talked to a pilot who flew for Exxon and found him close-mouthed, friendly but uncommunicative. The pilot would tell him nothing about the passengers he carried or how long they would be in Tokyo.

When he had finished the conversation with Lawson he found himself restless, frustrated. He went up to the executive dining-room. It was deserted. He took a small table next to a window in one corner of the panelled room, told the waiter to bring him a telephone and some coffee, then sat looking out over the wet grey dawn. He turned his mind to the meeting, putting together different combinations in search of a purpose. It was a corporate summit, he was certain of that, its importance gauged by the heavy security surrounding it.

There was a vast difference in the multinationals between staff and line officers and the majority of business was done by the line personnel so that the staff remained fixed in corporation headquarters in the United States, formulating policy, dealing with the company as a whole. Erikson was one of the few exceptions, like Geneen of ITT, who performed both functions ably and well, but now the other multinationals had found something important enough to dispatch staff officers on the long and gruelling trip across the Pacific.

He lifted the telephone, called Wilson. 'I'm sorry to get you out of bed,' he said.

'I wasn't asleep,' Wilson said. 'What's up?'

'I think there's a corporate summit going on in Tokyo right now,' Corbett said. He told him of his conversation with Mrs Seagraves, reproduction, transportation. 'I want you to track it down, find out where it's being held. I want to know the agenda. It's my guess that it's in one of two areas. Now, ESK may have a Chinese proposal that's too large to handle unilaterally and Erikson may have to lay off some of the deal with the other companies. That's the best bet. But it's also possible that he's considering washing out his whole Far East operation. Citibank holds a lot of paper on ESK/ PHILIPPINES. Exxon's got a large bite of the action in Indonesia. He could lay off the bulk of his holdings in one meeting.'

'Do you think that's possible?' Wilson said.

'Hell, anything's possible at this point.'

'I'll get on it right away.'

He was not much revived from the coffee. The sky changed from black to a leaden grey, and somewhere in Tokyo they would be meeting at this moment and the old man had not included him this time. Klein was with him instead, a sure indication of Klein's rising power in the corporation. He wondered if there was any connection between this meeting and the Korean business, the death of the Colonel. He could make no connections there. He dropped the idea.

He looked up to see Fenster coming across the carpeted dining-room in his distinctive angular gait, a rapid walk as if he had little time to waste in locomotion. He smiled humourlessly as he approached Corbett. 'My God, nobody ever sleeps around here. Do you mind if I join you?'

'No, sit down.'

Fenster sat down and Corbett could detect the concern in him, which expressed itself in a kind of forced cheerfulness. 'I don't function worth a damn at this time of morning. So maybe you'd better fill me in.'

'About what?'

'It's standard for legal to be notified whenever there's a police matter. Your secretary came in early and she found a couple of Japanese inspectors from the *gaijin* waiting in the anteroom. Do you want me with you? I need to know what's happening. You don't seem surprised.'

'A man was killed,' Corbett said.

'Oh?' Fenster said, not shocked, not startled, no,

117

ready to absorb facts, discard feelings. Corbett told him the whole thing while Fenster absorbed it with a concentrating frown, smoking a cigarette.

'Did you notify anyone?'

'I called the police, told them a man had been shot and killed in the Aoyama Cemetery.'

'Did you identify yourself?'

'No.'

'Good move,' Fenster said thoughtfully. 'My God, you wouldn't believe how complicated they make things over here for a person who's no more than a witness to something. How did they connect you with this?'

'I don't know. The car, perhaps.'

'All right,' Fenster said, frowning furiously, as if considering all the possible ramifications at the same instant. 'You're better off in the initial interview without legal representation. If I go with you, it's a sign that you're expecting something and it can be held against you. Play it easy. Show them you're willing to cooperate but don't tell them a damn thing. Find out what they have, what they want, and then call me.'

'I'm going to play it as it lays.'

'That's your prerogative, of course.'

When he reached his office his secretary intercepted him in the anteroom, a worried expression on her face. 'There are two Japanese officials waiting for you in your office, Mr Corbett,' she said in a hushed voice. 'I thought they would be less conspicuous in there than waiting out here.'

'Fenster briefed me,' he said.

As he entered the office both men stood up, bowing politely, both dressed in conservative Western business suits, the younger man taller than the other. It was not difficult to establish the dominance order here, for the younger officer introduced himself as Lieutenant Ito and then proceeded to introduce Corbett to Lieutenant Nakamura, a stocky man who nodded and sat down, looking to Ito as if to give him permission to proceed.

118

'Would either of you care for tea or coffee?' Corbett said.

'No, sir,' Ito said pleasantly. 'We regret the imposition on your time as it is. We are here only because our procedures require it.'

'What can I do for you?' Corbett said, sitting down behind his desk.

'We are interested in an automobile that is registered to your company,' Ito said. He took out a small notebook, read from a page. 'British registry, GB 37536. This car is owned by your company. Am I correct?'

'Truthfully, I don't know,' Corbett said. 'I can call transportation and verify it if you like.'

'It is registered to your company,' Nakamura said directly. 'And the ownership of the car is not really at issue here. Do you mind if we address ourselves directly to the facts?'

'Not at all.'

'The automobile in question is a black Lincoln Continental Mark Four,' Nakamura said. 'It was observed in Shinanomachi early this morning. It was also observed near Shinjuku station. We have checked with your transportation department and have learned that it was assigned to you last night.'

Corbett shook his head. 'I don't see any point in sparring with you. I have nothing to hide. You're here about the death of Colonel Pak. That's correct, isn't it?' If there was any surprise in either of the two officers, he could not see it. Nakamura simply shifted slightly in his chair.

'Yes,' he said. 'That is correct.' He scratched his chin. He was indeed discomfited, Corbett realised, because he had been prepared to track through the bits of evidence he had accumulated and now he was thrown off balance. 'Would you tell me what you know concerning this homicide?'

'I was there,' Corbett said. 'Our company has been negotiating with the Korean government and he was their liaison man. We met early this morning in the cemetery and while we were talking, somebody shot him.' He noticed that Ito was taking notes in little strings of Japanese calligraphy with a ballpoint pen.

'How many shots did you hear?' Nakamura said.

'I'm not sure that I heard any,' Corbett said. 'I've never heard a pistol shot with a silencer. I think there were two.'

'Two shots.'

'Yes.'

'And did you observe the person who fired the shots?'

'No. I didn't see anybody in the cemetery besides the Colonel.'

'Could you describe the direction from which the shots came?'

'No.'

'So you were speaking with the Colonel and two shots were fired and you do not know from which direction they were fired, or from what distance, or the person who did the firing. That is your statement?'

'Yes.'

'And then what did you do?'

'I found a telephone and called the police.'

'Why did you not identify yourself?'

'Our dealings with the Korean government are very delicate at this point,' Corbett said. 'I did not wish to be connected in any way with the Colonel's death and I still don't. Now, I don't know how you work, but I want to save the company any unnecessary publicity.'

'Certainly,' Nakamura said rather absently. 'I appreciate your candour in this matter. We have no intention of bringing unnecessary stress to anyone but we have been assigned to investigate a most serious business and there are certain procedures to be followed here. It is necessary at this point to establish a firm identification of the man who was killed. If you would come with us for as long as twenty minutes, it would be enough.'

'I don't have any objections.'

'If you would like to consult your company lawyers, that is permissible.'

'That's not necessary.'

Their car was parked in the lobby drive, a small blue Toyota, unmarked. Ito opened the rear door to permit Nakamura and Corbett to enter, then took his place behind the wheel. 'Out of curiosity,' Corbett said, 'how did you know the car was in the Shinjuku area?'

'We take pride in having the lowest crime rate of any large city in the world,' Nakamura said. 'This is because there is no animosity between the people and the police. Whenever there is a strange car in a neighbourhood, a citizen reports it. Yours is a very large and expensive foreign car, which created more interest.'

'Where did you learn your English?' Corbett said. 'You speak it quite well.'

'I was sent to London for special training,' Nakamura said. He lapsed into silence. The car turned into a side street and stopped at a compact and modernistic building that appeared to be a cube of concrete with a single door and no windows at all. Ito pulled up to the kerb and opened the rear door for Corbett and Nakamura. The rain had let up for the moment but there were scudding grey clouds across the sky.

'This should take only a very few minutes,' Nakamura said, leading the way into an office, a bare room with official-looking charts in Japanese on the walls, schedules, Corbett supposed. Nakamura spoke to an attendant in a white jacket and the attendant opened another door, a heavy chill pouring out. Corbett was handed a surgical mask, which he declined, but the two officers put them on as a matter of course.

There was a single gurney in the small room, the body covered with an opaque polyester sheet, and Nakamura pulled it away from the head. Ah, they were observing him at the very moment he was observing the body, looking for any change in his demeanour, but he displayed none for it seemed to him that he had never

121

seen the oriental who lay dead before him, the face puffy, waxy white, the Korean colonel certainly, transformed by death into a total stranger, no sunglasses now, no baggy uniform, the face distorted. He stood there looking for a long moment and then he turned away and without a word went back into the office, giving himself time to adjust. He was aware that Nakamura had rejoined him, sitting down in a chair. 'Can you make an official identification?'

'That is Colonel Pak, yes.'

'Regrettable,' Nakamura said. 'On what terms were you with the Colonel?'

'Beg your pardon?'

'My English phrasing is sometimes awry,' Nakamura said. 'I am merely asking if your relationship with the Colonel was a friendly one.'

'It was neither friendly nor unfriendly. It was a business relationship.' He realised that Ito was making notes again, standing in the background, that goddamned little notebook held in one hand while the pen whispered against the paper. And quite suddenly, he was aware of his irritation and the reason for it. 'My dealings with the Colonel have nothing to do with this matter,' he said. 'I am not implicated in his death in any way.'

'We must consider every possibility,' Nakamura said. 'Would you care for a cup of coffee? An experience like this can be very upsetting.'

'No,' Corbett said. 'I just want this finished.' His irritation was turning into anger and he checked it immediately. 'Look,' he said, 'I am willing to co-operate with you in any way that I can.'

'I appreciate that.'

'The Colonel and I were in an adversary position but there was nothing personal about it. Now, if I had wanted to see the Colonel dead, I wouldn't have done it personally. There would have been no advantage at all in that, especially when so many people knew we were meeting. If I had hired somebody to kill him, I wouldn't

122

have connected myself with it in any way.'

'Certainly,' Nakamura said.

'What does that mean?'

'What you say is sensible. You were meeting with him as a representative of your company; I can accept that. Now, I wish to know the specifics of your discussion with him last night.'

'That's certainly beyond the scope of this investigation.'

'Unfortunately not,' Nakamura said. 'There are unhappy times in Japan, especially in the connection between business and governments, foreign governments as well as our own. *Kuroi kiri*. Are you familiar with the phrase?'

'No.'

'It means "black mist", the corruption of business people. We have had our share of it here and so we are extremely sensitive to such matters. It is damaging to everything we believe in. Now, it would be interpreted by many people as an example of *kuroi kiri* that a representative of a company should have a meeting with a foreign government representative in a surreptitious manner and that one of the participants should be killed during that meeting. Under Japanese law it is my duty to investigate not only the homicide but the larger implications.'

'I can only repeat what I said before,' Corbett said. 'I will co-operate with you in any way that I can. But under no circumstances will I discuss company business with you. Now, is there any reason why I can't get back to work?'

'No,' Nakamura said with a shrug. 'But we must ask you to keep yourself available.'

When he reached the hotel and went up to his office he found a long list of calls waiting to be answered, various Asian managers, calls from Chicago and New York, and he knew the communications centre would be frantic handling attempts to check out the significance of the meeting in Tokyo today and its financial implications for various branches of the company.

He gave Wilson a call and could hear voices in the background, yes, the middle managers would have congregated there to exchange information. 'What's happening?' Corbett said.

'My God, it's a madhouse,' Wilson said. 'I've had calls from the financial editors of *Asahi* and *Marunichi*, another from the *Economic Review* in Hong Kong and more from various correspondents for the *Wall Street Journal*. They're all looking for "significance". The big boys couldn't have attracted more attention if they had taken a full-page ad.'

'Did you find out where the meeting's being held?'

'No. The latest rumour is that they've chartered a 747 and are currently cruising over the Pacific while they talk. I've drawn a blank on the other matters. Nobody thinks Erikson is selling anything, no vibrations anywhere for that. And the Chinese have all gone home so I don't think there's urgency in that direction.'

'Keep looking,' Corbett said. 'You'll find something.'

There was a tap on the door and Fenster poked his head in. 'I see that the Metros are through with you,' he said. 'Got a minute?'

'Sure.'

Fenster came in, slouched into a chair. 'What did you tell the police?'

'I told them I was there last night, at the meeting with the Colonel when he was killed.'

'Well, we'll work around that.'

'What's wrong?'

'Unfortunately, we are about to enter into a situation and I hate situations,' Fenster said. 'You seem to have a gift lately of attracting suspicions. Jesus, I can't explain it. You seem to be wandering around with a little black cloud over your head. Why don't you take my advice and go on vacation for a while.'

'I'm indispensable,' Corbett said. 'What's on your mind?'

'Well,' Fenster said, making a ritual out of unwrapping a stick of chewing gum, 'let's say that I have certain Japanese friends at court, not the Imperial, the legal.' He had called a friend, he went on, an attorney who was generally aware of everything that happened and what the attorney had told him had disturbed him greatly.

It seemed that the Koreans were not the least bit popular in Japan, and the Japanese public in general regarded them as inferior, but the Japanese business community was making a great effort to get along with the South Korean government because of vast Japanese investments in South Korea. News of the Colonel's death had circulated instantly when the Japanese police identified the body and Japanese business found itself in an embarrassing position. They were aware that the ESK plant in Seoul had been bombed. They felt the Colonel had been killed in reprisal for that bombing and they did not wish to be caught in the middle. The Ministry of Trade was currently drafting an official message to the Korean government apologising for the death of a Korean official on Japanese soil.

The proper Korean officials had already been apprised of the Colonel's death, of course, and as might be expected, they were expressing great indignation. 'They have already informed the Japanese that the Colonel came here to meet you,' Fenster concluded. 'So that puts you in what I would call an intensely vulnerable position.'

'Yes, indeed,' Corbett said. 'Most vulnerable. The

fact remains that I had nothing to do with the Colonel's death.'

'I know that,' Fenster said. 'I know you, Willie, and you don't have to convince me of anything. But they don't know you. And they are so damned sensitive about the Lockheed business and all the corporate graft, they would find it damned convenient to make a federal case out of you.'

'They had the opportunity to accuse me, to arrest me,' Corbett said. 'They didn't.'

'You can't be logical about the Japanese law. Who knows what they're going to do? Goddamn, sometimes I think they could close us down overnight if they wanted to. Klein's breaking every Japanese law in the books with his security force, his bodyguards. He didn't clear that particular plan through legal, I can tell you that. I wrote him a memo as a matter of fact, detailing the low Japanese crime rate, the high quality of the police, the fact that this is not a culture that tolerates foreign shenanigans for a moment. But he brought in those goddamned bodyguards, ex-Secret Service men, ex-military.' He shrugged as if dismissing the whole thing. 'We need to get back to your problem. I'll find out if the Colonel had a family. We'll send official condolences as a company, establish a scholarship for his son, if he had one. We will also send our official condolences to ROK, saying the world has lost a fine man, so on and so forth.'

The mental picture Corbett had of Fenster was of a sprightly man on a slowly sinking ship, running fore and aft with hands full of pitch, chinking the cracks with an almost ferocious zeal while the ship continued to settle slowly in the water. Corbett also had the feeling that as the ship continued to sink, he would be among the first to be jettisoned and he did not like that idea.

'At the moment I don't give a damn about your perambulations,' he said. 'If it comes to the point that I am either arrested or directly accused, then we will surface the Korean demands, the whole business.'

126

'Do you think that would make a damn bit of difference?' Fenster pursed his lips in a silent whistle. 'Christ, the nerve of the innocent.'

'I did not kill the Colonel.'

'The Japanese don't give a shit about the truth. They are wiser than we are in a great many ways because they know damn well that they're not likely to get at the complete truth of any situation. So they go after the strongest appearance of truth they can find. Do you understand what I'm saying? My God, the Korean government was putting the screws on the company and they blew hell out of one of our plants. There was a secret meeting and you were going to settle things with the Koreans and their emissary turns up dead. You are a loyal company man. The Japanese are very heavy on company loyalty, on corporate sacrifices. An open discussion of the Korean demands would only aggravate your situation. Now, I'm telling you that there aren't any formal charges yet and I'm telling you to leave the country and get lost for a while.'

'I don't think you're in any position to tell me what to do.'

'There's no point to your getting hostile.'

'No,' Corbett said. 'But there's a hell of a lot going on around here that I don't understand and I intend to. For starters, does legal know anything about the big meeting this morning?'

'That's a tricky one,' Fenster said obviously grateful for the diversion, his jaw working vigorously against the chewing gum. 'I can tell you something for absolute certain. There's no corporate business being conducted. We've been in touch with legal in every one of our headquarters and nobody was informed. They can't do business without lawyers, and that's for sure.' He stood up, stretched. 'One more thing,' he said. 'And this is just a recommendation, so don't take it the wrong way. If you won't leave, you're going to have the Japanese police crawling all over you for a while. If any one of them contacts you directly, in any way, you call me. We're at the point where legal counsel is vital.'

'All right,' Corbett said. 'I'll do that.'

Once Fenster was gone, Corbett began to feel the full impact of what was happening, and he found himself building the case against him as it would appear to the Japanese. He was still under the cloud of the Vietnamese arms business and that would colour any investigation of him. And the Colonel had recorded the first conversation in Seoul so it was highly possible the conversation in the cemetery had been transcribed as well. He could not remember what had been said, the tone of the conversation. Had it been brusque? Was there an undertone of hostility to what was said? Shit, it made no difference. He was sufficiently aware of the ambiguity of taped conversations. A listener could read any meaning into inflections that he cared to make.

He felt a slight panic, which gradually gave way to a general uneasiness and then to a realisation that nothing was going to happen to him. There was a sheltering power within the company itself, for he had long been aware of the preferential code for company officials in host countries. The company itself was often hassled as if there existed a perpetual adversary position between companies and governments, yet at the same time he could remember no serious prosecution of any individual highranking corporate officer by any country in the Far East.

A rational code was at work here. There was no reason at all why a man of influence would undertake any crime directly, not in an area where human life was esteemed so little and where men could be hired so cheaply for any purpose. His arguments to Nakamura had been valid ones; the police could not consider him suspect. There were no warrants against him, no charges, nothing but an indirect suggestion from Nakamura that he should be available for further questioning. He was quite free to leave the country at any time he

128

wished and ESK/INT with its immense resources, its armies of lawyers, would cover him.

He called his secretary and directed her to query Anderson in Mexico City for an update of the Petrosur situation. In a few minutes, she brought him an answer and waited for him to read it.

WE ARE STILL AWAITING GOVERNMENT CONFIRMATION. MARKET UP NINETEEN (19) PESOS. DO YOU WISH A DAILY REPORT?

ANDERSON

'Give him an affirmative,' he said to his secretary.

'Yes, sir. By the way, you had a call from Miss Benson. She wants to know when it would be convenient for you to meet her.'

'One thirty.'

'Fine. I'll let her know.'

By one o'clock there was still no word from either Klein or Erikson, so when Ellen arrived early he asked if she would mind if they went somewhere outside the hotel. The pressures were reaching to his office by now, with calls from his friends at the *Washington Post* and *The New York Times*, neither of which he accepted, giving his secretary orders to tell all callers that he was out of the office for the day. He called for the car and then had second thoughts and cancelled it, wanting to walk.

The rain had stopped; the sun was struggling through the clouds and a muggy heat had descended on the city, but once he left the hotel, he felt as if he had been reprieved. He stopped on the sidewalk, looking at Ellen in the bright sunlight. She was wearing a tailored suit, her long blonde hair straight around her shoulders. She put on her sunglasses, large circles with blue lenses. 'Where are we going?'

'To a coffeehouse, unless you want something stronger.'

'No, that's fine.'

He walked in the direction of the Ginza, wanting to put as much distance between himself and the hotel as possible. 'It's a goddamned madhouse today,' he said, slowing down to accommodate her. 'You heard about the meeting?'

'Yes. I also heard about the Colonel.'

'From whom?'

'The Japanese police were in communications all morning. Are you all right?' There was concern in her voice.

'No, I'm not all right,' he said. 'I'm functional but I'm not all right.' They had reached a crossing now, lights changing, the flow of traffic interrupted like the parting of the Red Sea. He pushed ahead, crossing the wide boulevard.

'How can I help you?'

'I appreciate the thought but I'm not sure anything can be done at the moment.' He looked up to see a glittering façade of windows overhead, one of Tokyo's innumerable chrome coffee bars. 'This will do.' He led the way up the stairs and allowed the hostess to seat them beside the window. Ellen sat down hesitantly, smoothing her skirt, brushing the hair away from her eyes with the back of her hand. She removed the sunglasses. Her eyes were incredibly blue.

'It's indecent, isn't it?' she said. 'Suddenly, everything changes, just like that.'

'Not everything,' he said. He took the menus from a mini-skirted Japanese girl and handed one to Ellen. 'The Korean plant gets blown up, the Colonel gets shot down, the old man is off wheeling and dealing and the routine chores still have to be done. What would you like?' He glanced at the menu. '*Sushi*,' he said to the waitress. '*Sushi* and American coffee, black.'

'Three dollars for a cup of coffee?' Ellen said, startled, looking up from the menu.

'The company can afford it,' he said.

'I'll have a coffee, light,' she said to the Japanese girl. Once the waitress had gone she folded her hands on the table in front of her, looking at him, and he realised suddenly that in everything that was happening she was primarily concerned for him. He was touched by it. He put his hand over hers.

'Look,' he said. 'It's not that bad. What did you decide about the job?'

'I was ready to turn it down,' she said candidly. 'I'm a direct person and I don't see any point to hedging. I liked being with you on the jet. In a way I guess you could say I felt proprietary about you. But I guess all that is going to change anyway, isn't it?'

'I don't know,' he said. 'I have no idea what's going to happen to me. But the job's a solid one.' As he looked at her he realised that she was about the same age Cristina had been when she first came with the company in the PR branch. Ellen was not the same, of course; she did not have Cristina's overwhelming vanity, but she was a beautiful woman in her own right. If she stayed with the company, she would not rise through the executive ranks, no, she did not have that kind of toughness, but she would very likely follow Cristina's route and he did not want that to happen. 'Do you remember talking about the north shore of Oahu?'

'Beg your pardon?'

'You mentioned it once, that you would like to live there.'

'Yes.'

'What would you do in Oahu?'

'Absolutely nothing,' she said with a smile. 'I would raise tropical plants, not commercially, but just because I enjoy them. I'd swim a lot, lie in the sand. I would just be. Can you understand that?'

'I can understand it,' he said, suddenly excited, his mind diverted from the company pressures for the time being. 'All right,' he said. 'You have it.'

'What?' she said. The waitress served the coffees and his *sushi*.

'You can have it,' he said. 'The north shore of Oahu, the freedom to do absolutely nothing. My gift to you. No strings attached.'

'You're not serious.'

'I'm completely serious.'

'I appreciate the gesture,' she said, sipping the coffee. 'I really do.'

'Hell, it's not a gesture,' he said. 'It would please me immensely to buy your freedom for you. I know how crazy this sounds, but I'm quite serious about it. I would expect a postcard from you every once in a while to let me know how you're doing.' Insanity, yes, he could feel a loosening within him, as if he had been wound tight for much too long, and quite irrationally, her acceptance had become desperately important to him.

She smiled. 'You really mean it, don't you?'

'Yes.'

'Why?'

'I don't know why,' he said. 'Or maybe I do and I don't want to admit it. You were right, you know, the company uses you up if you're not careful and I don't want that to happen to you.' He picked up an oval of seaweed wrapped around compacted rice, dipped it in a bowl of sauce. 'I guess none of this makes sense except that for once I have something I can give that nobody else will.'

She reached out and touched his hand again, her fingers warm. 'You really put me up against it,' she said. 'Do you know that?'

'Now I don't seem to be understanding you,' he said.

'I like to think about Oahu,' she said. 'When things get tight I say to myself, if only I could get back there, then everything would be all right. But if I really went, I don't know how long I'd last.'

'Why not give it a try and see?' Corbett said. 'How long would it take for you to get your things together?'

'You mean now?'

'I mean right now.'

'No,' she said. 'I don't think so. Not quite yet.'

'Why not?'

'You don't know why you offered and I don't know why I'm turning it down. Maybe it's because, in some way, I'm not through here.' She picked up her coffee again, looking at him appraisingly. 'Maybe you're the one who should head for the beach and give yourself some time.'

'No chance,' he said. He picked up another *sushi* and then, through the window, partially veiled by the wilting foliage of a chestnut tree, he saw the heavy bulk of a man standing next to a store window, hunched forward slightly, smoking a cigarette. Jesus, Nakamura certainly, and if he were here, it could only be for one purpose. He excused himself and half ran down the stairs, moving up the street to find that the man was no longer there. The window was full of Sony radios, loudspeakers blaring Japanese music on to the crowded sidewalk. He went into the store, looked around; a woman in a kimono, an elderly couple, a flock of teenagers, but no sign of the man. He went back up the stairs to the coffee bar, sinking down in the chair, winded.

'What happened?' Ellen said, alarmed.

'Nerves,' he said, trying to get his breath. 'That's all. I think I'm being followed. I thought I saw the Japanese detective who questioned me.'

'But you didn't find him?'

'No,' Corbett said. 'Maybe I imagined that I saw him.' He picked up his coffee and found it cold. He had no further appetite for the *sushi*.

'You don't need all this, Willie,' she said. 'It's time for you to get out. Why don't we both go to Hawaii?'

'I have too much of myself invested in the company, too many years. Can you understand that?'

'Yes,' she said. 'I don't like it but I understand it.'

He looked at his watch, aware of the passage of time.

It was nearly three o'clock and Erikson was either back at the hotel or would be, shortly, and he wanted to be there when Erikson made his announcement concerning the meeting. 'I need to be getting back,' he said, counting out sufficient oversized one-hundred-yen notes to cover the bill. 'I'd like to walk back by myself, if you don't mind.'

'I think I just propositioned you,' she said. 'Are you going to let it pass?'

'Yes,' he said. 'I don't want you involved in this. I want you to go to Hawaii. You can stay here a couple of weeks and cover the Asian meeting if you want to and then say to hell with it and take off. But don't wait too long.'

'You sound as if we're about to hit an iceberg,' she said. 'Or like an earthquake is going to tumble us all into the sea.'

'It very well could,' he said.

Once he left the coffee bar he intended to walk straight back to the hotel but instead he walked up towards the Emperor's palace and sat on a bench near the moat for a long time, watching the traffic, telling himself that he needed time to think but not really believing it. No, he had placed himself here, stationary, in a relatively open position, to see if indeed he was being followed. At any moment he expected to see Nakamura emerge from the crowds to sit down beside him and strike up a conversation. Nakamura would find him alone. Ellen would not be involved.

He smoked a cigarette and watched an elderly Japanese gentleman in a grey kimono bow stiffly towards the palace buildings in the distance. Loyalty, yes, a sense of obligation, and all the modernity in the world would never erase that characteristic from the Japanese personality. Erikson would have made a good Japanese businessman, he thought, for Erikson also possessed that innate sense of paternalistic authority and spent a good deal of his time reshuffling the structure of his

134

business empire so that none of his faithful retainers would lose their jobs. Corbett could not say that he really liked the old man but he did respect him.

He stayed on the bench until the suddenly thickening traffic reminded him that it was close to the rush hour and then he stood up and started walking back towards the hotel complex. He kept his eye on the crowds as he approached the hotel, making one final check to reassure himself that Nakamura was no place in evidence. Then he turned up the walk closest to the business entrance and the express elevators only to see Wilson coming out of the building very hurriedly, carrying an attaché case, and Corbett could detect a suppressed grimness beneath his rigidly placid exterior. 'For God's sake,' he said to Corbett in a low and agitated voice. 'Where have you been? We have to talk, but not here.'

'What's going on?'

Wilson's eyes were scanning the crowds, looking back towards the hotel door. 'Jesus, it's incredible,' Wilson said. 'Come on.' He headed down a sidewalk past a construction barrier marked in Japanese and then pushed past a group of Japanese workmen carrying sheets of plywood down a flight of stairs into what would eventually be a shopping arcade. Corbett followed him down a corridor and another flight of stairs to an empty landing where Wilson stopped, pausing to listen to make sure they were not being followed. Then he sat down on a step, rather wearily. 'Let me have a cigarette, please,' he said. 'I'm out.'

Corbett gave him a cigarette, lighted it for him. The smoke hung suspended in the still, damp air. 'I have things all set for you,' Wilson said. 'The jet's waiting at Haneda, gassed up. The pilot has filed a flight plan for Okinawa but he's been briefed.' He put his hand on the attaché case. 'Your passport and visa are here. And you do have resources in Mexico City, right?'

'What in the hell is going on?' Corbett said.

'They have you all wrapped up,' Wilson said.

'Wrapped up?' Corbett said, as if he were not hearing correctly. 'What are you talking about?'

'Listen, all hell has been breaking loose here in the past two hours,' Wilson went on, everything accelerating towards a point of collapsing confusion. He did not have the details, only bits and pieces. The Koreans had released Abernathy on the condition that he turn over all the company files to them, which he had done, and in those files they had found copies of communications between Colonel Pak and Corbett, suggesting that there had been some discussion of using Pak as an intermediary for the disposal of some of Corbett's Vietnamese arms. There was also a strong hint that there was collusion between the Colonel and Corbett concerning the payments that ESK would make to the Korean government, a suggestion that Corbett had insisted on padding the figure to be paid to ROK to allow for a large kickback.

'Incredible,' Corbett said, suddenly chilled.

'That's not all,' Wilson said. A Japanese family on a visit to Aoyama Cemetery had found a small-calibre pistol tucked away behind a stone and turned it in to the police. Ballistics had tied the pistol to the killing and registry had traced it to ESK security. When the police checked security they were told that the pistol had been issued to Corbett as part of a self-protection campaign in the company. There was an immediate search of Corbett's rooms and the suit he had worn to the cemetery was found, sent to the Metro labs where traces of human blood were detected. 'That's what they have,' Wilson said, rubbing his hands together. 'All very neat. Hell, the American government's suddenly moved into gear because they want to extradite you, sub rosa, back to the States and into the hands of the Senate committee before the *gaijin* detail exercises its warrant.'

Corbett shook his head, trying to absorb, to make a plan of action at the same time. Ah, the company had framed him perfectly, not a detail overlooked, so boxed

136

him in that there was no way out, for no reason that he could see. It could not be happening and yet it was. He glanced up at the harsh light of the single suspended bulb in the stairwell. 'The police have been here again? They talked with you?'

'They knew I was with you, Willie.'

'And what did you tell them?'

'I told them it was impossible,' Wilson said with a shrug. 'I told them you couldn't have done it.'

'Do you believe that?'

'Of course, I believe it,' Wilson said. 'I'm sure once you get away from here, you'll have time to straighten it out. And I'll work on it from this end.'

'I appreciate what you've done,' Corbett said. 'I won't forget it.' It was time to move, to force himself beyond the inertia that held him here.

'If I tie on to anything here, I'll leave a message with Rodriguez and you get in touch.'

Corbett watched him moving up the staircase and then he opened the attaché case that Wilson had left behind. The official documents, a thousand dollars in cash for any incidental expenses. Cristina. He would call her but first he needed access to a telephone. He walked back up the stairs to the first basement level, following it, the smell of fresh cement heavy in the air, approaching two workmen who were affixing a large sheet of plywood to a wall. One of them grinned at him, displaying a gold tooth as he bowed slightly. 'Telephone,' Corbett said, frustrated, searching his mind for the Japanese word. *'Denwa.'* He held an imaginary telephone up to his ear.

'Hah,' the workman said, and bowing again led him farther down the corridor to a telephone sitting on a small table.

Politeness, and he bowed to the workman and thanked him, his mind racing in a state of stunned confusion and still he followed normal routines, the finger

137

in the dial holes, the endless sounds of computerised clicking, the muted sound of ringing on the other end of the line and then Cristina's voice, answering. 'Hello.'

'Do you have a car?' he said. 'I can't explain what's happening, but I have to get to the airport.'

'The police have been here,' she said. 'Is it serious?'

'Very,' he said. 'Who's driving for you?'

'I have a Japanese driver,' she said.

'Can you trust him?'

'Implicitly.'

'All right,' he said. 'I want you to pick me up.' But where? That was the problem. Ironic. He had been able to walk into the hotel with great freedom and now had little chance of leaving it without trouble. 'The Imperial Hotel,' he said. 'There's a sculpture in front. Very controversial.'

'I've seen it. Are you all right?'

'No, I'm not all right,' he said. 'How long will it take you to get there?'

'Half an hour,' she said. 'Maybe twenty minutes.'

'That will give me enough time,' he said.

He put the telephone down and watched a workman trundling past with a large wastebin on wheels, manoeuvering to get down a narrow side corridor. In another thirty days the hotel arcades would be finished on these sub-basement levels, lined with expensive shops, soundproofed, with piped-in music, but now, in the raw concrete of the subterranean corridors, he could feel the hum of power from the massive machinery that provided the air conditioning and the heat to the complex of buildings. He was awed by the sense of it, all hidden and yet here, and on the upper levels in the suites with velvet walls and gold fixtures, the power that made them habitable was taken for granted.

And it would not be too difficult to leave here, no, for any complex of buildings like this was designed to the same end, that the unattractive necessities, the processes of delivery and waste disposal would be hidden from sight. He followed the general direction taken by the Japanese workman with the wastebin and eventually came to a loading dock where two refuse trucks were backed up to a concrete platform. The workmen were all deferential towards him, for he was wearing a business suit, carrying an attaché case. He was a visible symbol of power; he would not be here unless he had business here. Given the role, he assumed it, pausing to check a stencil on the side of a crate that had just been delivered. His heart was rapid; it had developed an uneven rhythm. His mouth was dry. He continued to check stencils and bills of lading, almost compulsively, nodding officiously, aware that one of the truck drivers was watching him with the keen eye of a responsible subordinate in the presence of a superior. His truck was loaded with pieces of scrap wood and he was about to move down the concrete steps to the truck cab when Corbett stopped him.

'Do you speak English?' Corbett said.

'*Skoshi,*' the man grinned, bowing slightly.

'What kind of truck is this?' Corbett said.

'Ah,' the man said, his eyes rolling upward, his face contorted with the great effort of translating. 'Honda,' he said finally with a great smile of relief. 'Honda.'

'Very good,' Corbett said. He walked around to the passenger side, opened the door and climbed into the seat. The driver slid in under the wheel, obviously mystified. Corbett leaned over and checked the speedometer. The numbers did not register in his brain. 'Fine,' he said. 'Drive on.'

The driver shifted into gear and the truck groaned up a concrete rampway, screened by heavy plantings on either side, finally pulling into a wider alley and then to the street. Corbett said nothing. The driver asked him a question in Japanese and when Corbett made no response struggled to put his words into English and then

139

shrugged and smiled as if to say that it was not important. The truck laboured past Hibiya Park and when it was forced to stop at a light, Corbett opened the door and climbed out. 'Very good,' he said to the driver. The driver smiled. The truck moved on.

Corbett crossed the street and sat down on a bench. From here he could see the gigantic sculpture, a massive construction of angled slats that from a distance looked like an abstraction of a pine tree. If she came, he would be able to see her limousine from here. Not *if*, he thought, *when*. For there had been no hesitation in her voice when he had called her.

A crow alighted in a nearby tree, feathers shining in the sunlight. A young woman walked by with her baby suspended from a sling on her back. Summer, he thought, and all the seasons became the same to him because they changed so often for him. In the jet he had a complete wardrobe, for at times in the course of a day he would move from summer to winter, from heat to snow. But no more. If he made it out of the country, if he made it to Mexico, if there was any way to find anonymity, he would sit in one place and watch the changing of the seasons.

He would not allow himself to deal with the problems that faced him now. They were too immense, too knotted, so incredibly complex that he could deal with nothing more than the matter of flight at this moment. He had never known another man in the same predicament. The expatriates he had met were all men obliged to flee through the force of their own errors compounded. Argentina was full of them, some of the most notorious embezzlers in the business world, the con men of reputation, manipulators all who had known at some time they might be forced to flee and so had made provisions for it, with villas in Buenos Aires and long low cars and dark-skinned bodyguards to keep the past from intruding. But he had been caught unawares and had made no such provisions.

Finally the limousine appeared, creeping along the street close to the kerb, and he waited until it was close and then emerged from the shrubbery and waved it down, climbing into the back seat while it was still moving. Cristina was there, looking pale, fragile, and distraught in a linen suit. She took his hand. Her fingers were icy. 'My God, darling,' she said. 'How did it happen? What's going on?'

'I don't know,' he said vaguely. 'I don't know who's doing what. Tell your driver to take us to Haneda.'

'He's already been instructed to take us there,' she said. The limousine was moving at a crawl. 'Would you like me to tell him to go faster?'

'No,' he said. 'Nothing to attract suspicion.'

'Would you like a drink?' she said, folding down the panelled bar in the back of the seat in front of her. 'God knows you look like you could use something.'

'Yes,' he said. 'Bourbon neat.'

She poured some into a glass and he downed it and returned the glass to her soundlessly. 'Have you spoken to Erikson today?' he said at last.

'Briefly, after the Japanese police had talked to me.' She poured herself a glass of wine. Elegant, he thought, even at a time like this, her movements, the picture she created of herself. 'He said he was powerless to stop them. I asked him why they were looking for you and he said you had been engaged in some unfortunate speculative activities.'

He smiled, despite himself. The whisky felt warm in his stomach. 'The son of a bitch does have a way of putting things,' he said.

'He asked me if I had any idea where you might be, what you might do. I told him no, of course.'

'And that's the big question I would ask, if there was anybody to answer,' he said. 'What I might do.'

'And you have no idea what's going on?'

141

He shook his head, no. 'Somebody's gone to a hell of a lot of trouble,' he said. He was having to deal with it now, having to sort it out, for it was possible that inadvertently she might have some small piece of information that would make sense out of what was happening. 'I think somebody made a very large deal,' he said, 'with a hell of a lot of money involved in it. And I am the cover for it.' Through the window he saw a police car on a side street, moving in the opposite direction. 'Did Erik mention the meeting today?'

'No,' she said. 'But I know it was important. He said last night that a lot depended on it.'

'And that's all he said?'

'I never push these things. He tells me what he wants me to know. Do you want another drink?'

'No. What are your plans?' he said, knowing the answer even as he asked it, accepting it.

'I will need to stay here a while,' she said. 'I owe that to Erik. And it depends on what you decide to do. Where will you be?'

'I'll spend a week or ten days in Mexico City,' he said. 'I'll hire a lawyer when everything surfaces but I don't anticipate it will do much good. I'll probably end up in Brazil or Argentina.'

'I'll want to know where you are. Perhaps I'll come.'

'Of course,' he said. But he knew that she would not. There had been a pact between them for a while, a kind of personal conspiracy, but he had known it would last only as long as he stayed with the company. For once he cashed in his stock and reached Argentina he would no longer be on the rise. He would have a comfortable existence in which there was no room for ambition. The limousine was wheeling up on to the expressway now.

'I'm going to miss you,' she said.

'Yes.'

He fell silent, aware that her hand was resting on his leg, but there was no real contact between them. He was also aware that she had no sense of fear, no urgency

142

about her, as if she had nothing to lose by helping him. He could project her reaction when her complicity was discovered. She would simply sit back on her sofa, crossing her perfect legs, looking directly into Erikson's eyes with that challenging innocence of hers and in a quiet voice, admit it. And Erikson would continue to study her for a moment, then nod and accept, for to him women were weak strange unpredictable creatures. If she accepted no guilt for her actions, he would press none on her.

They reached the airport, an unbelievable congestion of automobiles and a continual stream of jets lifting into the smog-filled sky, one at a time, regular intervals, as if the traffic never stopped. The driver moved into a space beside the private jet terminal and he could see the aircraft waiting for him. She put her face up to be kissed and he was startled to see tears in her eyes and he wondered if they were real.

'If there's anything you need, darling,' she said, 'you let me know. And if I hear anything, I'll pass it on.'

'Yes,' he said. 'Thank you. I'll be in touch.' He climbed out of the limousine with the attaché case and started out towards the jet, the hatch swinging down with the stairs, not turning his head to watch the departure of the limousine, for he knew she would not wait. He felt oddly detached, much as he did on any business trip except that in many ways it would be a relief to be out of it. He walked up the steps into the cabin and then stopped short. Stevens was sitting there, in one of the upholstered flight seats, looking perhaps more startled than Corbett felt, his face ashy, apprehensive.

'What the hell are you doing here?' Corbett said.

'Erikson sent me,' Stevens said nervously. 'For God's sake, this wasn't my idea.'

'How did you know I would be here?' Corbett said, sitting down, waving his hand slightly as if he did not need an answer to his question. Jesus, it was no wonder that Cristina had taken this whole thing so calmly, no urgency, none. 'What are your instructions?'

'I brought a car. I'm supposed to take you back to the hotel.'

'And suppose I don't choose to go?'

'Shit, Willie, I'm not going to make any attempt to force you.'

Corbett walked forward, looked into the cockpit. Empty, no pilot. He came back into the cabin and sat down. 'What makes you think I won't kill you like I killed the Korean?'

'I don't think you killed the Korean.'

'But you're not sure, are you?'

'For God's sake, I told him to send somebody else.' He fumbled with a cigarette, lighted it. 'I told him I didn't want any part of this.'

'You didn't say anything to the old man. No one does. You may have thought all those things, but you never said them. Now, exactly, what are you supposed to do?'

'He told me I would find you here. He said that you were bound to be upset because you did not fully understand the situation. I was to tell you that the company would stand behind you if you would come back with me.'

'And if I chose not to?'

'I was told to do nothing. After all, the Japanese police are looking for you.'

He looked out through a rectangular window at a 747 taking off, rising towards a low cloud layer. For a moment he considered his chances of finding a pilot and a way to follow that 747 into the air. If he was lucky, he might be able to swing it. But Mexico was closed to him now, Rio as well, and there was no part of the globe where the company did not have influence. He could deal with the threat of the police; he could even escape the influence of the American government. But if the company wished him uncovered, he would be.

'I'll go back with you,' Corbett said.

Stevens was visibly relieved. 'I really believe that Erikson intends to help you,' he said. 'I really believe it's the best thing for you.'

'I'll go back with you,' Corbett said. 'But I don't want any of your fucking reassurances. Not a word of it.'

Stevens said nothing.

Chapter 4

Old times, yes, and everything had changed and everything was the same and he sat in Erikson's reception room, waiting while Mrs Seagraves brought him coffee in a delicate china cup, no change of expression on her face to mark his change of status, filling the time with pleasant conversation about the weather, occasionally answering the beckoning lights on her soundless telephone, transferring calls, asking others to call back at specific times.

He was filled with a deep and burning anger he could not show. He had been betrayed, so thoroughly and so completely that his only hope of salvation lay in the hands of the old man in that office beyond the ornately carved oak door. He could not carry his anger into that room for it would put him at a disadvantage; the old man thrived on other people's anger, at times manipulated it to throw them off balance.

He looked up to find Mrs Seagraves smiling at his side. 'Mr Erikson will see you now, Mr Corbett.'

'Thank you.'

He went into Erikson's office, the rage cooled now, controllable, and he saw Erikson standing next to a chart mounted on an easel filled with numbers and specifications. Erikson often said that he could think better on his feet and Corbett remembered a time when he had installed standing desks in all his offices.

'It's good to see you, William,' Erikson said, shaking

his hand. 'It's been quite a bad day for you, and I'm sorry for that.'

'A hell of a day,' Corbett said.

'Sit down. Have a drink.'

'I don't want a drink,' Corbett said. 'I want to know what's going on.'

'This shouldn't take too long,' Erikson said. 'I'll want you to chat with Klein a few minutes directly. If you like, I'll order dinner for you in the board room. Do you remember the conversation we had the other day, about the inevitability of our decline in the Far East?'

'Yes.'

'I want a candid answer from you, William. If there were a decline in the Far East, if nationalisation of our companies did occur, would you be affected personally? I mean by that, would you regard it as a setback for democracy?'

'Democracy?' Corbett blinked, incredulous at the situation, for Erikson had placed him in an untenable position, one which could cost him the rest of his life, and now he was discussing abstractions, indulging in company rhetoric. 'What in the hell does democracy have to do with it?'

'Let's put it in other terms. Would it be a setback for the free world?'

Corbett shook his head, bewildered. 'I don't give a damn about democracy tonight, Erik, and I'm not much interested in freedom for anybody until I have it myself. I have some very hard questions that need answering and I think I deserve to have them answered.'

'Certainly you do,' Erikson said. 'And I'll answer any questions I can when the time comes. But I think we have to consider what's happening in a proper context.' He had wandered back to that goddamned ceramic dog sitting on a carved table, and his manicured hand reached out to pet the polished head. 'The origin of the temple dog is quite interesting,' he said, and Corbett realised he was off and running on one of his mini-lectures again, impervious to interruption. 'Originally, in primitive Korea, there were real dogs set outside the temples, vicious animals, protecting against intruders, against *real* evil, in a sense. But as the centuries passed, the real dogs were replaced by these symbolic ones, porcelain, ceramic. Now they are beautiful but they are also useless. Do you follow my meaning?'

Corbett said nothing.

'I have decided I do not wish to be a temple dog,' the old man went on. 'I have decided to draw the line. I don't intend to yield one of my companies to any country. I have decided to show them that ESK has teeth. There will be no nationalisation, no schedule of payments, no erosion of my position.'

And now Corbett knew the purpose for the meeting today, a wagon-train summit called to circle against the economic Indians. 'Did the other companies agree?' he said.

'There are some who will yield at present,' Erikson said. 'They will wait to see whether I am successful or whether I fall on my face, but once I show them that it can be done, they will go along. It is really up to us to show them how.'

The subtle shift from first person singular to plural, he was aware of it, the trick of inclusion. 'You don't need to sell me, Erik,' he said. 'This is your forte. You call the shots.'

'It is important that you believe it as strongly as I do,' Erikson said. 'The whole initial phase of this operation is keyed to you.'

'Then you've picked the wrong person,' Corbett said. He brought himself up short, on the edge of a diatribe, a personal declaration of independence that would serve no purpose. He could not extricate himself with speeches. 'I think you had better know where I stand, Erik. You have a brilliant gift for organisation, for putting things together. But I think you are being naïve if you think you're going to reverse the tide in the Far

East. You can stand as firm as you like and you may win a round or two. If you're here to make money, you can do that, absolutely enormous amounts. But if you think you're going to reshape politics in this part of the world, you're dead wrong.'

'I appreciate your opinion, William.'

'Which means you haven't heard what I said,' Corbett said with a half smile. 'That's not important. But I am going to ask you a favour. It's not a demand because I'm not in any position to demand a damn thing and you are not the kind of man to respond to demands anyway. I'm asking that you call off the dogs. I want you to put an end to it, now.'

'I know how you feel.'

'I'm positive that you can't know how I feel. But I have given you my best efforts and I expect yours in return.'

Erikson lighted a cigar, going through the ritual, the silver cutter, the rolling of the tip in the flame, the very light inhalation. 'I will make you a guarantee,' he said. 'You may suffer a slight discomfort for a while but you will have a complete exoneration within sixty days.'

'If,' Corbett said. 'I detect an if.'

'There is always an if,' Erikson said. 'Your belief in my methods is not absolutely vital. But I will require you to go along with what I have in mind.'

'I can't guarantee that, not until I have specifics.'

The old man's head turned slightly. Was he responding to some signal, some change in the lighting, some tone that Corbett could not hear, or was this another of his arbitrary devices, to pretend that he had been signalled? 'I think it might be a good idea if we go to the board room,' he said. 'Klein appears to be ready.' He picked up the telephone, as if by afterthought, calling the pantry and ordering dinner to be served in the board room. 'Come along, please,' he said. 'I think you will be impressed by what Klein has done.'

He led the way through an adjoining library and then

opened a heavy oak door and waited for Corbett to pass through before he followed. The board room had been enlarged, and now one solid wall was covered with various viewing screens around one larger television screen in the centre, absolutely enormous, at least five feet by seven feet, and Klein was standing at a console dial, turning a switch and watching a company logo appear on the centre screen. He turned to Erikson and Corbett, nodding.

'What in the hell is this?' Corbett said.

'It was developed by the Gould Company,' Klein said. 'The displays are all linked to central computers, a very intricate process, which I must say I don't fully understand. The idea was not original with them, of course. They call it a "war room" because it's a very precise way of summoning data for display and determining strategies. It's similar to those used by the military.' A telephone rang discreetly, a muted bell. Klein picked it up, spoke into it briefly, and then looked to Erikson. 'Mrs Seagraves wonders if you wish to cancel your oppointment with Farwell.'

'No, tell her I will be right along.' He looked to Corbett. 'Sometimes it takes hard measures,' he said. 'But I will leave Mr Klein to fill you in. And all I ask is that you trust what I'm doing and understand that you will not be hurt by it.'

Corbett watched him leave the room, closing the door behind him, and then he sat down at the large conference table in a semisprawl, aware that there was a definite purpose to all of this, not knowing what it was but determined to force Klein to move into an expository position. Klein sat down at the head of the table, resting his hands on a small console. 'I think we had better review your situation,' Klein said.

'You can spare me your impressive displays,' Corbett said. 'I've been through the soft sell, the declaration of principles. Now I want to know precisely and exactly what you expect out of me.'

'Your co-operation.'

'In what?'

'You will receive instructions as we go along. For a while, you will do nothing. We'll protect you from the Japanese police so they can't claim jurisdiction. After a short time, three days as a matter of fact, you will be flown back to the States to meet with a Senate committee, where you will testify.'

'About what?'

'You will confess to negotiating with the Vietnamese government for the purchase of abandoned American military hardware. You will testify that you moved those arms to a location in Africa in the hopes of selling them. You will also testify that you entered into a deal with Colonel Pak and that when he reneged in an abusive manner you shot and killed him.'

'Christ,' Corbett said, with startled amazement. 'The whole fucking thing is somehow your operation, all of it. What in the hell are you up to, Klein?'

'All of it will be revealed to you in due time.'

'It's rampant stupidity,' Corbett said. 'I won't go along with it for a moment.'

Klein's expression did not change; there was not a flicker of emotion on his face. 'I think you will change your mind.'

There was a light knock on the double doors of the room and a Japanese waiter in a white coat entered, pushing a cart, proceeding to set up a table service in front of Corbett. Corbett felt a sense of relief. He was on solid ground now, dealing with hard facts. The waiter lifted a silver cover from a rare steak, stood back from the table until Corbett dismissed him, and then trundled his cart out through the doors, closing them behind him.

Corbett unfolded his napkin and poured coffee from a silver pot. 'The untrammelled sense of power of the retired military,' he said. 'I can see why Erikson brought you aboard. The grandiose vision coupled with the machine of the military mind. Software and hardware. A perfect blend.' He cut into the steak, took a bite. 'You may have done a lot of things in your time, Klein, but this is one thing you can't bring off.'

'I think I can convince you,' Klein said. 'We can wait until you finish your meal, if you like.'

'No, go ahead.'

Klein's fingers moved on the console. A document appeared on the screen. 'This is a photostat of the agreement signed by you and the Vietnamese representative in Paris. There are various other pages detailing the equipment and agreeing on the price.'

'An exorbitant amount no doubt.'

'Very.'

He paused thoughtfully while he cut another piece of steak. 'And where did I get the money?'

'From various ESK/KOREA accounts, some others, all transferred to a Vietnamese account in Zurich.'

'All right. What else do you have?'

Klein pressed a button. The first document was transferred on to one of the smaller screens and the second document appeared on the large screen. 'This is the form you signed to set up Ludlow, Limited, in Liberia. It is not your name, of course, but we have handwriting experts willing to testify you wrote it and a Liberian official to identify you.'

'Rather shaky ground,' Corbett said. The steak was excellent, Kobe beef, probably. Beer-fed. 'You'll have a hard time proving that. I've had some experience in that field.'

'It's a minor item,' Klein said. 'A supporting document. But suppose we dispense with all these papers.' He manipulated the console again and suddenly all the screens contained documents, letters, memos, transscripts of conversations. 'You can examine them, if you like, but you'll find that, taken as a whole, they're pretty convincing. Too, there are a number of witnesses who will be called against you. Saperstein is one. He's currently in South America but he will fly to Washington on his own volition next week and make a statement to the Senate committee, which will also be released to the press. He will testify that he did authorise the sale of repair parts at your urging and that he was lax in double-checking the details and that now he wishes to clear himself, admit to error, and ask for understanding.'

'I always liked Henry,' Corbett said. He sipped the coffee, blotted his mouth with the linen napkin.

'And I think Henry returns that regard, but he's in poor health. He wants to retire and a government pension is pretty short money in these times. You can take my word for it that all the bases are covered. Once you are testifying, Kukler will be supplied all the documents he doesn't have as yet. He really believes all this material is authentic, by the way. And well he should. It's perfect.'

Corbett examined a small dish of baby peas. He decided he did not want them. There was a dessert on the table, something with chocolate, but the steak had satisfied him. 'Money,' he said. 'The witnesses. Every man has his price. 'I believe that, you know, not cynically but realistically. It's just a matter of offering a man the right rationale for selling out.'

'And what's your price?' Klein said. 'You do have one?'

'I suspect I do. But you're going about it the wrong way.'

'I don't think so,' Klein said. 'This isn't a matter of choice for you. We couldn't afford to leave you any alternatives.'

'You can't keep from it,' Corbett said. 'I'm willing to meet all your evidence head-on. I'm ready to refute Saperstein, Kukler, and whoever else you have in the wings.'

'The computer says you can't,' Klein said with quiet certainty.

'The most any computer can give you is probabilities,' Corbett said. 'You know that as well as I do. Now, the computer may give you a ninety-five to five probability but there's still that five per cent variable under the curve that you have to consider. Now, you can persuade, coerce, or otherwise convince enough key people to make a good case in front of the Senate. But there's also the possibility I can dislodge you there. Because I have allies in the company and you are also overlooking a key consideration. Your computer can't make mistakes, granted, but I can and have. If I made one log entry in error, either by putting down my itinerary a week later or just simply because I forgot and had my dates wrong, then your computer would be building on false data and the whole goddam thing would fly out the window.'

'There's always the matter of the Colonel. I think we have a good case there.' Klein pressed a button and a series of slides began to appear on the screen, flashes of Corbett outside the Public Information Office in Seoul, the glare of the Korean sun, pictures of the meeting in the cemetery, the Colonel's expression pensive, Corbett extending one palm upwards as if making a point. The Japanese students and their goddamned cameras.

'That proves nothing,' Corbett said. 'I have already admitted knowing the Colonel, meeting with him.'

'We have copies of messages transmitted between you and ESK/KOREA on the safe line that were delivered to the Colonel, at least half a dozen of them, demanding an immediate meeting, accusing him of bad faith, subtly worded, of course, but adding up to the fact that you were trying to force a sizeable kickback. Witnesses will testify that you sent the messages. Other witnesses at ESK/KOREA will testify that the messages were delivered.' He paused, lacing his fingers beneath his chin, his eyes half closed, as if he were meditating. 'The pistol,' he said.

'What about the pistol?'

'It was used to kill the Colonel. It was issued to you and you signed a receipt for it. Ballistics will show it is the weapon.'

Corbett tasted the coffee again. It was cold. He put the cup back on the saucer. 'Then you did kill him, didn't you? You arranged that. How far do you think you can carry this?'

'I want you to take this seriously,' Klein said. 'I want you to realise how far we are prepared to go. I can guarantee you that we haven't overlooked anything. Petrosur. You made rather a heavy gamble there, didn't you? I can show you the latest market position on the screen, if you like.'

'I'll take your word for it,' Corbett said. 'What happened to it?'

'Mexico nationalised it, made it a part of Pemex. There was an under-the-table payment to Guatemala. The big oil companies traded their shares early in France at a respectable price. Pemex will buy the equipment from Shell and Gulf, reimburse exploration costs. The common's being redeemed at ten pesos. Which means that you lose a total of something like six hundred thousand dollars. That makes it all the more difficult for you to explain your current financial position.'

Once again he touched the console and now, on the oversized screen, balanced neatly in columns, was a financial statement. Corbett leaned forward to bring it into focus, scanning the rows. Deposits in the Banco de Mexico, in Suissebanc, open accounts in various Zurich and Geneva banks, investments in foreign currencies, a running total of $1,900,000.

'That is supposed to be mine?' Corbett said.

'Yes. The money is traceable to various sources that will be revealed at the proper time,' Klein said. 'You made enough deals to put close to two million aside.'

The proverbial straw, Corbett thought, and he had been aware of the accumulating pattern of words on the screen, the pictures, even the damning evidence of the

155

pistol, but this one financial statement was enough to sink him. No one would be willing to transfer this much money to his account simply to make a case.

'What is the end result of this operation supposed to be?' Corbett said softly. 'Why in the hell have you gone to all this trouble?'

'The whys are unimportant at this juncture,' Klein said.

'You take a hell of a lot for granted.'

'Only because I'm in a position to do so,' Klein said. 'I don't like having to do this to you but in the end you will benefit by it. You simply follow through with the instructions that we will give you at the proper time and the hardships will be minimal. A temporary inconvenience, that's all it amounts to. Then you will be shifted to Europe and all of this will be behind you.'

'There's no way you can make that guarantee,' Corbett said. 'You have a lobby full of Japanese police, for one thing.'

'They will remain in the lobby,' Klein said. 'We don't intend to let them have you.'

'My God, your presumption amazes me,' Corbett said. 'Now you may have me cornered, you may have manipulated me into a bind, but I still have options. And if you think I'm going to allow you to control them, you're not as bright as you seem.'

Klein stood up now, systematically cutting off all the displays. The screens went dark, one by one. 'I can understand how you feel,' he said quietly. 'Nevertheless, there is too much at stake here to allow any margin for error. The Japanese would send you to prison with very little fanfare and that wouldn't do either of us any good.' He picked up the telephone. 'Mr Corbett is ready to go back to his suite now.' The door opened and a man in a conservative suit appeared, a very athletic man. 'This is Mr Goddard,' Klein said. 'He's one of the executive bodyguards we have put on the staff. Now, I want you to understand me completely

156

so you won't mistake my intentions. You will be restricted to the upper floors of the hotel. You may continue to work if you like. He will be with you every second, day and night, as long as I consider it necessary. He also has instructions, if you try to react in any adverse way, to kill you on the spot. We will simply claim that you came back, caused trouble, and were shot in the process. Do you understand me?'

Corbett stood up wearily. 'It won't work,' he said. 'You're wasting your time.'

'I never waste my time,' Klein said. 'Keep one thing in mind. You are only slightly less valuable to us dead than you are alive.'

Corbett said nothing.

2

As he came awake, Goddard was opening the drapes in the bedroom, permitting a flood of blinding sunlight to fall across the bed. He was immediately on guard. Goddard was a bulky man with the most impassive face Corbett had ever seen. It was as if he possessed no emotions whatsoever, perpetually cold, watchful.

'Mr Fenster will be here in fifteen minutes,' he said.

Corbett sat up in bed, running a hand across the stubble on his face. 'I want to get the ground rules straight. What am I permitted to do? Do I have the freedom of the executive floors?'

'Yes,' Goddard said. The single word, nothing more.

It would be hard going, yes, but he had to make an attempt to move around this mind, to discover the soft spots, the weaknesses. He had not encountered a man like Goddard before, a man who had been instructed to kill him under certain conditions and who would not hesitate to do so. While Corbett shaved, brushed his teeth, he could see Goddard reflected in the mirror, standing near the bedroom door. Something about his attitude was familiar, the posture of eternal readiness.

'Secret Service, right?' Corbett said as he came out of the bathroom and picked up his shirt. 'You used to be one of the men in sunglasses with the coloured code pin in the lapel.'

'Yes,' Goddard said.

Corbett put on his pants, sat down to put on his shoes. 'Do you know that I'm being set up?' he said. 'But I don't suppose that would really make any difference to you, one way or the other.'

'I have my orders,' Goddard said.

Ah, the first small triumph and he had succeeded in coaxing a full sentence out of Goddard. It was not much, but it was something. He went into the sitting-room to find a thermos of coffee and copies of newspapers laid out for him. He picked up the *Wall Street Journal*, confirmed the collapse of Petrosur, thumbed through *The New York Times* and the English edition of *Asahi*. The *Times* devoted no coverage to him, but *Asahi* contained a long and rather restrained article on the death of the Colonel and the diplomatic ramifications. The Koreans were claiming that the Japanese were dragging their feet. The Japanese government was saying nothing at all; the Metropolitan Police were saying that they had a prime suspect and they expected to make an arrest shortly.

As he read the papers he was aware that Goddard had taken a seat near the door where he did absolutely nothing except sit with his legs crossed, his arms folded across his chest. Corbett wondered how he occupied his mind in this state of perpetual watchfulness when there was indeed nothing to watch. Layers, of course, there had to be some drifting; no mind could be trained to be perfectly inactive.

There was a knock on the door and Goddard answered it immediately, opening the door a crack and then admitting Fenster, who came in with his attaché case, smiling, full of energy. 'Good morning, Willie,' he said.

'Sit down. Have some coffee.'

'No more coffee. I have to limit myself. But I will have a glass of water. I'm trying to drink a gallon a day, for the kidneys.' He approached the wetbar, drew a glass of water from the tap, then placed it on the coffee table in front of him while he sat down opposite Corbett, perched on the edge of the chair. 'We might as well get to it,' he said. 'We have a lot to do.'

'A lot of what?' Corbett said.

'I've been assigned your defence,' Fenster said. 'You're smiling. Is there a joke? Am I missing something?'

'The world grows more unreal by the moment,' Corbett said. 'First, the company manufactures charges against me in such complete and overwhelming detail that I am absolutely engulfed. And then it assigns legal counsel to defend me against those charges.'

'That's not going to do us any good,' Fenster said. He took a cigarette and inserted it into a filtered holder, drawing smoke through it with great effort. 'These goddamned filters are supposed to cut down on the tars and nicotines. They do it by not permitting any smoke to pass through.' He sucked on the filter. 'I think we have a number of lines of defence, Willie, but you're going to have to level with me or we won't get anywhere.'

'I'm serious,' Corbett said.

'And so am I,' Fenster said. He removed the filter, dumped it in the ashtray and stuck the cigarette in the corner of his mouth. 'In the first place, I don't think you're in violation of any federal statutes in the Vietnamese business. You were acting as a private contractor, not for ESK, and none of your shell companies are American, no stockholders, no listing on the exchanges, so there's nothing they can pin you with. Yours is an offshore operation so you don't have to be registered as a munitions dealer. I can't see any complications in this area.'

Ah, there was a Kafkaesque quality to this business,

a *Catch-22* insanity. He said nothing, pouring himself coffee.

'The only possible violations concern your dealings with Saperstein and DOD. The question is whether you represented yourself as ESK and even if he testifies to that, he doesn't have a damn thing to support it. We've made a search and there's no paperwork to indicate that he didn't make a bogus assumption if he regarded you as ESK. You bought through Ludlow, Limited, after all. I take it that none of the vouchers were drawn against any ESK subsidiaries.'

'You are out of your fucking head,' Corbett said, filled with a sudden and despairing anger. 'There are no forms, no goddamned vouchers, no payments.'

Fenster sneezed. Taking out his handkerchief, he blew his nose, then carefully folded the handkerchief and put it in his pocket. 'Technically, however,' he said, ignoring Corbett's outburst, 'it will play better if there is a charge against you in the States. The American government will insist on priority on the grounds that your offence in the United States is more grievous than the alleged offence in Japan and therefore takes precedence.'

Corbett shook his head. Anger was useless, he realised, for Fenster was totally immune to it. 'I want you to listen to me for a minute,' he said quietly, forcing calmness. 'Can you do that?'

'I'm listening.'

'I did not do any of this,' Corbett said, enunciating his words with an exaggerated precision. 'I had nothing to do with the Vietnamese arms. I did not shoot the Colonel. The whole thing is an ESK project.'

'Are you saying that you acted on behalf of the company?'

'No. I was not involved in any of this, in any way.'

'No one will believe that,' Fenster said. 'The second way to handle it is to mount a defence here. We have Japanese lawyers who say they could make a good case

160

for you. Since hearsay is admissible, we would simply have to produce witnesses who could testify that the Colonel held ill will towards you and might have considered doing you bodily harm. He was a military man, after all, trained in the martial arts, so that you can always claim that he attacked you and that you shot him in self-defence.'

'You're wasting your time. I won't co-operate with you.'

'Are you telling me that you won't provide any of the information we need for your defence?'

'Since I was not involved, I have no information.'

Fenster shrugged again, finished the water. He frowned. 'You're making a hell of a mistake,' he said. 'But I'll do my best to put something together.'

Corbett watched him leave. He looked at Goddard, still sitting at the door. 'Have you ever killed anybody?' Corbett said.

'No,' Goddard said.

'Have you ever shot anybody?'

'Yes.'

'Without emotion?'

'It was necessary. I didn't worry about it.'

'Do you have to repeat what goes on in this room? Is that a part of your job?'

'Yes.'

'I've been given permission to work. What does that entail?'

'Any of your normal duties,' Goddard said flatly.

'Is my telephone monitored?'

'Yes. You're limited to in-house calls.'

Corbett shrugged. He picked up the telephone. Almost immediately Stevens answered. 'Yes?'

'I want to see Ellen Benson.'

'Why?'

'She's making arrangements for the Asian meeting,' Corbett said. 'Shit, if I'm not to engage in any further work, you let me know. Otherwise, locate her and send her up.'

'I think that will be all right.'

'In the meantime connect me with Wilson.'

There was a pause on the line while Stevens thought it over. Obviously, he was checking against a list of approved names. 'All right,' Stevens said. Corbett heard a series of muted clicks, a number being dialled.

'Wilson.'

'Corbett here,' he said, rushing ahead, giving Wilson no time to say anything that might involve him. It was necessary to communicate to him that they had to talk on a level beyond Stevens's capacity to understand. 'I want you to brief Ellen Benson on all the ramifications of the Asian meetings before I see her.'

'I already have,' Wilson said, picking up the intent. 'You will find that she's fully informed.'

'Good. Have you put together the cost figures?'

'Yes. I'm available to go over them with you any time you like.'

'I'll need them later today. So stand by.'

'Will do.'

Corbett put the telephone on the cradle with a feeling of relief. Wilson had not been implicated in his abortive escape effort. And Ellen would know what was going on.

In a few minutes there was a knock on the door and Goddard opened it cautiously before he admitted Ellen. She glanced at him curiously and then looked at Corbett. 'I didn't realise you were busy,' she said.

'I'm not,' he said. 'Ignore Goddard.'

'Ignore him?' she said. But Goddard had taken his heavy perch on the chair by the door again and she sat down, crossing her long legs, putting papers on the coffee table. 'Honestly, I don't know when I've enjoyed doing anything as much as I have doing this. I have a list of the delegates here with key points about each one. They've all booked accommodations at the New

Atami. Their general meetings will be held in the ball-room. Now I would like to arrange for two hospitality suites, one on the same floor as the ballroom, the other on the fifteenth floor. None of the other companies have anything above the third floor.'

He could not tell whether her plans were real or improvised but she was quite good at it either way, he decided, and she was positively glowing with her talk of caterers who would provide delicacies from each of the countries for the delegates. She was also arranging for the printing of invitations in each of sixty-three languages with the logos of local ESK companies on the covers. 'I have it all here,' she said. 'Will you look it over for me?'

'Certainly,' he said, picking up a sheet. Across the top, written in a lightly pencilled handwriting, she had written: 'Are you all right? Is there anything I can do for you?'

'I like your ideas,' he said. 'I do have a suggestion for the caterers.' He took a pencil from his pocket. 'Wilson. Three o'clock. Roof garden,' he wrote across the top of the paper, making certain she could see it as he wrote. Then he scrubbed it out with an eraser, removing her writing as well. 'No,' he said. 'I want you to handle this one strictly on your own. I'll critique it when you get through.'

Had Goddard observed the passing of the message? Was he aware of the subtle shift of expression on Ellen's face? No, Corbett thought not, for Goddard remained implanted in his chair, slowly scratching the back of his right hand with the index finger of his left.

'Do you have a schedule of the agenda for their meeting?' Corbett said. 'That's a little beyond your scope, but I'd like you to see if we have anything.'

'We have the exact time of their sessions but no agenda,' she said. 'It's a crazy business. They are getting together to come up with a unified plan of action against corporations and yet they're willing to take whatever

163

extras we're willing to give them while they're doing it. Exxon is paying for their final banquet. We're putting up fifteen thousand dollars to rent a hydrofoil so they can have a morning's outing.'

'There's no logic to it,' he said. 'There's no logic to anything connected with it. I'll look these over and get back to you if anything's terribly wrong.'

'Do you want me to get together with Wilson?'

'Yes. He will approve your budget for this one.'

Once she had gone, he settled in with the papers she had brought him, only half aware of the content, instead studying Goddard and his restlessness. With nothing to occupy him, Goddard could not sit still. After an hour of sitting in the chair he stood up, stretching himself, walking over to pour himself a cup of coffee and to take a stance at the window, where he could look down at the street. Athletic, yes, the well-conditioned body of a man ill-suited to inactivity. He moved on the balls of his feet, rocking back and forth as he stood at the window. It would be necessary to loosen him up in order to get past him. Corbett continued to go through the papers until noon.

'Am I allowed to go to the executive dining-room for lunch?' Corbett said.

'Certainly,' Goddard said.

Corbett went to the bathroom to wash his hands, examining the slot window. No, he was not agile enough for that, forcing himself through a narrow opening to find himself eight floors above the street. Whatever he did would have to be inconspicuous enough and timed to give him a few minutes alone with Wilson before he was picked up again. He washed and dried his hands and then rejoined Goddard, who was waiting for him.

They took the elevator up to the executive dining-room and Corbett paused in the doorway. Five or six of the tables were occupied by men who pretended not to see him; the word had been passed. Corbett was in difficulty and they would just as soon not get involved in it. Corbett took a table in the corner, Goddard sitting with his back to the wall. He ordered a bourbon and water and trout, then turned his attention to the windows and the tiny figures on the terraces of the building opposite, the Japanese men driving golf balls during their lunch hour, the air full of them, a swarm of insects from this distance, arcing into the giant nets.

'Do you play golf?' Corbett said.

'When I have time,' Goddard said.

'Can I buy you a drink?'

'No.'

'Duty, yes,' Corbett said. 'I don't blame you for that. It's a good practice. Now, me, I'm just passing time so it makes no difference whether I drink or not.' A waiter served his bourbon. He lifted the glass slightly in Goddard's direction. 'The question is, what am I waiting for? You don't happen to know what they have in mind for me, do you?'

'No,' Goddard said. He was watching the golfers now and Corbett could almost see the tension in his body, the slight wistfulness with which he regarded those men and the driving range.

'I take it you don't want to talk.'

'No.'

Corbett shrugged. When the fish came, he ate half of it and then ordered another drink while Goddard consumed his club sandwich, his powerful jaws working against the triangles of bread and meat. God, he was a persistent man and Corbett felt claustrophobic around him. They finished eating in silence and Corbett took his time over the drink, then walked back down the corridor to the elevator.

'How many Japanese police are in the lobby?' he said.

'Enough,' Goddard said. 'They're very efficient. You'd never get past them.'

Corbett forced a smile. 'And where would I go if I did?'

165

Once they were back in the suite, Goddard resumed his position at the door again and Corbett lifted the telephone.

'Yes, sir?' Stevens said.

'Connect me with Klein.'

'He's not in his office at the moment.'

'How soon will he be back?'

'He's having lunch.'

'Interrupt his goddamn lunch,' Corbett said. 'I want to talk to him.'

The line went dead and at first Corbett thought that Stevens had hung up on him but then he heard a click and Klein's voice came on the line. 'You want to talk to me?'

'Yes,' Corbett said. 'I've had second thoughts about the whole business. I'm willing to give you my co-operation but there are a number of things I want in return.'

'I'm pleased to hear it,' Klein said, his voice curious.

'I'll be at your office in thirty minutes. I want to stop at accounting first.'

'Very good.'

Corbett began to assemble the papers on the Asian meeting, placing them in an attaché case, playing it casually now, already feeling the sense of relaxation in Goddard. 'Maybe you'll have the chance to drive a few balls this afternoon after all,' he said. 'Shit, I don't know why I was holding out. A sense of pride, maybe. If you ever move up in the hierarchy, Goddard, keep in mind that it's important to allow a man to save face. That's sometimes worth more than any amount of money.' He snapped the case shut. 'Would you really have shot me?' he said.

Goddard shrugged. 'Yes.'

'I suppose you would have,' Corbett said pleasantly. 'After all, you have your job and I have mine.'

Accounting was on ten, a labyrinth of offices and corridors, and in the elevator Corbett tried to remember the exact setup, the precise arrangement of the file room. He had been there no more than a couple of times – there was always someone to bring him what he needed – and yet now his life would depend on how well he remembered it, on whether he had guessed right. For he had no doubt that Goddard would shoot him if the occasion arose, automatically, with no more thought than he himself would give to the termination of a file. Idiocy, yes, and this man who stood at his side in the elevator, smelling faintly of lime cologne, could within minutes be the cause of his death.

'I've been with the company most of my adult life,' Corbett said. 'They've taken good care of me so far. There's no reason why they won't continue to.' He was exuding rationalisations now, the proper sounds, in the hope that Goddard would be perceptive enough to pick them up.

The elevator stopped; the door hissed open and they were faced with the frosted glass doors of the accounting office. He walked down a corridor to the left, moving through rows of desks and men at their silent calculators to another door marked FILES. Goddard opened it for him, allowing him to pass through, keeping close to him as he approached the counter and a woman whose face he knew but could match with no name.

'What can I do for you, Mr Corbett?' she said.

'I want to look at the weeklies for Kyoto Ceramics,' he said, pulling a name out of his memory at random.

'You'll need to go to computer for that,' she said. 'We keep a running file here for twenty-four hours and then they go into computer storage.'

'It's the daily figures I'm interested in,' he said. 'Where are they kept?'

'If you'll follow me,' she said. She led him through another corridor to a small room with an open area surrounded by walls of metal filing cases. She pulled one open. 'I think you'll find everything you need here.'

'I'll need one thing more,' he said. 'A chair.'

167

'We'll need to bring one from the office.'

Corbett began to thumb through the folders. 'You can bring a chair for yourself if you like,' he said to Goddard. 'We may be here a few minutes.'

Goddard hesitated, then left the room, appearing less than a minute later with a single chair, which he placed by the file. Corbett sat down, pulling out a pair of folders marked 'Kyoto Ceramics', thumbing through the papers without seeing them. Goddard took a position near the door, leaning against the wall. It was all a game, Corbett realised, even this, and he had probed Goddard's weaknesses and established a single precedent upon which he would attempt to capitalise. Goddard had left the room to bring the chair, the visual contact broken, and Corbett was now one up.

'Kyoto Ceramics is a good company,' Corbett said, lighting a cigarette. The room was poorly ventilated, obviously pressed into service to take care of a filing system that demanded more space than was originally designed for it. The smoke seemed to hang in the air, suspended. 'If you had invested ten thousand dollars in their company a couple of years ago, you would have enough money to retire today.' He removed a pencil from his pocket, making check marks by the meaningless columns of figures, finishing one cigarette, lighting another, aware that Goddard was growing increasingly restive. Finally he pinched the bridge of his nose and closed his eyes. 'Do you have an aspirin?' he said to Goddard.

'No.'

'I need an aspirin and a glass of water.'

'We'll get you one when we leave.'

'Jesus Christ,' Corbett said. 'I'm going to be here another half hour. Look, if you won't get it for me, I'll do it myself.' He realised that Goddard was looking over the room for any sign of a telephone, an intercom, but there was none.

'I'll get it for you,' Goddard said.

The moment he was gone, Corbett moved to the door, waiting until Goddard made the turn towards the central file room, and then he ran down the hall in the opposite direction, his heart pounding, the goddamned attaché case weighing down his arm. He opened one door, found himself staring into a broom closet, fled down the hallway again, opening another door filled with filing cases, passed through it and out a door that led into the elevator hallway. He forced himself to act casual as a pair of men alighted from the elevator. He stepped inside, holding the door open, and then pressed the button for three and stepped out again, just as the door hissed shut and the elevator began its descent.

He moved through a fire door into the staircase and then ran up to the next landing, where the steps reversed direction, leaning against the wall to steady himself, dizzy. He had neglected his body and he could feel the fatigue running through him. It would not work. Goddard would see the descending lights on the elevator panel and would not be fooled and in a moment Corbett would hear the fire door open and Goddard would find him here and kill him. Yet he could not move, not for a moment, not until he had calmed his breathing.

A minute passed. The fire door did not open. Goddard had been diverted, at least for the moment. But Corbett had not thought it through, had not determined where he would go, what steps would be taken against him now. Undoubtedly, hotel security would be alerted, but how would they go about looking for him? He looked up the stairs, realising he did not have the stamina to walk to the roof garden. He was being foolish. He had made his move now and it was not reversible. Slowly, he climbed three flights of stairs and then cautiously cracked the fire door and looked out into the hallway. It was empty.

He straightened his tie and ran his hand over his hair, then stepped into the hallway, crossed to the elevator, and pressed the up button. The door opened and he was inside, alone, and he took the elevator to the roof, following a path through the potted shrubbery until he found a secluded table screened by a growth of bamboo. He sank into a chair, relieved to be safe for the moment. A waiter approached, Japanese, solicitous.

'Bring me a beer,' Corbett said.

'Which brand do you prefer?'

'Any kind of beer.'

In the shade of the bamboo he tried to relax, to bring his mind up over the level of physical panic sufficiently to create some course of action for himself. He could think of nothing constructive. When the beer came, he drank it slowly. Through the smog the sun was hot. Nothing was irreversible. If he stood up now and took the elevator down to Klein's office, absolutely nothing would happen to him. He could always claim that he felt oppressed by Goddard's presence, demeaned – which was true – and that he wished to meet with Klein on his own, not because he was being coerced. He was appalled at the stupidity of his own position, which had moved to the point of physical flight from a man who might or might not shoot him. His own thinking had become infected with the same sense of paranoia that had pervaded the company, the animation of fears into a kind of compulsive behaviour.

He had been there no longer than ten minutes when Wilson came down the pathway, his suit rumpled, a rather strained expression on his face. 'Goddamn,' he said, 'I didn't know whether you would be here or not.'

'They're looking for me then?'

'With a vengeance. Hotel security covered the lower three floors of the hotel in a matter of minutes. The Japanese are raising hell because they were not informed that you were in the building in the first place. But they're all convinced that you made it out.'

'How?'

'One of the Japanese cops was assigned to the service

170

elevator. He's got a bladder infection and when the detectives checked, they found the poor bastard in the can. So they covered all the bars, restaurants, any place you might have been in the lobby area and concluded you had gotten lucky and hit the service elevator at exactly the right time. But the poor cop is off the hook with his superiors because they weren't informed. It's a crazy business, Willie.'

'That will give me a few minutes anyway,' Corbett said. 'What did you find out?'

'They're really out to zing you,' Wilson said. 'They have a witness who's going to put the whole thing together against you.'

'Who?'

'Your old buddy, Abernathy.'

'No,' Corbett said flatly, refusing to believe it. 'You're dead wrong. I just pulled his ass out of a hole in Korea. He's not the man.'

'There's no such thing as gratitude anymore,' Wilson said. After taking Corbett's call Wilson had remembered something from the examination of the cash flow of ESK/KOREA, a rather minor item for the expense of investigating the proposed acquisition of a large complex of phosphate and coal companies owned by Standard Chemicals with plants in Korea, Japan and Singapore. The expense money had been directed into Eastern Technico, a company supposedly based in Tokyo, and when Wilson investigated, he found that Eastern Technico was a dummy corporation, a funnel for some rather large sums of money from seven different ESK/KOREA enterprises. The money had been poured into Technico and then to another holding company owned by ESK/INT in Switzerland. 'That's as far as I could trace the funds,' Wilson said.

'How much?'

'In excess of three hundred million.'

'Jesus.'

'I called Korea and found that Abernathy had left

171

there and is presently someplace in Japan. Now, I don't have any concrete proof but he sure as hell knew that money was being transferred. And I believe that when the time comes, he's going to surface and blow you out of the water by testifying that you engineered the transfer of funds for your Vietnamese deal.'

'I need to get out of here and find the son of a bitch,' Corbett said. 'Can you get a fix on him for me?'

'I think so, yes.'

Corbett ran a finger across the top of the table. It had been clean when he sat down and already a fine residue of what appeared to be ash had covered it. 'I think I know how to leave the hotel,' he said. 'But it would take a hell of a risk on your part.'

Wilson stared off into the distance. 'I don't have any faith in the company,' he said. 'I enjoy negotiating. I'm fascinated by it but I don't like this kind of operation. If they're allowed to do this to you now, it would just be a matter of time before the same kind of thing happened to me.'

'All right, then,' Corbett said. 'I want you to call Ellen. Have her go to one of the shops in the tourist wing and buy luggage. Then she's to meet me on the mezzanine in the tourist wing. I want you to call the tourist desk and talk to the Japanese day manager. Tell him that an important client of the company is checking out and that he and his wife are to be treated with the greatest courtesy. The company is picking up the tab. Have a bellhop waiting in the lobby and a taxi at the door.'

'You're going to try and walk out?'

'Yes,' Corbett said. 'I think it will work.'

'That depends on the lobby,' Wilson said. 'I'll scout that before I do anything else. What if the police are still around?'

'Have Lieutenant Nakamura paged. He's the only one I'm really concerned about. If he's there, then we'll scrub this and try something else. And make it clear to

172

Ellen that I will understand if she opts out of this.'

'Right.' Wilson stood up. 'I'll get it done as soon as I can. You'll know I'm ready when the Japanese waiter brings you a bourbon and water on the house. If it doesn't look possible, I'll be back.'

Once Wilson was gone, Corbett was left with a feeling of apprehension. In the distance he could hear a man's voice, low guttural Japanese, and the response of a woman laughing. He thought of Cristina and wondered if she had the slightest pang of regret at betraying him. Probably not. She was a conduit for emotions; they swept through her and left her clean, leaving no after-effects. And sooner or later she would run across another man and resume her sexual conspiracies.

He finished the beer. The shadow of the bamboo moved almost imperceptibly against the top of the table, crawled an inch, and he realised that he had no sense of time, no idea how long Wilson had been gone. Then he saw the waiter approaching, the glass of bourbon on the tray, setting it before him, saying something inaudible. Corbett bowed slightly, smiling until the waiter had gone.

He drank the bourbon and then stood up, leaving money on the table. He was steady now; he would regard this as preparation for one of his business meetings where the odds were stacked heavily against him. An air of confidence was all-important. There were two elevators on the roof garden, one serving the executive wing and the other, at the far side, leading down to the tourist lobby.

He waited patiently at the latter, casually lighting a cigarette, nodding to a pair of Japanese businessmen, who acknowledged his presence with broad smiles and no words. The doors hissed open. He ground his cigarette out beneath his heel, motioned for the men to precede him, but neither of them moved and finally he entered first. His breathing was shallow, his throat dry. It would there are businesses in Tokyo that do not welcome

173

thing different, the linens elevator maybe, or the arcade through which he had departed before.

They would catch him; Wilson and Ellen would be implicated as well. The elevator slowed at the sixth floor. A couple from India entered, an ugly woman with a black caste spot on her forehead, the man hirsute, bearded, turbanned. Corbett watched the descending numbers and when the elevator reached the mezzanine he pushed his way out, slightly sick with fear.

He saw Ellen and Wilson standing near one of the pillars, overlooking the lobby below. He put his hand on Ellen's arm. 'I appreciate this,' he said.

'Anytime,' she said, attempting a smile, but something was awry here and he could feel it. Wilson nodded towards a squat man sitting near a gigantic tapestry of the rising sun. 'I didn't page Nakamura,' Wilson said. 'I decided against it. Now that man is a detective. One of the bellboys pointed him out. There are no other police in this wing. The question is, is that Nakamura?'

Shit, the man was sitting at an angle so that his face was not visible but from this distance Corbett could swear it was Nakamura. 'He's right in front of the elevators.'

'I'll get him out of there,' Wilson said. 'There's a taxi waiting for you outside. I don't know whether I'll be able to move him all the way out of the lobby, so take your break whenever it comes.' He moved off down the stairs and Corbett watched him as he approached the Japanese. Nakamura, yes, turning slightly now, his face quizzical as Wilson engaged him in conversation. Wilson was selling something at the moment, that expression of concentrated earnestness on his face as he waved his hand towards the house telephones. Nakamura stood up, giving the lobby a sweep with his eyes before he lumbered along after Wilson.

Corbett picked up his attaché case in one hand and the suitcase in the other, surprised at its lightness. He escorted Ellen to the elevator. The door hissed open

174

to reveal a party of Aryans and their wives, all speaking German, squeezing together to make room for Corbett and Ellen. Corbett was pressed close to her in the elevator and he was surprised to find that he picked up no sense of fear in her whatsoever. She was unusually calm as the door opened into the lobby and they swept along with the Germans. Corbett could see no sign of Wilson and Nakamura from here. Ellen took his arm as they crossed the lobby. The automatic doors opened noiselessly. They crossed the sidewalk and climbed into the taxi.

The moon-faced driver looked at him expectantly. 'Where?' he said. '*Doko, ne?*'

'Just drive,' Corbett said.

PART II

Chapter 1

There were times when Klein missed the military, the sharply delineated chain of command in which the power of his will passed unchallenged down through the table of organisation. He had fought in three wars, and there was a cleanness about action in the field he had not found in any other place, for there was always a visible objective, the capture of a city, the destruction of an enemy regiment, a winning that expressed itself in the death or capitulation of the men ranked against him. He did not miss the bureaucracy of the Pentagon, the civilian side of the military, the endless wrangling over numbers, the muddied philosophy of men too keenly attuned to power and promotion to be able to see the real threats to civilisation that were spreading like cancer through the world.

In the end he had grown unfashionable and was labelled a hawk in a time when the doves were in ascendance, and when he had been approached by Erikson with an opportunity to put some of his beliefs into action, he had hesitated no longer than a couple of days before he moved to ESK, taking nothing with him except his aide and mementos of the past, a few pictures of the highlights of his career.

But now, as he sat in his office, he was not so sure that he had made a wise choice, for he was not getting the cream of the crop, no, not the masses of good men he had approached to quit the military and follow him into the private sector, and he was having to politic the old man to keep him from swerving away from his beliefs. There were times when he wished he himself had not been so single-minded, that he had preserved his marriage and raised children along the way and moved into retirement, but that would have been to abandon the field and that he could not do.

Miller buzzed him to announce that Goddard was here. Klein continued to stare out the window as Goddard came in to stand uncomfortably before the desk. 'He caught you off guard,' Klein said.

'He appeared to be co-operating,' Goddard said.

'Appeared?'

'Yes.'

'But obviously he was not. Obviously, he was setting you up.'

'Not obviously. No, sir.'

Klein swung around, facing him. 'Stop making excuses for yourself,' he said. 'He caught you flat-footed. That's the truth of it. I don't give a damn about you now. I'm only concerned about what he intends to do.'

'We've been through this before. I told you everything he said.'

'You have told me everything you heard. That's not the same thing. I want you to put the whole thing in writing, everything that you can remember. That's all, Goddard.'

The military reflexes were still there. Goddard made a slight pivot as he turned to leave the room. The intercom buzzed on Klein's desk. 'Yes?' he said.

'Mr Erikson wishes to see you in the board room,' Miller said.

'Tell him I'll be right along. Then come in here, please.'

'Yes, sir.'

He stood up. The leg pained him continually and he welcomed it because it kept him aware. It always took a moment before he could nerve himself to put his full weight upon it and take the larger jolt that then tended to subside. Standing at his desk, he was aware that he was favouring the weakness, the bulk of his weight divided between his right leg and his two palms flat against the desk top. Miller came into the room. 'We had a call from an upper-echalon Japanese official with the Metropolitan Police,' he said. 'He's filing a written protest against the fact that we did not inform them that Corbett was on the premises. I told him it was inadvertent and inexcusable and we were looking into the matter to see who was responsible for not notifying them.'

'What did you find out about the Japanese policeman?'

'His name is Naito and he's a veteran on the force. The Metro Police doctors examined him less than an hour ago. He does have a bladder infection, which he didn't report for fear it would be interpreted as weakness. He has no possible connection with Corbett.'

'Very well,' Klein said. Now, with Miller looking directly at him, he allowed his full weight to settle on his left leg, the pain passing through his thigh and hip like electricity. He controlled himself successfully; Miller could not see the pain.

He walked into the 'war room', where Erikson was sitting next to the console, rolling an unlighted cigar in his fingers, staring pensively at the blank screen. 'We're beginning to get responses from the other companies,' Erikson said thoughtfully.

'Are they what we expected?' Klein said, knowing full well that they were, intending to disarm Erikson before the collective will of the business community could weaken his resolve.

'Pretty much,' Erikson said.

'Do you have summaries?'

'Yes.' Erikson pressed a button and the summary flashed on to the screen.

181

SHORTFALL SUMMARY RESPONSE/ADLER/11756/G
FIVE OUT OF EIGHT RESPONSES AS OF 1200 LOCAL
HOURS EXXON TAKES BASIC NEGATIVE VIEW. GULF
BASIC NEGATIVE. ITT NEUTRAL NEGATIVE. CITICORP
STRONGLY NEGATIVE WITH VIEW TO COUNTERACTION.
INTERNEL INCLINED POSITIVE.

'What does all this mean?' Klein said. 'What is a basic negative view? What in the hell is a neutral negative? Are these your in-house terms?'

'Yes,' Erikson said. 'Adler's been making these summaries for me for a long time. It's developed into shorthand. The "basic negative" means they will decry any actions we take but that's as far as they will go. "Neutral negative" means that ITT wouldn't instigate any such activity on their own, nor would they really support ours, but if we decide to go ahead, they will stay out of it. Intertel's all for it. Citicorp would blow the whistle, if they had the chance.'

Klein studied the old man, who was lighting his cigar now, his face glowing with good health and a balanced physical care, the assurance of power, for Erikson had it all and knew that he had it. Klein had learned about power in his years with the military, realised its gradations, its subtleties, its applications, and at the moment he knew Erikson was dangerously close to calling the whole thing off, following the inclinations of the majority, for he was an old man and he was suggestible.

'I knew Herbert Hoover quite well,' Erikson said. 'He was one hell of a fine businessman. A poor politician. I offered Herbert a chance to head my European operations in the thirties but of course he wasn't interested. A man who has tasted absolute power is not interested in modified power.'

A light blinked on the telephone and Klein picked it up, grateful for the interruption. It was Miller. 'We just received a teletype from the South Korean government.' Miller said. 'Do you wish to have it on display, sir?'

'Yes, put it on.' Klein flipped the open channel switch and the message appeared on the screen.

TO: ERIKSON-ESK/INT/TOKYO
FROM: GIE/DEPUTY FOREIGN MINISTER/ROK/SEOUL
A FORMAL PROTEST WILL BE LODGED THIS DATE WITH
THE AMERICAN AMBASSADOR IN SEOUL CONCERNING
THE IMPLICATIONS OF THE DEATH OF A KOREAN
OFFICIAL AT THE HANDS OF YOUR COMPANY. OUR
REPUBLIC HAS ALWAYS BEEN DEVOTED TO THE
SOLUTION OF PROBLEMS WITH THE FOREIGN SECTOR
IN A PEACEFUL AND RESPONSIBLE MANNER, ABHORRING
THE POLITICS OF ARTIFICIAL SOLUTIONS DEPENDENT
ON NONPEACEFUL MEANS. IT IS IMPOSSIBLE FOR OUR
NATION TO BE SO INTIMIDATED/END.

'Very good,' Klein said. 'They did get the message after all. They didn't even bother to polish the language. The phraseology is typically Korean.'

'I had no doubt they would get the message,' Erikson said. 'If you strike a man with a hammer, it's pretty certain that he's going to get the intent. But that still doesn't resolve for me the reluctance of the other companies. I don't think we can bring this off unilaterally.' He studied the ash of his cigar. 'What do you think?'

'I think we can bring it off or I would never have gotten us involved in this,' Klein said. 'We agreed, you and I, from the beginning, that there would be reluctance on the part of the other companies to commit themselves to this. They are not as heavily involved in the Far East as we are. We also have a computer prediction, based on their past policy, that all of them will be willing to accept what we do once it has become a fait accompli. Now, I am perfectly willing to abide by any decision you make, but that decision has to be made now.'

'You don't seem to understand the way I have made

a successful corporation,' Erikson said. 'There's no such thing as an irrevocable decision. Even if the shoe is dropped, we still have alternatives.'

'Certainly,' Klein said, backing off, reversing himself. 'But in this particular case if the shoe is to be dropped at all, there are certain things that we must do. And in this case timing is critical.'

The old man nodded. 'Did I ever tell you about the time I met Woodrow Wilson?'

'No, I don't believe that you did.'

'My father took me there,' Erikson said. 'It was after the sickness had begun to make itself evident. My father had been asked to the White House, for what purpose I can't remember except that it had to do with European trade. At no time did the President rise from his chair. He simply sat there, grey pallor, his colour terrible, and I knew at that moment the United States would not join the League of Nations, because he didn't have the strength to carry through. That was the key to his failure, the key to any failure, and I have made it one of my cardinal rules. I never enter into any action if I do not have the strength to carry it through to a satisfactory conclusion.' Erikson stood up. He snuffed out his cigar in an ashtray. 'We will proceed as if we are going to carry through. I will leave the details up to you, your best choice. But I ask you to be aware that there is the possibility that at the last moment I will tell you to cancel. And, if that is the case, you will have everything covered so that ESK/INT is not implicated in any way.'

'I can do that,' Klein said.

'I'm sure you can,' Erikson said, a note of finality in his voice. He left the board room and Klein remained seated, the smell of cigar smoke in his nostrils. He felt a slight antipathy towards the old man, for everything was totally dependent on the way Erikson happened to be thinking at the moment, how his mind was working, whether that brain was clear or muddied with the memories of Presidents and kings, past glories and triumphs, and Klein could not count on the old man's clarity to make the final decision. In the end, the computer would have that final say, balancing all the factors fed into it, working with an indisputable logic and a capacity for synthesis. If he had been given this computer in Vietnam and no interference from the politicians, the whole course of history in Southeast Asia would have been changed.

He caressed the console, punched into the SHORTFALL programming, began to put the computer through a practice run, asking first for a printout of the traffic in the kidney-shaped inlet north of Atami. The computer complied instantly, first flashing the outline of the inlet and then a grid that covered it, the figures beginning to fill in the squares. Over a hundred fishing boats in the past four hours, the regular runs of the sightseeing boats making an irregular but predictable pattern. He pressed in a time, 001201. The figures rolled and gave him the destiny of boats at the precise second, a rectangular blip giving him the precise location of the sightseeing boat, slowing for a turn near a high bluff, with at least six fishing boats within a quarter-mile area.

Now he asked the computer for an average position for that sightseeing boat on any Monday at precisely 001201 hours and there was a random scattering of dots near the bluff, all within five hundred yards of the shore, the central cluster about a hundred yards offshore.

He asked for the SPRAY pattern and an oval engulfed the majority of the dots, and when he asked for the addition of wind drift the oval encompassed the better part of the sector. No, that was out, for it covered too much territory. He asked for the modified CBU 55, the CAN pattern, and was given a more tightly confined oval. He watched it gyrate under different wind conditions, but in no case did it move into an overly wide spread. He would go with that, of course, just as he had deter-

185

mined in the beginning. But he felt better with the constant confirmation of the computer to back his decision.

He ran the computer through the coded reports of the Group Readiness Headquarters at Atsugi, military traffic arriving and departing. He projected 001146 at a Monday time and asked for an average and he received a heavy pattern of aircraft departing, for weekends were used to log air time for air force desk personnel. In addition there was a training session going on with the Japanese Self-Defence Forces.

He thought of Webster. He had no doubts at all concerning the man because they had been together under battle conditions and Webster had demonstrated not only his courage but his loyalty as well. Once Webster had completed his assignment in Shortfall, Klein would see that he was absorbed into the company, in a European assignment where he would be completely untraceable.

There were immense benefits to the modern technology, not only in the vast ability of the machines to calculate alternatives but in the sense of control that it gave him. That had been his trouble in the Pentagon, in the spacious office on the E ring, for in truth, control was in no one's hands. Any concept, however significant it might be, however new or novel, would come into immediate conflict with the concepts of men who had more power. And there remained, even after the in-house battles were settled, the larger fight with Defence and the battles with Congress, so that his own ideas, gained in the field, were always either lost or so watered down and vitiated as to be useless by the time they had gone through the mill.

But now, feeling the electronic hum of the power at his fingertips, the immediate responsiveness, he was indeed answerable to no one except Erikson himself and even then after the fact. For he saw the old man for what he was, semirigid in concept, ageing, his arteries losing suppleness, his brain ossifying with the old patterns rigidly set. He could admire Erikson; he could defer to him, knowing that Erikson had the power to terminate any action he wished to end, but Klein reserved the freedom to make the final determinations here, for only he could see the full scope of the problem and the steps necessary to correct. The computer itself would protect him against the old man's inquiries. Among the dozens of programmers and technicians, there was not one who was capable of putting all the pieces together to know what was about to happen. The light blinked. He picked up the telephone.

'We have something from a police contact,' Miller said. 'I can punch it up, if you like.'

'Yes,' Klein said.

INTCPT/TMP/001413/SUMMARY
TELEPHONE CONVERSATION BETWEEN INSP. G. NAKAMURA, TMP, AND W. ITO, FOREIGN MINISTRY, THIS DATE. WHOLE TAPE TRANSCRIPT AVAILABLE/ADD ONE. CALL INITIATED ITO FOR INFORMATION HOMICIDE COLONEL PAK. NAKAMURA EXPRESSES DOUBTS THAT CORBETT COMMITTED ACT. ITO ASKS FOR EVIDENCE AND NAKAMURA HAS NOTHING TO SUBSTANTIATE. ITO EXPRESSES PERSONAL FEELING THAT THE HOMICIDE HAS LARGER IMPLICATIONS POLITICALLY AND INTERNATIONALLY. NAKAMURA INSTRUCTED, ONCE CONTAINMENT OF CORBETT ACHIEVED, TO HOLD FOR QUESTIONING WITH ENTRY INTO OFFICIAL RECORD UNDER GOVERNMENT ORDER. ADD ONE/MORE.

Corbett again, and there was a new perspective to the business now. He shut down the screen and wandered back to his office, the pain in his leg nagging at him until he could reach his specially constructed chair, conformed to the contours of his back. He elevated the painful leg on to an ottoman, needing to think this through.

He had calculated what would happen if Corbett fell

187

into the hands of the Japanese police. There would be a trial, of course, a laborious and drawn-out procedure, but long before the trial took place all of the pertinent evidence would have been leaked, sufficient to convince Washington that Corbett was solely responsible for the arms business. But the Japanese Foreign Ministry had thrown him a curve, for if Corbett were swallowed up by the Japanese bureaucracy, he would disappear for a time without a trace, becoming totally inaccessible. That could not be allowed to happen.

He unlocked the file drawer in his desk and removed the dossier on Corbett, flipping through the pages in search of something he might have overlooked. He needed leverage now, something to bring Corbett into line, but he could find nothing. For Corbett had been a dedicated company man with no life outside its perimeters. There was a marriage listed here, so far back it did not count. There were no permanent liaisons of any sort, only a long list of positions that Corbett had filled with distinction.

He leaned back in his chair, propping his leg up again, closing his eyes, bringing his fingertips together, thinking. The answer did not lie in any of the statistics in the dossier but rather in the character of the man himself, in his propensities, in the way he reacted to situations. If there was a weakness, in terms of Corbett's usefulness, it lay in the individualism he expressed that allowed him to pinpoint weaknesses in company operations with no fear of reprisal.

There was a basic dichotomy here, in that Corbett was highly resistant to the structure of authority and yet always yielded to it in the end, questioning the old man's decisions at times far past the normal boundaries of insubordination, yet in the end abiding by Erikson's decisions. It was partially because of this dualism in his nature that he had been selected for this project (a selection confirmed by the computer, which predicted cooperation after an indeterminate time for adjustment).

But as far as Klein was concerned, all of the computer predictions and the rationale for singling out Corbett were secondary. For in the end it was absolutely necessary that Corbett be cancelled out. From the very beginning he had known this, for Corbett was antithetical to everything Klein believed in, and left to himself with the realisation of what was being planned, Corbett would have blocked it. Klein had encountered enough of these men in the military, intransigent sons of bitches who refused to yield their positions. In the majority of cases he had been able to shuffle these men off to the periphery, into smaller offices out of the mainstream, where they passed judgement on unimportant papers and made inconsequential decisions that were never implemented. But in the end Klein himself had been outpowered by men with little sense of daring and even less vision, and the country's military strength had suffered as a result.

He was determined that this would not happen here. Corbett was the only man of sufficient strength in the company (excluding Erikson himself) who could block the new policy, and Klein could not afford to underestimate him. It was necessary to maintain a delicate balance here, to keep Corbett open to outside definition, to make of him a convenient vehicle to carry the consequences of any crimes the company wished to assign to him. Klein wished him dead and permanently out of the way but there were certain indisputable advantages to keeping him alive and Corbett did not have the power to confirm, to be questioned and reply and make himself believed. The problem at hand was the means by which he would be brought to the point of co-operation.

Klein picked up the telephone, punched the numerals for Security Estimates, asked for the estimates supervisor, a man named Shulman. 'I have a question,' he said. 'If the Metropolitan Police arrest Corbett and decide to keep him in cold storage, what procedure will they follow?'

'A simple one,' Shulman said. 'They will hold him on an open bench warrant, a John Doe. It won't be registered until they make a formal charge. They'll probably hike him off to one of the houses run by TMP where the Foreign Ministry can have access to him.'

'Do they have to make a charge within any given time?'

'Technically, yes,' Shulman said. 'Actually, no. They could have him a couple of weeks before they filed anything against him.'

'Do you have any contacts within the department?'

'It's a hell of a big department. We can't cover all the bases.'

'Then how can we determine if they have him?'

'We can't. Not immediately, anyway. Since the Foreign Ministry is interested, there should be routine telephone inquiries every second day as long as he's loose. Once he's picked up, the FM will be notified by runner and the inquiries will stop. They won't noise it around because they don't want any conflict with the American Embassy.'

'I want you to extend your sources,' Klein said. 'I don't care what it costs but I want the whole department covered.'

'I'll give it the best try,' Shulman said. 'But I'd be less than candid if I tried to give you any guarantee.'

'I don't care how you do it,' Klein said. 'But I want it done.'

He terminated the conversation to answer the intercom. It was Miller, announcing that the daily estimates had just come up and Klein asked that they be brought in, along with a cup of coffee. He removed his leg from the ottoman. It was unwise to demonstrate weakness any more than was absolutely necessary. In a moment Miller entered, carrying the coffee in one hand and the dispatches in the other. Klein accepted the mug and leaned back in his chair. 'What kind of an update do we have?'

Miller sat down, scanning the sheets. 'India has decided not to send a delegate to the meetings. We had estimated that earlier. Nepal and Bangladesh have come aboard as has Sri Lanka. Estimates predicts that the other countries will key to those three. Japan is hanging back with a wait-and-see attitude. They'll send token delegates but not on a Foreign Minister level.'

'Very good,' Klein said, sipping the coffee. 'What new proposals have they come up with?'

'Malaysia and Indonesia are suggesting not only a flat gross percentage rate but a payment based on their evaluation of foreign companies. They are also suggesting a percentage of gross to be paid into Bangladesh and Nepal, into development funds. Estimates call that proposal firm because it guarantees that Bangladesh and Nepal will also vote the negative line.'

A political game, Klein thought, no more than that, a daily tally of the forces in one direction and the counter-forces in another. These nations had the right idea, consolidating against what they considered a common enemy. There was still one complicating factor. 'What of China?' Klein said.

'There seems to be no change in their position,' Miller said. 'Our China hands think they are influencing the position of some of the smaller countries, encouraging them, but the Chinese will do nothing to jeopardise their position with the United States, not actively.'

'How many observers will they have?'

'A couple.'

'But not official.'

'No.'

'Fine,' Klein said. He had heard enough and was terminating the report. Later he would go over the papers, which Miller laid on the edge of his desk, to make certain he was overlooking nothing. But for now he had more important business. 'Call Goddard and tell him I want to see him.'

'Yes, sir,' Miller said.

191

Fifteen minutes later Goddard arrived, slightly out of breath, clearly uneasy at being summoned again. 'Sit down,' Klein said.

Goddard sat, folding his massive arms, a little easier in this stance. 'I've been working on the report,' he said.

'What do you make of Corbett?' Klein said.

'We've been through that.'

'I am looking for something different now.' He shifted in his chair. The leg was paining him again. 'You were with the Secret Service a long time, Goddard. You had an excellent record. As I remember it, you left the Secret Service with the highest commendation of your chief officer.'

'Yes.'

'Which demonstrates your capacities. You are a trained observer. You were with Corbett long enough to form some strong opinions. Now, I want to know what you think it would take to gain his co-operation, given the fact that he thinks he has been betrayed by the corporation, sold down the river.'

'Has he?' Goddard said.

'Has he what?'

'Been sold down the river.'

'Yes,' Klein said, without hesitation. 'Does that make a difference to you?'

'Only in determining his reactions. You won't get him back until he's convinced that your plans for him have changed.'

'And what would it take to convince him?'

Goddard displayed a slight shrug. 'I don't know.'

Now the questioning was moving on to touchy ground and Klein was aware of it. He would move around the subject without approaching it too directly, for it was imperative that he should know Goddard's reactions before he came to the point. 'You were in the Korean War.'

'Yes,' Goddard said.

'Your record states that you were awarded a silver star after Pork Chop Hill.'

'Yes.'

'Did you at any time consider it to be a stupid war, one that the United States should never have been involved with?'

'That's not for me to say.'

'You fought it, for God's sake,' Klein said. 'Who should have a better right to an opinion?'

'I've never had any interest in international politics,' Goddard said.

'But you fought in Korea.'

'I was ordered to.'

'You did not volunteer?'

'No. It was my job and I did it.'

'Do you hate the Koreans?'

'No.'

'Do you hate the Chinese?'

'No.'

'What feelings do you have towards Corbett?'

'None. I would like to ask a question.'

'Yes.'

'What's the point of all this?'

'That's for me to determine,' Klein said, testing now. There was no reaction from Goddard, no bristling. 'How much do you earn a year from the company?'

'Thirty thousand.'

'With benefits?'

'Yes. Of course.'

'Do you feel you're worth thirty thousand a year?'

'I think so. You wouldn't be paying it otherwise.'

'That's correct,' Klein said. 'We wouldn't be paying thirty thousand if we didn't feel you were worth it. And I'll give you an answer. There's a point to all these questions. I have a very special mission that I want you to undertake, one that is sufficiently important that I can't entrust it to any man who I think will have second thoughts about it later. You will do this one thing cleanly and then you can be transferred to any part of the world you wish. I'll place you in charge of a security section at forty thousand a year.'

There was a faint glimmer of understanding in Goddard's eyes now. He cleared his throat. 'You want somebody terminated then,' he said. It was not a question.

'Yes, I want somebody killed. It is imperative that he be killed, not from any personal malice but because a much larger operation depends on it.'

Goddard stared at the wall, his thumb working against his palm as if trying to smooth away a surface roughness. Finally he looked directly at Klein and Klein could see no emotion in his face whatsoever. 'Forty-five thousand,' he said calmly.

'It's a deal,' Klein said.

2

He sat alone in the apartment, looking down at the narrow lane outside, the paper lanterns glowing in the warm darkness of the summer night, thousands of them, a congestion of Sunday people off from work, in costumes, streaming banners and torches in the heart of the city. He glanced at his watch. Ten minutes after nine and she should have been back by now. He was restless. The weekend had brought nothing but indecision. He paced through the three rooms looking for a direction to take. He distracted himself by going through the closets and the drawers, putting together the character of the airline pilot who kept this place for his stopovers in Tokyo. His name was McGuiness and he was a friend of Ellen's from her days with Pan Am. From the uniforms in the closet, Corbett could tell that McGuiness was a large and fleshy man.

There was a photograph of him in the bedroom, his arms around a Japanese girl in front of a temple. They were both smiling into the camera lens, McGuiness with

194

his mass of curly red hair and a flowing moustache. He was a great lusty man, who kept various sizes of lingerie stocked here, and Corbett wondered if he had a wife in the States, if he had other apartments like this scattered around the world. The liquor cabinet was filled with brandies and cordials and four bottles of Scotch, none of the scrounged airline mini-bottles for McGuiness, everything oversized.

How much did McGuiness make a year? Fifty thousand? Sixty? It was foolishness that the question should even have occurred to him at all. McGuiness was going to be the saving of him, that was all that mattered.

He went through the contents of a small chest of drawers. Letters here, more photographs, different women, and then his fingers touched something cold and hard. A pistol, yes, a very small pistol, chrome-plated, shining, with Japanese engraving on the barrel. It was a twenty-two calibre, he supposed, although he knew nothing about pistols and had not touched a firearm since a socialised skeet shoot in France four years ago, on the country estate of a French politician, with the clay birds rising from beyond a low hedge. He had been lucky enough to hit a few but he had not been interested by the sport and had sensed little connection between the shotgun kicking against his shoulder and the exploding clay discs.

He examined the pistol, managed to open the cylinder. It was loaded but he could not see that it had ever been fired. He found a repulsive comfort in the weapon although he could foresee no possible circumstance in which he would use it. He pictured Nakamura in his mind, bowing to him and informing him in a polite voice that he was to be taken into custody. He could not imagine pointing this pistol at Nakamura and pulling the trigger.

Nevertheless, he put the pistol in the pocket of his suit jacket, noticing that there was little weight to it. He searched through the drawer and found a small box of cartridges, again Japanese, each shell polished to a high sheen, and they reminded him in some way of the mock plastic vegetables outside Japanese restaurants, a representation of the real thing that was more faithful to art than to reality.

He turned on the television set and sat down on the edge of the bed, scanning the channels with a remote-control switch in the hope of hitting a news broadcast, but there was none. On one channel was a Japanese documentary and on another was a monster movie, with a giant reptile emerging from the sea. He turned the television set off and went into the living room just as the door opened and Ellen came in, carrying a pair of large bundles. She smiled when she saw him.

'My God,' she said. 'The streets are packed. But I managed to find us something to eat.' She went into the small kitchen and began to set out cans and a loaf of French bread. Domestic, yes, she acted very much at home, minimising the reality of anything that lay beyond the walls of this apartment.

'I missed you,' he said, coming into the kitchen. 'You've been gone for hours.'

'I called Carl,' she said. 'He will be coming over after a while.'

'Carl?'

'The navigator I was telling you about.'

'What did you tell him?'

'Nothing specific. Carl's a romantic. He likes challenges. I remember once he brought back a diamond ring for an airline executive from Hong Kong, smuggled it through by wearing it on his little finger, just to see if he could get away with it. Are you hungry? I can offer you a small steak, French bread – which is a rarity by the way – or if you don't want anything formal, I can go down the street to McDonald's and bring you back a hamburger that tastes slightly like fish.'

'I'm not hungry,' he said. 'Would you like a drink?'

'Yes,' she said.

'You have a choice between Scotch and brandy.'

'Brandy,' she said. She came into the living room and sat down. He found a crystal glass and poured her a brandy. She leaned back on the divan, cradling the glass in her hands, kicking off her shoes. He was filled with a sudden gratitude for her and a concern for her safety. It had been a mistake to involve her in this.

'And what happens if Carl doesn't buy the package?' he said quietly. 'What happens if he decides to take the whole thing to the police?'

'He won't,' she said.

'But if he does.' He put his glass down. 'I don't want you in this,' he said.

'You keep forgetting. I already am.'

'Then I want you to extricate yourself. I want you to go back to the hotel.'

'That wouldn't work,' she said. 'You're a very dense man sometimes. I'm here because I want to be.'

'Why, Ellen?'

'Because you need me.'

'I don't understand that.'

'I don't suppose you would,' she said with a smile. 'I know you far better than you know me, remember? I've seen you on the jet and I know how you operate. You're a very self-contained man. You pride yourself on that, on not needing anybody.' She was looking at him and very slowly he took her into his arms and began to make love to her and she came against him as if she had been waiting for a long time, peacefully, no urgency, her mouth moving to meet his, alive, mobile, lifting her body away from the couch to allow him to undress her. He knew that she was giving him a gift and he took it gratefully, entering her, filling her lovingly, one of her hands cradling the back of his head, the other pressing against his back, and he could not tell where she stopped and he began.

When it was done, he continued to lie beside her, peaceful for the first time in weeks, as if everything had

197

come into perspective. 'I want us to go to Hawaii together,' he said. 'Only it can't be Hawaii, not now. We'll have to make it South America.'

'I would like that,' she said. No questions now, no probing into motives. There was a solid bond between them that had been there all along and only now been realised.

'How soon do you think Carl can arrange it?'

'His next flight. I don't know when that is, but it's bound to be within twenty-four hours.' Her arm moved across his chest. 'I love you, Corbett. I'm not exactly sure what that entails but I think you should know it.'

'I love you too.'

'That's a very good arrangement. I never thought it would happen to me again.' She was quiet a moment, touching his face. 'You had better know that I am a very possessive woman,' she said. 'But I also realise you have a mind of your own so I won't interfere if I can help it. I have the feeling that you're not going to be content to stay here until Carl comes.'

'I don't know,' he said. 'I want to make it possible for us to live on a beach somewhere.'

'But?'

'They have me avalanched,' he said. 'And I don't like that. If we're going to have any freedom at all, I've got to stop them.'

She shook her head slowly. 'I love you, darling, but I don't think you're omnipotent. I've been around the company long enough to know that anything they start, they have the power to carry through.'

'What would you suggest?'

'I won't suggest anything because I know you'll do what you feel you have to do. But you've said it yourself, they have nothing against you personally. You're just a convenience to them. And if you disappear, then they will have to find some other way to do what they want to do.'

'I don't want to let them win,' he said.

'Can you stop them?'

He was distracted by the pounding of drums, the shrillness of discordant flutes. The procession was passing beneath the window now. 'The odds are very long against it, but I would like to try.'

'All right,' she said tenderly. She kissed him briefly. 'What can I do to help?'

'Call Wilson for me,' he said. 'His phone will be tapped. So tell him your name is Annette and you met him in Mexico. Before he has a chance to say anything, tell him there's somebody at the door, give him your number and ask him to call back. He'll get the message and use a safe telephone.'

She sat up reluctantly, brushing the strands of blonde hair away from her face. 'We have to have an agreement,' she said. 'I want to be living with you for a long, long time. So if you see that what you're trying to do is impossible, I want you to put aside your pride immediately and abandon the whole thing.'

'All right,' he said.

She picked up the telephone and dialled, carrying off the whole thing perfectly, affecting a slight Southern accent. 'He got the message,' she said.

The telephone rang within two minutes. 'Answer it,' he said. 'They may be checking the number.'

She picked it up, spoke into it, and then handed it to him. Wilson was on the line.

'Are you clear?' Corbett said.

'Yes. It's safe,' Wilson said. 'Where are you?'

'I couldn't tell you if I tried. An apartment. Someplace. Do you have anything?'

'A hell of a lot,' Wilson said. 'First, I've located Abernathy. He's here in Tokyo.'

'Where?'

'Erikson has a house here.'

Of course, logical, and Cristina would be there as well, convenient, on tap, Erikson's holding pen.

'Are you still there?' Wilson said.

199

'Yes.'

'Do you want the address?'

'I have it.'

'I wouldn't advise going there, friend,' Wilson said. 'No hard information, but I think Klein will have him pretty well covered. I have something else. I don't know how much sense it makes but I'll pass it on anyway.' He had been nosing around PR, he went on, and a new man named Brach who had transferred in from American Airlines PR in New York City approached him with a problem.

He had been asked to write a news release that ESK/INT was going to release at an indeterminate time. It made no sense to Brach and he was looking for guidance, an interpretation. Wilson sat down and read it through, thoroughly alarmed but showing no sign of it. It was a draft of an official expression of condolence, nonspecific with blanks to be filled in later, but the implications were clear. Some figure of international importance was going to die (the release presumed him already dead) and this release was a reflection of Erikson's personal abhorrence of violence and a pledge on the part of ESK/INT to support the expressed sentiment of the people of Asia.

'Hell,' Corbett said. His hands were moist now. 'Klein can't be serious about this.'

'Then it means the same thing to you as it means to me?'

'Stupidity. Goddamned stupidity.'

'Who do you pick as the chief candidate?'

'Any one of a half dozen men,' Corbett said, his mind sorting now. 'I'd split my money two ways. Either the Philippine Foreign Secretary or the Foreign Minister of ROK.'

'I'd have to go with the Philippines,' Wilson said. 'Brach told me there's a special PR delegation leaving for Manila right away. They wouldn't beef up the operation there unless there was a hell of a lot of extra flak coming.' He paused. 'What do you think we should do about this?'

'Do you have a copy of the release?'

'No.'

'We can't do a damn thing until we're sure it's Carlos. But Abernathy can confirm it.'

'I still wouldn't advise it,' Wilson said. 'Do you have a way out of the country?'

'I think so.'

'Then take it. Leave the rest of this to me.'

'Do they know about Ellen?'

'No, I covered. As far as they know, I sent her to Atami.'

'I need time to think,' Corbett said. 'Memorise this number. If you wrote it down on anything, burn it.'

'Done.'

'And call me back at midnight.'

'Will do.'

Corbett put the telephone down and leaned back on the couch. Ellen was dressed now. He told her what had happened. 'The goddamned military mind,' he said abruptly. 'My God, I should have guessed it.'

'What?'

'More retaliation,' he said. 'They can't protect against what the delegates are going to do but the corporation will show them the consequences of any move against the globals.' The delegates had begun to assemble at Atami, he went on, and the first informal caucuses would take place and power would begin to centre on one of the delegates, most likely Carlos, the most eminent of the lot. And then, with no warning, the leader would be terminated, killed, blown away, wasted, in as blatant a manner as Klein could conceive. And the rest of the delegates would know full well why he had been killed, regardless of whatever story Klein put out to cover it. It would signal them that the business community was prepared to use violence.

'Are you serious?' she said.

201

'Stupidity,' he said. 'It won't work. If he kills one, it will unite the rest of them.' He lighted a cigarette. He would have to go out, he knew that, and he did not want to go. He wanted to remain here with her until the arrangements were made and then board a plane with her and leave the machinations of the corporation behind him. The company would destroy itself in the end, without any doing on his part. He stood up, putting on his tie. He fumbled through the wallet until he found the card with the Japanese directions to the house written on the back of it. 'How soon is Carl coming?'

'I don't know,' she said. 'You're going out?'

'For a while. Can you make the arrangements without me?'

'Yes.'

'I should be back in a couple of hours.'

'What are you going to do?'

'I'm going to find out who Klein is after, that's all,' he said. 'Once we have a name, we inform the Japanese police and let them handle it.'

She put her arms around him, kissed him. 'Just remember our agreement,' she said.

'I won't forget. I'll do what I can. If I see I can't do anything, I'll back off. That's a promise.'

Once he had gone down the stairs and into the street, he was certain that he was making a mistake for there was every possibility that Wilson had made a mistake in his conclusions and that Corbett had followed the same false lead. The procession had passed, whatever ceremony that was being celebrated was finished, and the narrow lane was full of people. He realised how immensely visible he was here, a head taller than any of the people in the street, aware that they would report his presence to the police in the next few hours. He bowed to an elderly woman in a kimono, maintained a perpetual smile, moving at a deliberately slow pace until the lane emptied into a boulevard, the traffic so heavy that he felt claustrophobic, surrounded by it. He picked up his pace, walking a couple of blocks to a business district before he hailed a cab, raising two fingers to signify that he was willing to pay double fare. He climbed into a small kamikaze taxi, handed the driver the card, and then settled back against the seat.

Foolishness, yes, and if he managed to see Abernathy, how could he possibly pry the information out of him, Abernathy with his squint and his painful teeth and his habit of sucking air through the slight frontal gap of his incisors. Abernathy had concealed his secrets well. Corbett suddenly became aware of the solid lump of the small pistol in his pocket. Insanity. He could no more use this pistol to coerce information out of Abernathy than he could gain the information of Abernathy's own free will.

He looked out at the lights of the central business district, the great loops and whorls of neon, the stream of car lights on the street, and the normalcy of the night made his plan seem absurd. The taxi paused at a light. A man passed in the counterstream of traffic on a bicycle, a high pile of noodle trays balanced behind him. A rickshaw moved along the kerb, pulled by a lithe old man, carrying tourists. It was madness that Klein could have gone as far as this. The Colonel's death had had no effect on the international situation and Erikson would countenance no more violence, Corbett was sure of that. There were too many effective alternatives, multiple techniques, proven ones, that the company could use, the most efficient of which was bribery. The right money in the right hands at the right time and the work of the conference would be stalled for a while, delayed until an effective compromise could be negotiated.

He had the presence of mind to stop the driver some distance from the house and then he extracted a handful of hundred-yen notes from his wallet, pressing them into the driver's hand despite his protestations, his insistence on calculating the correct fare and returning the precise difference to him. He climbed out of the taxi and stood on the street alone, watching the tail lights disappear in the distance. His apprehensions returned.

Wilson had insisted that the house would be guarded and so he walked down the narrow street slowly, staying in the deep blackness of the shadows next to high fences. But he saw nothing, no signs of cars or people, no evidence that anything was out of the ordinary here. He could hear the sound of a radio or a television, layered over unintelligible voices, the barking of a dog, the far-off energy of heavy traffic, multilevelled sound, and he wondered if any place in the city was completely silent.

He stood motionless down the lane from the house for a long time, smoking a cigarette, certain now that Wilson was correct and Klein's men were around here, present but not in evidence, well concealed. He ground out the cigarette and approached the gate, realising that they could take him here with no commotion whatsoever. He pushed against the rough wooden gate door with the palm of his hand and to his surprise it yielded, opening noiselessly, admitting him to the garden, which was partially illuminated from the lights blazing in the lower floor of the house. He stood beside a tree, waiting again. He could see no movement in the muted light falling across the garden. Through a window he saw two figures sitting at a table but from this angle, his view partially obscured by the folded thickness of a gossamer drape, he could not identify them.

Finally he went directly to the door and found it unlocked, letting himself into the entry hall where a new pair of ceramic temple dogs flanked the staircase to the second floor. The sounds came from the room to his right and as he stood outside the half-opened door he recognised the voices. Cristina laughing. Abernathy speaking in low measured tones. He opened the door and just stood there, blinking. They were playing backgammon. Abernathy had the dice cup in his hand, rattling it absently before he spilled the dice on to the table. Cristina examined them, frowned at him, and then smiled up at Corbett as if she were not at all surprised to see him, a radiant smile, absolute elegance in a white silk gown falling away from bare shoulders, a double strand of diamonds around her pale neck.

'Come in and protect me, darling,' she said. 'You do know Edwin, of course. He's a terrible cheat.'

And quite suddenly a terrible anger passed through Corbett and he grabbed Abernathy by the front of his shirt and half lifted him from the chair and then pushed him backward so that Abernathy fell sprawling to the floor, in no hurry to get up, rolling over slightly, his face grey, a slightly bewildered expression in his eyes. 'You son of a bitch,' Corbett said. 'You really set me up.'

'My teeth hurt,' Abernathy said, getting to his feet, very unsteadily. He was drunk, Corbett realised.

Abernathy picked up his drink from the table, rolled the cold glass against his bony jaw. 'I apologise,' he said. He took a drink, washing the whisky back and forth in his mouth before he swallowed it. 'They made all the plans. All of them. All I did was to confirm, go along. There were a half dozen others who would have done it. Have you ever had any dealings with a goddamned Japanese dentist? Totally different from the Koreans.'

The anger was evaporating within him. He felt very cold.

'Will you listen to me, Willie?' Cristina said.

'To what?'

'I talked to Erik about you,' she said. 'Today, as a matter of fact. He takes some understanding, darling. He's very single-minded about his business, but he really doesn't want to see anything happen to you.'

Ignoring her, he looked to Abernathy, who was fumbling with a cigarette. 'I want to know what's going to happen at Atami,' he said.

'I never asked for any details,' Abernathy said. 'I should have stayed in the States. I should never have come to the Far East. I don't like orientals. My marriage is on very shaky ground, did you know that?' He flicked the lighter twice with his thumb before he could coax a flame from it and then he edged the tip of the cigarette into the fire.

'I know that someone's going to be killed at Atami. I want to know who.'

'I don't know,' Abernathy said vaguely. 'I really don't care.'

'We need to talk,' Cristina said. 'Just the two of us.' He followed her into a smaller sitting room. 'You're taking this much too seriously, darling.'

'You're a bitch. You knew Stevens was waiting for me at the jet.'

She sat down, crossing her legs, giving him the direct expression he had seen so often, that quizzical smile, the implication of complete openness, as if he were special and she had nothing to hide from him. He could not tell whether it was authentic or not, whether it was real now or ever had been. 'Does it matter?'

'No,' he said. 'It doesn't really make any difference, not at this point.'

'That's intelligent of you.' She stood up, her silk dress rustling, an intimate, feminine sound. 'I like you, Willie. That's a rather large compliment coming from me because I don't like many people, especially men. And I did know someone was waiting for you. I told them what you were planning to do.'

'Why the sudden burst of truth?'

'Because you're in trouble,' she said. 'They're going to make you another offer. I don't know what kind. But if you take it, then you're home free. And if you don't, they're going to kill you.'

And now it was beginning to come clear to him, a knowledge that had been his all along. He had simply refused to recognise it. They had leaked Abernathy's

206

location to him, knowing that he would come here, and she was the softener, the persuader, making the initial pitch for them. They had given him open access but they would not let him out. He could almost feel Klein's hovering presence here. Or perhaps it would be Goddard instead, waiting to take him back to the hotel.

'All right,' he said. 'You've been a hell of an experience for me, the whole business has. Let's leave it at that. He's here, isn't he?'

'Who?'

'Klein, of course. They couldn't leave the details to you. You don't have the power to bargain. Or maybe I'm supposed to go back to the hotel myself, as an act of contrition.'

'He's here,' she said. 'But if you don't want to talk to him, you don't have to. You're free to leave. I insisted on that.'

'You insisted?' he said with a laugh. 'Do you really think your insistence means a goddamned thing? Where is he?'

'Upstairs. Will you see him?'

'Bring him down.'

She left the room, walking with infinite grace. He looked at the room, the collection of art objects, an intricately carved screen along one wall, mounted with small ivory and jade animals. The opulence here was a proper setting for high-level talks and he wondered if he could make it out of here, leaving now, through the garden. Perhaps. But he did not have the will to leave. Cristina was correct, he did have a streak of stubbornness within him and he could not leave them uncontested. Quid pro quo, something for something, a bargain, and at the least he would cause them an inconvenience.

He heard the tip of the cane click on the tiles of the foyer and Klein came in, a pleasant hard expression on his face as if he had just been informed of the presence of an old friend he did not particularly want to see.

207

'Well,' he said to Corbett. 'I'm glad to see you back.'

'I'll bet you are,' Corbett said.

'I'm glad to find you in a reasonable mood.'

'Negotiation is my business,' Corbett said. 'There's no point in beating around the bush with you. I know what you're planning at Atami.'

'Oh?' Klein said. Was he startled? Corbett could not be sure. 'And exactly what is it that we're planning at Atami?'

'You don't have a chance of bringing it off,' Corbett said. 'Now, this may be a minor exercise in terrorism for you, General. Because you have the firepower. That is the right term, isn't it? But I've been in this part of the world long enough to know that you can't bluff a country like Bangladesh or Sri Lanka because they don't have anything to lose. You give the Asian countries a martyr, a rallying point, and you might as well fold up and go home.'

'The role of political pundit doesn't suit you,' Klein said.

'I don't give a shit for your opinion. I'm negotiating now, trading.'

'And what makes you believe you have anything to trade?'

'The fact that I'm alive,' Corbett said. 'You knew damn well I was coming here. You could have had me shot the moment I walked in but you didn't. No, you need my cooperation or neither one of us would be here.'

Klein paused by the carved screen. Leaning on his cane, he peered at it closely. 'Have you seen this screen?' he said. 'It's fascinating. There is not one animal here that does not have a natural enemy nearby. The hen is shadowed by the fox. But the artist has put it all in order, created his own natural balance.'

He abandoned the screen and lowered himself into a straight-backed chair, extending the bad leg, wincing slightly. 'I make a point of disguising my pain most of the time,' he said. 'I damn near lost this leg to a land mine, a mechanical contrivance, but I don't regard it impersonally. No, a human being purposefully planted that mine with the express hope of blowing my legs off, or somebody like me. That was his duty because he was my enemy. Violence is my business, Corbett, and I know damn well that the world is full of it, either potential or real. It's a fact of life. The hen survives because she knows instinctively the destructive capabilities of the fox. No politics there. I think it's quite within my power to bring at least a temporary sense of order to this part of the world.'

Corbett waited, said nothing.

Klein held his cane between his knees, both hands folded over the head of it. 'What do you think is going to happen at Atami?'

Cristina came into the room, carrying a silver tray. 'I brought you a drink, darling,' she said to Corbett. He lifted the glass from the tray, almost automatically. 'Would you care for anything, General?'

'Nothing,' Klein said, a trifle impatiently.

'Poor Edwin is totally drunk,' she said. 'I would like you to have him put to bed.'

'Directly,' Klein said.

'Soon,' she said. 'This is my house, after all.'

'I have a proposal,' Corbett said after she was gone. 'I will cooperate with you to a certain degree. I will go back to the States and meet with the Senate committee and take my chances. If your case against me is as thorough as you seem to think, then you won't have anything to lose. In return, you call off your plans for Atami.'

'Interesting,' Klein said, but the word came out flat and Corbett knew he was not interested at all. His mind was already set on a course of action and he was simply going through the verbal motions. 'Unfortunately, that won't work. There are a great many other companies that will be affected by the Atami meeting. There's no way we can take any unilateral action.' He shifted his leg slightly as if seeking a way to make it more comfortable. 'I have a counterproposal. I want you to fly back to Washington tomorrow. In return for your testifying before the Senate committee, I'll see that you're cleared of any connection with Colonel Pak's death.'

'You are full of self-assurance, Klein. And how do you suppose to bring this off?'

'We have a man who confessed to killing the Colonel,' Klein said. 'The evidence will simply be rearranged.'

'Now you see it, now you don't.'

Klein went through the laborious process of standing up, raising himself against the prop of his cane. 'I would like to show you something that I think will make my point clear. If you will come upstairs with me.' He led the way from the room into a foyer, contemplating the stairs with a grimace, passing beyond them to a small elevator. 'I will caution you in advance not to do anything foolish. It will help if you can see matters objectively.' He slid back the folding gate of the elevator, allowing Corbett to precede him. 'Emotionally, it will be something of a shock and you should be prepared for that. But in the larger view it makes very good sense.' The elevator crawled to the second floor and when he opened the gate, Corbett was aware of Goddard standing in the corridor against an immense French tapestry. His arms were folded across his chest. He was completely passive.

Klein stopped at the first door. 'I think you will be able to see the logic of what we have here.' He opened the door and Corbett followed him into the darkened room, waiting while Klein turned on a small lamp. The room was a library, walls covered with shelves of books. In the glow of the lamp, he was slow to become aware of the figure sitting at a corner desk, slumped over, and all the feeling went dead within him as if he were in a wax museum and the man at the desk was not Wilson at all but a construct, the replication of a man with the

210

side of his skull blown away, the spread of blood on the leather blotter not real at all. But there the dead man who was not Wilson sat, legs splayed out at the knees, one foot askew and resting on one side of the shoe, one arm dangling limply, as if pointing to a pistol on the flowered carpet. The drape behind him was stained with flecks of blood.

Corbett stood transfixed. A slow sigh escaped him, akin to a moan. He was aware that Klein was talking, voice low, hushed, funereal. The focus had shifted, Klein was saying, for Wilson had exactly the same pattern of movement as Corbett – Korea, the Aoyama Cemetery — and he could have killed the Colonel, no, he *had* killed the Colonel. For all the evidence was here and Wilson had put the blame on Corbett and tonight Corbett had confronted him with the facts, the proof, and Wilson had taken the only way out that appeared to him. He had killed himself.

'Proof,' Corbett said, echoing. He looked at Klein's face in the half light, the sharp angles of his cheekbones, the lamp reflecting on the heavy silver head of the cane.

Klein's voice started again, the words moving in a different direction, a reversal of the tide, and Corbett could comprehend even though it seemed as if the voice was speaking to him from a far distance. Everything in the room could be interpreted in a different light, to prove that Wilson had known of Corbett's guilt and had not testified to his certain knowledge until his conscience had weighed too heavily and he had informed Corbett that he was going to testify against him and Corbett had killed him.

Facts were liquid, they could run in any direction, prove anything, and Corbett could now have the choice of double incrimination or none at all. But the figure in the corner would never move again.

The fingers on the dead suspended hand were half curled. Were the eyes open or closed? The face mashed, lying on one fleshy cheek, distorting the mouth, causing it to be agape. Not real, no, and he shook a cigarette from the pack and lighted it, turning slightly, his eyes registering an ashtray and the title of a book, gold letters impressed into red Moroccan leather. Gibbon. *Decline and Fall.*

He stood smoking, ashes dribbling down the front of his suit, smoke stinging his eyes, and he reached out and picked up the heavy crystal ashtray, balancing it in his hand, and then, almost as if he had nothing to do with the act and were only witnessing it, he pivoted and with all his weight behind his arm drove the ashtray towards Klein's head, catching it in the act of turning. Klein staggered, cane dropping to the floor, falling backwards, blood churning from his cheek, a table falling with his weight. Corbett grabbed the cane, stout wood, heavy, and as the door opened and Goddard came in, he met the full force of the cane glancing off one shoulder and catching his thick neck.

And now Corbett stood with the cane, the breath pumping into his lungs in great painful heaves. His cigarette was on the floor. A wisp of smoke curled from the contact of the live coal with the carpet. He stepped on it, entrapping it with the sole of his shoe. Goddard was moaning slightly, his body trembling on the floor. Not dead, no, neither of them, and Corbett stripped the belt from Goddard's waist and bound his hands behind his back.

He took the pistol from Goddard's shoulder holster and put it in his own pocket, then he searched Klein, taking everything from his pockets, keys, wallet, a small notebook, loose change, stuffing everything into his own pockets. He did not look back towards Wilson. He stepped out into the hallway and closed the door, moving automatically now, the cane still in his hands. He went down the stairs and into the room where Cristina and Abernathy had been playing backgammon.

Abernathy had passed out in his chair, his head lolling to one side, emitting a low snore. Cristina was on the telephone. She turned slightly as Corbett came in and when she saw the cane, a flicker of alarm shadowed her eyes. He reached out and pressed down the cradle, severing the connection.

'What in the hell is wrong with you?' she said. 'I was talking to Erik.'

He grabbed her wrist, feeling the fragile bones in his grip, knowing he could break them. 'You will not raise your voice,' he said with effort. 'You will not cause the slightest trouble. Do you understand me?'

She grew very still. 'Yes.' she said.

He released her. 'Go through his pockets. See if he has any money.'

She did as she was told, pulling back the side of Abernathy's coat, removing a slim wallet. She removed a half dozen ten-thousand-yen notes, a couple of hundreds. He took them from her, folding them, putting them in his pocket.

'Can you tell me what's going on?' she said, subdued.

'Your Japanse driver. What's his name?'

'Yamaguchi.'

'Where does he sleep?'

'I don't know where he sleeps. I suppose we have quarters. Anyway, he's out tonight.'

'But you do know where the cars are kept?'

'Yes.'

He took her elbow. 'Move,' he said. 'I want to see the garage.'

There were four automobiles in the garage, space for two more. He opened the garage door in front of the Datsun. 'This will do,' he said. 'Get in.'

'I deserve to know what's going on,' she said once they were in the car.

The motor kicked to life. 'It doesn't matter, Cristina,' he said. 'You don't matter.'

She said nothing.

Under the brightness of the lights he was semiblind, fretting under the hands of the goddamned Japanese surgeon, who wore surgical gloves and a gauze mask, and he wondered why the Japanese had such a fetish about gauze masks. 'All right, go ahead,' he said to Nakamura, who sat on the far side of the emergency room, stolid, patient, Ito sitting next to him.

'You were informed he was at the house, with Wilson?'

'Yes.'

'By whom?'

'Abernathy.'

'And what time did you arrive there?'

'Eight o'clock, approximately.'

'And you discovered what conditions?'

Klein could feel the curved needle plucking at the flesh of his cheek. There was no pain. He was aware that Ito was taking down his words. 'You saw the conditions.'

'And Corbett was still in the room?'

'Certainly.'

'He admitted the killing?'

'Yes. He was incoherent. Wilson had called him. He had come to the house, argued with him, killed him, and tried to make it appear like suicide.'

The surgeon had finished with the stitches and was applying a bandage now. He said something in Japanese to Nakamura. 'He says you should take rest for forty-eight hours,' Nakamura said.

'How is Goddard?'

'They will hold him overnight. He was struck on the neck and the skull behind the ear. There is some concussion. Are you familiar with the automobiles at the house?'

'No.'

'Do you know the name of the driver employed there?'

'I'll provide you with any information you need once I get back to the hotel.'

'That will be satisfactory.' Nakamura handed him a card. 'If you will call this number and give the information to the policeman on duty.'

With Nakamura and his aide gone, the surgeon called out in Japanese and a nurse trundled a wheelchair into the room. Klein shook his head. 'No,' he said firmly. 'I'll walk.' He stood up, putting his weight on his feet, everything in control, his mind a bit hazy from the sedatives but his body manageable, even without the cane. He walked down the tiled corridor to the exit from the St Luke's emergency room. Miller was standing beside a limousine under the portico. He opened the back door.

'Are you all right, sir?' Miller said.

'Yes, thank you.'

Klein used the trip back to the hotel to collect himself, to sort through the pieces and put them into place. He had not handled this properly and he could see that now, but there was no self-recrimination in that recognition. There was no such thing as perfect decision making; the competent man examined his mistakes and allowed them to work for him. Twenty-four hours now, that was all the time he needed and then it would make no difference whether Corbett was alive or dead.

The limousine pulled into a subterranean parking garage and Miller accompanied Klein to the express elevator. 'Mr Erikson called at the hospital,' he said. 'He asked about your condition and requested that you call him when you feel up to it.'

'Tonight?'

'Yes, sir.'

Klein nodded. Once they reached his suite, he asked Miller to get Erikson on the telephone while he examined himself in the bathroom mirror. A bloody mess, his shirt and jacket caked with dried blood, the bandage covering an irregular rectangle beneath his left eye, along the cheekbone and back to the ear.

'Mr Erikson is on the line, sir.'

'Yes,' Klein said. He took the call in the sitting room. 'Klein here.'

'I was sorry to hear about your unfortunate accident, General,' Erikson said. 'They tell me you're all right.'

'Yes.'

'Have you met Jorge Carlos? He's here with me now. He was gracious enough to drop by and talk before the conference. Are you in any mood to have a drink with us? If you don't feel up to it, please feel free to say no.' Carlos, yes, the Philippine Secretary of Foreign Affairs, a patrician man. Klein had met him in some sort of ceremony in Manila.

'Fifteen minutes,' Klein said.

He allowed Miller to help him remove the bloodstained clothes and sponge him down, then he put on a fresh suit and selected another cane from the wicker holder. 'If you'll pardon my saying so, sir,' Miller said, 'you don't need to be in a long meeting, in your condition.'

'An hour or two,' Klein said. 'Time is running out.'

When he reached Erikson's suite he shook hands with Jorge Carlos, remembering him perfectly now for a face that wore a perpetually shrewd expression, as if Carlos were privy to information that no one else possessed. 'I heard of your accident, General,' Carlos said. 'I hope it is not too painful.'

'No,' Klein said. 'How are you, sir?'

'A bit confused at the moment,' Carlos said.

'Jorge and I are old friends,' Erikson said. 'He was economic minister when we put our first plants in the Philippines. That doesn't mean we're in total agreement, but we are perfectly open with each other. We just received a rather distressing call. It seems that someone informed the police that there is to be an attempt on Jorge's life in Atami.'

'Oh?' Klein said.

'The caller was not certain that I would be the target,' Carlos said in his brittle English. 'I am being considered a probability.'

'I don't understand,' Klein said, sitting down. 'Who made the threat?'

'An anonymous caller to the police,' Erikson said.

'That's not what I mean,' Klein said. 'Who is supposed to be threatening Mr Carlos's life?'

'We are,' Erikson said.

'Ridiculous,' Klein said.

'Not so ridiculous,' Carlos said, pouring himself a glass of wine from a decanter. 'Not from the point of view of your competitors.' He coughed slightly, covering his mouth with his hand. 'Let us suppose, hypothetically, that one of your competitors wished to assume your favoured position in the Philippines. Suppose that they make an attempt on my life, perhaps successfully, and that act is attributed to your company. Now certain retribution would be taken against you and your competitor would be given more than a favourable status. Do you follow my reasoning?'

'Certainly,' Klein said. 'But we have an excellent security system and we know what other companies are planning and not planning. Believe me, Mr Carlos, there is no such plan in the works. The rival companies are competitive, but not to that extent.'

Erikson was relaxed, easy, and Klein doubted that anything could throw him off balance. 'I think we can take the General's word for that, Jorge. We'll follow up, of course, but I doubt that there's anything to it.' He sat down. 'Before the call, Jorge was making an interesting point about the meeting. I think we all need to take a second look at financial conditions in the Philippines in particular and in all of Southeast Asia as well. It seems that there is a tide of antiforeign senti-

217

ment, a natural resentment. I must say, I can understand your point of view. But I don't think we're going to solve anything by making our differences greater than they are. If there are difficulties between your country and my companies, we'll iron them out.'

'These are desperate times,' Carlos said, raising his wine glass to the light. 'The old ways of doing business are not satisfactory anymore. There must be international equity, so it is the policy of my government to seek a unity of purpose with other small nations.'

The establishing of positions, that was what was occurring here now, more than political rhetoric, and Carlos was approaching Erikson as he would another national entity, not a company, no, for ESK was beyond that category. Carlos was defining the Philippine position and making a try for understanding at the same time, in the event that the Asian Conference failed to reach consensus.'

Klein tuned them out except for the general tone of the conversation. The feeling had begun to return to his cheek, not only the surface pain but a deeper ache that encompassed the whole left side of his head. There was a great deal remaining to be done, a multiplicity of details, but the final decision was in his mind and the certainty of that pleased him. Even Corbett's abortive attempt to communicate with the police would prove useful in the end. He came around with a start; a question had been asked of him.

'I beg your pardon,' he said.

'Jorge wants to know your opinion of the National Rural Police.'

'They are a highly efficient organisation, your Excellency,' Klein said.

'I have no doubt of that.' A furrow of concern crossed the smooth brow, the colour of olives. 'The question is how efficient they will wish to be. I have been a frequent and outspoken critic of the Japanese, especially in the past few years.'

218

'I was thinking that we can offer Jorge the Lincoln,' Erikson said. 'It is in Japan, isn't it?'

'Yes,' Klein said.

'I would not want it to appear that I was taking extra precautions to protect myself,' Carlos said.

'It's an unobtrusive limousine,' Klein said. 'Armour-plated, thoroughly bulletproof, but with an ordinary appearance. If you like, we can assign you a good security force.'

'The automobile will be quite sufficient,' Carlos said. 'My own men are quite adequate.'

Carlos was afraid, Klein realised; under this calm exterior was a keen anxiety and despite his protestations to the contrary, Carlos was taking this warning very seriously. Klein picked up the telephone, called Miller, and told him to have the limousine serviced and ready to go by morning. 'Your driver can pick it up at eight o'clock,' he said. 'Have him contact Mr Miller in my office.'

'Thank you,' Carlos said, standing. 'And now, if you will forgive me, tomorrow is to be a busy day.'

'Certainly,' Erikson said. 'I'll see you for breakfast.'

After Carlos had gone, Erikson lighted a cigar. 'What do you think?' he said, but Klein knew that the question was rhetorical, that the old man was processing information in his mind and not looking for an outside opinion. 'I don't think the conference is going to be able to reach a concensus. He wouldn't have come here otherwise.'

'Nothing has changed,' Klein said. 'I have participated in three wars in this part of the world. I fought the Japanese and the North Koreans and the North Vietnamese, so I know how they think in an adversary position. There may not be a total concensus at the conference, but there will be a partial one. And the end result is that they will have us by the balls. What will you do if the Philippine government decides to take over your operations?'

'They're not ready to make that move.'

'You can't be certain of that. And if they do, you can't do a damn thing to stop them.' He was overstepping himself now and he knew it, but he was aware that the old man was vacillating and he could not have that. 'There is no more American force in the Far East. You know that as well as I do. So nobody outside is going to back you up. There's nothing to stop the Philippines and South Korea from cramming their new policy down your throat.'

'You're out of line, General,' Erikson said firmly.

'Of course,' Klein said, backing off instantly. 'It's your decision to make.'

'I want you to put everything on hold,' Erikson said. 'We'll see how things work out tomorrow.' There was a finality in his voice. Klein stood up stiffly.

'I think I will call it a night,' he said. 'I am feeling some discomfort.'

'Get off your feet, General,' Erikson said. 'Take care of yourself.'

'Thank you.'

He did not go back to his suite but instead went to the board room, restless, switching the computer on line, punching into the programme. He sat down in a deep leather chair, requesting the weather report for Atami for the day after tomorrow. The map appeared on the display screen, pressure isobars appearing, the contours of the upper atmosphere, and the words flashed on the lower part of the screen.

WEATHER PREDICT/SHORT RANGE/ATAMI PREFECTURE/
1100 PROJECTED 48///
TYPICAL SUMMER WEATHER PATTERN WILL PREVAIL FOR
THE MORNING HOURS WITH SSW WIND, FIVE KNOTS TO
CALM, BAROMETER 30.02 STEADY. LATE AFTERNOON
WINDS INCREASING TO FIFTEEN KNOTS, GUSTS TO
TWENTY-FIVE, WITH SIXTY PER CENT (60%) CHANCE

OF THUNDERSTORMS AS A LOW PRESSURE TROUGH
MOVES EASTWARD FROM THE INLAND SEA.

He ran the computer through the checklist. There
was no change in the traffic pattern at Atsugi, nothing
to block or complicate, precisely correct conditions. He
made an estimate run of the Chinese, the Russians,
and the Americans, current position. The Russians
were making no preparations whatsoever, neither recognising nor rejecting the power of the conference to
set new policies; the Americans were taking four suites
of rooms at the hotel for a diplomatic force.

He punched in Japanese security precautions and a
map of Atami came on to the screen, with markers for
Japanese units. The government was placing a thousand Japanese police in the area (they would increase
by 50 per cent with the new warning) heavily concentrated in areas around the New Atami Hotel, providing
escorts for any planned excursions beyond the hotel. He
was pleased at the deployment of forces represented on
the screen. The Japanese were compulsive rather than
ingenious in their security arrangements. They had
developed a pattern that they considered adaptable to
any situation and they had not departed from it here.
Consequently, they were highly predictable, easily out-
manoeuvred. After the incident they would seal off the
area immediately and filter out all the individuals within
their cordon. There would be a mass resignation of all
their senior officers.

He rang Miller. 'Look in my bathroom,' he said.
'Bring me the prescription on the lower shelf, the one
for pain.'

'Do you want me to get the hotel doctor, sir?'

'No.'

In a few minutes Miller arrived with the bottle of tab-
lets. Klein took two, washing them down with water from
the carafe. 'Sit down, Miller,' he said. 'I want to talk.'

Miller sat down.

'How many men have full knowledge of what we're doing?' Klein said.

'Half a dozen,' Miller said. 'Some of the programmers have partial information but not enough to put anything together.'

'Corbett called the police,' Klein said. 'So somebody leaked something. Not that it makes much difference at this point, but I want to make sure that no more information goes out. Can you take care of that?'

'Yes, sir.'

That was the trouble with the Pentagon,' Klein said, reflectively. The pain in the side of his face had begun to ease. 'It made no difference how effective a plan we came up with, because too many people had to know the details, initial papers, give their approval, and the moment you began an operation, you could count on resistance. Because everybody was out to cover his ass in case anything went wrong. There's no strength in numbers because there's always somebody who can countermand the order to do what has to be done.' He closed his eyes, pinched the bridge of his nose. 'Erikson is having second thoughts. He's an inflexible old man and he doesn't know it.' His head was relaxed now. It was as if he could still detect the pain, it was still there, yes, but he could ignore it. His mind was floating free, soberly euphoric. He would be able to sleep soon. 'When is the next contact with Webster?'

'Ten hundred hours tomorrow.'

'I want to talk to him. When is his final check time?'

'Sixteen hundred hours.'

And now Klein knew what he was going to do. His whole life had been aimed towards this moment; the multiple frustrations of years of the military had accelerated his determination. 'I intend to give him a green light when I talk to him in the morning. From that point on, we will sever contact unless something comes up he can't handle.'

'Yes, sir.'

Klein yawned. 'As far as anyone else knows, the mission is scrubbed. If Erikson says anything about it at all to you, you will tell him that I issued a hold order with an automatic abort, unless he should say otherwise. I don't expect any inquiry, but I want to be sure.'

'Yes, sir.'

'And now,' Klein said, 'I'll think I'll go to bed.'

4

Corbett took one of the uniforms from a hanger in the closet, measured himself against it. It would not be a perfect fit, no, but it would do for the time being. Cristina was sitting in a chair in the corner of the bedroom, smoking a cigarette, a petulant frown on her face.

'There's no way you can make it darling,' she said. 'I'm a very good judge of your capabilities. I know you better than you know yourself.'

He said nothing. He found a flight bag in the closet and began to unload his pockets, sorting through the things he had taken from Klein. The wallet contained fifty thousand yen and an assortment of credit cards. Goddard's wallet held less than five thousand yen. All in all, he would have cash enough for a couple of days, no more than that. He thumbed through the scratchings in Klein's notebook, a record of financial transactions for the most part. He placed it in the bag along with Klein's keys and the two pistols.

The door opened from the living room and Ellen came in, collected but obviously under a great strain. She looked at Cristina coolly, appraisingly, and then turned to Corbett. 'I want to talk to you in the other room,' she said.

He checked the window first. It could not be opened. He picked up the flight bag and went into the other room. 'There was nothing about Wilson on the English newscast,' she said. 'They mentioned that the police had

223

received a telephoned threat against the Philippine Foreign Secretary.'

'Are they taking it seriously?'

'They just said that the police were taking added precautions.' She fell silent a moment. 'I know this is a rotten time to bring it up, but I need to know if she's the woman you were involved with.'

'Yes,' he said. 'But that's all finished.'

'Are you sure?'

'Positive.'

She nodded, accepting. 'I'm pleased for that, but it doesn't change anything. I want you to think about something, and don't interrupt me, please. Facts are facts. Wilson is dead.'

'Yes.'

'He was a fine man and we can grieve for him and that's all either of us can do. They killed him and sooner or later it will catch up with them. I believe that, because life is a great leveller, but you can't bring it about. Are you listening to me?'

'Yes. I hear you.'

She took his hands. 'Carl was here. He can arrange to get you on a flight tomorrow noon. I told him we were running away together, a very complicated situation. You'll go aboard as a part of the crew and then move into the first-class section. At Mexico City you'll debark as a member of the crew. We can go together.'

'There's nothing I would like better,' he said. 'But it will have to wait until I get back from Atami.'

'What can you do there? You have called the police.'

'I don't know. For one thing, I may be able to recognise Klein's people. He's bound to have men there.'

'And suppose they see you first. What's to keep them from killing you?'

He looked towards the bedroom. 'She's my insurance,' he said. 'She belongs to Erikson. He won't do anything to jeopardise her.'

'Then there's nothing I can say to persuade you.'

'This has to be finished,' he said. 'When it is, I promise you we'll leave here together.'

'All right,' she said. 'I won't make it any more diffi-cult for you. What can I do to help?'

'I want you to stay here in case I need a backup, somebody outside the area. I should be gone forty-eight hours, no more than that. Also, get in touch with any of your airline friends. Find out if there's an inn or an hotel in Atami where I can check in with no questions asked.'

'If that's the way you want it.'

He went back into the bedroom, began to strip off his clothes and to put on the uniform while Cristina ground out one cigarette and lighted another.

'What do you intend to do with me?' she said.

'You're coming along.'

'Where? You don't need me. You know how trouble-some I can be.'

He said nothing, putting a leg into the pants.

'I had nothing to do with any killing,' she said.

'No?'

'No.'

'You didn't hear the gunshot. You didn't suspect any-thing was going on. Klein and Goddard simply came into your house.'

'They told me you would be coming, that's all.'

'And Abernathy, you knew nothing about what he was doing to me?'

'I don't know anything about the company, you know that. Erik simply asked me if he could stay at the house for a few days.'

They were bickering, no more than that, and she would dissipate the strength of his feelings if she could, bring him back to her own reality. But in his mind, in-delible, was the picture of Wilson dead and he main-tained that image, refused to let it go. There was power in it.

He knotted the tie, examined himself in the mirror.

He did not fit the image of a pilot, no, and yet the uniform was only a trifle too large for him. With any luck, he would pass. He found shaving paraphernalia in the bathroom, added it to the bag. One thing at a time. He functioned best with concrete plans, a linear progression. He took the small pistol from the bag, put it into a pocket of the uniform. It created a small bulge but it was not especially noticeable.

'Who owns the car?' he said to her.

'The company.'

'Which section of the company? The hotel, the rental agency, ESK/JAPAN, who?'

'I don't know. What difference does it make?'

'I want to know how long it will take them to trace it.' He was back in the labyrinth again, trying to estimate the unknowable. If the police had the chauffeur, they would already have a description of the car and if they did not, it might take them days. In any event he would have to use it. He could not take the chance on public transportation. 'Into the other room,' he said.

Ellen was still on the telephone, writing something down on a piece of paper. 'Are you sure that's the name of the place?' she said. 'Okay. Thanks a lot.' She put the telephone down and turned to Corbett. 'A Japanese motel, would you believe it? Water beds. X-rated television. It's called the American Jazz Motel. The rooms are rented by two-hour rates, cheaper if you stay longer.'

'How close is it to the New Atami?'

'I didn't ask.'

'I'll check it out when I get there.'

'Some of the flight crews use it regularly. They say the management is discreet.'

He found the small car still parked in the street. He opened the door to admit Cristina and then turned to Ellen, who was standing on the sidewalk. He touched her hand. 'I'll be back,' he said.

'Sure,' she said, close to tears. 'I'll be here.'

He put the flight bag in the back seat and then slid

226

under the steering wheel and closed the door. He started the engine. 'I think you had better know something up front,' he said. 'Don't make any mistakes. If anything happens to me, the same thing happens to you as well.'

He could not see her face in the darkness but he had the distinct feeling that she was smiling. 'Of course,' she said.

He shifted into gear and pulled out into the light traffic, heading in what he assumed was a general south-westerly direction in the hope of intersecting the Tokaido Expressway, which would take him south to the Izu Peninsula and Atami. On the main thorough-fares the traffic was heavy as usual; the Japanese appeared never to sleep, and there was a stratum of smog hanging just above the pavement, making driving difficult.

He had always considered himself to be a good driver but within a half hour his nerves were tight and he was forced to pull into the left lane and slow down. He passed two accidents, minor, cars hunched into each other, red lights flashing, the police much in evidence. He passed both of them with his heart racing, fully expecting to be stopped. It was only a matter of time until they picked him up, methodically, dispassionately, their organisation perfect, inescapable.

Finally he came to the expressway on-ramp and began to settle into the steady monotony of the slow lane, the air heavy with diesel fumes. He was aware of Cristina sitting beside him, very close in the small car, strangely quiet but very much alert. 'Tell me something, William,' she said. 'This may sound foolish to you, but was a man really killed in my house tonight?'

'Do you doubt it?'

'I don't like the thought of death,' she said quietly. 'To be alone. To decay. I can't believe that Erik would permit something like that to happen.'

'It's not the same world,' he said.

'That doesn't make any sense.'

227

'He lives on two levels,' Corbett said. 'He collects oriental art and considers himself a man of peace but he sets up a slush fund for paying ransoms for executives kidnapped by terrorists in any part of the world and he knows damn well that terrorism works. And he's going to give it a hell of a try. Klein's picked a big target and I helped him inadvertently by notifying the police. Because the word will get out and when the Foreign Secretary is killed, the countries involved will know damn well who did it. Erik's going to find himself knee deep in blood before he's through.'

'I don't want to talk about it,' she said. 'It has nothing to do with me.'

Hell, she had approached reality and was now choosing to withdraw. He could understand that, and given her preference, she would move back into her house and follow her daily routine, the massages, the gowns and the receptions, with no real world beyond the surface of her mirror.

The traffic had thinned now except for a steady stream of heavy trucks. He felt very much alone, powerless; he knew he was operating from a position of no strength. He had always prided himself on being a realist; now he must admit that he could not bring this off alone. He should have called the head of AP in Tokyo or fed the story to one of his contacts at the American Embassy, leaving the matter to be resolved on a higher level. With the story made public, the American government could not afford to ignore it, to pretend it did not exist. Very well, the first thing in the morning he would find an Embassy official and set things into motion, on another track.

It was very late by the time he reached Atami and he spent another hour driving through the narrow streets, vision limited by the patches of night fog in the hills, a heavily forested area with paper lanterns glowing like fireflies through the trees. He was exhausted; Cristina was asleep on the seat beside him. He found the New

Atami Hotel, a sprawling four-floored structure at the edge of an inlet, a floodlighted pier jutting out into the water, the cruise boats at anchor. He did not drive too close because he could see clusters of Japanese police stationed at various points around the approaches to the hotel. He turned into a road that skirted the inlet and continued to drive until he saw a discreet electrical sign flanked by Japanese lanterns. THE AMERICAN JAZZ MOTEL. FOR YOUR MOST ULTIMATE. XXX

He turned down the lane, parked in front of the long low wooden building, which appeared to be perched on the edge of a steep bluff. When he killed the engine the silence was overwhelming. Cristina stirred but did not come awake. He had difficulty moving; his legs were cramped, his mind was cottony. But he forced himself out of the car. The air was cool here with a slight breeze moving in off the water.

The office was ersatz American with a coffee machine and a young Japanese clerk sitting behind a chrome counter, reading a magazine.

. 'Welcome,' he said to Corbett. 'You have selected the correct place, Captain. We have it here what you need and desire.'

Corbett cleared his throat. His mouth was dry. 'What are your rates?'

The clerk slid a rate card across the counter, tiny figures in a grid. Corbett had trouble making them out, outrageous prices, 15,000 yen for two hours, a special rate of 180,000 yen for a twenty-four-hour day. He was not going to have enough money for a long stay. He rubbed his hand across his mouth. 'Steep,' he said, and knew immediately from the blank expression on the clerk's face that his English was limited. 'Expensive,' he said.

'For true value received,' the young man said, smiling. 'The best experience costs more.'

Corbett consulted the chart again, the rate for twelve hours, 87,500 yen. He took the money out of his pocket, counted out eight 10,000-yen notes, seven thousands and five hundreds. 'Twelve hours,' he said.

'You will never have regrets, Captain.'

Corbett signed the registry card under the name of McGuiness.

'We also have a bar which is never closing and a fine eating place overlooking the water.' He gave Corbett a key. 'Do you wish baggage service?'

'No.'

'It will cost you no adding on by tips. The special service charge is already totaled in your payment.'

'No bellhop,' Corbett said. 'Where's the room?'

'Number five. You will not be able to miss it by driving to your left when you exit this door.'

Once he was outside, he proceeded to leave the car where it was. He opened the door and put his hand on Cristina's shoulder. She came awake, gracefully, startled. 'Where are we?'

'Atami,' he said. 'Come on. I have a room.'

He took the flight bag from the back seat and led her across the narrow gravelled parking area, moving down the row of doors until he reached number five. The room smelled slightly of pine oil disinfectant. If he had not been so tired, he would have burst into laughter at the expression on Cristina's face as she regarded the mirrored ceiling and wall, the water bed covered with fur with the television set at its foot. There was a small intricately lettered sign above the water bed that read ENJOY!

'My God,' she said, astonished. 'What in the hell is this?'

'The Japanese extension of American sexual fantasies,' he said. He passed beyond the water bed through a narrow hallway to a Japanese toilet with a bidet and a shower and beyond it a door that opened on to a small private terrace. From here, he could see the waterfront side of the New Atami Hotel up the inlet, the lights reflecting in the water. An official-looking Japanese patrol boat was lying off the end of the pier, anchored. The officials were taking no chances. He went back into the room to find her sitting on the edge of the bed, the furred surface in motion, contained swells moving beneath the surface.

'I can't stay in this place,' she said. 'It's impossible.'

He clicked on the television, searching for news, but the screen was alive with a Japanese pornographic film, two couples in passionate calisthenics. He switched channels, found an American movie dubbed into Japanese, another channel of pornography and nothing else. He clicked it off.

She stretched out on the bed, very tentatively, looking miserable. 'How do you expect me to sleep?' she said. 'I'm getting seasick.'

'You don't have any choice,' he said. He put the flight bag next to a chair and surveyed the room, sorry now that he had insisted on bringing her along. For she was quixotic, unpredictable, and he would have to sacrifice any hope of comfort in order to guard her. He moved the chair against the door, put his flight bag behind it.

'What are you doing?' she said.

'Making sure you stay put.'

'I'm not going anywhere.'

'That's for sure,' he said. He took the telephone off an end table. The cord was just long enough to allow him to put the telephone under the chair. He sat down, trying to get comfortable. 'The terrace is over a steep bluff,' he said. 'A drop of fifteen, maybe twenty feet.'

Ironic, he thought, that in this setting, at this time, the most exquisitely sexual female he had ever known was totally without any sexuality at all, simply a very uncomfortable woman trying to adjust to a bed that would not stay still. She fell silent and he slumped down in his chair, determined to stay awake until she went to sleep. His mind drifted. Time, four in the morning, and he could rest a while and still be able to make it to

231

Haneda in time for the Mexico City flight, and he would have to call Ellen and let her know. The Plaza de la Reforma. No, incorrect, the Paseo de la Reforma, an avenue named for revolution, and he jerked awake in sudden panic. He had dozed off. But Cristina was asleep now. The room air conditioner put out a gentle soothing sound. To hell with it. He went to sleep.

When he came awake, there was daylight in the room and for a moment he was disoriented and did not know where he was, and then he saw the empty bed and rose to his feet, half running down the narrow corridor. He stopped at the door to the terrace. She was sitting there, her hair mussed, her gown rumpled. She merely glanced at him and then stared out over the inlet. The water was full of boats, Japanese fishermen for the most part, putting out from the side of the inlet opposite the New Atami. The Japanese patrol boat remained in the same position.

'How long have you been up?' he said.

'Since daybreak,' she said. 'I couldn't sleep.'

And now, by daylight, he saw something he had not noticed the night before. A narrow flight of steps led down from the terrace to a path below. He lighted a cigarette, sat down. 'You could have gotten away,' he said.

She nodded. 'I do not want them to kill you, Willie.'

'Thank you for that.'

'I don't want to be responsible for your dying.'

'Hell,' he said, with a shrug. The cigarette smoke was brackish, stale.

'Don't take this for weakness, William.'

'All right.'

'I want you to call me a taxi and send me to the New Atami,' she said. 'I'll check in and sleep. I'll get my hair done and then I'll call Erik and have someone pick me up.'

'You betrayed me before. You'd do it again if the circumstances were right.'

232

'That was before your friend was killed. I won't betray you. I could have left on my own.'

'You couldn't explain how you got here without betraying me,' he said. 'Erik knows you left Tokyo with me. He would know I was here. Besides, as long as you're with me, I'm not worried about Erik.'

She gave him an appraising look. 'May I have a cigarette?'

He lighted one, handed it to her. She inhaled deeply, leaned her head against the back of the chair, and blew smoke at the sky. In the thin morning light he could see the almost invisible network of lines around her eyes, the slight, almost imperceptible sagging of flesh in her cheeks. 'I had a chance to marry into a European royal family last year,' she said. 'It was a small country, a duchy, I think. A real prince, literally. He commanded his own troop of horse guards in ancient uniforms and he had a flaring moustache. A bachelor of forty, wealthy, second in line to the throne.'

'Why didn't you marry him?'

'I had a long talk with the Queen Mother. She invited me in. An honest woman. She informed me that I would have a generous allowance and be impregnated by a vigorous man of her choosing in order to produce a child. It was all designed to quiet the rumours. Her son, the Prince, was a flaming faggot, a notorious homosexual.' She put out her cigarette. 'Is there a shower in this passion pit?'

'Yes,' he said.

She went into the bathroom and he returned to the room, putting the chair back in its place, returning the telephone to the table, trying to remember the name of the man from AP. He could not. He picked up the telephone, asked the motel operator to connect him with the New Atami, and then asked for the American pressroom. In a moment, an American voice came on the line.

'Is there anyboby there from AP?' Corbett said.

'Not yet. This is Fisher of the Tokyo Bureau of *The New York Times*. Can I help you?'

'You'll do,' Corbett said. 'Does the name William Corbett mean anything to you?'

There was a momentary pause and he was aware that Fisher was covering the mouthpiece with his hand, asking around. When he came back on the line, his voice was sharply interested. 'Corbett of ESK?' he said.

'I have a story to give you,' Corbett said. 'But I have certain conditions.'

'What's on your mind?'

'I want the name of somebody from the American Embassy.'

'He has to be here, in Atami, right?' Fisher said pointedly.

'Yes, I'm willing to give you an interview but there must be an American official present. And no Japanese police.'

'That's a tall order, Mr Corbett. There's a lot of heavy pressure around to pick you up. Why don't we talk alone? That way, I can guarantee you security.'

'No.'

'All right. I don't know about the Embassy but there's a delegation from State here. Try Kenneth Cummings. I have his number here. Hold on a sec.' He looked up the number and Corbett wrote it down. 'Give me a minute to call and brief him. I think he'll be reasonable about this.'

'I'll call him in three minutes,' Corbett said.

'You'd better give me your number, just in case.'

'No.' He severed the connection. He lighted a cigarette, feeling very apprehensive. Fisher would know he was here, in Atami. Very well, it was a calculated risk. He waited three minutes and then called the number he had been given. There was an immediate answer.

'Cummings here.'

'What's your official position, Mr Cummings?'

'Deputy Undersecretary, Far East.'

234

'All right. I won't waste any time. There's to be an attempt on the life of the Philippine Foreign Secretary today. I'm willing to give you full details, but only in the presence of a reporter. The information has to be published.'

'I don't know,' Cummings said. He had a heavy Boston accent. 'I'm sure you can understand the complications, from a diplomatic point of view.'

'Screw your diplomatic point of view,' Corbett said. 'My life is at stake. What's about to happen is going to turn this part of the world upside-down.'

'I can understand your feelings, Mr Corbett, but I'll have to clear a procedure through Tokyo.'

'There's a promontory north of the New Atami Hotel, about a quarter of a mile,' Corbett said. 'It's nine o'clock now. Meet me there at eleven thirty, unofficially. Just listen to what I have to say and make up your own mind.'

'I suppose I could do that,' Cummings said.

He called Fisher again. Fisher agreed to the meeting at eleven thirty.

Cristina came out of the bathroom now, naked except for a towel turbaned around her hair. She stood in front of the mirrored wall, examining herself dispassionately.

'I'll see if I can't get some breakfast sent around,' Corbett said.

'I don't eat breakfast,' she said. 'I can't afford the calories.'

'My God,' he said, smiling.

'My breasts are much too large,' she said, almost to herself. 'When I was much younger they were in fashion, but not anymore. Small breasts are very chic now.' She turned slightly, running a hand over her hips. 'I need to take an inch off.' She abandoned her appraisal. 'I think I'll get some sun.' She retrieved a larger towel from the bathroom, wrapped it around her, and headed for the terrace.

In a moment he followed her on to the terrace. The

235

hot sun had burned the mist off the inlet and the water was cluttered with sailboats. One of the hydroplane excursion boats was just beginning to move, making a wide, slow swing around the inlet until it cleared the traffic, then it gained speed, lifting to skim the surface of the waves as it angled out into open water. It was headed for the island of Oshima, yes, he had taken that trip once with an ESK group. He sat down beside Cristina, propping his feet up on the railing, feeling the warmth of the sun against his face, able to relax for the first time in days. He had a clear course of action now. He would meet with the two men at eleven thirty and pass on the information he had. It made no difference what they did with it; the responsibility would no longer be his. He would find a way to get back to Tokyo and Ellen. She had been able to arrange transportation once; she could do it again.

Cristina stirred slightly, her eyes closed against the glare of the sun. 'Everything is all finished between us, isn't it, William?'

'Yes,' he said. 'I'm not sure we really had anything in the first place.'

'Don't discount the physical,' she said. 'That was good.' She scratched the tip of her nose. 'I wasn't completely honest with you earlier. My days with Erik are about over, I know that. And I think he will use my going with you as an excuse to end it. So the question is, where do I go from here?'

'You shouldn't have any money troubles.'

'I could always marry, I suppose. There's a man in New York City who controls Scotch whisky imports into this country. He's very old, very wealthy.'

He looked out over the inlet, watching a Japanese couple raising a sail on a small boat. The knowledge of what he was about to do was already in his mind, for he had known from the very beginning that he would not be able to use Cristina to cover himself. He would never be able to hurt her and any threat to that effect was bound to ring hollow.

'I want to make a deal with you,' he said. 'I'll leave you enough money to hire a car to take you back to Tokyo. In return, you can tell Erik that I forced you to go with me, kept you in Tokyo until you could make a break for it. You don't know where I am.'

She sat up. 'Why would you do that?' she said.

'Masculine pride,' he said. 'A gesture, maybe. I don't know.'

'How do you know I won't betray you again?'

'You probably will,' he said. 'But by the time you get back to Tokyo, it won't make that much difference.'

She held out her hand to him, smiling. Her fingers were warm. 'We could always make love one more time,' she said. 'For old times' sake.'

'No,' he said. 'We'll leave things as they are.'

He went back into the room, counted out sufficient money for the hiring of a car, and then picked up the flight bag and went out the front door. The sunlight was blinding and he had the beginnings of a headache. In the office a different young man was on duty, a sober Japanese with owlish eyes. 'Do you speak English?' Corbett said.

'Yes, sir.'

'Where can I buy a pair of sunglasses?'

The young man removed a card of sunglasses from below the counter. 'We have much call for sunglasses here.'

They were all slightly too small but he picked a pair of them and doled out the yen. 'I want coffee sent around to Number Five,' he said.

'Yes, sir,' the clerk said. 'We have complimentary coffee and Danish pastries here, if you wish.'

'I'll have it here. I still want the coffee sent around. And the lady will need a car to take her back to Tokyo. You can arrange that?'

'Yes, sir.' The clerk poured coffee into a china cup

237

and placed a pastry on a paper plate, then turned to the telephone. The coffee was weak, the pastry cold, but Corbett consumed both, hungrily.

Outside, he put on the sunglasses and the glare was eased. It was only as he started the car that he realised he had not shaved and there was a slight stubble on his cheeks. It made no difference, not really, because they would be no more inclined to believe him if he were well groomed.

He drove no more than an eighth of a mile and parked the car in a lane where it would be sheltered by trees from the main road. Carrying the flight bag, he began to walk, following the path along the bluff around the inlet, falling into an easy pace, amazed at how deceptive the darkness had been. With the fog and the lanterns there was a certain charm to this countryside that had disappeared with the daylight.

The trails were littered with paper, crowded with Japanese tourists out walking in their *happi* coats with the ideogram of their inns stamped on the back, families for the most part. On the far side of the inlet he could see bulldozers at work, clearing trees for land development, for new hotels and country houses, and there was an occasional muffled boom of dynamite as the builders attacked a rocky ridge. One day in the not too distant future the whole area would be paved with buildings and all that would remain would be the view of the bay and the islands off the coast, only because that was something beyond their power to change.

In the heat of the advancing morning he worked up a sweat. He could feel the shirt clinging to the small of his back beneath the uniform jacket. He approached the promontory and sat down on a bench near a small Shinto shrine built into the side of the rock. A hundred yards below him he could see a narrow beach through the trees. Decrepit houses, Japanese fishermen repairing their nets in the bright sunlight, a make-shift pier cluttered with wooden boats. Across the inlet he could see a dining terrace at the New Atami, people at tables beneath brightly coloured umbrellas. The conference would be underway now, delegates around a long table, interpreters in a glass booth, the presentation of preliminary position papers, the first rather desultory approaches, and nothing much would be accomplished this morning. He had attended enough of these meetings to know the pattern. Real progress would come tonight, in the bars and private rooms, and tomorrow, on the excursion boat to Oshima, out of range of reporters and the onus on officiality.

Odds were that the meeting would never get that far. Klein would already have a man in position somewhere in that hotel, undoubtedly Asiatic, with ready access to the Philippine Foreign Secretary. He would be armed with a pistol and a silencer perhaps, and the attempt would be made before the day was out, and the Foreign Secretary would be dead. At that point the meeting would recess but he was convinced it would not end, no, for there were swarms of delegates and subofficials from each of the participating countries. Telephone contact would be made with Manila, authorisation would pass to a deputy, and the meeting would proceed. Ah, shit, madness, and perhaps he would be able to change the course of things a little, to deflect Klein's plan, if he could persuade the official from State to take him seriously.

He could see the Japanese police dotted around the terrace; the patrol boat still stood offshore. He was convinced that they could flood the area with men, increase security tenfold, and still they would not be able to defend against one man determined to kill. For in the end human beings were such fragile creatures, capable of being killed in so many ways, a bullet tunnelling through the brain, the severing of nerves, the rupture of the heart.

He checked his watch. It was nearly time. He climbed the path through the trees to the promontory. By the

239

time he reached the top he was winded. He stood near a park bench in the cover of the trees until he saw the car approaching, small, black, American economy. There were two men in the front seat. He emerged from the trees, uneasily, placing the flight bag on the bench, suddenly aware of the small pistol in his pocket. He was not reassured.

The car pulled to a stop near the bench and the two men climbed out. The shorter, older man with distinguished grey hair he assumed to be Cummings; the taller, rangy-looking young man with short black hair would be Fisher. They both approached him hesitantly. He was reassured. They were as wary as he was.

'Mr Corbett?' the older man said. 'I'm Cummings and this is Peter Fisher.'

Corbett shook hands and sat down at the far side of the bench. 'I want to get this over with,' he said. He told them about Wilson, the killing of the Korean colonel, the preparations in PR for a disaster.

Cummings was obviously uncomfortable. 'And you say this is an ESK operation?'

'Certainly.'

'Can you offer any substantiation?'

'I think the events are sufficient.'

Cummings shrugged. 'All right, let us suppose for the sake of argument that what you suggest is true. What do you think we should do about it?'

'I don't give a damn what you do about it,' Corbett said. 'A man is going to be killed down there. So the monkey is on your back now.'

'I can understand your impatience,' Cummings said. 'But you are a man of considerable experience in matters like this. So I think you can understand our position. We are, in a real sense, guests on foreign soil. At this meeting we have no function at all. This is an Asian conference, and if we were to interfere, to intrude in any way, our action would be wrongly interpreted.'

'Then you will allow him to be killed.'

'Let me put it another way,' Cummings said, 'First, the Japanese police were alerted last night, by a telephone call from you, I assume. Secondly, by your own admission, you have no hard evidence of a conspiracy here, nothing I can offer them. That does not mean that I don't believe you, but the Japanese authorities would discount anything you say as an attempt to get yourself out of a dilemma by shifting the blame. Thirdly, the Philippine Secretary is being chauffeured in a bullet-proof limousine supplied by ESK. That may mean nothing, of course, but over here, among the Asiatics, that implies that ESK will go to unusual lengths to protect him, simply because there has been a rumour to the contrary.'

Corbett looked to Fisher. 'When it happens, I want you to print this,' he said. 'I want it on record that I have advised an official of the United States Government and that nothing was done about it.'

'We'll print it, of course,' Fisher said, in a flat voice. He had a broad nose, which appeared to be slightly crooked, as if it had been broken at one time and improperly repaired. 'There's another matter I would like to ask you about, Mr Corbett. There's a set of rumours that say the Vietnamese arms are somewhere in Asia, ready to be used. Another story has them in Africa.'

Incredible, Corbett thought, and what he was doing was wasted here, and quite suddenly he was aware that something was wrong, for the voice coming out of Fisher was not the same voice he had heard on the telephone. This man who was so calmly inquiring into the matter of the Vietnamese arms, this newspaper reporter, was taking no notes. Of course, betrayed, and he took a deep breath and rubbed his hand over his eyes, refusing to panic. He took a cigarette out of his pocket, leaning over to allow Cummings to light it for him and at the same moment slipped his hand into the jacket pocket, his fingers touching the small pistol.

'The Vietnamese arms,' he said, straightening up.

He was calm now, contained. He would do nothing to provoke reaction from the man pretending to be Fisher. He looked directly at him, smiling. 'Suppose we put all our cards on the table first,' he said. 'I know that you're not who you say you are, Mr Fisher. I would guess, just offhand, that you would be with American intelligence. Am I correct?'

'Let's just say that I can get you off the hook,' the man said. 'We are no more anxious to see you picked up by the Japanese police than you are.'

'Good,' Corbett said, nodding. 'Then we agree on that, at least.'

'We will take you back to Tokyo and see you safely removed to the States. If you cooperate with the Senate committee, I'm authorised to guarantee that you will not be extradited for trial in Japan.'

'What's your name?' Corbett said. 'I can't keep calling you Fisher.' His fingers had closed around the pistol now.

'Evans.'

'All right, Mr Evans. We may be able to work something out. But first, there's the matter at hand, Mr Carlos.'

'I should not be a part of this conversation,' Cummings said rather vaguely. 'After all, I openly represent the government of the United States. So whatever transpires between the two of you has to be considered strictly unofficial.'

Evans ignored him. 'Is Mr Carlos a friend of yours, Mr Corbett?'

'No.'

'Then what do you suggest?'

'I want an official note hand-delivered to Mr Carlos, advising him that the United States Government has definite evidence of a plot against his life. I want a similiar warning delivered to whoever is in charge of Japanese security.'

Evans lounged back against the bench. 'I could pretend to go along with you, Mr Corbett,' he said. 'You know that. But I don't intend to bullshit you. It's my business to know what's going on and I don't believe there is a plot. That's only my opinion, of course. On the other hand, suppose it does happen. We have to determine whether such an action would be converse to our best interests over here.'

It was laid out before him and he felt a perverse delight in his own stupidity for not having predicted what the American response would be. My God, he had been dense, for the American government would not be especially keen to see a new coalition form among the Asian countries. And if Carlos were to be murdered, the meetings delayed, the American government would make an appropriate expression of outrage and be secretly relieved. Further down the line the government would tend to do nothing to stop Klein, for he would be doing privately what the American government had been doing for many years and was no longer strong enough to do.

'I see your point,' Corbett said. He puffed on the cigarette. Far down the hill a band of Japanese bicyclers had dismounted against the steep gradient and were pushing their machines up the slope. Overhead, a seagull banked in the still air. His mind was sluggish. He had difficulty thinking. It would be to his best interest to let the matter rest here, to accept Evans's offer and be taken back to Tokyo and go through the normal course of giving evidence, seated at a table in an air-conditioned room, entering what would be an intellectual exercise with plenty of sleep to fortify him.

And in the end what did it matter whether this unknown man was killed at the New Atami or not, whether the meetings continued or stalled, for he would be out of it. But there was always Wilson. Where was he now? On a slab in a Tokyo morgue? Flown back to the States, in cold storage, embalmed? It was the rational course but he knew he would not take it. Now, at this moment, he preferred the irrational.

'What is good for General Motors,' he said.

'What?' Cummings said.

'It doesn't matter,' Corbett said. 'But if you are interested in seeing the Far East remain as it is, then why should the Vietnamese arms concern you?'

'That depends on where they are,' Evans said. 'That depends on who has them. Now, if you are willing to give us a full disclosure, we may be able to take care of the matter without going to a public hearing. If they're in Africa, they can cause problems.'

'Africa,' Corbett said. 'Yes, a troublesome area. Millions of barbarous blacks. I can see why you would be concerned. All right, you have a deal.' He stood up and then, as Evans began to rise, Corbett drew the pistol from his pocket, knowing even as he did so that Evans would have to react, his hand moving towards the inside of his jacket. Corbett's finger jerked against the trigger and the pistol made a loud pop, not an explosion, no, and the bullet caught Evans in the shoulder and he seemed to freeze where he was, his hand motionless against the front of his shirt, a rather dull look in his eyes as if he could not believe he had been hit. Slowly, he sank down, sitting on the bench. The blood had begun to stain the light fabric of his suit. Cummings was transfixed, making no move at all. The bicyclers were running up the hill.

Corbett backed away, still holding the pistol, picking up the flight bag before he ran down the path. He ran automatically, without feeling, the Japanese hikers along the path giving way, making room for him to pass. And then, a hundred yards from the car, he slowed down, stopped dead in his tracks. Through the brush he could see the Japanese police car parked next to the Datsun, the men in uniform going over the car. How many of them, two, three? It made no difference. He reversed direction and went down the path towards the beach.

Klein was having luncheon in the dining-room with Erikson when the waiter summoned him to the telephone. Miller was on the line. 'I think you'd better get right down here, General,' Miller said.

'What's going on?'

'It's too complex to explain on the telephone, sir,' Miller said.

'All right,' Klein said.

He excused himself and went directly to the board room, where Miller was waiting, a harried expression on his face. 'I've taken the liberty of calling Webster and telling him to stand by,' Miller said. 'We have trouble at Atami.'

'What kind of trouble?'

'Corbett,' Miller said. 'He arranged a meeting with a reporter but the government sent an intelligence agent. Corbett ended up shooting him.' Corbett had gotten away but the Japanese police had located the Datsun he had been driving. Putting the two incidents together, they had brought in a special force to comb the area and requested the foreign delegates to close down their meetings for the afternoon, until Corbett had been captured. 'So the Foreign Ministers decided to reverse their schedule,' Miller said. 'They're taking the hydrofoil down to Oshima.'

'What time?'

'Fifteen thirty.'

'I see.' He sat down in the leather chair. 'Get Webster for me.' He had been in situations like this many times before, the vagaries of chance, the stray accident that shot a perfectly conceived plan to pieces, but he had learned to take no action before an alternative plan could be thoughtfully arranged. Miller handed him the telephone.

'Webster here.'

'Has Miller filled you in?' Klein said.

'Yes, sir.'

'How soon can you be in the air?'

'We have problems here,' Webster said. 'I had a practise mock run scheduled. I think we can do it and still make the drop this afternoon, but I can't give you an unqualified affirmative.'

'I want an unqualified affirmative,' Klein said. 'I don't care how you do it.'

'I'll arrange it somehow. When can you give me a target approach?'

'I'll run it through the computer. You have to be over the target at exactly fifteen thirty.'

'I can make that.'

'Get on it. Call me back and verify when you're clear.'

He severed the connection, leaned back in his chair, closing his eyes. At the moment he had to consider the possibility that Webster could not bring it off. Should that happen, he would have to find an alternative.

'Get Goddard for me,' he said to Miller. 'And I want a computer update of projected traffic at Atami this afternoon.'

'I have programmers working on that,' Miller said. 'They should be feeding in late data from Atami now.'

'Very good,' Klein said. He turned to the terminal, requested an Atami grid with the new estimate for 15.30. It came on to the large screen and he shook his head at the congestion of dots on the display and asked the computer to check itself, to verify the data. When there was no change in the density, he relayed the information to Miller and asked him to find out what in the hell had gone wrong with the machine. It was imperative that the computer be kept in perfect running order; he would have to rely on it heavily through the afternoon.

He called for current weather and was pleased to see that this function of the computer was still operative. The data was printed on the top smaller screen to his left. No significant changes since the last check.

In a few minutes Goddard came into the board room and Klein was amazed at the resiliency of the man. Less than twenty-four hours since he had suffered a concussion and yet he appeared to be in perfect health, not a mark on him except for a slight redness on his neck just above his shirt collar.

'How are you feeling?' Klein said.

'I'm feeling fine,' Goddard said.

'No aftereffects then?'

'No.'

'Sit down, Goddard. We have a special problem.'

'If it's Corbett,' Goddard said, 'I heard the business about him on the news.'

'He's part of the problem,' Klein said. 'We had been counting on his co-operation, but after what happened at Atami I can see that we're not going to get it. So it will be necessary to take him out, one way or another. As long as he is at Atami he can recognise members of our team. So we will make him first priority.'

'Do you want him alive or dead?'

'It makes no difference. I just want him neutralised.'

'All right,' Goddard said.

Klein paused, searching for the right words to outline the action he wanted Goddard to take without giving him an overall view of the plan. 'Suppose I asked you to come up with a plan to waste some of the delegates at the Asian meeting. How long would it take you to get ready and how would you go about it?'

'Which men?'

'Let's just say any six, at random.'

Goddard rubbed his chin, staring off into space towards the screens on the wall without really seeing them. 'The main problem is going to be the Japanese security,' he said finally. 'I take it you would want the strike to be clandestine.'

'Certainly.'

'We have a six-man team. Thrash knows every foot

247

of the Atami area.' He paused again and Klein could almost hear the laborious working of his mental processes. 'I can't give you any definite plan until we make a survey of the area.'

'All right,' Klein said. 'There's a possibility we won't have to go this direction but I want you at Atami, just in case. Take anything you need. Once you've established a base, get back in touch.'

'Will do,' Goddard said flatly.

Miller came back into the board room. His face was pale and he waited until Goddard had left before he said anything. 'I think you had better have a look at your Atami grid, sir,' he said.

Klein punched up the grid. The density of the black dots representing boat traffic had more than doubled since the last check. 'What in the hell is going on?' he said. 'Can't they correct the computer error?'

Miller sat down. 'It's no computer error,' he said. There was no way it could have been figured in advance, he went on, because the plans had not been made until yesterday afternoon. It seemed that the All Japan Sailing Association was having their annual regatta in the bay fronting Atami, and at the last minute, realising that so many distinguished visitors were coming to the New Atami, they had requested permission from the Japanese government to sail into the inlet, a form of paying their respects.

'How many boats?' Klein said, rubbing his chin.

'About two hundred and fifty,' Miller said. 'Jesus, they're mostly Japanese families from the greater Tokyo area, General. Men, women, and children. I think we can figure an average of three people to a boat.'

Klein turned to the console. He projected the course of the hydrofoil and a solid curved line appeared on the screen, arching from the New Atami dock to the bluff on the far side of the harbour before it began to pick up speed and head for the open water. He punched in the weather, dead calm, yes, but when he superimposed the

248

CAN pattern, he could see that the strike was going to take at least a hundred of those small boats. Allowing three people to a boat would give him a civilian death rate of three hundred. He checked the grid position at the bluff and jotted down the figures.

'I would suggest that we call for a new target position,' Miller said with effort. 'There's no reason he shouldn't make the drop after the hydrofoil's in open water.'

'There's every reason,' Klein said. 'The hydrofoil slows to a crawl when it makes its turn at the bluff. In open water, with the hydrofoil at full speed, it would escape the pattern altogether.'

'Then I would suggest a strike when it pulls in at Oshima.'

'We don't have any co-ordinates for Oshima.'

'You will have your team at Atami,' Miller said, his voice very subdued.

'They're strictly for contingency,' Klein said. The telephone rang. Webster was on the line, his voice calm.

'No trouble at all,' Webster said. 'Everything's on.'

'Good. Your grid co-ordinates are Seven George Fourteen. Have you got that?'

'Yes.'

'You have dead calm so you make your approach at a hundred and fifty feet coming in from the north northeast. The hydrofoil will be making no more than ten knots in its turn near the bluff.'

'I have it,' Webster said.

'Once you have made the drop, you will cross the peninsula and traverse Suruga Bay at an altitude not to exceed two hundred feet. That will avoid their coastal radar. When you pass Omaezaki at the southwestern tip of the bay we will make a visual sighting and alert the boat at Ikobe. It will proceed due south and stand off at approximately ten miles. You will key on that boat. If there are fishing craft in the vicinity, it will lead you to open waters. Then you can ditch the plane and the boat will pick you up. Once you have begun your run, you will maintain total radio silence. We've been over this before but I want to make sure you understand it.'

'You can count on me,' Webster said.

'I'm sure I can. Just make sure of your altitude and the checkpoint at Omaezaki. Good luck.'

Klein shut down the computer and the screen went dark and he realised that he was depressed and exhilarated at the same time. There was a great deal to be done but he could accomplish it quickly because he had planned for this moment a long time and everything was in place. He did not like the idea of the civilian casualties but he had faced this problem before, many times, and he refused to allow himself to think of them in human terms at all but rather as dots on a screen, numbers, a price that had to be paid for any military operation in a civilian area.

When he had made certain everything was operative he would call the hotel doctor and have the dressing changed on his cheek (the wound was seeping; he could feel the wetness of the bandage) and then he would sleep for an hour or two and prepare himself for the siege that was certain to come. He closed his eyes, pinched the bridge of his nose.

'You have the checklist,' he said to Miller. 'We will hold the press releases until sixteen thirty when we have a partial list of the casualties. Then have them Telexed to our appropriate offices. I will schedule a press conference at seventeen thirty for Erikson. But don't send him a copy of the statement he's to make. I'll hand-deliver that. Right now alert Omaezaki and Ikobe.'

He was aware of silence and he opened his eyes to find Miller looking at him, just sitting there, hunched forward slightly, his hands clasped between his open knees. 'Call it off, General,' he said quietly.

'I beg your pardon? I didn't hear you.'

'Jesus, you can't do it. Three hundred civilians?'

'We are not responsible for their being there,' Klein

250

said. 'If there was another way, I'd be the first to take it. But there isn't another way, none at all. There's no will in the United States anymore, no strength. If we don't take action, they will eventually strangle us.'

Miller said nothing.

'Can you think of some other method?' Klein said. 'I respect your opinion. If you have another solution, I'd like to hear it.'

Miller shrugged, shook his head slowly. 'No, I don't have another way.'

'I understand how you feel,' Klein said. 'It's an unfortunate business all round. I'll be in the doctor's office and then in my quarters. Let me know when you have the affirmatives from the list.'

'I'll do that,' Miller said.

6

Goddard had never felt comfortable with people. When he had been with the Secret Service, his supervisor had called him in one day to have a friendly conversation, assuring him up front that there was nothing wrong with his performance, no. But there was something Goddard should know. The other agents, when requesting assignment to teams, always had Goddard at the bottom of the list. This was not because Goddard lacked efficiency but because of a certain personality deficiency. He was considered overly taciturn, silent; he did not socialise nor did he engage in conversation. His face never changed; the other men could never tell what he was thinking. He made them uneasy.

Goddard had worked on it. He had gone through a couple of special courses in Washington in which he was required to memorise names of people and something about them (this was not difficult; his memory was perfect, he never forgot the detail of a face) and to make extemporaneous talks on a variety of subjects in front of a group of men. This he could do well enough and when he had finished the course, he immediately dropped back into his former habits.

He did not really mind, for he realised that he was different from most people, with an entirely different set of skills, perceptions that even his highly skilled compatriots did not possess. In an earlier age he would have made a good tracker, for he had a single-mindedness that was not easily distracted. Now, standing by the Datsun, which had not yet been moved, watching the Japanese police going over the car for prints, meticulously collecting useless evidence, he was in touch with that ability, that sense of logic that made it possible for him to reconstruct Corbett's actions in this situation. He looked up the path that led towards the promontory, squinting against the bright sunlight.

Corbett was not a physically strong man; he smoked too much and he would not have good lungs. He had come from someplace a good distance below the hill and parked as close as he could to the promontory to spare himself the rigours of a long uphill hike. He had spent the night in one of the inns around here, that much was certain, for the American official had described the uniform Corbett wore as clean. And the woman was nowhere in evidence. He had stashed her someplace. If the inn had been on the upper ridge, he would have parked the car on the same level as the top of the promontory.

He could picture the event in his mind, Corbett shooting the American agent, scrambling down the narrow trail to this road, proceeding to the first point at which the car was visible (the very spot where Goddard was now standing). Panicking, he would have struck off on the trail downslope, towards the beach, but he would not have gone near any of the habitations. From here, Goddard could see a hiking trail halfway up on the bluff, visible only in patches between the trees.

252

He walked back up to the promontory, where Thrash was on the car radio. Thrash was a small man with a wiry build and he spoke fluent Japanese. He looked up as Goddard approached. 'We can eliminate all the Japanese inns,' he said. 'On weekends they're heavily booked in advance and have a policy against accepting foreigners. That limits us to the Atami Hotel, the Atami Fujiya, and the New Fujiya. Williams covered the first two, Voigt the third. Negative.'

'He wouldn't have checked into a well-known one,' Goddard said. 'He had to have someplace private. What kind of uniform was he wearing?'

'Some airline,' Thrash said. 'Evans thinks it was Pan Am but he's in a state of shock, very confused.'

'So the question is, where did he get it?' Goddard said, half to himself. 'Does Pan Am have a tie-in with any of the resorts here?'

'No.'

'Do you know that for sure or are you guessing?'

'I'm positive.'

There was a weakness in such certainty, because if a man was certain then his mind was closed to any other possibilities. 'Is there a place where airlines personnel hang out in Atami?'

'I'll check it out,' Thrash said. He began to speak in Japanese into the radio while Goddard looked down the path Corbett had followed in his flight. He could feel Corbett's presence, not close, no, but he sensed that he was somewhere in the area, somewhere in the panorama of trees and hills. Thrash was off the radio again. 'Airline personnel frequent the porno places here,' he said. 'The massage parlours, a few quasi-inns that rent rooms by the hour.'

Yes, that was it, of course. 'I want a list of those around the inlet here,' he said. 'Nothing in the city of Atami. He wouldn't have risked that.'

Thrash was on the car radio again, taking notes this time. 'I have three,' he said. 'The Big Times, the

American Jazz, and the Old St Louis. I think we can eliminate the Old St Louis. They keep strict records. It's run by a former Tokyo policeman.'

Goddard nodded. He picked up a road map of the area around the inlet. The roads were in his favour, for this area was still under development and there were only two paved roads that ran around the top of the ridge. One went straight across the spine of the peninsula and the other ran back to join the main highway to Tokyo. Corbett would scarcely try to make it on foot. If he decided to make a run for it, he would have to be in a vehicle of some sort. 'I want Williams and Voigt to cover these two roads at this point,' he said to Thrash, pointing out the two spots on the map. 'I don't think he will try a run, but we will make sure.'

'The Japanese police have already set up blocks,' Thrash said. 'They're checking all outgoing traffic.'

'Then that will make our job easier, won't it?' he said evenly. 'If the Japanese police get him first, we will at least know where he is. I want them up here within ten minutes.'

He walked away, standing in the shade of a tree, looking across the water at the New Atami. The inlet was full of small sailboats, staying well behind a line some fifty feet out from the dock and the Japanese patrol boat. He uncased his binoculars, made a sweep of the dining terrace. The police were much in evidence there but the tables were crowded with Asian men in business suits. It would be possible to station sharpshooters on this side of the inlet to squeeze off a dozen shots apiece and still make an escape. Even at this range he could count on a high percentage of hits.

He went back to the car. 'Patch me in with the General,' he said. He waited patiently and in a few minutes Thrash handed him the car telephone. 'This is Blue Runner,' Goddard said. 'We're all set up here.'

'I'm going to cancel you out,' Klein said. 'We have

254

everything under control here. You can shut down and return to base.'

Goddard shook his head. There would be no attack on the hotel, but he felt Klein did not fully understand the situation. 'I get your message,' he said. 'But I think we can pin down what we're looking for.'

'That won't be necessary. I want your team out of the area.'

The line went dead. He handed the telephone back to Thrash and then turned away, looking at the country-side. He had been given a direct order and he was con-ditioned to accept immediately, without question. But there was a difference in this case because there was more than the company interest at stake here. Corbett had outwitted him twice, once in the hotel, drawing him off balance, and then escaping him again in the house, when he had rushed into the room too quickly, off guard, decked, out like a light.

There was a strong sense of balance in Goddard. Not to get Corbett would leave things uneven and it was always possible that they could blame him for it later, for when things went wrong there was always recrimin-ation and they would be able to claim that he wasn't alert, not on his toes that Corbett should have gotten away from him. It was therefore necessary that he get Corbett, not from any sense of personal vindictiveness (he did not really know the man; he had no feelings to-wards him one way or the other) but because the balance of things required it. The other members of the team knew Corbett had taken him twice and if he gave up, they would certainly regard him with less respect.

'We have been directed to disregard the delegates,' he said to Thrash. 'But we will still get Corbett. I want Page and Guthrie to take the trail along the bluff. I want them to talk to everybody they meet who might have seen Corbett.'

'Whatever you say,' Thrash said. 'In the meantime I

suggest we check out the inns on the list. The American Jazz is the closer of the two.'

'We'll get to that directly,' Goddard said. 'After we check the trails.'

Chapter 2

He had no idea how far he had walked but he knew it was not much farther than a mile, for from his vantage point on the side of the bluff he could still see the New Atami Hotel and the pier. He was still above the fishing village and beyond it, in a rocky area where the winds had hollowed holes in the rock face of the bluff, not caves, no, they were not deep enough for that, but scallops in the hard stone. He was soaked through with sweat; the uniform jacket was dirty where he had fallen during the run.

He sank down in the shade of a tree, listening to the waves breaking below him. The air was stifling; there was not a hint of a breeze. He could hear the distinctive sound of Japanese sirens in the distance and from here he could catch an occasional glimpse of the police cars on the opposite side of the inlet. They had sent a van south of the hotel, the doors opening to disgorge a platoon of policemen who dispersed immediately. On the inlet another patrol boat had appeared and the two had assumed positions a hundred yards to either side of the New Atami pier and they were slowly edging out to increase the security area, talking through bullhorns to the dozens of sailboats becalmed by the lack of any wind.

He heard a babble of voices, looked up to see a group of Japanese Boy Scouts coming along the path. He forced a smile and a wave and they waved back at him and moved on. Time limits again, always time limits, and now a fresh one had been imposed on him. A half hour perhaps before the Scouts reached the fishing village or their bus and heard what had happened and began to chatter about the man they had passed on the path, the word relayed to the police, the shifting of forces to this side of the inlet. He would have no place to go. He would have to move now.

He stood up, examining the uniform, doing his best to brush it off with his hands, picking up the flight bag and taking a narrower path that led in a steep and winding course to the top of the bluff.

As he topped the ridge he stopped, startled. In front of him, in an opening in the trees, a van was parked and a family, European, he supposed, had spread a blanket and a picnic lunch on the grass. The man was nut brown from the sun, wearing ragged trousers that had been cut off at the knees, and he was sitting cross-legged at the end of the blanket, squinting while he tried to re-thread the laces in a hiking boot. The woman was young and lean, as brown as her husband, and the children were small, tow-headed, throwing a ball back and forth at the edge of the clearing. The man squinted up at him, not hostile, no, and spoke to him.

At first Corbett did not catch the language, for in the back of his mind he was considering this family as a means of escape, thinking how simple it would be to draw his pistol and hold that clear-eyed girl-bride hostage against a ride back to Tokyo.

'Quelle heure est-il?' the young man was asking, flat Parisian French, upper class, words formed in a polite fashion, and Corbett managed a smile, taking off his sunglasses, blinking against the bright sunlight as he polished the lenses with a handkerchief.

'My French escapes me,' he said. 'Do you speak English?'

'He wishes to know the time, if you please,' the young woman said, catching one of the children by the arm, applying a handkerchief to the small nose. Corbett rolled his wrist, checked his watch. 'It's approximately three thirty.'

'Thank you very much,' the woman said. 'You are American?'

'Yes, American.' Any thought of using the pistol faded. He would not resort to violence with this family, but he could see himself safely hidden in the back of that van, sharing space with the bedrolls and the cooking utensils. He would have to find a way to bridge the gap between the wish and the reality to persuade them to give him a ride. But the language barrier was there, the husband and wife were chatting back and forth and he felt excluded, standing in a spear of shade from a tree, his mind at a loss for language, for plausible stories, for excuses, for any rationale that would make it possible.

'My husband wishes to know if you are with the Pan American Airways,' the woman said.

'Yes,' he said. 'I'm a navigator, on layover.'

Now the husband began a tirade to his wife, waving the single boot he held in his hand while she nodded and absorbed and Corbett witnessed her struggle to translate what he was saying into English.

'We have come to Japan by your airways,' the woman said. 'And the baggage that contained the boots of my husband has been misplaced somewhere. He wishes to know where he can place the proper complaints in which section. For he has not received satisfaction.'

Corbett shrugged, coughed slightly, placing the sunglasses back on the bridge of his nose, distracted now by the small airplane that seemed to lose altitude almost directly overhead. It was military, American, a small Beechcraft, perhaps, canted at such an angle that he could not read the numerals on the underside of the wings, but his first thought was that it was in trouble and had lost power. It banked slowly, hung suspended for a moment, and then seemed to fall away to begin a sweep of the inlet, almost at the level of the bluff on which Corbett stood. He watched, perfectly quiet, as the plane swept low over the water. Some children were waving, yelling at it from the deck of a sailboat.

The plane angled as if to graze the top of the hydrofoil which was making a turn near the bluff, its blatant horn working against the congestion of sailboats directly in its path, which had forced it to slow to a near halt. And then, from the aircraft, he saw the oblong canister drop, tumbling end over end as the plane accelerated and began to climb, and almost at once the whole area around the hydrofoil was enveloped in a kind of mist that seemed to hang for a moment before it erupted into an explosion, a giant fireball and he made a dive for the two children and took them flat with him as the earth shook.

When he stood up, one of the children was crying, and the inlet was full of steam from the explosion. The hydrofoil had been mangled, the bridge blown away, the decks aflame. As he watched, it continued straight ahead, out of control, smashing through a cluster of burning sailboats until it crashed on the rocks. He could see dozens of sailboats aflame through the mist and he heard the sound of people screaming in agony. The patrol boats were rocking crazily in the heavy swell and the pier was beginning to fill with police and the shrill bleat of whistles.

It was impossible; it was inhuman and yet Klein had done it; that was the first thought to flash through his mind. He had been wrong to underestimate Klein. He had not been after just one delegate. Klein had intended a massacre and here it was. He did not know what kind of weapon had been used, but there was no one left alive on the hydrofoil.

The Frenchman was dancing around on one leg, trying to cram his free foot into the boot while he shouted at his wife who was herding the children into the van before she turned to gather up the blankets and the plates.

'I want to ride with you,' Corbett said to the woman. 'I have to get back to Tokyo.'

The woman said something to her husband, who nodded abruptly and motioned towards the van. Corbett moved into the back with the children. One of them was throwing up and the mother took the sick child on her lap as the Frenchman slammed the van into gear. The roads were congested with traffic, ambulances screaming down towards the inlet, police cars, and throngs of curious tourists who lined the bluff to look down into the holocaust. A heavy pall of smoke had coiled up from the water now and was beginning to drift inland.

'Do you know what happened?' the woman said to him.

'An accident,' Corbett said. 'It appeared to be an accident.'

'My husband says the airplane dropped a bomb.'

'It could be. I don't know.' He leaned back against a pile of sleeping bags. The van lurched to a stop and reflexively, his hand went to his pocket and the small pistol. But through the windshield he could see an ambulance that had smashed into a small car. No injuries. Crowds of Japanese were pushing the ambulance aside to allow the traffic to flow through.

The van lurched forward. The Frenchman turned on the car radio, turned the dial until he found a broadcast in English. The Japanese were fast, Corbett thought, for there was already a bulletin from Atami on the explosion of a hydrofoil containing delegates to the Asian conference. The woman was doing her best to translate for her husband but she had fallen hopelessly behind and he turned the radio off in exasperation. Not one assassination, no, multiple murder, neatly done, and the sweep of events had passed him by now, for the accusations against him were minuscule indeed, compared to this.

And quite without thinking about it, he knew what he had to do, what he would do. The Frenchman was cursing under his breath as the van reached the open highway and headed north. The woman had a sympathetic expression on her face as she smoothed the hair of the sick child with her hand and glanced back at Corbett. 'My husband's feet are hurting,' she said. 'When the baggage was lost by your company, he was forced to buy Japanese boots. They are too small, much too small.'

2

Klein had leaned back in his chair to rest a moment when the fatigue caught up with him and he had dozed off. He had been dreaming that he was in Washington, waiting in a bare room with no doors and a single telephone that would not work. But it took him no more than the fraction of a second to become alert and he picked up the receiver.

'Klein here,' he said.

It was Miller. 'We've just had word from Atami, General. It's already on the wires. There was an explosion on the hydrofoil.'

Klein cleared his throat, sat forward in his chair. 'What's the head count?'

'First reports are unclear. There's an estimate that there were approximately fifty delegates on the boat.'

'Names?'

'No, sir. Not yet. The Japanese police are checking the New Atami to see if they can determine which delegates stayed behind. No, hold on a minute.' There was a pause on the line. 'We have more coming in. Witnesses identified an aircraft, a light plane with American Air Force markings. They say that the aircraft dropped an explosive device.'

'How many civilian casualties?'

'Two hundred and twenty-five dead, at least a hundred wounded. It's a guess at this point.'

Klein did not trust that estimate. Early reports of casualties were always exaggerated and he was sure that the final tally would be considerably lower. 'I want printouts as they come in,' Klein said. 'Take a lead time of thirty minutes and then send out the release to the PR offices. Tell them to hold until we have a definite identification. Has the old man heard yet?'

'I'm not sure,' Miller said. 'He was scheduled for a meeting with the American ambassador this afternoon.'

'Here or at the Embassy?'

'Here.'

He severed the connection, raised himself off the bed, and went into the dressing room to put on fresh clothes. He propped the statement he had prepared for Erikson on the dressing table and scanned it while he put on a conservative suit. Yes, it would do nicely. Once he had dressed he examined himself in the mirror and then he rang Mrs Seagraves. 'This is Klein,' he said. 'Has Mr Erikson completed his meeting with the ambassador yet?'

'As a matter of fact, the ambassador just left,' Mrs Seagraves said. 'And Mr Erikson asked me if I could locate you.'

'I'll be there in a few minutes,' he said.

He put the statement in an envelope briefcase and then took the elevator to Erikson's floor. Mrs Seagraves smiled at him (the old man could be preparing to murder and she would still present the same calm and pleasant façade) and told him Erikson was waiting.

Erikson was standing by the window, looking down at the street, his hands clasped behind his back. 'You son of a bitch,' he said quietly. 'We had an agreement.'

'Yes,' Klein said. He placed his briefcase on a table, proceeded to unzip it.

'I should have known better than to bring you into the company,' Erikson said, turning now, his face calm but flushed deep red. 'As of this moment you are terminated, General. And I intend to turn every scrap of evidence I have over to the prosecuting authorities. Goddamn, how could you underestimate me so completely? You've murdered over two hundred people.'

'That was regrettable,' Klein said. 'I don't like casualties any more than you do.' And briefly he remembered another meeting in the Pentagon, staff Generals, civilians from DOD, and he had been making a presentation, and from the moment he saw their faces he knew the decision had gone against him, even before he spoke a word, even before they had examined any of the evidence. He was in no such position of weakness now, for Erikson could rage all he wished and in the end he would have to acquiesce, one way or another. 'I think you had better hear me out, Mr Erikson. Because there is a lot at stake here.'

The telephone rang. Erikson picked it up. 'No,' he said. 'I haven't agreed to any such goddamned thing.'

'If that's concerning the press conference, I would suggest that you reconsider,' Klein said. Erikson put a shielding hand over the mouthpiece, waiting. 'Now, if you intend to denounce me,' Klein went on, 'that press conference will be the perfect place to do it. ESK is very involved, Mr Erikson. You had better consider that.'

'All right, then, five thirty,' Erikson said into the telephone. 'I'll meet them in the Crystal Ballroom.' He replaced the telephone, continued to stand. 'I'll give you five minutes,' he said.

'It won't take that long. If you will forgive me, sir, I think I will sit down. My leg is hurting me.' He sat down next to the table. 'Now, I can guarantee you that there is no possible way that the aircraft can be connected with ESK. The pilot will ditch off the coast of Honshu and be brought back to Tokyo in the black. The wreckage of the aircraft will be discovered later tonight and it will be assumed that he crashed at sea. In an examination of the pilot's records at Atsugi, it will be discovered that he had a distinguished war record in Vietnam, but that he also underwent psychiatric treatment in Washington and that the treatment was considered successful. The Air Force will come to a conclusion that he had a psychotic episode and that the dropping of the explosive device at Atami was an act of random violence.'

The old man was listening now. He was leaning on a pair of extended hands flattened against the table but his normal colour was beginning to return.

'The Japanesse press will soon discover that there was a summit meeting of executives from major multinationals here in Tokyo and there will be an attempt to tie this despicable act to that meeting. The denials will fall like rain all over the world because no one can afford to admit that violence was even discussed at that high level. At your press conference you will not even mention it, of course. But the countries affected will know damn well what has happened. They will realise that this has been a well-planned operation, not a quirk, not an irrational act. And they will have absolutely no recourse whatsoever. It was a military plane that dropped the device but they can't attack the United States Government. And there's a clear line between the United States and ESK. Who the hell can they blame for this?'

'I would never have approved a strike like this,' Erikson said. 'If you had consulted me, I would have told you to go to hell. I've never done business based on bloodshed. I don't intend to begin now.'

Revisionism, yes, but if Erikson's selective memory included none of the past discussions, Klein would not contradict. He decided to take a different course, to move around Erikson's pride instead of confronting it.

'I take full responsibility for what has happened,' Klein said.

'That's not good enough,' Erikson said. 'The others know goddamned well that this is my operation. I called the meeting.'

'A meeting to discuss parameters of action,' Klein suggested. 'Nothing more than that. They are caught in the same squeeze that affects you. And I would suggest that you wait until you get their reactions before you do anything. I would also suggest that you take the re-action of the South Korean government, whatever it is, as a bell-wether. If they are prepared to contest what you've done, my God, you'll know it within twenty-four hours. They will come down on ESK/KOREA like a ton of bricks. But I don't think they will. Because we have made a forceful preemptive strike. They will sus-pect, and rightfully so, that any action on their part will lead to further counteraction.'

Erikson had turned away. He was pouring himself a brandy, a rather stiff one, Klein realised. 'All those dead and wounded people,' he said softly, thoughtfully.

'Which may prevent a thousand times that many deaths in the long run. If these countries do develop a solid alliance, we'll be in for hit-and-run tactics for the next twenty years. I know these governments. They would not hesitate for a moment to burn our plants and slaughter our people if it would gain them an economic advantage. This is a war, Mr Erikson, a totally different kind of battle, but a war just the same.' He could tell that he had reached the old man now, the processes of rationalisation and pragmatism had begun to take hold in his mind. Erikson was absorbed in thought. He poured a second glass of brandy, placed it in front of Klein.

'I will make a concession,' he said. 'If this action is connected in any concrete way with ESK, I will have you skinned alive, General. I will make it known that I hired you to investigate alternative methods of dealing with political pressures in Asia. I will let it be known that you alone are solely responsible for the slaughter at Atami. I don't want you to have the slightest doubt that I can or will do it.' He finished his brandy. 'Now, I had better consider what kind of statement I am going to make to the press.'

'I have prepared a suggested text,' Klein said, reaching into the briefcase. He put the sheets of paper on the table. 'In brief, you are expressing shock at the outrageous incident at Atami. You are decrying terrorism of any sort and calling on international agencies to draft an agreement between nations on the punishment of terrorists. You are also putting up one hundred thousand dollars reward for anyone furnishing information that will lead to the arrest and conviction of the perpetrators of this act.'

Erikson unfolded his reading glasses, put them on his nose, scanned the text. 'I'll work on this,' he said. The telephone buzzed. He picked it up, spoke into it, then extended it to Klein.

'Yes?' Klein said abruptly.

'We have heard from Thrash,' Miller said. 'He has lost contact with Goddard but he says Goddard is following Corbett. Corbett's in a van with a French family on the Tokaido Expressway, coming back into Tokyo.'

'Goddamn it, I ordered Goddard to move his team out of there.'

'That's what I told Thrash,' Miller said. 'He said he is under Goddard's orders unless he hears directly from you to the contrary.'

'I'll take care of it,' Klein said. 'I'll be there in a few minutes.'

'What's going on?' Erikson said, when Klein was off the telephone.

'We have Corbett spotted. He's on his way back to Tokyo.'

Erikson removed his glasses, stared into space. 'That's too bad,' he said, as if he were speaking to himself. 'I should have known from the beginning that he was too independent to go along. Do we have any word of Cristina?'

'No.'

'Very unfortunate. But she has a remarkable aptitude for survival. I'm not really concerned for her.'

'Yes, sir.'

'I want Corbett,' Erikson said, matter-of-factly. 'I think it will demonstrate our attitude if we hand him over to the American government. But I want it done publicly. I don't want any goddamned intelligence operation sucking him underground. I want to call Senator Hyden personally when we have him.'

'That makes sense.'

'One more thing,' Erikson said. 'When the casualty list comes out, I want the head of operations in any affected country to make a personal call on the family of the deceased to express condolences. We will also send fruit, flowers, whatever is appropriate.'

'That should be most effective,' Klein said, standing up, concealing his elation. 'And now, if you will excuse me, I have a lot of details to take care of.'

3

It was somewhere in Yokohama that Corbett realised the van was being followed. The sick child was asleep on a pile of bedding; the small boy was sitting on a box and watching the traffic through the rear window. The couple were arguing in the front seat, the man muttering in fitful bursts to his wife, who was obviously under attack. Enough of Corbett's French had returned that he could catch the drift of the argument. The husband was suggesting that it was their duty to contact the authorities as witnesses to what had happened and she was countering that this was a part of his sick desire for self-importance, that they had seen nothing that a thousand other people had not seen more clearly. They were supposed to drive to Nikko in the morning, and to get tied up in a fruitless interaction with the police would ruin their vacation.

Corbett was only half listening, for he had seen a small maroon car some distance back in the stream of traffic. Over the miles it seemed to maintain its position relative to the van, slowing when the van slowed, picking up speed when the van accelerated. For a while it was hidden behind a large truck laden with heavy earth-moving equipment and Corbett was almost able to persuade himself that his imagination was distorting reality when the maroon car edged out from behind the truck just long enough to take a sighting and then drifted back in again.

It was neither the Japanese police nor American intelligence, no, for either of these agencies would have taken direct action, the Japanese blocking off the highway, pulling the van to the side, the Americans boxing him in. This would be Klein's men, patiently tracking, for what reason he did not know, an extension of the insanity at Atami, perhaps. He tapped the woman on the shoulder and asked her where they were going and she informed him that they were going to Nikko. 'Where would you like for us to drop you?' she said.

'Any place in the city,' he said. 'It doesn't matter.'

The husband began to swear. The van had been trapped in an exit lane from which it was impossible to escape, egress on the right side blocked by a line of trucks. The van descended into a swarm of traffic clogging narrow streets while the Frenchman leaned on his horn and shouted imprecations out of the window. His wife was on him in a moment, demanding to know what he was doing, what he was thinking, to put them in a situation like this.

Corbett checked the rear window. The maroon car was still following, midway down the off-ramp, seven or eight cars behind now, visibility partially blocked by a panel truck. The Frenchman slammed on the brakes at a red light and in that moment, with no word to anybody, Corbett opened the door and climbed out, carrying his flight bag, threading the slight space between two cars to reach the kerb.

Instantly he realised his mistake; he saw a figure emerge from the maroon car, which was stalled at the foot of the exit ramp. Goddard. If he had stayed with the van, the traffic might have worked in his favour. But now he was on his own with Goddard in pursuit and he ran down the street and into the first wide doorway, finding himself in a department store, totally disoriented. He moved ahead blindly, through crowds of people. A pretty Japanese girl in uniform stood by the escalator, cleaning the moving handrail, and he stepped on to the stairs rising towards the second floor.

Halfway up, he looked back and saw Goddard coming through the door, not swiftly but relentlessly, as if nothing could stop him. His massive head raised and for a moment Corbett was looking into his face, recognition established, and then Corbett stepped off the escalator at the second floor.

He walked into a bank of colour television sets, piled one on the other in a solid wall, all of them alive with film of the destruction at Atami. Time, yes, he needed a few minutes to collect himself, to come up with a plan, for if he acted impulsively, he was lost. Goddard was trained to anticipate the moves of a man running, conditioned as a bird dog to sniff out any place where he might logically come to rest. He moved past the television sets and through the stereos and then ducked into a doorway with a Japanese sign and a smaller misspelled legend: EMPLOYES ONLY.

It was a stockroom, a large area filled with cartons on metal racks, and he zigzagged down the irregular aisles to the far side of the room, sinking down behind a stack of cartons on a loading dolly. He opened the flight bag, hands trembling, seeking the heavier pistol, encountering the mass of papers and credit cards he had taken from Klein. Finally he pulled the pistol from the bag and rested it on his knee.

He could hear two Japanese stock clerks talking, one of them laughing, then the echo of footsteps moving away. A door opened and closed. Silence. Not even piped-in music here. He was alone. He waited, his breathing almost suspended as if he were compressing himself into a very small space. Goddard would be on this floor by now, looking around, trying to psych out the direction he had taken. Impossible, there were too many alternatives, too many ways he could have gone, no visible tracks. He breathed deeply, trying to relax. He had no idea in which section of Tokyo the department store was or how to reach the apartment but he would rent a taxi and play it by ear. He had driven to the apartment once, he could certainly find it again. Cristina came into his mind. She would be back in Tokyo by now.

He went through the yen in his pockets, little left, less than ten thousand yen. He could not have spent that much, but for the first time his mind had lost its capacity to deal with figures. He could not remember how much he had paid for the room in Atami, whether the clerk had given him the right change. He rummaged through the bag, found a five-thousand-yen note, and went through the pages of Klein's passport in the random hope that one of the banknotes had lodged there.

He froze. The door opened. He listened. The door closed. There was someone else in the stockroom, he was sure of that. Motionless, listening. He heard no footsteps. Could he hear the sound of breathing? No, the room was too large for that. He waited. No further sound. Perhaps he had imagined the opening and closing of the door. He was tired; his mind could be deceiving him. He closed his eyes, his ears straining. He jumped slightly, soundlessly.

'I know you're here,' Goddard said in a conversational voice. Corbett did not move. Where was he? How far away? Was he approaching? 'It's my job to take you in and I'm going to do it.' He was moving as he talked. Corbett could detect the change in the pitch of his voice, a shift in acoustics. He lifted the thirty-eight. As he did so, the fabric of his knee scraped a box, no more than a whisper.

Goddard fired, a whomp of compressed gases released through a silencer, the bullet ripping through boxes, the muffled implosion of a crated picture tube. Corbett could not tell where the bullet had gone, how close it had come; he could see nothing from here.

'I have my reputation, you know,' Goddard said, closer now, his voice slightly constricted, not so easy. 'I care what other people think about me. I would rather walk you out of here. But I'll do what I have to.'

Corbett knew he could not stay here. He could not match himself against Goddard's experience. The best he could hope was one wild shot before Goddard closed and killed him. Quietly, he returned the pistol to the bag. He braced himself and then, in a single concerted effort, threw all his weight against the cartons stacked on the dolly, a little startled at their heaviness. They toppled into the aisle with a crash and he scrambled away, running in a half crouch to the door, which opened and spilled him into a corridor.

He could hear the whir of business machines, the clatter of typewriters. Two Japanese secretaries in short skirts stared at him from a coffee machine. The executive wing. He moved around a bend in the corridor, straightening up now, running a hand over his unruly hair, realising how unkempt he looked. Goddard would be right behind, out of the stockroom and into the corridor. A frosted door appeared to his right, marked with Japanese characters, and he went through it, closing it behind him.

An attractive Japanese woman smiled up at him from behind a desk. He went blank for a moment and then cleared his throat and said the first thing that came to mind. 'I want to see the manager of the store.'

She said something in Japanese, apologising, pressing buttons on the desk, and he realised she was summoning someone on the intercom who could speak English. He sat down in a chair partially shielded from the door by a large ceramic lamp. He sat with the bag in his lap

272

and his fingers curled around the butt of the revolver. The positions had been reversed now. There was no way Goddard could come through that door without exposing himself. He willed Goddard to come through that door. He would not hesitate to kill him on the spot.

But Goddard did not come. Instead, in less than a minute, a door opened behind the secretary and Corbett could hear the sound of men singing. A man in a business suit approached him, bowing slightly, a very distinguished-looking man with iron-grey hair. 'I am Mr Yoshida,' he said. 'May I be of service?'

'Are you the store manager?'

'I am the assistant manager,' Yoshida said. 'Mr Watanabe is currently in a meeting.'

That explained the singing, the executives gathered together for a pep rally and a verse or two of the company song. Corbett felt easier now, back in a world he could understand.

'I suppose you can take care of it,' Corbett said, extemporising. 'I have a complaint to make against your store. I realise you can't be responsible for all your employees, but I have been poorly treated.'

'We try to provide an unexcelled standard of service,' Yoshida said. 'If you will come with me, I am certain we can resolve the problem to your satisfaction.'

Corbett followed him through the door behind the desk into a narrow corridor. Yoshida opened a door off the hallway, bowing him in. The office was airy, with a pair of windows overlooking the street. There was an abstract painting on one wall, a massive splash of yellow on a field of red. An abacus sat on the wooden desk, the beads polished with usage. 'Would you care for tea, sir?'

'No, thank you,' Corbett said.

'Then please sit down and tell me your problem.'

'I will ask you to be candid with me,' Corbett said, dissembling slightly, allowing himself room. 'I read the manual before I came to Japan and I'm aware that there are businesses in Tokyo that do not welcome foreigners. If that's your policy, then let me know.'

'We have extensive business with Western visitors,' Yoshida said. 'Our gentlemen's furnishings department is noted for our stock of suits designed to the proportions of the American and the English gentleman. As you may know, the Japanese male is of different proportions and consequently the size printed on a garment is sometimes not accurate by your standards. How have you been offended by our personnel?'

Yoshida was off balance, talking too much. Corbett reached in his bag, pulled out an assortment of Klein's credit cards, spread them on the desk. 'Are any of these accepted in your store?'

'Certainly,' Yoshida said, puzzled.

'And this is my identification,' Corbett said. He placed Klein's passport and ESK identification card on the desk. 'Now, I want you to tell me if this is sufficient identification.'

Yoshida tapped the passport with the tips of his fingers, took only a cursory glance at the ID. 'What is the problem, Mr Klein?'

'I have just flown in from Panama,' Corbett said, the shape of the lie forming itself. 'I am very tired and I need a shave and I am in desperate need of a business suit for a conference. I am suffering from jet lag. My luggage has been lost. So I come in here and I explain what I need to one of your girls and she is totally unco-operative. Do you understand what I mean?'

'She refused to honour your credit cards?'

'She didn't tell me one goddamned thing. She just stared at me.'

'Ah,' Yoshida said, as if he had solved the problem. 'The language. Some of our staff do not speak English. We have language classes, but some of our employees are not yet proficient.'

'It's possible you're right,' Corbett said, allowing himself to be mollified. 'I was expecting everybody to speak

274

English, I guess. I feel rather foolish about this complaint.'

'No, not at all,' Yoshida said earnestly. 'If you can tell me which girl, she would be pleased to have the opportunity to issue you a formal apology.'

'I think I'll let it drop,' Corbett said with a smile.

'You are very generous with your understanding,' Yoshida said. 'I would take it as a personal favour if you would allow us to be of service to you.'

'I appreciate that,' Corbett said. 'Do you have a barber shop?'

'In conjunction with gentlemen's furnishings we have a hair salon.' Yoshida stood up. 'If you will please come with me, I will conduct you myself.'

He followed Yoshida down the corridor to a small elevator. The singing had stopped now and he could hear the store manager talking to his men in the manner of a commander exhorting his troops. Corbett felt reprieved for now, the time for battle past, but only temporarily. There was a lesson here for him and he would pick up on it instantly and base his future upon it. He would never be able to outpower the men like Goddard but he could outwit them and, in the balance, wits were more important than strength. He would outfit himself in the kind of clothes he was not used to wearing, something jaunty perhaps, out of character, and he would have his hair cut short.

The elevator came to a stop on the fourteenth floor and he was ushered into a special room where Yoshida introduced him to a splendidly tailored man named Nogayama. 'Mr Nogayama will bring suits for your inspection to this room,' Yoshida said. 'If you wish, alterations can take place while you are in our hair salon.'

'Good enough,' Corbett said. 'I think I may buy a couple of suits while I'm here. I take it that there's no limit on my credit card?'

'None at all,' Yoshida said. 'We are happy to serve you, Mr Klein.'

4

It was the proper setting for it, Klein realised, for Erikson had picked one of the smaller ballrooms for the press reception, a room decorated in the French manner. Overhead, reflecting the intense lights of the television and film crews, was a gigantic crystal chandelier, patterned after one at Versailles. In such a setting Erikson thrived. From the beginning of the statement, standing behind the polished wood of a podium emblazoned with the company logo, he had reflected an elegant and autocratic certainty. He was very much on command.

Klein sat in the back of the ballroom on a Louis XV chair that he found stiff and uncomfortable, but he was too immersed in Erikson's performance to care. Erikson was just finishing the statement that Klein had prepared for him, adapting it to his own language so perfectly that it seemed extemporaneous.

'Now, if you have any questions,' Erikson said, and immediately a young Japanese reporter from *Shimbun*, known for his incisive attacks, was on his feet.

'Is it not true, sir, that your corporation has grown on an exploitation of the peoples of the Fourth World?' The voice was shrill, challenging. 'Is it not true that you are antinationalistic?'

'I think I can answer that,' Erikson said contemplatively, as if he were considering a response to a difficult query, but Klein knew he was working a draw play, pulling the reporter into an opening.

'The profits from ESK/PHILIPPINES are estimated at two hundred twenty-five million dollars for the current fiscal year,' the Japanese said. 'Is it not true that you are removing a quarter of a billion dollars from this one nation each year?'

'That is a considerably exaggerated figure,' Erikson said easily. 'I do know that we have gone far beyond the guidelines established by President Marcos for employee benefits. We have contributed over twenty million dollars to Program Compassion. In Quezon City we have established low-cost public housing for our workers and a free clinic, by the way, not just for employees but for the general public as well. The infant mortality rate has dropped sixty-three per cent. The minimum wage we pay is five hundred per cent higher than the median weekly household income in Manila.'

He was a statistical orator, fascinating to watch, the torrent of figures pouring out of him until the Japanese correspondent was awash in figures. The press conference was shaping up very well indeed. The company would come out of this meeting with a stronger position than it had occupied before. The television lights reflected in Erikson's reading glasses; he seemed to radiate light. Klein waited for the planted question to arise and now it came, through an American correspondent who stood up to be recognised by Erikson.

'Your company has been requested to testify before the Senate Multinationals Committee concerning the purchase for resale of American arms abandoned in Vietnam. Do you intend to comply with the Senate request?'

Erikson leaned forward slightly, placing both hands before him on the lectern. 'I'm glad to deal with that question. I think we had better clarify the situation, however, because the company has not been asked to testify. The charges, if you can call them that, have been made against one employee of ESK, one of a quarter million employees, I might add. Any of us, and I speak for all of the men and women who are a part of ESK, any of us will be glad to co-operate with the United States Senate at any time, in any way. Because we realise that such a magnitude of weaponry could be used

277

to equip a terrorist operation against one of the smaller countries, for whatever reason, and that country would have little chance of defending itself. If those weapons are in the Far East, for example, they could very easily determine the balance of power. The incident at Atami today is a powerful indicator of what devastation even the smaller weapons technology can cause in the wrong hands.'

There it was, the spelling out of the new policy in terms that any astute Asian politician could understand, a very subtle conveyance, to be sure, but unmistakable. Klein raised himself up on his cane and left the ballroom. He took the elevator up to the computer floor, not bothering to go through security but limiting himself to the nonsensitive area, where Miller and Stevens were taking printouts from three chattering terminals, sorting them into piles.

'We're catching hell,' Stevens said. 'South Korea and the Philippines are putting pressure on both the United States and Japan to investigate any possible connection we might have with Atami.'

'What's the position of the Japanese government?'

'They're boiling, to say the least. They're having to deal with thousands of Japanese students snake-dancing in front of the American Embassy. They all feel that their territory has been fouled. They have the plane tagged from Atsugi. My God, they have enough pictures of the bombing to cover a wall. But the American military is stonewalling it for the time being. The word's leaked out that they had a wacko who ran amok. That's all they're going to have. They'll be forced to give that much to the Japanese government tomorrow.'

'Any mention of the plane yet?'

'No. They won't get on that track until everything else simmers down.'

'Do we have a confirm on Webster?' Klein said to Miller and recognised immediately that something about

278

Miller had changed. Miller did not look up; he continued to shuffle through the printouts.

'He was picked up at seventeen twenty-two hours. The plane was ditched without a trace. He should be in Nagoya by now.'

'Come with me,' Klein said. 'I think we could both use a drink.'

In his quarters he poured a Scotch for Miller and then one for himself. 'What's wrong with you, Jack?' he said. 'Are you getting yellow fever?'

Miller shrugged. He rolled the ice in his glass and then drank, his head tilted back. His neck was scrawny, birdlike. 'I'm going home, General,' he said. 'I can give you two weeks' notice, a month if you like, but I've had enough.'

'I can't replace you, Jack,' Klein said. 'You've been with me how long, over ten years, isn't it? My God, we've been through a lot together.'

'I'd like another drink.'

'Sure.'

He sat slumped over, the glass cradled in his hands. 'I managed to take it in the military, you know that, General. I never backed down.'

'No, you never quit on me.'

'I never liked the military,' Miller said. He drank the glass halfway down. 'Some parts of it were all right but I never got used to the killing.'

He finished the drink and Klein filled the glass again. He knew what was troubling Miller. He had seen it before, the inability of a man to disassociate himself from the consequences of a military action. But of course it would not do to have Miller going back to the States because he was a potentially lethal weakness. He knew, he had been a part of, he had witnessed, and despite his professed good intentions and the loyalty of a long relationship, the time would come when he had had too much to drink in that small town in California and out would come the guilts, the doubts, and along with them a few shreds of fact, and the elaborate scheme could begin to unravel.

'Have you seen the Japanese pictures?' Miller said. 'Jesus, they have this shot that was taken of a family sailing, a man and his wife, and their little girl. And they have another picture after the blast, the sailboat burning, blood and flesh blown all over everything, scraps of people. Now, I ask you, General, what in the shit does that have to do with anything?'

'Nothing,' Klein said. 'It was a terrible thing, a mistake.'

'You admit it, then?' Miller said, startled. His glass was empty again. Klein filled it. 'You admit the whole goddamn thing was a bloody mistake?'

'A very bad one,' Klein said. 'You know me better than anybody alive, Jack. I make bad judgements sometimes, like anybody else. So I have to live with them. But we can avoid another incident like that.' He fell silent, watching. Miller was very drunk now. He had probably been drinking all evening. 'I think you need a couple of weeks R-and-R,' Klein said.

'No, sir. Edna's back in California. Her husband died, someplace in New Jersey, I think. There's a chance we might get together again.'

'Bring her over here. We'll send a plane for her.'

'She won't come. We used to have bitter fights about my going overseas. No, that wouldn't work. I'm going back and I'm going to open a hardware store.'

'I won't try to talk you out of it, Jack,' Klein said. 'I hate to see you go, but that's your decision after all. I would appreciate it if you would give me a month to try to fill in the gap.'

He sent the bottle with Miller, knowing that he would finish it off and be out for the next eighteen hours. Once he was alone, he realised that the time had come to begin to implement some of the procedural plans he had been making, for the structure he had created was sufficient for only a small-scale operation and his preliminary plan was outgrowing its original boundaries.

He went to his office and punched into the programme on the terminal, asked for material on Thrash, G. P. In a moment the display rolled on to the screen and he leaned back in his chair, pressing the tips of his fingers together as he studied it. Thrash was a physically small man but very quick-witted. Klein had been impressed by his regard for orders this afternoon in his insistence on following Goddard's instructions until directly countermanded by Klein himself. Thrash was in his late thirties and had been trained by the FBI, serving as a special agent in Florida until he was recruited by ESK. Klein put in a tracer call for Thrash and within minutes Thrash was in his office, openly curious.

'Sit down,' Klein said. 'Do you know where Goddard is?'

'No,' Thrash said. 'That's not my business to know.'

'He's off on his own chase,' Klein said. 'What do you think of him as a team leader?'

'Do you want my candid opinion?'

'Of course. I wouldn't ask otherwise.'

'He's just short of being psychotic,' Thrash said. 'He's obsessive and so goddamn spaced out that he makes the men nervous. We have some good boys, General, but Goddard spooks them.'

'That's my opinion as well,' Klein said. 'So from this moment I am making you my special assistant. You will be working closely with me and you will be in direct charge of the security personnel.'

'I see.'

'You don't like the idea?'

'I like it very much,' Thrash said. 'But I don't know what it entails. I would like to know the chain of command, the policy, and how much authority I'm going to have.'

'That's a simple matter,' Klein said. 'You will take orders directly from me. I will be making the policy. Now, as to how you carry out your assignments, that will be up to you, but I will expect you to clear any major changes with me first. As to the personnel under you, you can hire and fire and rank them any way you wish. I want you to enlarge the security force, first of all, fifty men to be assigned here. Within the next month, you will be putting together large security teams to be stationed in Manila, in Seoul, and a number of other places. We have been advertising for ex-military men with specialised skills, so we have a sizeable file.'

'Security teams,' Thrash said, a knowing glint in his eye.

'I think we understand each other,' Klein said.

'This policy of yours,' Thrash said. 'How much of it will I know about?'

'Very little at first, if you're talking about overall plans. You'll be replacing Miller as my aide and Goddard as well. As the situation develops, you will be fully informed. I need a decision right away so I suggest you think about this tonight and we'll talk more in the morning.'

'Fine.'

The telephone rang and Klein picked it up. Stevens was on the line. 'The lost sheep has been heard from,' Stevens said.

'Goddard?'

'Yes. He just called computer, requested a patch on the Metro interface. He wants to know what the Tokyo police have picked up on Corbett.'

'Go ahead and give it to him,' Klein said.

'Give it to him?' Stevens said, startled. 'I thought you wanted him recalled.'

'He's of no further use to us,' Klein said. 'Let him track Corbett down. If we're lucky, he'll find him and cancel himself out.'

'All right,' Stevens said. 'Will do.'

5

The visual disturbances had begun to return again, migraine, and Goddard's vision was distorted. It seemed as he sat in the small Japanese bar that he could not focus his eyes properly. There was a blind spot in the centre of his vision and smaller jagged bars across the retina that were apparent even when he closed his eyes. He had learned to go into them rather than to resist. The trick had been taught to him by a doctor at Bethesda, a young man fresh out of medical school, who had attributed these episodes to stress and told him to relieve them through relaxation, through experiencing rather than denying. So he continued to look straight ahead, at a hostess perched on a bar stool, the shape of a woman dressed in black satin. Her face was blurred. He could only see it peripherally.

He signalled a waitress to bring him more coffee. He felt that they would be quite pleased if he left, for he did not see another white face here and he had the feeling the bar was exclusively Japanese. But he could not leave because the circle was narrowing, constricting, closing in, and he was determined to be at the centre of it when it finally closed.

He had not lost his head after the incident in the stockroom. Instead, he had taken an available seat in the credit office and waited for the destruction in the stockroom to be discovered. It did not take long. In less than five minutes the corridor was buzzing with minor executives and store detectives and then he approached one of the officials, a thin man with a gold tooth, and suggested that he could be of service in this matter and told the official to call Nakamura of the *gaijin* detail. In the interim, while waiting, Goddard was served Japanese tea and a kind of pastry that he did not like, but he ate it anyway, knowing that if things went well he would probably not have the chance to eat again for many hours and his body required fuel, calories.

When Nakamura arrived, he asked Goddard into a private office, politely, and closed the door.

'I am Goddard, ESK security,' Goddard said. And he launched into his story. He had never been good at extemporising a fiction because he felt more comfortable with hard facts, but in a way what he said was true, with no more than a few alterations. He told Nakamura he had trailed Corbett into this store, that Corbett had spotted him and moved into the stockroom, that when Goddard followed, Corbett had fired at him with a pistol and made his escape into the executive corridor. At that point Goddard had lost him.

Nakamura looked puzzled. 'Why did you not tell all this to the store officials earlier?' he said, lighting a cigarette, almost delicately, placing it to his lips as if he were tasting rather than smoking it. Wisps of smoke trailed out of his nostrils.

'They are not competent to handle this,' Goddard said. 'I wanted them to call you because I think Corbett is still in the building.'

'*Ah, so desuka?*' More smoke wisping from the apertures in the broad face. 'How do you come to that conclusion?'

'I know his pattern. I think he's still here,' Goddard said.

'I don't mean to offend you,' Nakamura said, 'but this store is a very large place. Do you have any idea where he might be hiding?'

'No,' Goddard said.

When Nakamura began his search Goddard returned to the waiting room, sitting on one of the chairs, which he found slightly too small for his build, a chair designed for the smaller frame of the Japanese, he imagined. He sat there for what seemed like hours while the Japanese police went through the building. Finally Nakamura had returned, summoning him to the office again, lighting up another cigarette.

'Klein,' Nakamura said.

'Klein?'

'The name of your superior.'

'That's correct.'

'Do you know if Corbett had occasion to come into possession of his credit cards?'

'That's possible, yes.'

'He has charged some clothing here in the name of Klein.'

'You have him then.'

'No, unfortunately, he left some time ago.'

Goddard's pulse quickened but he made no show of it. To reveal too much interest now would be to blow the whole thing. 'What kind of clothing did he buy?'

'That is a matter for the Japanese police,' Nakamura said. 'I appreciate your efforts, Mr Goddard, but our laws have priority here.'

'I wouldn't interfere with you,' Goddard said. 'I'm under orders to co-operate fully, as a matter of fact. We have a number of men looking for him and if we spot him, we'll forward the information to you and let you handle it.'

Smoke again, oozing from the contemplative mouth. 'He bought two suits of informal styling,' Nakamura said. 'When he left the store he was wearing a coat with blue stripes against a white background and blue trousers.'

'Royal or navy?'

'I beg your pardon?'

'Light or dark blue?'

'A medium colour. He also had his hair cut short and the colour changed.'

'What colour?'

'A tint. Red.'

'Red?'

'Yes.'

Goddard nodded appreciatively. Corbett had been extremely clever to take the opportunity to change his

285

appearance at this point, to shuck the airlines uniform and alter the gestalt. It made Goddard feel much better to be up against a worthy adversary, somebody with imagination, not just a businessman in a state of panic. For in the end that would have been no victory at all, not nearly enough to balance the episode in the hotel kitchen in Los Angeles. Who would have suspected that small dark man with no record of violence whatsoever, a man of rather simple ideas, as it turned out, would have produced a pistol out of nowhere and destroyed one of America's last hopes while Goddard was still blocked in by the crowd trailing after the man Goddard was assigned to protect? A stupid act, a senseless one, carried out by a man who was meek when captured, mute when interrogated, simplistic in his political theories, and no one would have suspected him because this insignificant man was unworthy of being suspected.

But Corbett, on the other hand, had proven himself sophisticated. There was more to him than Goddard had thought there was. To bring him down would involve skill. Goddard looked at Nakamura. 'Do you mind a word of personal advice?'

'No,' Nakamura said.

'Cigarettes will kill you,' Goddard said. 'That's not just opinion. It's scientific fact.'

'True,' Nakamura said. 'It is a dirty habit. Nevertheless, I am addicted. Now, I wish to have your guarantee that from this moment on, Corbett is a matter for the police. Our claims have precedence.'

'Certainly,' Goddard said. 'He belongs to you. We intend to help you net him.'

'I am pleased that we understand each other,' Nakamura said.

He needed nothing more from the Japanese, for there was an intercept on all police communications and the information was fed into the computer. All that remained now was for Goddard to insure that he had access to that information.

He felt it necessary to demonstrate to the Japanese that he had no further interest in the matter so he left the department store and walked down the boulevard until he found a small movie theatre. He bought a ticket and went inside, certain that Nakamura would have him followed and that this act would be sufficient to mollify the police. He took a seat in the back. The theatre stank of fish and he saw three workingmen in baggy coats sitting in front of him, eating rice and fish out of flat tin boxes, watching the giant images of ritualised violence on the screen, two medieval warriors exploding into a series of apparently aggressive motions, swords swinging without clashing, falling into immobile posturing before they repeated the action. Only this time a razor-sharp blade glided across flesh, elicited a keen red line that oozed drops of blood, and the action was repeated again and again, more slashes, more blood, until in a final burst of effort, holding the long handle of the sword with both hands, the smaller of the warriors swung with all his strength, a wide slicing sweep and the glittering blade cut his opponent in half.

Not real, no, screen tricks, or perhaps it was that modern violence on a one-to-one level was simpler. The killing of the man in the library, no sweat, the pressure of a finger on a thin trigger, a resultant single hole with life released, the body jerking forward to the desk, convulsive. The man did not matter to him one way or the other for he had been ordered to do it and the decision-making power was the larger force and he assumed there was good and sufficient reason for the man to be killed.

Corbett, however, was a different matter, a personal symbol. Let Corbett represent x and the equation would then be $x - x = 0$, the equation representing the preferable state. Or representing himself as y, $x/y = 0$. And Klein was testing him here, of course, not really calling him off but pretending to, in order to determine whether he had the stuff to bring it off by himself. Klein did not think he could do it; that was obvious. This supreme expression of doubt was at the same time the strongest challenge to his abilities and he was obliged now to follow through and prove himself.

When he left the theatre it was dark and he was sure that whoever had been following him had long since moved on. The whole sky was ablaze with reflected lights on the low clouds. The migraine had begun to set in; he could feel its approach, the general uneasiness in his skull. He would not let it stop him. He resolved to be patient, knowing that the Japanese police did not move with any great speed. The city was huge and their department was stratified (he could remember an instructor in Washington referring to their process as a series of filters, progressively smaller, so that at the bottom they were always left with the man they wanted) and despite the computerised central headquarters, they would have to wait until all the reports came in from taxi drivers and block captains and local residents concerning unfamiliar foreigners in their neighbourhoods.

It was only as he found the bar and went in to order coffee that the migraine came upon him in full force, the terrible heaviness in his head, the split vision, the slight queasiness in his stomach. He drank coffee for a while and waited and then decided to call computer contact to see if they would co-operate with him. If they refused, he would find a way to get the information out of Nakamura. He would not give up. There was no telephone in the bar so he went outside and found a red plastic box phone.

When he called computer contact Stevens answered. He did not like Stevens, for Stevens was an intellectual, and in his knowledge of computers exuded the feeling that he possessed secrets to which no other man had access.

'This is Goddard. I want a patch into Metro.'

'I don't think you're going to get it,' Stevens said. 'It

288

has to be cleared through Klein himself and I don't know if he's available.'

'Tell him I can find Corbett.' He looked towards the street, the lights of the cars. His vision was still blurred. It pleased him that there was no way Stevens could know of his present weakness.

'Hold the line,' Stevens said. Goddard stood by the telephone, considering the future. Once he had proven himself again, he could go back to the States and take a long rest in New Hampshire and then go back to Washington and take up his career again, for they had not fired him. They had simply recommended that he be moved to a less critical position. He had liked Washington, the small apartment in Georgetown.

'Are you there?' Stevens said, finally, coming back on to the line.

'Yes.'

'You have permission to go on line with the Metro patch. I'll give you the telephone number for direct access. Do you have a pencil?'

'I can remember it.'

'All right. Zero three, seven six five, nine two.'

He depressed the connection, inserted another aluminum coin. That was one of the reasons he did not like Japan, their coins, all aluminium, lightweight, insubstantial. A man could not balance a pile of them in his hand and know that they were money. He dialled the number. A woman was on the line, no greeting, just a repetition of the last four digits of the number.

'This is Goddard. I have authorisation,' he said. 'I want any data you have on Corbett, William J.'

'Just a moment.'

She was clearing him now and he could envision the workings of the machine, the computer that picked up all the Japanese messages and translated them and kept the information filed and sorted.

'You have been cleared,' she said. 'We have a dispatch, time eighteen thirty-two, filed by Ito Abe, Taxi

289

Registration one seven nine six Zebra. He picked up a Caucasian matching the Corbett description in Ginza Ward Seven Cho Six at fifteen twenty-two and left him at the Tokyo Tower. Do you want the Ward number?'

'No.'

'At eighteen thirty-three, the information was logged into the Metro Central Computer and dispatched to seventeen precinct police stations under their standard watch order. There have been no precinct reports.'

'Thank you,' he said. He replaced the telephone and moved away from it. From here he could see the peak of the Tokyo Tower in the distance, the lights flashing from the antennae, not directly, only peripherally, for the centre of his vision was smudged. And somewhere in that general area, Corbett would be holed up, for he had little freedom of movement and would not trust public transportation. He would have walked and in that perambulation somebody would have seen him and sooner or later the word would be flashed. He would have to make certain he was in a position to act on it as quickly as the police.

He waved down a taxi and with some difficulty managed to convey to the driver that he wanted to go to the Tokyo Tower. Then he leaned back against the seat and closed his eyes. An hour, perhaps two, no more than that, and then he would go back to the hotel. He could picture the clean, cool sheets, the chill of the air conditioner and the silence. He needed sleep and soon he would have it.

6

Corbett lay on the divan, watching the films on television, and it did not surprise him that the Japanese had so complete a record. They were notorious camera freaks, and there were films of the air attack from three different angles. He watched them, mesmerised, one in

290

slow motion from the Ned Atami dock, the hydrofoil moving sleek and silver against the blue waters of the inlet, beginning a wide slow sweep through the triangular multicoloured sails, and there was the indistinct figure of a man on the deck, waving back towards the camera. When the plane approached, it was no more than a dark speck in the air that gradually took the form of a light military aircraft and it was in the picture for a moment above the bluffs and then it went out of frame. When it entered again it was flying low, wobbling slightly, and the canister that tumbled out of it looked like a small garbage can, tumbling end over end.

The can itself did not explode. Someplace over the hydrofoil it seemed to rupture, releasing a spray of gas, very light in colour, a gas that expanded rapidly into a cloud hanging over and beyond the hydrofoil while the can tumbled past the bow and into the water. And then the whole cloud of gas ignited instantaneously, a single bright flash, which in an instant crushed the hydrofoil and set the sails of the small craft ablaze.

'My God,' Ellen said, sitting down on the couch beside him. 'How many times will they run that horrible thing?'

'Until they can absorb it,' he said, taking the drink from her.

There was a still photograph on the screen now, the face of an air force Major in uniform, a clean-cut man in his thirties, sincere eyes, the hint of a smile.

'Is that the man they think did it?' she said.

'I don't understand Japanese that well,' he said. 'But I'd bet that he's the man they've picked for it.'

'Is it all right with you if I turn the set off? Have you seen enough?'

'More than enough.'

But as she reached the set he stopped her, for there on the screen was his own face, a company photograph, his passport picture, he could not remember which, and he listened intently to the Japanese newscaster as if by sheer concentration he would be able to understand

291

something of what was being said. But he could not.
They showed another picture of him, with changes made
by an artist, his hair now close-cropped red, wearing the
suit he had worn on leaving the department store. Somehow under the artist's brush his face had become menac-
ing.

She turned the set off. The screen went dark but he
was left with the heaviness of the imprint. The search
for him would be intense now. He tried to remember all
the people he had seen on the walk here from the Tokyo
Tower but he could remember no more than the vast
crowds of people around the tower itself and a few
Japanese in the less congested lanes. Would any of them
remember him, connect him with this face on the television screen?

Ellen sat down beside him again, a perplexed expression on her face. 'There must be somebody you can
call,' she said. 'Somebody.'

'Who?'

'I don't know who. Friends in the company, maybe.
Friends in other companies.'

He shook his head, drank from the glass. 'There are
one or two in Paris, maybe, another in Washington. And
if I called them, all they could do is to commiserate. I
have two governments and the company after me now.'

'All right,' she said. 'Then I'll use my friends. We'll
find somebody else to get you aboard a plane.'

'No,' he said.

'What kind of answer is that? I don't see that you
have a hell of a lot of options at this point.'

'Some,' he said, drinking again. He did not like what
he was about to do. He did not approve of it because he
would have liked to be able to handle things by himself but the time was past when that was possible. Now,
despite the fatigue, a general lack of feeling, he knew
he was going to have to move or be trapped. It was as
simple as that. If the Japanese found him first, he would
spend years in Sugamo Prison, for they would release

against him the accumulated outrage from the Atami incident. If the Americans caught him, he would be taken back to Washington and they would find laws to convict him for the sale of the Vietnamese arms, for the level of frustration in the world was far too great for them to do otherwise.

If the company found him, he was convinced he would be killed, quickly and simply; he would cease to exist and the evidence of his guilt would be produced to stand uncontradicted.

'I don't see any of your alternatives,' Ellen said.

'They're not the best, I'll admit that,' he said. 'I'm a great believer in looking at things the way they really are. Now, I don't intend for them to catch me sitting. I intend to put up a hell of a fight in some way but I have very little conviction that it will make the slightest bit of difference in the end. The most that I can do, probably, is to be a temporary embarrassment.'

'Then listen to me,' she said, taking hold of his hand. 'The odds are very long against you, true?'

'Very long.'

'Any way you go.'

'Yes.'

'Then why not try it my way? There's a possibility we can get to South America. I care about what happens to you, Willie. I may not tomorrow or next week and a year from now I may not like you at all, but right now I happen to love you. I don't want you to stay here. I want to live with you for a while.'

'I would like that.'

'Then it's settled.'

'No,' he said.

'Your attitude doesn't make any sense.'

'It's not logical,' he said, putting his hand against her face. 'Nothing at all is logical to me at this point. I saw a great many people slaughtered at Atami, just for the sake of Klein's goddamned escalation. Somebody I liked very much was killed minutes before I saw his body. I was angrier than hell at that because Wilson had done nothing against them. And maybe I felt guilty because he wouldn't have been killed except that he was associated with me.' He shrugged. 'I don't have that burning feeling any longer. I don't have any feelings at all. I am damn well going to do as much damage to Erikson and Klein and the company as I can, but that's a decision, not a feeling. Does that make any sense to you?'

'No,' she said.

He smiled slightly. 'I want you to do something for me.'

'What?'

'There's a restaurant a couple of blocks from here. I want you to bring us noodles from that restaurant but I want you to take time doing it. I want you to be aware of the traffic on the street, the people, whether there are any taxis in this district. And I want you to see if the police have moved in.'

She stood up, putting on her shoes, looking at him rather wistfully. 'You're not just getting me out of the way, are you?'

'No,' he said, candidly. 'I would like to get you out of the way, but I can't afford to.'

Once she was gone, he poured the contents of the flight bag on to the coffee table to tally his resources. First, the two pistols: he took the small one, wiped it carefully with a towel and returned it to the drawer from which he had originally taken it. The thirty-eight he laid to one side. It was easy to fall into the same position as the rest of them, to become like Goddard, who was capable of killing on a small scale, or Klein, whose scale was a large one. He himself was capable of violence. He had demonstrated that. It was likely he would have further use for the weapon.

The only thing comparable with force (direct or threatened) was money and he had little of that left, no more than twenty thousand yen. Klein's credit cards were now useless to him. The wallet itself was empty, a quality lizard skin, oversized to accommodate the large Japanese banknotes.

The small memo book was bound in the same kind of lizard skin. He found it intriguing. Klein had headed the first page TEMPLE DOGS in minuscule block letters and beneath the words were a series of numbers which, from their arrangement, Corbett assumed to be birth-dates. That was a standard company practice to conceal confidential operations, stemming, Corbett supposed, from the days during World War II when Geneen of ITT had coded the cities of the world according to the first names of company managers resident in those cities. There was a certain appropriateness in Klein's labelling his security forces TEMPLE DOGS after Erikson's pre-occupation with those silent guardians of the Japanese shrines.

Another page was headed SHORTFALL in the same block letters. Beneath it the word was separated into two, SHORT FALL, and there were six groups of numbers below that. They could have great significance or none at all. *Shortfall*, as one word, was a financial term. Perhaps *short fall*, as two words, was a play on words, a code name for the strike at Atami, the dumping of the low-level canister bomb. The numbers were obviously coded, but what they represented was beyond him.

On other pages of the notebook, hastily scrawled in contrast with the precise lettering on the first two pages, was trivia, a reminder to have a prescription refilled, a telephone number blocked in with doodles that re-sembled teeth, obviously drawn while he was on the telephone. On another page was an itinerary, names of Japanese towns, written in haste. Important or signifi-cant, something or nothing, he had no idea. He put the notebook in his pocket, set the flight bag aside in favour of the attaché case.

He heard a sound at the door. Reflexively, he picked

up the pistol. A key turned in the lock and Ellen let herself in. Her face was pale.

'I didn't get to the restaurant,' she said. 'There are Japanese police out on the boulevard.'

'How many of them did you see?'

'I walked to the end of the lane. There was one police car parked down towards the restaurant, another in the direction of the tower. The men around them were just waiting.'

'They're moving in faster than I thought they would.'

'What do we do now?'

'Call the hotel, the tourist side. Make a reservation for Mr and Mrs Richard McGuiness.'

'The hotel?' she said, startled. 'You're out of your gourd.'

'It's our best shot,' he said. 'I don't think they'll expect that. And find out the rates. I only have twenty thousand yen left.' He went into the bedroom, taking a suitcase from the closet. He threw in the rest of the clothes he had bought at the department store. The thirty-eight he put into his pocket. He found a formless Irish tweed hat on a shelf, jammed it on to his head. It was slightly too large but it covered the hair. Jesus, he was tired and guilty at the same time, guilty because he was exposing her to all this and he wanted to tell her to go to someplace safe but to do that would leave him to the mercy of the Japanese police. They would be looking for a man moving by himself.

When he went back into the living-room Ellen was on the telephone. She covered the mouthpiece with her hand. 'They only have a suite.'

'How much?'

'Thirty-two thousand.'

'Jesus Christ.'

'I have some money. I think we can cover it between us.'

He nodded and she confirmed the reservation, then proceeded to go through her purse. She was an organised, efficient woman. The bank notes were folded in her purse and she smoothed them out, one by one. She had approximately twenty-five thousand yen, more than enough.

He moved to the window, looked out, but he could see no stir of movement in the lane. He turned back to her. 'Now, listen to me carefully,' he said. 'I think it's about a mile and a half to the hotel and we're going to have to walk. There's not a cab driver in the area who hasn't been alerted by now.'

'All right,' she said.

'I'm not through. We'll stick to the side streets, the lanes, the alleys as much as possible. Now the odds are better than fifty-fifty that they're going to spot me. If they do, if I see that I have to make a run for it, we split up on the spot. You go into the first restaurant, the first store, any public place that's open and you stay there until the police clear out of the area. Understood?'

'Who's to decide that?' she said.

'I am.'

'No,' she said. 'I'll make my own decision.'

'Look,' he said, frustrated. 'We don't have time to argue.'

'Then you're going to have to take me on my own terms, aren't you?' she said.

He shrugged, accepting. He moved through the apartment, turning out the lights in the bathroom and the bedroom, finally clicking off the lamp in the living room. He pulled back the drape, looked down into the lane. There were two Japanese university students, shaggy-haired, dressed in dark blue uniforms, standing in the soft spill of light from an open gate. There was the flare of a lighter; one of them was lighting a cigarette for the other. He waited for them to move but they did not. A conversation on a summer night and it could last for hours. He had no time to wait.

'We'll have to risk it,' he said. He picked up the suit-case and the attaché case and followed her out into the darkness locking the door behind him. They approached the students and one of the boys looked up at him, smiled, bowed politely.

'Good evening, sir.'

'Good evening,' Corbett said, pleasantly, continuing to walk but he was brought up short by the student's voice, another question, and he knew he could not walk away without arousing suspicion, without implanting himself in the student's memory.

'Excuse me, sir,' the student said. 'But are you American?'

'No,' Corbett said. 'English.'

'Ah,' the student smiled. 'Thackerlay.'

'I beg your pardon?'

'Thackerlay. The very famous novelist.'

'Thackeray,' Corbett said, his eyes moving past the student. On the distant boulevard there were lights. He could see a police car moving.

'Yes, Thackeray. Do you English agree in our fine estimate of his talents?'

'Quite so,' Corbett said. There was irony here, for he felt pinned by the conversation, rooted to the spot, as if he could not leave to save his life except by permission of these two students who wanted to practice their English. A question, yes, that was what he needed to break free. 'How long would you say it would take to walk to the Tokyo Tower?'

The two students lapsed into Japanese, discussing the question. 'Not very far,' one said. 'Ten minutes.'

'Thank you. Have a pleasant evening.'

'Excuse me, sir. Do you have the correct time?'

'I'm afraid I can't help you. My watch is broken.'

'Ah,' the student said.

'Have a good evening.'

He left the students behind and walked on, keenly aware of the woman whose arm was linked in his. Very soon he realised that the police were not going to pick him up on the streets, not now, for the whole of Tokyo

298

was as some gigantic maze teeming with people, especially at this time of night. With so many foreigners in the crowds the odds were immense against the police being able to sort him out so quickly.

The problem then was the hotel, which loomed before him after a twenty-minute walk, the twin towers, and even from a distance he could see that the night traffic was no lighter than the day's. There was a string of limousines in front of the company tower; high-level meetings were in progress, the pace of business continued unabated. There was a swarm of taxis in the circular drive approaching the tourist wing and his chances of passing through unrecognised would be small indeed. She sensed his apprehension. Her fingers tightened on his arm.

'I don't think this is such a good idea,' she said.

'It'll have to do,' he said. 'I'm going to put you in a taxi. Use a bellhop, complain a lot, look bedraggled. I want you to appear like a tired tourist who wants your room right now.'

'I won't have to pretend. But aren't you coming with me?'

'No. But if I have any luck, I won't be far behind.'

He stepped to the kerb, held up three fingers to indicate he would pay triple fare and in a few moments a small kamikaze taxi darted out of the solid stream of traffic, the automatic back door hissing open. He put the bags beside her in the taxi, feeling terribly alone and yet relieved at the same time as the taxi pulled off down the street.

Something was aquiver within him, a visceral trembling as he contemplated the space between him and the impersonal safety of the hotel room. How far was it, a horizontal quarter of a mile, a couple of hundred vertical feet? He decided on the service entrance of the unfinished arcade, counting on the propensity of the Japanese contractors to work night shifts, around the clock. There would be workmen who would see him, of course, but he did not believe he would have any trouble getting past them.

He did not follow the main boulevard but instead took a winding alley that he hoped would lead him to the service entrance in a circumspect manner, but within minutes he found himself in a typical Tokyo labyrinth of noodle stalls and fences and small business buildings, all jumbled together with a complete lack of uniformity, and down one of their narrow side streets another of their goddamned festivals was in progress, the din of tight drums, the throaty squeal of the wooden flutes, masses of young men naked to the waist, bearing a platform and a portable shrine. Nearby, blocking off motorised traffic, was a pair of uniformed Japanese patrolmen.

He reversed his direction and in a few minutes found himself near the service entrance to the hotel, recognising with a sinking hope the absence of the crowds of workmen on which he had been counting. There was no activity at the loading dock, none, the empty platform illuminated by batteries of floodlights.

He lighted a cigarette and waited, hearing in the distance the irregular beat of the drums and the shriek of the flutes against the steady roar of the traffic from the distant expressway. He stood in the shadow of a dumpster, a trash container the size of a small shed. As he watched the loading platform, an old Japanese emerged from the door to the side of the dock and proceeded in a slow and methodical gait down the platform, testing the handles of each of the overhead docks in turn until he had reached the far end of the dock where he stood looking up at the sky. He took a pinch of tobacco from a small tin, inserted it in the bowl of a tiny pipe, and lighted it with a match. A relic of the past, the old habits, the conservation of cigarette butts for use in pipes.

The old man did not realise how close to death he was, standing there, for Corbett meant to have access

300

through that door, despite the cost. He was single-minded now. He could picture the room, Ellen waiting for him, the door locked securely behind him. On impulse, he lifted one of the metal flaps on the trash container and, seeing the masses of paper and crushed cardboard inside, flicked his lighter into flame and ignited one protruding corner of the paper. He moved off to the opposite side of the alley, his heart pounding.

At first it seemed that the flame would not catch; the paper appeared to smoulder and then, quite suddenly, there was a flash and flames leaped out of the rectangular opening. He ran towards the loading dock, yelling fire, and the old man took note now, a delayed reaction, not moving, as if he could not immediately comprehend what was happening.

'A telephone,' Corbett yelled at him. '*Denwa*. There's a fire.'

The old man nodded and leaped down from the platform with a surprising agility, running towards the trash bin. Corbett went through the door, moving quickly down a deserted corridor, breath heaving from the exertion. Few lights, piles of lumber, hallways branching into cubicles full of boxes and he lost his bearings and came to a dead halt. He doubted that the old man would report him or be able to provide a coherent description if he did, but he could not count on it. He would have to hurry but make no mistakes in the process.

He could hear the hum of machinery off to his left so he opened a heavy metal door and went down a service corridor, stopping when he heard the sound of voices speaking Japanese. Around the corner he could see through open double doors into the power centre of the building, the banks of transformers, the masses of air conditioning and heating equipment.

Two Japanese men in coveralls were standing at a display board near the door, checking something against a list on a clipboard. He backed off, moving towards what he thought to be the centre of the building. He found a work telephone mounted on a wall and picked it up. He could hear a voice saying, *'Moshi, moshi,'* and he asked to be connected with an English-speaking operator. A man came on the line. 'May I help you?'

'Yes,' Corbett said. 'Connect me with the hotel desk.'

'This is the maintenance division,' the Japanese said. 'Maintenance only.'

'I don't give a goddamn what you are,' Corbett said. 'Connect me with registration.'

Silence. A series of clicks. 'Registration,' a feminine voice said.

'I want the number for Mrs Richard McGuiness.'

Another pause. 'I'm very sorry. We have no person registered with that name.'

The heat was oppressive in the corridor. His hands were sweating. 'She should be there now. She just checked in.'

'One moment, please.' Another pause. 'Oh, I am very sorry, sir. She is here. Her room is twelve fourteen. May I ring it for you?'

'Yes, please.'

She answered on the first ring. 'William?' Her voice was apprehensive.

'Yes. I'm in the hotel.'

'Stay away from the lobby, for God's sake. There are two policemen there, checking new arrivals. I told them my husband would be arriving tomorrow.'

'All right,' he said. 'I'll try to find a service staircase or an elevator.'

'I've ordered steaks and a bottle of bourbon.'

'I'll be there.'

He severed the connection and then jiggled the cradle until he was connected with maintenance again. He asked the man where he would find the service elevator and was told that it was near the power room. He retraced his steps, located the elevator, which was oversized to accommodate cleaning equipment, then he pressed the button for the twelfth floor. The doors hissed, closed; the elevator moved upward. He examined the control panel, hoping for a button marked EXPRESS. There was none. The elevator approached the lobby level, came to a halt and he placed his hand in the pocket with the pistol as the doors slid open and he was confronted by a pair of Japanese cleaning women dressed in shapeless *mompei*, cloths tied around their heads. They bowed to him and giggled as they tried to manoeuvre an oversized linen cart into the elevator.

He could see past them into the lobby and he spotted the familiar form of a man standing near the entrance, Nakamura, patiently waiting, well out of the mainstream of traffic entering through the large glass doors, eyes moving in a continual sweep of the lobby. And there was a moment before the elevator doors closed that he was sure Nakamura had seen him. The elevator moved very slowly, the Japanese maids continuing to chatter, only slightly subdued by his presence. The third floor was passed; he waited for the fourth, sweating, knowing that if he had been spotted, he was effectively trapped here while hotel security spread out through the corridors.

The elevator stopped at the fifth floor. With much bowing, the Japanese maids manoeuvred the linen cart out into the corridor. The elevator crept upward again. Nakamura had not seen him and as the lights counted out the successive floors his sureness increased. At twelve the elevator stopped and he moved down the corridor until he found the room. He rapped on the door lightly.

She let him in instantly, closing the door behind him. 'You're not cut out for this kind of business,' she said to him. 'You're white as a sheet.'

'Has the bourbon come yet?' He slumped down in a chair.

'Yes.' She had prepared a drink for him and he took

303

it gratefully, the whisky warm against his throat. She put a hand on his head. 'The food's here if you're hungry.'

'I don't want to eat now.' He needed time to think. Boldness was required, the unexpected; nothing else would do. 'I want you to call Stevens for me in the other building. I want you to find out where he is, whether he's alone.'

'How do I do that?'

'I'm not sure,' he said. 'Would he recognise your voice?'

'I don't think so.' He told her what he wanted done and she picked up the telephone and asked to be connected with Mr Stevens in the ESK office. He could tell that she was being shunted from one operator to another until she was finally connected with Stevens himself.

'Mr Stevens?' she said. 'I am very sorry to be troubling you at this hour, but this is Elsie in communications and I've just had a very strange call with a message from Mr Corbett.' She paused, listening. 'No, sir, I'm not supposed to do that. He said there is no such thing as a private telephone and that I was to deliver the message to you personally and confidentially. Now, I will give it to you on the telephone, if you insist, but it's rather embarrassing since it concerns Mr Erikson.'

Good girl, he thought, she had hooked him now. He could not run from that one.

'Yes, sir, I can meet you. I know where that is. Yes, sir. Knox. Elsie Knox, K-N-O-X.' She put the telephone down, a thoughtful expression on her face. 'I'm tired, Willie,' she said. 'Now, Stevens is sitting by himself in the Dragon Bar on the lobby floor of the other building and he's alone and you can go over there and do what you want. But I want to make one last pitch.'

'For what?'

'Any alternative,' she said. 'I don't care what it is. But I don't see any sense in all this.'

'Oh, there's sense in it all right,' he said. 'I lost my nerve for a while, but it's back.'

'And what do you have to gain by it?' she said.

'Considerable, I think,' he said. 'It's possible I can hit them where they're most vulnerable.' He lifted the attaché case, testing. It had the right heft to it. It would do.

She shrugged slightly. 'All right, then I accept. I won't even ask what you're going to do. How can I help?'

'Sit tight,' he said. 'Stay here, in this room. If you don't hear from me in the next three hours, leave. Don't check out, just walk away.' He stood up and took her in his arms with the sudden and certain conviction that once he left this room, he would never see her again.

He kissed her. 'Three hours,' he said.

'Three hours,' she said.

7

The Dragon Bar was a dark cave with a garish phosphorescent mural of a serpentine dragon glowing above the polished bar and along one wall. He walked into the twilight of the entry with a feeling of relief, almost anticipation, for he was to have a direct adversary now, and a stronger sense of purpose was beginning to form in his mind. A hostess bowed to him and he told her he was here to meet somebody and moved past her, letting his eyes become accustomed to the darkness, the glow of candlelight on dark tables. Then he saw Stevens sitting in a booth on the far side of the room, the candlelight reflecting on the burnished surface of the half-bald head with the strands of hair swept across it in a vain attempt to cover. Vanity, vanity, he thought, his mind exceptionally clear. He realised he had never seen Stevens before, not as a man.

He wandered past the bar coming upon Stevens from

behind. He slid into the booth while Stevens blinked at him, startled, half rising.

'Sit down,' Corbett said. He placed his attaché case on the leather seat beside him with exaggerated care. 'I have a pistol in my pocket, Sam. But you know what I've done within the past twenty-four hours. I don't have to tell you.'

Stevens sagged slightly. 'I can't do you any good, Willie.'

'I think you can,' Corbett said. 'First, you're going to buy me a drink, bourbon and water, and keep it congenial.'

Stevens raised a hand, summoning a waitress, saying nothing until the drinks were delivered and the waitress had departed. 'I mean what I say. It's all gone to hell in a handbasket, Corbett. I hoped you had made it out of the country.'

'No,' Corbett said, sipping the drink.

Stevens lighted a cigarette, his hand trembling slightly. 'Do you want me as a go-between, is that it?'

'I don't have many options, Sam. I think you would be wise to consider me a desperate man and past any manipulation. I am vengeful, angry, determined. And the first thing I want is information. The Vietnamese arms. Do they exist?'

'Yes.'

'Where?'

'I don't know where.'

'Better than that.'

'Honest to God. They're all in the Far East, scattered around, I think. Some in the Philippines, some in Borneo. Only Klein knows all the locations.'

'How did Klein buy them?'

'A third-person deal. ESK made the arrangements through a Liberian company.'

'Then he intends to use them,' Corbett said.

'I don't have a goddamn thing to do with policy,

Willie,' Stevens said, his eyes drifting up to the mural on the wall.

'He intends to use them,' Corbett repeated firmly.

Stevens drank from his glass, wiped his mouth, nodded slowly. 'He's putting together his own security force, his own army. That's what the word is. I didn't think he really intended to use them. I thought it was all a colossal bluff.'

'It's no bluff,' Corbett said. 'He took the first step at Atami. It's a whole new business concept. It was bound to come.'

'I don't know anything about that.'

'The hell you don't,' Corbett said. 'You choose to stay out of it but you know goddamn well what he means to do. Why shouldn't a company use force to protect itself? The Asian countries make demands and Klein answers in a way none of them can mistake. But there's nothing to tie him or the company to any of it. Now, how is he going to get his men? Where is he bringing them into the company? How does he intend to train them?'

'I don't have any answers.'

Corbett lifted the attaché case carefully and placed it on the table. 'Now, I want you to listen to me very closely, Sam,' he said. 'We are going upstairs. You are going to carry the attaché case. If you're wise, you will handle it like eggs. You won't let it bump into anything. You won't try to run or make any sudden moves.'

Stevens's eyes were staring at the polished leather surface. He shook his head soundlessly for a moment. 'Don't do this to me, Willie.'

'You know the computer backwards and forwards.'

'They'll never let us in there. Klein's put in a new security system. Anybody wanting access has to call preliminary security on nineteen. They issue the magnetic cards there. There's a second security guard on twenty. There's no way to get past it.'

'You're very inventive. Now, pick up the attaché

case by the handle. You'd better stand up first.'

Stevens slid out of the booth, stood up, looking very weak. Slowly, tentatively, he reached out and touched the handle, took hold of it, and lifted the case very slowly. The persuasiveness of illusion, Corbett thought, and in an insane world, craziness was quite believable. He followed Stevens out of the bar and down the lobby to one of the house telephones. 'There's a new man on preliminary security,' Stevens said. 'His name is Merriam. Have you met him? Does he know you?'

'I haven't met him but that's no guarantee,' Corbett said.

'I can try. That's all I can do.' He picked up the telephone, cleared his throat, obviously trying to clear his nervousness, to move beyond it. He rang the nineteenth floor and asked for Merriam. 'This is Stevens,' he said. 'Clearance for myself and Squires, J. R.' He covered the mouthpiece with his hand. 'If he knows Squires, there's no way we can get in there.' He responded to the telephone again. 'Right,' he said, and put the telephone back on the cradle.

In the harsh light of the elevator Corbett could see the fear on Stevens's face. He was pale to the point of chalkiness. 'Shit, Willie,' he said, his voice hoarse. 'I'm a machine man, you know that. That's all I am.'

'What's the procedure if we get past nineteen?' Corbett said.

'If Merriam clears us, he will call ahead to twenty. There will be another guard at the desk to log us in.'

'What kind of alarm device does he have?'

'There's a pressure plate built into the kneehole of the desk. If he has the slightest suspicion, he moves his knee and sets off a silent alarm and closes down access to the computer room.'

'Then you're going to have to be pretty goddamned convincing,' Corbett said.

Stevens said nothing. At nineteen the elevator stopped and the doors opened into a hallway where

Merriam sat, a man in his late twenties, uniformed. And from the moment they left the elevator Corbett was certain that Stevens was not going to be able to carry it off, for Stevens launched immediately into a tirade against the company and the necessity for being on call around the clock. But Merriam did not pay any attention to him, giving Corbett only a cursory glance as he rotated the circular file on his desk and took out the two magnetic cards. He pushed a receipt form across the desk. Stevens scrawled his name and handed the pen to Corbett and for an instant his mind went blank. The name of the man he was supposed to be. Squires, yes. Initials? J. R. He signed the alien name.

Merriam picked up the telephone and called the twentieth floor.

Once the elevator doors closed behind them, Stevens slumped slightly, still holding the attaché case with great care.

'Will the guard on the computer floor be behind the desk?'

'He's supposed to be.'

'I want him standing up, away from the alarm.'

'I can only do my best, Willie.'

The door opened to the twentieth floor. The guard was sitting behind the desk, a large burly man. He put down the telephone and looked up as Stevens approached, a tired smile on his face. 'How's it going, George?' Stevens said.

'Can't complain,' George said. He produced the log sheets, placed them on the desk.

Stevens placed the attaché case on the far end of the desk and leaned over to sign the log sheet. 'You'd better check the attaché case,' he said offhandedly. 'We might as well follow these goddamned regulations all the way.'

The guard looked directly at Corbett now and Corbett's hand covered the pistol in his pocket and he wondered if at this moment the guard's knee was moving imperceptibly against the alarm panel, in a single instant putting an end to the whole thing. 'How are you, Mr Squires?' the guard said.

'Tired,' Corbett said.

The guard stood up and approached the briefcase, and as he reached out to open the attaché case, Corbett pulled the pistol out of his pocket. The guard froze where he was, a puzzled expression on his face. 'What's going on?' he said to Stevens.

'Just do exactly as he says,' Stevens said, his voice almost inaudible. 'No heroics, for God's sake.'

'I don't want any sudden movements,' Corbett said. 'I want you to take the pistol out of the holster and lay it on the desk. Now, if there are any alarms, if you don't follow my instructions, I'll kill you.'

The guard hesitated a long moment and then slowly, reluctantly, he unsnapped the holster and withdrew the pistol, laying it on the desk. 'Now,' Corbett said. 'Back away, into the middle of the hallway. You are not to touch the wall.'

Unruffled, not the slightest hint of fear in that broad face, the mind sorting through alternatives, obviously finding none. He backed away from the desk and Corbett picked up his pistol, pocketed it. He waited until Stevens had picked up the attaché case, then he nodded to the guard. 'You lead the way,' he said.

The guard walked down the centre of the hallway, making the bend in the corridor to a heavy door, windowless, with a pair of parallel slots where the doorknob should have been. There was a television camera mounted at the top of the corridor, above the door.

'What's that?' Corbett said.

'A closed-circuit monitoring camera for the computer room,' Stevens said.

'Open the door.'

Stevens inserted the magnetic cards. There was a click and the door opened slightly. 'Now,' Corbett said to the guard, 'there are certain things you should understand. First, I won't hesitate to kill Stevens if I'm inter-

310

fered with. You call Klein. Tell him to ring me in the computer room in exactly ten minutes. I'll talk with him then.'

The guard nodded. 'All right,' he said.

8

When the call came, Klein was asleep on the couch in his quarters. He came awake grudgingly, the book falling from his chest to the floor as he sat up, blinking. He cleared his throat, allowed his mind time to adjust before he picked up the telephone, listening to the guard on the line, the dry, flat tones of his report. And now, with Corbett in the centre of his mind, he began to plan what he would do.

'All right,' he said, accepting immediately. 'How many people are in the main computer room?'

'Only Corbett and Stevens.'

'How many on the computer floor?'

'Six night personnel.'

'Where?'

'In data programming.'

'Get them out of there but don't let them know anything is wrong. Tell them a repair crew is coming in. How is Corbett armed?'

'A thirty-eight police special, sir. And Stevens was carrying an attaché case. I think it contains a device.'

'What kind of device?' Klein said, trying not to lose his patience. 'What makes you think it was a device?'

'From the way he carried it. He was terrified. As I say, that's only a hunch.'

'All right.'

'Once the people are cleared, what do you want me to do?'

'Stay at your desk and wait for further instructions. If Corbett contacts you again, tell him I will call in exactly ten minutes.'

311

'Yes, sir.'

The moment he severed the connection the telephone rang again. It was Thrash. 'Goddard is here, sir.'

'All right, I want him in the board room, now. I also want you, Phillips, a couple of lead computer technicians, the building supervisor, and all blueprints and schematics for the twentieth floor.'

'Yes, sir.'

Klein stood up, his body rather stiff from the inactivity. He retrieved the book from the floor, Clausewitz, and placed a marker where he had stopped reading. He placed it on the end table. His leg was hurting again, the attack from within, and he required himself to think above the pain as he moved to the bathroom and regarded himself in the mirror.

He looked tired, drawn, dark hollows about the eyes, a faint stubble on his cheeks. The bandage gave him the appearance of a casualty. He removed it, examined the proud flesh, the alien substance of the stitches. Wetting the shaving brush, he whipped up a lather in the mug. It was going to be a long night and he must appear to his men as a leader who needed no rest, who knew exactly what he was doing, no edge of uncertainty to him.

He took the straight razor from the cabinet and with smooth strokes whetted it against the leather strop. He shaved automatically, with pride in the sureness of his hand, close to the red flesh of the wound. He washed his face and applied a fresh bandage, a smaller one, not so obtrusive. He knotted a tie into place, put on his jacket, gave himself a final critical examination in the mirror before he selected a cane and went to the board room.

Thrash was at the head of the table, on the telephone, and Goddard was sitting nearby, looking gaunt and fatigued. Klein sat down across from him, placing the back of his hand against a coffee thermos, which he found warm. He filled a styrofoam cup and pushed it across the table towards Goddard. Then he filled one for himself.

'I apologise,' Goddard said. 'I overstepped.'

'Yes.' Klein sipped his coffee.

'I can understand why I was replaced.'

'I have some questions,' Klein said. 'So we will save any discussion of what you did or did not do until later. You know the situation.'

'Yes.'

'In the past twenty-four hours, to your knowledge, has Corbett had the opportunity to get hold of any explosives?'

Goddard nodded. 'Yes, but I don't think he did.'

'Where?'

'There's a lot of construction blasting going on at Atami.'

'Then we can assume the possibility of an explosive device.'

'I've studied his files,' Goddard said. 'He doesn't know anything about explosives. I don't think he has a bomb.'

Thrash turned from the telephone. 'Phillips is on his way. The rest of the men should be here shortly.'

Klein checked his watch. It was time. 'Ring the computer room for me.'

'Yes, sir.' Thrash dialled and handed him the telephone. Corbett answered on the third ring. 'All right,' Klein said, in a comfortable voice. 'I must admit that you've surprised me. What are you up to, Corbett?'

'I'm indulging myself,' Corbett said.

'Are you open to talk?' Klein said, detecting what he perceived to be a slight weakness in Corbett's voice. 'I think we had better take things one at a time. I am aware that you have explosives.' He waited. Corbett said nothing. 'I want you to consider the ramifications before you do anything. If you set off an explosion, a great many innocent people could be killed.'

'Yes,' Corbett said. 'I saw that happen at Atami.'

'All right, consider things on a pragmatic basis. The Japanese have no idea where you are. Neither do the

Americans. I don't want to see you do anything that removes the possibility of negotiation.'

'That possibility does not exist in this moment.'

The line went dead. Klein pinched the bridge of his nose, his eyes tired. He knew damn well what Corbett was doing, how he was feeling, for he had been saddled with a couple of junior officers in Korea and Vietnam who had followed the same pattern, their units chewed up around them, the pressures so great that they had entered a dangerous numbness, a blind destructiveness that placed them beyond words or reason. He could not categorise Corbett, not yet, for Corbett had really not refused negotiation but was merely stalling for time.

Phillips came in with Adair, Phillips a tall spare man in his early forties, Adair short, compact, iron-grey hair, crew-cut, heavy glasses. Adair spread a blueprint of the twentieth floor on the table, unrolled a separate diagram of the computer complex. 'You'd better give me the full problem,' Adair said in a flat Rhode Island voice.

'We have a disgruntled employee who has gained access to the computer centre,' Klein said. 'He has a device, probably explosive.'

Adair whistled softly. 'What quantity explosives? What kind?'

'They're contained in an attaché case. I don't know what kind.'

Adair shrugged slightly. 'If he has simple explosives, he could create a hole. Some of the new stuff, he could cause a hell of a lot of trouble. Is he after the computer?'

'I don't know. Assume that he is.'

'How bright is he?'

'Very bright.'

'Are you sure the case contains explosives?'

'No.'

'He could put an electromagnet in a briefcase. He could put it near the central processing unit and if he's

314

got the right kind of equipment he can really mess it up.'

Klein turned to Phillips. 'If the computer goes out, what would happen to world operations?'

Phillips shrugged. 'It would create one hell of a mess.'

'How much damage would it do to ESK?'

'I don't know,' Phillips said. 'This is our central terminal, worldwide. Everything is fed into our storage. Now, the standard rule is that all offices preserve twenty-four-hour records except for New York, where they have a month on tape. If he takes out the computer, we have backup records, tapes and programmes in the vault.' Phillips lighted a cigarette, thinking. 'The financial loss would be enormous but we could be back on line in a couple of weeks.'

'Go with the possibility that he can take the vault too.'

'Then the damage might be irreparable. Erikson would have to assess that. Have you informed him?'

'I don't want him informed. We can handle this.' He turned to Adair again. 'I want an estimate of blast damage based on maximum. I also want to know if we can get men in there.'

'No,' Adair said.

'Can we feed gas through the air-conditioning system?'

'Possible. But it would take a while to find something he couldn't detect, even longer to make the computer air system leakproof.'

'Get on that,' Klein said to Thrash. 'See what you can get from the Japanese companies.'

'I think you're forgetting something,' Thrash said. 'Stevens is in there with him.'

'Check it out anyway.' He stood up now, putting his weight on the head of the cane. He needed to be out of here a while, to give himself time to think. Adair was leaning over the table, working intently with a pocket

315

calculator, examining the specifications through his thick glasses. Goddard was no longer in the room. 'As far as I'm concerned, this room is sealed,' Klein said. 'The problem will remain with us. Nobody is to be informed. Is that clear?'

Phillips nodded. Adair grunted assent. Thrash followed him to the door. 'I need to understand you,' he said quietly. 'What do you intend to do about Stevens?'

'I want Corbett taken out, whatever the cost.'

'I understand.'

'One more thing.'

'Yes, sir?'

'Get your boys after Goddard. I want him locked in a room until this whole business is finished.'

'Will do,' Thrash said.

9

It was as if his mind had become suddenly linear, so that the ideas came trailing to him one at a time. He also found that, now that he was here, there was no place for him to go. He was overwhelmed by the physical presence of the computer, the banks of machinery covering the walls, and he was in the physical centre of the company power and could do nothing about it. He felt some empathy for Stevens, who had carefully placed the attaché case on the floor next to the console in the centre of the room, but he did not show it.

'I have some questions,' he said to Stevens. 'First, is there any way that the information stored in this computer can be transferred to another one?'

'Certainly.'

'I want that capability cut off.'

'I'll have to de-energise all the input interfaces.'

'Do it.'

Stevens moved to the console. He appeared to be relieved that now he had something physical to do. He

316

cut off some circuits and some lights went dead. 'All right, we are self-contained.'

Corbett prowled the room, paused at the vault door in the corner. 'How do you open this?'

'A palm print on the plate.'

'You're authorised. Open it.'

Stevens placed his hand against a polished plate in the door and Corbett heard the muted whirring of a motor, and the door swung open. Inside were long rows of metal racks laden with boxes of computer tapes. The whole company was here, all of the financial transactions for the past ten years. The company was as vulnerable as he himself was, at least for now. Until they figured a way to get to him he was very much in charge.

He returned to the console, sat down. 'I want all input from Tokyo terminals shut down,' he said to Stevens. 'I don't want anybody to be able to control the computer from any place beyond this console.'

'They can bypass local terminals.'

'How?'

'If you shut them down here, they can call Seoul, for instance, feed in from any of the terminals there.'

'Then shut them all down.'

Stevens nodded. 'This is all shit,' he said, almost to himself. 'I've never had anything against you, Willie.'

'But you did nothing to stop them.'

'How in the hell could I stop anybody?' He turned from the console. 'All inputs are closed down.'

'Did you know in advance that Wilson was to be killed?'

'No. I swear to God. I liked him. Can I have a cigarette?' He accepted the cigarette and the light, leaned back, looking around at the machinery. 'I'd have a man's ass for smoking in here. But it's all down the drain anyway.'

'Did you know about Atami?'

'I knew something was going to happen there, yes.

317

I thought there was to be a protest of some sort. Nothing like it was.' He pulled his lips back from his teeth in a humourless grimace, as if his teeth were hurting. 'Hell, I'm a technician and that's all I am. I've never asked to be anything more. I don't have any taste for intrigue.'

'It's all here,' Corbett said, laying his hand on the console. 'Everything Klein has done, everything that he has left to do. He's put the information in. I want it out.'

'Can't be done, Willie.'

'I think you can manage it.'

'A physical impossibility,' Stevens said. Klein had eight technicians at work full time, putting material into the computer, Stevens went on. Reams of it, army technical manuals, political speeches, shipping schedules, even sections of the Tokyo telephone directory. To keep a technician from having any conception of the true nature of a project, it was common practice to swamp him with trivia so that he could make no sense of it, even if he talked with other programmers working on the same project. 'He's been doing it for months,' Stevens said. 'I registered a modification memo with the comptroller, suggesting a simplification of Klein's grand project. There are a hell of a lot of ways to feed a confidential programme that cost less money. But I never received any answer so I dropped it.'

'What's his project code name?'

'BIG DEAL,' Stevens said. 'But that won't do you any good. The computer has been programmed to transfer any data put in under BIG DEAL into another code name.'

'You're sure of that?'

'I tried it once. I wanted a printout of data under BIG DEAL. There wasn't any. I requested the computer to give me an access code on BIG DEAL data. There wasn't any.'

Corbett rummaged through his pockets, found the pages from Klein's notebook. 'Try these,' he said.

Stevens turned to a keyboard, began to type instructions to the computer. 'Nothing,' Stevens said. 'I get

318

garbage from either TEMPLE DOGS or SHORTFALL. I've directed the computer to give me all possible letter combinations and to check any of them as an access code. But he could have a book of random numbers and letter combinations and simply change his access every morning.'

Ah, shit, the power of the intellectual process, and where Stevens had been afraid before, now he was intrigued, caught up in a battle of wits, not with the machine itself, no, but with the man whose secret he sought to uncover. He passed the eraser end of a pencil against his teeth, ran a hand over his balding head. 'No, he wouldn't work that way,' he said, scratching his head. 'I've known other men who worried about their programmes. They used random number access for a while but that required record-keeping, so they settled in on a particular combination.' He began to work on the keyboard again.

Corbett sat back in a leather swivel chair, leaning his head against the back, listening to the hum of the machines surrounding him. He watched the rotating tape wheels turning fitfully through slot windows, the battery of lights on the console, an immense power surrounding him, enormously cold. Somewhere in these machines, these miles of tapes and discs and microcircuits, the information was hidden and he tried to picture the form it was in, electrical impulses, variations in magnetic fields on a ribbon of tape.

Suddenly the printout machine began to chatter. 'I've hit something,' Stevens said. Corbett walked over to the machine, where printed lines seemed to appear miraculously on the striped paper. Long chains of chemical formulae. They had tapped into something, one small portion of Klein's hidden data, probably from an army technical manual fed into the computer.

'Are we in?' Corbett said.

'Possible,' Stevens said.

10

'I have a projection,' Adair said, looking up from the blueprint. Klein sat down in the chair next to him, the pain so persistent he knew he would have to take something for it very shortly. But he forced himself to concentrate on what Adair was saying, forced his eyes to follow the finger moving across the blueprints. 'The twentieth floor is heavily reinforced to carry the weight of the computer equipment. Now, if he places his explosive charge here, where it will do the most damage to the computer, the thrust of the blast will be transverse, that is, it will tend to blow the walls on the twentieth floor, the interior partitions. It will cause a minimal damage to the twenty-first floor. There is a possibility it may rupture the exterior wall, here, in which case there will be a danger to street traffic from flying debris.'

Thrash came in, cool on the surface, agitated underneath, his face flushed. Klein leaned back in his chair, shifting his leg slightly as if he could escape the pain by finding the right physical position.

'Are you all right?' Thrash said.

'Certainly. What do you have?'

'One grand goddamn bluff,' Thrash said. 'There's no way he could have explosives. He opened the flight bag in the presence of department-store personnel. Nothing but papers. He couldn't have gotten explosives at Atami. The Japanese are so damned security conscious, their construction explosives are pitted, fenced, locked. Once Corbett left the department store, there was no place he could have picked up the stuff.'

There was an ironic symmetry to all this, Klein thought, and he had to give Corbett credit for ingenuity in the face of immense odds. Now the possibilities were reduced to two. Either Corbett intended to damage the computer, the assault of one man against a machine, or he intended to use it to clear himself. If he had decided on the first course of action, he would have already commenced. Since he had not, he was obviously compelling Stevens to operate the machine.

'I want six men with automatic weapons,' he said. 'I want them tactically deployed on the twentieth floor. There is an emergency fire door here.' His fingers found a place on the blueprint. 'I want two men there. I want another two men at the main door. One man is to cover the elevator and another the staircase.'

'Do you mean to force him out?' Thrash said.

'We won't have to,' Klein said. 'He's a corporation man after all and he won't commit suicide just to make a point. He's in there now trying to find a way to save his ass. Sooner or later he will realise that's impossible and a simple show of force will be enough to bring him out.' He stood up, balancing on the console, looking to Phillips, who was working the console with no effect.

'He's blanked it out pretty well,' Phillips said.

'Is there any way you can shut the computer down altogether?' Klein said. 'What if you cut off the main power line?'

'The storage capacitors hold the power long enough to permit the auxiliary to come on.'

'How can we shut down the auxiliary?'

'If we remove all the power, the magnetic fields collapse and we lose all the information in the storage banks. If you simply want to cut the auxiliary, you simply turn it on.'

Alternatives, and he might have to resort to that, but each step now created fresh hazards. Each action would precipitate another action, a whole chain, irreversible. He needed an easing of the pain in his leg, a careful sorting through of so many details, and his mind was not as elastic as it had been when he was younger. 'Thrash?'

'Yes, sir.'

'Did you find Goddard?'

'No, sir. I didn't disperse security beyond the hotel.'

'Are the Japanese police still in the lobby?'

'Yes.'

'Very well, I'm going to my office. When you have the team ready let me know.'

He went from the board room into his office, where a small lamp was burning; sufficient, he could see. He opened a packet of powders, shook them into a glass, and added water, drinking the mixture. Goddamn the leg; a part of his body was betraying him, refusing to hold him. He sat down, waiting for the pain to ease. Hell, he had relied too heavily on the computer instead of carrying details in his mind as he once had done.

The damned machine with its infinite capacities and no predictable biases, none, and when Corbett had taken the notebook from him, Klein had realised the foolishness of putting anything on paper, changing the access, moving back to memory. Eight digits, and what were the odds that Corbett, even with the aid of a man like Stevens, could crack it? A million to one. Greater, perhaps. But even at these odds he could not accept, for he wanted to take no chance at all that what he was doing would be aborted. Enormously successful, yes, a new policy, independent of nationalism, private success where the government had failed, and all this was jeopardised by one man playing a numbers game on the computer.

He lifted the telephone, called the computer room. Corbett came on the line. Klein was feeling easier now. The pain killer had begun to take hold. 'I think the time has come for us to talk,' he said.

'I'm listening.'

Klein closed his eyes, the better to concentrate on the sound of Corbett's voice, the better to articulate his own thoughts. 'I would like to summarise your position as I see it. I'm sure you will correct me if I'm wrong. I believe that you entered the floor intending to destroy the computer but thought better of it, realising that if you destroy it, you will have no proof either against me or the company.'

'Your grasp of my intentions is nonsense.'

'Perhaps,' Klein said. 'Now you also have some things going for you. You're armed. You have a computer expert who is co-operating with you, under duress or not. You have physical possession of the room, of the machinery. We're aware that you have no explosives but we are also aware that you can cause great damage. I'm also aware that the odds are very long against your finding what you want.'

'We're closer,' Corbett said. 'We're zeroing in.'

'You're talking to an expert,' Klein said. 'You can't zero in. You either have it or you don't.' It was his job to close down the options now, eliminate them one at a time. 'Suppose for a minute that you do get lucky. You'll have enough pounds of printout to fill a small truck. I assume that you would either have to get them out and into the hands of somebody appropriate, or you would have to get somebody in. Now, you must know that I won't let that happen.'

'Ah, you are one cool son of a bitch, aren't you?' Corbett said.

Klein could feel the beginning of capitulation. It was always signalled by the flurry of assault that came from a man who was trapped. 'Not cool,' Klein said. 'Determined. I'll give you two options, letting you know in advance that I prefer the first. If you give up now, at this point, we can find a solution that is mutually acceptable. I can guarantee that you will face no prosecution in any way.'

'So we are back to Wilson.'

'That's possible. Dead. Regrettable. But he can't be hurt by any of this.'

'And what about your plans?'

'They can be modified. I'm willing to admit that a mistake was made. I'm willing to discuss alternate means.'

A pause now, and was Corbett considering, balancing? Klein believed so. There was no way he could avoid such a consideration. 'And if I don't buy any of your bullshit?'

'I have six professionals ready to move in on you.'

'You're forgetting. I have a hostage.'

'Expendable.'

'How long do I have?'

'Let's say ten minutes, fifteen at the outside. But figure the odds against you before you make a decision. You have always led a rather peaceful life. The six men are combat veterans. I wouldn't want it to come to that, of course, but I'd be less than truthful if I didn't spell it out.'

'Go to hell.'

The connection was severed. He replaced the telephone. The pain was almost gone from his leg. Time, he only needed a small amount of time to guarantee Corbett's surrender. He would give him eight minutes and then make another call. He lifted the telephone and rang Thrash in the board room. 'I want you to check with Phillips, see if auxiliary power can be destroyed without damaging the computer. Also, how long can all power be shut down without damaging the computer?'

'Hold on.' Thrash was gone from the line for a moment. 'All right,' he said. 'We can destroy auxiliary power without affecting primary. Any shutdown of power will result in some damage. We might suspend five minutes without significant damage.'

'What the hell does that mean?'

'Do you want to talk to Phillips?'

He checked himself. 'No. Have your men ready to move.'

'Yes, sir.'

He put the telephone on the cradle, looked up with a start. Erikson was standing in the doorway, his face in shadow. 'I want to know the situation,' he said. Klein could feel the steel in his voice.

'Sit down and I'll fill you in,' Klein said. He watched Erikson sit down, rolling a cigar in his fingers. For a brief moment, his face was illuminated by the flare of the lighter, his expression more curious than hostile. Klein told him what had happened, only the facts, none of the plans.

'How did he get past you?' Erikson said. 'How did he get through this marvellous security system of yours, past the Japanese police in the lobby? And I was under the impression that computer security was foolproof.'

'Nothing is foolproof,' Klein said. 'And at this point it isn't important how he got into the hotel.'

'No, I don't suppose it is.' The smoke drifted up through the semidarkness. 'I have been getting calls all afternoon, interesting calls from the other companies represented at the meeting.' None of the calls had been addressed explicitly to the subject at hand, he went on, because no communications were secure anymore and what a man said jokingly, off the cuff, could rise to haunt him in an investigative committee later. So these had all been social calls or concerned with minor business, but they were all supportive. 'No indignance,' Erikson said. 'They figure a move like this has been long overdue.'

'Then they will co-operate with us,' Klein said. It was not a question.

'Very soon,' Erikson said. 'We're already seeing results in South Korea. I had a call from the Korean ambassador. He said that he had just become aware of the problem that was causing friction between his government and private business interests. He wants to get together to seek an equitable solution.' He drew in on his cigar. The coal glowed brightly. 'The Japanese are extremely angry and we will have to guard against their coming into possession of anything tangible that they can use against us. The Philippines still appear to be recalcitrant. So I would say, offhand, that you

325

will have to continue your move in that direction.'

'I agree,' Klein said, pressing his fingertips together. 'Now we have the question of Corbett.'

'What's your plan?'

'To take him out in the most expedient way.'

'And suppose he gives up, decides to surrender?'

A tricky point here, yes, and he could not decide how to play it because he did not wish to lose the old man's support, yet there was no way he could equivocate. 'He knows that the material is in the computer,' Klein said dispassionately. 'Now, even if we make the case against Wilson and buy Corbett off, he will always remain a potential threat.'

'So what do you propose?'

'I'll try to get him out with minimal damage to the computer.'

'Before you do anything I have something I think might bring him out to you. But what do you suggest once we have him?'

'I don't see that we have much choice.'

'Meaning?'

'We will do it as quietly as possible. Nothing to alarm the Japanese police. But Corbett will have to be terminated.'

Erikson studied the cigar thoughtfully. 'Corbett is a good man and he's been with the company a long time. But I think we are at the point where neither sentiment nor service can be allowed to count. These are bad times, Klein. The whole world as we know it is going down the drain. A damn shame.'

'The trick is to survive,' Klein said. 'That's all that matters in the long run.'

'I suppose so.'

'Then you agree with his termination?'

'I prefer the more direct word,' Erikson said. 'Killed is what we are talking about here.'

'Yes,' Klein said. 'Killed.'

Erikson nodded. 'As quickly and quietly as possible.'

11

The telephone rang and Corbett picked it up, expecting Klein to be on the line. He was surprised to find that it was Cristina. 'Darling,' she said. 'It seems that you're causing quite a fuss.'

'That's my intention,' he said. 'What do you want, Cristina?'

'To help you. We go back quite a way, William, and you've been good to me. I owe you for that.'

'You don't owe me anything.'

'All right then, it's important to me. I want to come down there and talk to you.'

'Impossible.'

'Erik suggested it. It won't do any harm.'

Erik, yes, a last-ditch effort. 'If Erikson has anything to say to me, have him call me.'

'You know he won't do that. I'm coming down, darling.'

Before he could respond, the line went dead. He turned to Stevens, who had a scowl on his face. 'Garbage,' Stevens said, watching the printout pour from the machine to fold itself in a bin. 'We've tapped into an access for his army technical manuals. We're running a complete printout of TM 3-1040-207-15P, a manual on the M10 airplane smoke tank.'

It was all a grand puzzle, Corbett thought, an intellectual exercise that Stevens was taking very seriously. He checked the television monitor as Cristina came around the bend in the hallway, wearing a soft dress, the thirties look, strolling very casually as if she had no urgent business. The hallway was clear behind her. He waited until she reached the door and then opened it, allowing her in before he closed it behind her.

She nodded to Stevens, who ignored her in favour of the printout, then she looked around the room. 'Fascinating,' she said. 'So this is what the battle is all about, all those millions of pieces of information inside the machinery. I can feel them in the air.'

He leaned against a table. She did not look well; there was something terribly awry with her. Cristina did not react well to stress that was not of her own making. Her eyes were tired. Her voice was slightly shrill. Try as she would, she could not make this conversation light.

'What does Erik want?' he said.

She turned to him with a forced smile. 'Peace,' she said.

He smiled despite himself. 'That's pretty goddamned incongruous,' he said. 'What's his offer?'

'I think it's pretty generous,' she said. 'We had a very long conversation and he has known about us for a long time, darling, and he is perfectly willing to allow it to continue, as long as we're discreet about it.'

'Oh?'

'He's willing to give you a European company, in Belgium, and I can maintain my permanent residence in Antwerp when he doesn't need me. There's a marvellous country house twenty minutes from Antwerp that I visited once. You would love it. There's a formal garden and a gateman's cottage.'

The words were coming too quickly, spilling out of her, and her eyes were large and sad even while the forced smile remained fixed on her face. Conflicted, yes, and he was touched by it, for she was doing this for Erik but she had felt something for him once, something so strong that she could barely keep from weeping in the process.

'It's all right,' he said. 'I understand.'

She stopped short, shaking her head. 'I don't know what you mean. You understand what?'

'You're not very convincing, dear. I'm grateful for that.'

Suddenly, she was weeping, a short burst, quickly brought under control. 'I really don't want anything to

328

happen to you,' she said. 'I want to get you out of this if I can.'

'There's nothing you can do to help me,' he said.

'Erik is a very stubborn man.'

'So am I.'

He put his hands on her shoulders, looked directly into her face. For once, he thought, she was not posing and any artifice she had was gone. He held her to him for a moment and then let her go. 'You watch out for yourself, Cristina. Tell Erik that you did your best but that I wouldn't listen. All right?'

She shook her head sadly, wordless, and he opened the door and let her out, watching the television monitor until she rounded the corner and disappeared from sight. Stevens shrugged as if what had happened was none of his business. He terminated the printout, sat down. 'Goddamnit, there has to be a way.'

'Look,' Corbett said. 'I apologise to you, Sam. This isn't your battle and I shouldn't have involved you in it.' He gave the attaché case a shove with his foot. 'No explosives. It was all a bluff.'

Stevens pursed his lips. 'You son of a bitch,' he said, without giving it much thought.

'Klein is about to mount an assault to blow me out of here. So I suggest you haul ass. You're a good man and there's no point to your going down with me.'

'Hell, I think you're wrong. Klein isn't about to wreck a fine piece of machinery like this. Besides, as long as I'm here, you have a hostage. That gives you leverage.'

Corbett smiled. 'I tried that. He said you were expendable.'

'Expendable?' Stevens said with a grimace. 'Well.'

'If I were you, I'd find a good sound company back in the States and retire from the wars. Because that's what the General is here for, one grand and glorious military operation. Or maybe a series of little wars, all so cleverly fought he'll never be caught at it. He knows military operations backwards and forwards.' And there it was, another lead, a hunch. 'You say he probably keyed to numbers.'

'Yes,' Stevens said, openly curious.

'Can the computer give up his personnel file?'

'Certainly.'

'I suggest you show me how to punch it in and then get the hell out of here.'

'I'll stay for a while,' Stevens said. 'You couldn't do it yourself. You'd fuck it up.' He moved to the keyboard and began to punch in a series of numbers. Almost immediately the display screen began to fill with data, the whole life of Brig. Gen. George B. Klein, United States Army. Retired. And numbers by the hundreds, street addresses going back thirty years to his days as an enlisted man, dates of services in various theatres of war, APO numbers, telephone numbers of references, Social Security numbers for himself and his ex-wife.

'Jesus,' Corbett said. 'Infinite possibilities. He could have combined three APO numbers to give him nine digits. He could have reversed an old telephone number.' He shook his head. 'All right. Let's start from the top. Take the numbers as they are.'

'I don't think the bastard is that obvious,' Stevens said. 'I have the feeling he used a number substitution for the letters of his name or a phrase.'

Corbett stirred, listening beyond the whir of the machines. He was aware of another sound, similar to a metallic banging, coming from someplace on this floor. Klein had moved his forces in, on the same level, a different room. The clock was running. There was no time for intellectual experiments, for complicated variables. 'Punch them in straight from the top,' Corbett said.

Stevens began. He punched in the numbers of Klein's birthdate. The display responded immediately. INSUFFICIENT DATA. He hunched over the console, face distorted in a frown, clearly expecting nothing, displeased with what he was doing, falling into a kind of blocked rhythm, feeding the number, flicking his eyes at the

330

INSUFFICIENT DATA before he entered another number. The sounds outside were unmistakable now, the muted shuffle of feet. And at any moment they could storm the door, smash it in, and both he and Stevens would be dispatched in seconds.

INSUFFICIENT DATA.

He thought of Ellen waiting in the room and he wanted to call her, to hear her voice, to let her know what was happening, but he could not, of course. He could not bring her into this.

INSUFFICIENT DATA.

Where was Erik at this moment? In his suite, perhaps, cigar clenched in his teeth, magnifying glass to his eye, examining another of his acquisitions, able to separate his mind into compartments, one section assessing this small piece of oriental art, another thinking of what was happening on the computer floor. But not truly disturbed, no. For if Erik willed something, he believed that he could bring it about.

INSUFFICIENT DATA.

Stevens pushed back from the console, rubbed his eyes. 'I think we're barking up the wrong tree,' he said. 'If I were doing this, I'd pick a random ten-digit number and let it remain constant. Nobody could crack that.'

'But you're not Klein. He had to use something he could remember instantly, something not obvious, something he couldn't forget.'

Stevens raised his head. Now he could hear the noises too. 'You call it. I'll give it a try.'

'We'll eliminate combinations and numbers of less than six digits.'

Stevens began again.

INSUFFICIENT DATA.

Corbett leaned back in his chair, stared at the ceiling. Another five minutes at the most, and he considered abandoning the search and doing as much damage as he could before they finally reached him. Would the magnetic tape burn? Could he destroy the records in

331

the vault? Possible. Now there was a low sound from Stevens and Corbett had to look at him before he realised that Stevens was quietly jubilant. 'Son of a bitch,' Stevens said. 'We have it.'

///38787513/ACCESS SHORTFALL AND TEMPLE DOGS CONFIRMED///

'What number is it?'

'His enlisted serial number,' Stevens said. 'Jesus, no imagination.'

'Now comes the crunch,' Corbett said. 'They won't let either one of us out of here, especially now. We can take a thousand precautions and the odds are that we will still both be dead by the time we leave the twentieth floor.'

'There's always a catch,' Stevens said, reflectively.

'We'll have to come up with some options.'

'All right,' Stevens said, after a pause. 'We'll come up with something.'

12

Goddard sat at the bar, waiting for some sign, keenly alert and aware, his senses finely honed, his ears picking up every wisp of sound, the laughter of Japanese businessmen in a booth, the almost crystal sound of women's voices, and his eyes moved in a slow and continual sweep of the mirror behind the bar, recording patterns of movement, colours, the brilliant red of a dress, the scarlet slash of a mouth, and he looked at the glowing form of the dragon mural, the great mouth open, teeth shadowy, white. His nostrils picked up the scent of perfume from a hostess seated on a bar stool next to his and he regarded her in the periphery of his vision, without looking at her directly.

Her golden flesh seemed to radiate light and the black silk sheath dress she wore seemed to absorb it, a polarity there, white, black, light, darkness, and his nostrils picked up another odour as well, the smell of the kitchens, stainless steel and the slight pungency of disinfectant, and he was sure that in this dark room full of tobacco smoke and the smell of bodies and candlewax, no one but he could smell the kitchens, and there was the direction for him, indicated so subtly that he would have missed it altogether had he not been so aware.

For the polarities represented positive and negative and made no sense at all except in the evasive kitchen odours, and on that night in Los Angeles in that frantic procession across the kitchen when the shots were fired he had been in a negative position, cut off by the narrowness of a corridor and the crush of newsmen, but in the essential rightness of things, the tendency of life to correct itself, he had been negative there so he could be positive here. There was redemption in being indispensable and at the moment he was indeed indispensable for he had been removed from his other responsibilities to free his mind for this one act.

The balance within him would not be restored completely until Corbett was dead, and by his hand. He took a wad of hundred-yen notes out of his pocket and dropped them on the bar, then slid off the stool and made his way towards the exit.

13

'Do you have the men in position?' Klein said to Thrash.

'Yes, sir,' Thrash said.

Klein picked up the telephone, rang the computer room.

'Yes?' Corbett said.

'The time is up,' Klein said. 'Which way is it to be?'

'I want to talk.'

'Very well, I'll be down,' Klein said.

He put the telephone down and decided to counterbalance the sedatives, which had removed the pain and taken the edge off his thinking in the process. He took two pills and washed them down with a glass of water from the carafe on his desk. 'We'll make him wait now,' he said to Thrash. 'It's hard for a man to bluff when he's on the defensive.'

'You're really going to meet with him?'

Klein flipped the switches on the console, as if by some miracle they might have begun to work on their own, but the screens remained blank. 'I am his only hope of getting out of here,' he said. 'I have conducted surrenders before. There was a Japanese garrison, for instance, that appeared to wish to surrender, but none of the officers . . . ' His voice trailed off; he checked himself. He did not wish to become loquacious, anecdotal. He needed to think and speak with precision. 'You have the silencer?'

'Yes.'

'This is a tableau,' Klein said. 'It must look right. When we have finished talking, we will come out of the computer centre. I will be leading the way and he will have a pistol in my back. There will be a man in the corridor immediately in front of the computer room with an automatic weapon. I will tell him to put his weapon down and he will lean it against the wall, precisely at the corner where the corridor makes a sharp right turn. Do you have that?'

'Yes, sir.'

'At the moment he turns the corner I will distract him and give you a clear shot. You will be on the blind side of the corridor and the moment you see his head you fire. If you miss, you will have time for two more shots. His reflexes will be slow and you will already be in firing position.'

Thrash was checking his pistol. Clean, immaculate hands, long supple fingers. Youth, the clear-eyedness of the mid-thirties. Klein felt a tinge of excitement, the first stirrings of adrenalin, the combined effect of pills and an approaching confrontation. 'We'll cut off the auxiliary power first,' he said, leading the way to the elevator.

'Is that necessary?'

'Yes. He must be unnerved. He has to come to the conclusion that there is nothing that is not expendable.'

The elevator opened on the twentieth floor. There were three men standing at the desk, all armed with automatic weapons. He looked to Thrash. 'Call the hotel desk. Tell them to be prepared for possible calls from guests complaining or reporting gunfire. All callers are to be reassured that there is a mechanical malfunction on one of the upper floors and no reason to become alarmed.'

'Yes, sir.'

'You men come with me,' Klein said, leading them down a corridor, through the wide data-programming room, down another hallway to the power-room door. It was locked, solid, requiring two magnetic cards to open. 'All right,' he said to the men. 'You will fire into the lock, short bursts, staggered. I want noise.'

He stood back as the automatic weapons fired, the sound overwhelming in the corridor, the air heavy with the acrid smell of cordite. The door shattered, flew to pieces, opened.

'Cease fire,' Klein said. He led the way into the room. The generator was enormous, humming, the wiring in cased pipes radiating down the side of one wall, leading into a switching box. He threw the master switch and the generator began to wind down. He shut down the battery source. The auxiliary system was now inoperable.

He walked back to the central desk, where Thrash was just hanging up the telephone. 'A couple more things,' Klein said. 'If I am in there longer than twenty minutes, you are to close down the main power on the computer and put it out of commission. If I can persuade him to come out, before I leave the computer room I will call you on the telephone and tell you to have the men put

335

down their weapons and clear the area. I want the man at the turn of the corridor to time it so that the minute he sees us come out, he will lean his weapon against the wall and retreat.'

'Yes, sir.'

Klein took out his handkerchief to dab at his stinging eyes. He made a list-minute inspection of himself, straightening his tie. He was ready. He braced himself with his cane and began the walk towards the computer room.

14

It was the gunfire that did it, Corbett decided, for when it came it echoed through the air vents, vibrated through the walls, sharp staccato bursts. With the sound of the shots he felt his stomach begin to shake, and he remembered Wilson and he remembered Atami.

'Jesus Christ,' Stevens said with a start. 'What in the hell are they doing?'

'Klein is now calling my bluff. Look, there's no reason for you to stay any longer. I brought you in here at gunpoint.'

'He has troops out there,' Stevens said, as if he had not heard. 'The sorry son of a bitch has troops.'

'On the other hand, you're as safe here as any place, I suppose. I forced you to co-operate.'

'Shit, he won't kill us,' Stevens said with little conviction. 'We have him cold.'

'All the more reason to do it. But we will have stopped him. Flip the switch.'

'That doesn't leave you any bargaining power.'

'None,' Corbett said.

Stevens shrugged, leaned forwards, flipped the switch. The computer began to hum. There it was, Corbett thought, finished. A great feeling of release came over him, a burden removed. 'How long will it take?'

'Fifteen minutes, more or less,' Stevens said.

'We can hold that long.' There was a knock on the door and he checked the television surveillance. Klein was alone. Corbett let him in. Stevens did not get up from his chair. He did not look at Klein.

'You've made a good decision,' Klein said to Corbett.

'It had to come to an end,' Corbett said.

'I agree with you,' Klein said. He sat down in one of the chairs at the console and Corbett sat down opposite him.

'Stevens came here because he was forced to,' Corbett said. He placed the pistol on the console in front of him. 'So we will take it for granted that he returns to status quo. He's not at issue here.'

'Certainly,' Klein said. 'May I have one of your cigarettes?'

Corbett handed him the pack, provided him a light. Klein leaned back, inhaling the smoke. 'It's a strange bit of business,' he said, 'the joy of breaking the rules. These machines are so damned delicate. But everything has a tendency to change.' He tapped the cigarette. The ash shattered and showered on to the floor. 'We are both professionals,' he said. 'There's no need to prolong this. I think it's customary to disarm at this point. So I will take your pistol.'

'No,' Corbett said.

Klein shrugged. 'It doesn't matter. Keep it then, if you like. I don't need to spell out our comparative positions. I take it that you have decided on the Wilson approach. I don't think there's any point to your going further than a deposition to the Japanese police supporting the evidence against Wilson. Then we will prepare a statement to satisfy the Congressional investigating committees. We will have to make a corporate mea culpa concerning illegal payments. But the world moves very swiftly and other problems take precedence.'

'And the Vietnamese arms?'

'They will become a part of corporate folklore.'

Corbett was amazed at the assurance of the man, dressed in a business suit but still very much the general, at home with power and manoeuvering. 'No,' Corbett said. 'Not folklore, fact. We have the printout, if you would care to see it, the names of subsidiaries, the freighters used for transport, the stops they made in Southeast Asia before they even headed across the Pacific. We have the location of the weapons in the Philippines, in Malaysia.'

'I don't believe you,' Klein said, but his hand was poised in midair, the cigarette smoke wisping up in a blue plume.

'Give me the printout,' Corbett said to Stevens. He placed the folded sheets in front of Klein, who examined the first page rather absently.

'I should have been more cautious with access,' Klein said. He opened the printout. 'Yes, you do have the Vietnamese arms pinned down, don't you?' He closed the printout, gently. 'What else do you have?'

'The names of the companies that attended Erik's summit plus their positions on your operations.' He extended his hand to Stevens, who supplied the separate printout, which Corbett placed in front of Klein. 'We also have the Atami operation, the connection with Atsugi, the projection of the flight into the Inland Sea. I think it's all quite convincing. There are holes, of course, gaps, but not so many that they can't be filled.'

Klein grew very still and Corbett could almost see his mind working as he sucked on the cigarette, exhaling the smoke in shallow breaths. And Corbett was also keenly aware of the men waiting outside, for now Klein would have to be considering a fresh plan of attack. How many minutes had passed since Stevens had flipped the switch? Not enough. He needed more time. Corbett looked to Stevens and then back to Klein. 'Pick up the telephone and tell them to pass Stevens through.'

Klein hesitated. 'I don't see how we can do that. He

338

may have come in here against his will, but he still has the knowledge. We will have to come to some understanding.'

Corbett picked up the pistol. 'Make the call.'

'He goes empty-handed,' Klein said.

'Agreed,' Corbett said. 'I want you to make your instructions simple. No booby traps. No extra instructions.'

Klein nodded. He picked up the telephone and dialled a single digit. 'Thrash, Stevens is coming out. Let him pass through.' He severed the connection. Stevens stood up, a trifle unsteady on his feet. Klein looked at him evenly. 'We will talk about arrangements later,' he said. 'For the moment I would advise you to discuss none of this with anyone.'

Stevens brushed a hand over his balding scalp. 'You going to be okay?' he said to Corbett.

'Fine.'

Stevens nodded, went out through the door, leaving behind him a heavy silence, broken only by the steady whir of the machines. Fine now, yes, a few minutes to see Stevens clear, a rationale for waiting. Klein cleared his throat. 'I know you neither like nor approve of what is going on,' he said. 'Nevertheless, it is necessary. I think that beneath your resentment, you can see this is the case. Now, the question is, what will it take to satisfy you?'

The appearance of reality was so convincing that he was almost tempted to believe, to accept Klein's sincerity at face value, and he would have to appear equally as sincere in his responses.

'I don't give a damn about your international policies,' Corbett said, 'except in a perverse and personal way. I want your personal guarantee that what happened at Atami won't happen again.'

'We won't need another move like that,' Klein said, his eyes watering from the sting of the cigarette smoke.

339

'That's bullshit,' Corbett said. 'I know about your plan for the Philippines.'

'That's nothing but a contingency plan.'

'Which you will scrub.'

'Which is now unnecessary.'

The conviction of argument, the battle for moot points, and Corbett felt a sudden rush of fatigue. 'All right,' he said. 'I will accept that. Now, how do I know that I will get out of here alive? What assurances do I have?'

'I can see that would be a large concern for you,' Klein said. 'But you do have a pistol, after all. And I value my life equally as much as you value yours. I am perfectly willing to remain your prisoner until you reach a position of safety.' He sucked the last shred of smoke from the cigarette, ground it out beneath his heel. 'You won't be able to use any of your information, of course. Once we leave here, I will reprogramme, eliminate all of the material from the computer. The Vietnamese arms will be dumped at sea within hours. You won't be able to establish a case against either me or the corporation. And we'll follow the Wilson approach to the Korean business.'

Tidy, everything falling into place. He would take Klein with him and perhaps there would be a slight chance he would leave here alive. If he could make it to the safety of the hotel room, he could hold Klein prisoner for the time he needed.

He would concentrate on the survival of egress from this floor. And he was equally resolute that if he reached the point where he could see he was not going to survive, he would kill Klein. He would see him dead.

He walked over to the television monitor. There was a man at the turn in the corridor, resembling nothing so much as an athlete on a playing field, the weapon held casually, pointed at the ceiling, jaws in motion, chewing gum, now looking at the door, now back towards the desk in front of the elevator, checking signals.

'All right,' Corbett said. 'Call off your man. Clear the floor.'

Klein picked up the telephone. 'Thrash,' he said. 'Tell the men to put down their weapons and get off the floor. We're coming out.'

In the television monitor the man at the corner paused, listening to something being said to him from the desk. Then he removed the ammunition clip from the automatic carbine and laid it on the floor, next to the wall where he leaned the weapon, and disappeared in the direction of the desk.

'Now we go,' Corbett said. Klein raised himself on the cane, his limping pronounced as he crossed the room. Corbett opened the door and left it wide. 'You had better understand that there is no way they can kill me without your dying too.'

'Yes.'

'You go first.'

Klein proceeded out the door, relying heavily on his cane, moving very slowly, and Corbett thought ahead no farther than the elevator now. Once he reached the elevator, once the doors slid shut behind him, the worst part of the journey would be over, the most dangerous section. Klein stumbled slightly, caught himself, moved on. Delusions, yes, he had been deluding himself, for this man who limped ahead of him was a military general who had commanded troops in the field, and he would not allow himself to be in a hostage position unless it was a temporary posture. Corbett felt a fear approaching exhilaration, for he knew he would not reach that elevator alive and he also knew that he would kill the General before he died.

They were approaching the corner now and as they reached it Klein's leg appeared to give way, a feint, yes, and the cane came around in a wild swing as Klein threw himself to the floor. Blurred, the sudden appearance of Thrash's face, sighting down the pistol held in two hands, pointed at his head, and Corbett dropped reflexively, stumbling over the cane, the sound of Thrash's pistol filling his ears. The plaster of the wall exploded behind him.

And now there were other gunshots coming from the elevator area and he saw Goddard come lumbering down the hall, firing his pistol until Thrash turned and with the grace of a conditioned athlete shot him three times at almost point-blank range. Goddard stopped dead in his tracks, collapsing on knees that failed to hold him, crumpling awkwardly. And by the time Thrash had turned again Corbett had his pistol pressed against the back of Klein's skull.

'I'll blow his fucking head off,' Corbett said. 'Believe me.'

Thrash's arms lowered, his mouth half open, breathing heavily.

'Let it fall,' Corbett said.

Thrash's pistol hit the floor, the silencer separating from the muzzle, spinning crazily on the polished tiles. Thrash's arms hung limply at his sides.

'Now, get the hell off the floor,' Corbett said. 'Move.'

Thrash paused a moment, looking at Klein, then he turned and walked back down the corridor, carefully stepping over Goddard's body. The elevator doors opened to swallow him and then he was gone.

Corbett moved away from Klein, sliding back to sit against the wall. Klein stirred, raised himself to a sitting position, his eyes unrelenting. Under the gun, the corridor a bloody shambles, and still Klein was unruffled. 'You bloody son of a bitch,' Corbett said. 'You goddamned son of a bitch.'

Klein looked at Goddard's body sprawled out on the floor. 'There are always complicating factors,' he said, as much to himself as to Corbett. 'He was overzealous to the point of psychosis.' He took a breath, looking to Corbett. 'You still won't make it,' Klein said. 'Dying doesn't particularly disturb me so it makes no difference if you kill me. You can't stop the project.'

342

'I have stopped it,' Corbett said exultantly. 'Do you hear the computer, General? We reversed the interface on the Japanese police computer and lined up all the company terminals. The computer has been sending the whole goddamned content of your package to a dozen different countries. At sixty thousand bits a minute, it could have translated an encyclopedia by now.'

Klein's eyes were glazed, his head cocked to one side, as if he could not believe it. Slowly he rose to his feet, listening to the clicking whir of the computer. And suddenly he lurched down the hallway towards the computer room, half dragging the offending leg in a kind of grotesque run. Corbett stood up and in a moment followed and when he reached the door, he saw Klein's cane in the act of smashing a display screen, which imploded with a shower of glass. And the cane continued to rise and fall, wood against metal and glass, until Klein's strength was gone. And still the computer whirred.

Corbett picked up the telephone on the desk. 'Get me Lieutenant Nakamura,' he said.

Chapter 3

Corbett sat at a window table in the airport lounge, sipping a drink, watching the monstrous jets waiting in line on the distant runway while one gained momentum and with a roar climbed at a steep angle over the bay, leaving plumes of black smoke hanging in the heavy air. A hand touched his shoulder and he looked up to see Nakamura standing there. 'I think it is a most pleasant day,' Nakamura said. 'Do you mind if I sit down, Mr Corbett?'

'Not at all,' Corbett said. 'I take it this isn't official?'

'In my business most things are a mixture,' Nakamura said. He ordered tea from the waitress. 'I am here on another matter but I had hoped to see you one last time.'

'I'm sorry things happened as they did,' Corbett said. 'I respect your country.'

'It is not what I would have chosen, of course. Have you seen the morning papers?'

'No.'

'Your company is denying everything, but I would have expected that. They are claiming that the computer data transmission was nothing more than an elaborate attempt to link them with the worldwide scandals. I made an attempt to have your Mr Klein and Mr Erikson held here for trial but my government saw fit to yield to the desires of your government to have them testify before various government committees. I understand that Mr Stevens will be testifying against them as a government witness.' He paused, his eyes following a 747 rumbling down the runway, the roar so loud it made conversation impossible. After the jet had lifted into the haze Corbett put his drink down.

'Yes, he's going to testify,' he said.

'But you are not. Is my understanding correct?'

'Very correct. I won't be needed.'

'But you have the opportunity for a *coup de grace.*'

'Nothing has really ended,' Corbett said. 'Nothing beyond one paramilitary operation by one corporation in one area. Everything's wide open now. The small countries are going to feel they can move in any direction they please, with impunity, and the big companies will continue to respond, one way or another. The Vietnamese arms have been uncovered and they will be destroyed but the companies can afford to put full-scale mercenary armies in the field before they're through.'

'These are perilous times,' Nakamura said. 'Where will you go?'

'Hawaii, for a while. But I'm not through over here, not by a long shot. Erikson doesn't know it yet, but I'm going to take over his operations in the Far East and find a way to make them work without a series of military battles.'

Nakamura's tea was served. He contemplated it in silence for a moment. 'When you return,' he said, 'I would suggest that you take us into your full confidence. We are different in many ways, of course, but in the end we want the same thing.' He looked out the window, stood up. 'I am afraid that I must turn my attention to official duties now,' he said, extending his hand. 'But I wish you to know that I hope you are successful.'

'Thank you,' Corbett said. He watched Nakamura moving towards the elevator and then, through the window, he saw what had prompted Nakamura's departure. The ESK jet was moving into a loading position at a private terminal and he saw Erikson walking towards the lowered stair hatch and he was somehow moved, for even from this distance Erikson appeared to be no more than any other tired old businessman off to fight another skirmish in the company wars. And Cristina was with him, her arm linked through his, and Corbett hoped that the old man had sense enough to appreciate the one thing he had bought that was truly his. Below the window Corbett saw Nakamura emerge on to the field, keeping his distance but very much in evidence as if he had to insure the departure of an evil from his country. A temple dog, Corbett thought.

He was aware that Ellen was standing beside him, looking off towards Cristina, who was just boarding the plane. 'Any regrets?' she said.

'None,' he said, putting his hands over hers on the table. God, she was a radiant woman, dressed in yellow, cheerful at a time when he needed it.

'The Hawaii flight's ready to board,' she said. 'But I think we should discuss something first.'

'What's that?'

'I realise you're a proud man, William.'

'So?'

'I have arranged a loan from some friends at the airline.' She opened her purse and displayed a cheque. 'Twenty-three hundred dollars. It will do us for a while.'

'Look . . .'

'No, please. You offered me my freedom in Hawaii once. I'm giving us both the favour. It won't last a hell of a long time, but I'm sure you will come up with something. You're a very resourceful man.'

He held the cheque in his hands and thought about telling her that he was a rich man now, for the money that ESK had placed in his Mexican and Swiss accounts to set him up was still there, his. He decided against it. Telling her now would devalue a loving gift and there were too few loving gifts in this world.

'Yes, I'll come up with something,' he said. 'Thank

346

you.' He leaned across the small table and kissed her, aware that people were watching and that he did not care. 'And now,' he said to her, 'let's go catch our plane.'

Also available from Sphere Books
by Robert L. Duncan

DRAGONS AT THE GATE

A coveted Japanese treasure trove lost since World War
II . . . a chilling, awesome plot to incite international up-
heaval . . . a beautiful girl using sex for blackmail and betrayal as her way of life . . . a brilliant, cynical CIA agent
caught in the jaws of a treacherous hoax, on the run across
the throbbing, exotic landscape of Japan, where there is no
place for a man to hide, but many ways for him to die . . .

DRAGONS AT THE GATE is one of the most riveting
thrillers to hit the bestseller lists in recent years. And in its
brilliantly authentic portrayal of the terrifying inner workings of the world's most powerful secret intelligence agency,
it reaches new heights of grim topicality.

'Highly recommended: one of those rare thrillers that are
subtle, intelligent and literate'   *Sunday Express*

'A tense, cool, wise book, with Mr Duncan's searching
intelligence producing fine chiaroscuro effects'   *Scotsman*

'Suspense, followed by even greater suspense, is the hallmark of this tightly-plotted, fast-moving and timely story . . .
Another winner'   *Publishers Weekly*

'LIKE LE CARRÉ, THE AUTHOR KNOWS THE DARK
WORLD OF WHICH HE WRITES'   *Washington Post*

0 7221 0487 1   ADVENTURE/THRILLER FICTION   95p

THE MITTENWALD SYNDICATE

Frederick Nolan

THE FACTS:

A fantastic fortune in gold and jewels lay buried in the mountains above the village of Mittenwald at the end of the Second World War. It comprised the last of the Reichsbank reserves, removed by the Nazis too late for shipment abroad. None of it has ever been recovered. And no one has ever been arrested for its theft.

THE NOVEL:

Frederick Nolan's brilliant thriller dares to speculate on what could easily have happened to the Nazi treasure. It explores a violent world of greed, intrigue, betrayal, killing and revenge – especially revenge. And, all the way, you will ask yourself where compelling fiction ends and terrifying fact takes over . . .

'A splendidly exciting novel'   *Daily Express*

'Genuine excitement'   *Sunday Times*

0 7221 6427 0   ADVENTURE/THRILLER FICTION   95p

HELL SHOT

Joe Poyer

'Mr Poyer is very, very good'   *Alistair Maclean*

Satellites patrolling the earth's skies, watching for illicit fields of poppies, had virtually wiped out opium traffic. Then suddenly, the world was again being flooded with lethal heroin. But Spacewatch II couldn't detect the poppies that were its source . . .

Cole Brogan, special investigator for the International Narcotics Control Commission, thought he had the answer: a crop more precious than emeralds might be growing in Ireland. But nobody believed his fantastic theory, even when his girl friend was kidnapped and Brogan himself barely escaped assassins' bullets.

It was only after a nightmare pursuit across Ireland that Brogan uncovered the truth about his opponents – and about the deadly double-cross that was designed to end his luck. And his life . . .

HELL SHOT is a power-packed thriller by one of today's greatest names in adventure fiction, internationally best-selling author Joe Poyer.

0 7221 6994 9   ADVENTURE/THRILLER FICTION   95p

Craig Thomas's Bestselling Paperback

FIREFOX

Soon to be a major film

The Soviet Mig-31 is the deadliest warplane ever built. Codenamed **FIRE FOX** by NATO, it can fly at over 4,000 m.p.h., is invulnerable to radar – and has a lethally sophisticated weapons system that its pilot can control by thought-impulses. There is only one way that British Intelligence and the CIA can counter the threat it poses: a scheme more desperate and daring than any undercover operation since the Second World War –

HIJACK THE FIREFOX!

'Simply won't allow you to put it down until you reach the last page' Jack Higgins, author of *The Eagle Has Landed*

'A marvellous read – a gripping, believable thriller that flies at Mach-5 speed' Ira Levin, author of *The Boys from Brazil*

'I devoured Firefox instantly. An excellent, exciting book!' Arthur Hailey, bestselling author of *Airport*

0 7221 04456 ADVENTURE/THRILLER FICTION 95p

A selection of Bestsellers from Sphere Books

TEMPLE DOGS	Robert L. Duncan	95p ☐
THE PASSAGE	Bruce Nicolayson	95p ☐
CHARLIE IS MY DARLING	Mollie Hardwick	£1.25 ☐
RAISE THE TITANIC!	Clive Cussler	95p ☐
KRAMER'S WAR	Derek Robinson	£1.25 ☐
THE CRASH OF '79	Paul Erdman	£1.25 ☐
EMMA AND I	Sheila Hocken	85p ☐
UNTIL THE COLOURS FADE	Tim Jeal	£1.50 ☐
DR. JOLLY'S BOOK OF CHILDCARE	Dr. Hugh Jolly	£1.95 ☐
MAJESTY	Robert Lacey	£1.50 ☐
STAR WARS	George Lucas	95p ☐
FALSTAFF	Robert Nye	£1.50 ☐
EXIT SHERLOCK HOLMES	Robert Lee Hall	95p ☐
THE MITTENWALD SYNDICATE	Frederick Nolan	95p ☐
CLOSE ENCOUNTERS OF THE THIRD KIND		
	Steven Spielberg	85p ☐
STAR FIRE	Ingo Swann	£1.25 ☐
RUIN FROM THE AIR		
	Gordon Thomas & Max Morgan Witts	£1.50 ☐
EBANO (Now filmed as ASHANTI)		
	Alberto Vazquez-Figueroa	95p ☐
FIREFOX	Craig Thomas	95p ☐

All Sphere books are available at your local book shop or newsagent, or can be ordered direct from the publisher. Just tick the titles you want and fill in the form below.

Name ....

Address ....

....

Write to Sphere Books, Cash Sales Department, P.O. Box 11, Falmouth, Cornwall TR10 9EN

Please enclose cheque or postal order to the value of the cover price plus:

UK: 22p for the first book plus 10p per copy for each additional book ordered to a maximum charge of 82p.

OVERSEAS: 30p for the first book and 10p for each additional book BFPO and EIRE 22p for the first book plus 10p per copy for the next 6 books, thereafter 4p per book.

Sphere Books reserve the right to show new retail prices on covers which may differ from those previously advertised in the text or elsewhere, and to increase postal rates in accordance with the GPO.